Just Beyond the Garden Gate

A Highland Gardens Novel
Book 1

Dawn Marie Hamilton

ISBN: 978-0-9899642-2-7

In memory
of
Agnes and Rodger Hamilton

Thanks, Mom, for the gift of reading.
Thanks, Dad, for encouraging me to dream.

ACKNOWLEDGMENTS

So many individuals have helped bring this book to fruition, and I thank you.

My dearest thanks to the Hamilton ladies for being my first readers—Agnes, Kim, Lois, and Lynn.

Thank you to Cindy Davis for editorial guidance. To Eliza Knight for critique. To the Celtic Critters, past and present, for critiques and vital encouragement. Words cannot convey how important you are to me.

Thank you to the members of Celtic Hearts Romance Writers and From the Heart Romance Writers for keeping me sane. To all the judges who've judged the manuscript for *Just Beyond the Garden Gate* in RWA® chapter contests and provided constructive feedback. Priceless.

With all my heart, I thank Frank, my husband, best friend, and personal hero.

PROLOGUE

Strathlachlan, Scottish Highlands, 1506

Your parents are missing.

The seneschal's words reverberated inside Patrick's head, louder and more insistent than the white-capped waves crashing against shingle at the foot of Castle Lachlan. *Your parents are missing.* He gripped the battlements' cold stone and watched two galleys approach through the thickening haze, bows cutting through the turbulent water of Loch Fyne.

MacLachlan banners snapped.

Your parents are missing.

His stomach churned. Did his clansmen bring news?

Raw wind ripped Patrick's hair free of its restraint. Damp from the salty spray, the strands stuck to his eyes and the sides of his face. With a growl, he pulled the thick mass back and secured it again with the leather thong.

A mighty clap of thunder echoed, and he shifted his weary gaze to the sky. Dark clouds hurled lightning bolts at distant hills. *Damn the weather.* He slammed a palm against stone. The imminent storm worsened his already foul humor. He'd traveled night and day in response to his father's urgent request to return home, only to find his parents gone from the castle.

His clansmen whispered tales of strange happenings in the forest, afraid to utter the words aloud. Good Lord, he prayed the rumors about his parents proved false.

He arrived at the shore as the first galley beached. Briny air filled his nostrils. He stiffened when Donald MacLachlan lumbered over the side and strode forward. Well known for a lack of loyalty, his uncle was the last person he expected to see. Sudden apprehension crept through Patrick—the same wary readiness he felt before battle.

He wiped sweaty palms on his *plaide* and embraced the older man.

"'Tis good you have returned, lad." His uncle thumped him hard on the back.

"My father's missive stated I was to travel in all haste. What news?"

Donald's gaze bored into him.

The eyes Patrick stared back at mirrored his own. Many folk said he and his twin brother, Archibald, resembled their father and uncle. Same chestnut hair, blue eyes and broad nose, except Archibald's eyes held more silver than blue. They shared an identical cleft in their chins. Patrick wished his brother were home, but he traveled for King James and couldn't return.

Donald sighed heavily. "I fear 'tis bad. You should have come sooner, before the trouble began. If only you honored the betrothal agreement and wed the Lamont lass." He shook his head. "Now 'tis too late. Your father and his..." a scowl twisted his upper lip, "woman have gone missing."

Patrick's chest tightened and he clenched his fists so tightly his blunt nails cut into his palms. "My parents are missing and yet you belittle my stepmother. Have you no conscience, man? Can you not even say her name?"

"Neither she nor her Campbell kinsmen be friend to me."

With effort, Patrick refrained from uttering further angry words at the insult to his sweet stepmother. "Tell me what

2

happened."

"We tracked them to the Fir-wood near the deserted hut. Three MacLachlan horses grazed there, but nary a sign of your parents. Heavier tracks made by other horses headed off to Lamont country and Toward Keep. We followed and crept as near as we dared."

Donald tilted his head in the direction of the beach, and the two burly men working to secure the galley. "The MacEwen twins posed as Maclays to gain entry. A band of Lamont clansmen claims they chased your parents into the wood, intent on holding them for ransom. The Lamonts pursued, but when the clouds uncovered the full moon, your parents disappeared afore their eyes. They searched, but found naught. They tell all who are willing to listen Fir-wood is faerie-cursed."

Staring across the rough seawater of the loch, Patrick struggled against soul-wrenching pain. As the eldest living son of the chief of the ancient Clan MacLachlan, he knew what the clan expected. He trained from the cradle to be a fierce warrior. Discipline demanded he show no emotion.

No fear.

But he couldn't assuage the fear for his father and stepmother churning within him. Patrick hid his angry confusion and turned back to his uncle as an especially bright, jagged streak of lightning lit the man's face.

Donald's gaze wandered. He shifted from one foot to the other. "When we returned to Castle Lachlan, I believed you were still on the Continent. Not trusting the Lamont tale, I thought it best to take the galleys across the loch to Campbell country to search and seek word of the chief and his *lady*-wife there. Ach, lad, 'twas a waste of time."

Patrick braced against a gust of wind, jaw tight. The tale made no sense. People didn't disappear without a trace.

A loud scraping noise caused him and his uncle to look toward the water where the second galley beached. The rest of the lads jumped from the boats onto shore and made haste to secure the two galleys before the storm's full rage fell upon them.

Patrick whirled and strode to the castle. He would find his parents.

CHAPTER ONE

Present Day, Anderson Creek, North Carolina

Wet *skin glistened golden across his broad back in the sunlight. Muscles flexed with each stride as they climbed the waterfall. The enticing sight of water splashing over and caressing strong thighs and a tight butt the way she wanted to touch him had her licking parched lips in anticipation.* Laurie moistened her lips along with the heroine and tightened her grip on the e-reader as if it were the hero's backside she squeezed. It was easy to get lost in the web of the story—the only way she experienced romance.

The nearby crunch of gravel made the hairs on her arms stand on end. She snapped her gaze up. At the edge of the secluded garden enclosed within yellow forsythia stood the tall, willowy woman she'd seen earlier at the inn. The woman watched Laurie through intense green eyes set in a face smudged with dirt. She wore grubby work clothes and boots, and an equally grubby wide-brimmed hat.

"Oh, hi." Laurie smiled and placed the e-reader on the cedar side table. "You startled me."

The woman continued staring, eyes narrowed.

"I'm Laurie Bernard, a guest at this inn."

The intruder crossed her arms over her chest. "I ken

that."

"Who are you?" Laurie asked, trying to remain civil.

"Caitrina."

"Is something wrong?" Laurie didn't understand the woman's rude behavior. Who was she? Why was she just standing there, staring?

"You're sitting in my garden."

"I see." But she didn't. Laurie shifted her weight in the chair, wishing the woman would get to the point or leave so she could finish reading her favorite author's latest romance novel.

"I've many here and about." The woman waved her arm in an arc. "Do you like gardens? If you do—"

"I do." Okay, she'd pushed the right button. Laurie loved gardens. Dreamed of having one to care for.

"Then walk along the trail through those woods and you'll find a special place."

The trail appeared overgrown. Didn't look like anyone had walked that way in ages. "Is it safe to walk in the woods alone?"

Caitrina pursed her lips. "If you'd rather not—"

"I didn't say that. I want to make sure it's safe to explore alone. I've heard there are bears in this area."

"Bears wouldn't dare bother you. This land belongs to Himself."

"*Himself?*" Laurie creased her brow, puzzled by the strange term.

"Iain," Caitrina said matter-of-factly.

Then she disappeared. Poof. Gone.

"What the—" Laurie clutched her chest over her fiercely-pounding heart. She jerked her gaze around. *Where the hell did the woman go?*

She squeezed her eyes shut, rubbed them with trembling hands, snapped them open and scanned the area again, but couldn't figure out where Caitrina had gone so fast.

Think logically. The woman didn't just vanish. She must have gone somewhere.

A deep breath eased Laurie's panic. The bright afternoon light must have caused a moment of blindness as Caitrina walked away through the thick shrubbery.

Silly to overreact. Laurie shook her head. She really was dangling from a thin thread.

Well, that's why she was here, wasn't it?

She needed this vacation. Deserved it.

Curiosity piqued, she rose from the chair, flipped shut the cover of the e-reader and tucked it under her arm then headed for the woodland trail the woman indicated. As she made her way into the woods, a soft giggle from behind made her shiver.

Laurie looked back along the path. Nothing but sun-drenched woodland. Great. Now she was hearing things. With a shrug, she continued in the direction of the special garden.

"*Beware. 'Tis magic in the wood.*"

She swung around. "Who's there?"

Nobody replied. No one lingered nearby. Feeling ridiculous, she shook off the uneasy sensation. She wasn't hearing voices. The wind and her anxieties made her imagine things. That's all.

She must be more stressed than she thought from all the tiresome business trips over the last several years. From the brutal brow beating during contract negotiations. From the constant client catering after deals closed. From the lack of a social life.

If only she'd handled things differently. Too late for that. Laurie sighed. She hated rehashing a past she couldn't change. Would be better to look to the future.

Well, she had a month reserved at the inn. A month should be plenty of time to get over the stress that triggered her professional meltdown. She continued into the woods, hoping to find the *special* garden.

The meandering trail led past clusters of evergreens and small groves of broad-leaved rhododendrons. She stopped a couple of times to marvel over early spring wildflowers poking up through the carpet of last year's fallen leaves. This place was peaceful, the quiet broken every so often by the melodic call of a bird, so different from the rat race that was her life.

She skirted a couple of large boulders and disturbed a squirrel. The little critter scolded before scampering away. A chuckle bubbled up Laurie's throat. The forest pulsed with magic, a healing kind of magic. Magic she needed.

The trail entered a large meadow; an old stone cottage came into view. She gasped in surprise. Goosebumps prickled and a chill teased her spine.

The cottage called to her. Called to a romantic need within her soul.

Stomach tight, she hurried through the calf-high amber grass and into the yard. The quaint little house had leaded windows and a heavy oak door carved with a Celtic design. She tiptoed to one of the side windows and peered in. The room was empty. The cottage appeared deserted.

Creeping to the front door, she knocked. When no one answered, she glanced around to see if anyone watched then twisted the knob. "Darn, it's locked."

She made her way through overgrown shrubbery at the left of the house to a high stone wall. Compelled to learn what was on the other side, she tried the rusted iron gate. It wouldn't budge. She pushed harder, until the metal grille creaked open. Easing it farther, she walked through. Yay! A neglected garden was enclosed within the wall. Another gate at the rear led to more woods.

Sunlight shimmered outside the gate, tempting her to discover more of what lay beyond. A shadow suddenly darkened the area, giving her a chill. She rubbed her arms and studied the sky. When had clouds blown in?

Warmth returned with the sun, and Laurie dropped onto a concrete garden bench. *This must be the garden Caitrina meant. What a mess.* Weeds and brambles choked the garden, although a few bulbs bloomed, and scattered about were early season herbs. Laurie recognized chives and caught the tangy scent of lemon balm when she teased aromatic leaves with sensitive fingertips. She leaned down to scoop a handful of rich soil. Possibilities ran through her mind. As the dirt slipped through her fingers, an idea blossomed.

She'd always wanted to live in a cottage with a lush garden. When young and foolish, she'd imagined such a place, and a special man sharing her life. Laurie snorted. Like that would ever happen. She gave up on the dream years ago and concentrated on her career...or had she?

Maybe she'd remained a romantic after all.

She would find out who owned this place and make it her own. Heck with staying a month. She'd stay longer. Maybe start a small business.

Caitrina was right—the garden was special.

Laurie's head swirled with ideas on the way back to the inn. The Victorian painted-lady with the Blue Ridge Mountains as a backdrop belonged to a bygone era. She stopped, awe inspired by the vermillion sunset. With a smile, she rushed to her suite, quickly freshened up and hurried downstairs to the dining room. The lamps were dim, but the room glowed with candlelight. Windows filled the far wall and nearby a fire burned in the hearth. Still early in the tourist season, there were few diners.

Mairi, the fortyish woman who'd checked her in earlier, stood at the hostess station arranging yellow daffodils in a ceramic vase. The silky strands of her strawberry blond hair hung loose around her shoulders with casual elegance and laugh lines edged her silver eyes when she looked up and smiled.

"Great to see you this eve'n," she said with a Scottish burr. "Would you like to be seated?"

"Yes, please."

Mairi waved over a fellow from the bar area. "This is my husband, Iain."

So this is Himself. Amusing attire. He wore traditional Highland regalia like her cousin Finn often did—belted plaid kilt, shirt and vest, leather sporran—complete with a *sgian dubh*, a small knife, inserted in his knee-high hose. A good ten years older than Mairi, he stood tall and broad, his chestnut hair spiced with a hint of gray, worn long and secured at the back with a leather strap.

He grinned at the inspection and his deep blue eyes glimmered with mischief.

For an older man, he certainly was handsome.

"We've been waiting for you to arrive for a long time," he said.

"What do you mean?" It had only been two days since she made the reservation, not that long ago.

Mairi cleared her throat and exchanged a stern glance with her husband. "He's teasing. Iain, I'm sure Miss Bernard wishes to go to her table."

He guided her into the dining room, his back stiff. He and his wife were a curiosity.

"I like your Scottish getup." Laurie hoped to ease the awkward moment. "Mairi told me you moved to Anderson Creek from Scotland and opened the inn three years ago."

"Aye, 'tis a fact. This place reminds us of our homeland with its rowan trees and thistles and frequent mists. Mairi gets melancholy at times, missing the old place and the children, but I like the modern conveniences."

"You must also miss your children."

"They have destinies to fulfill." His features closed, end of subject. Then he smiled. "Have you visited Scotland?"

"A couple of times on business."

"Did you enjoy our culture?" He leaned closer, seeming eager to learn the answer.

"Yes, the people and the countryside are pleasant." She had found the Scottish people and their country lovely, at least the few she'd met and the little bit she'd seen between business meetings.

"Glad to hear it. Here we are." He sat her near the hearth and handed over a menu. "May I bring you something from the bar? Whisky perhaps?" He jigged his eyebrows, grinning.

She chuckled at his antics. "A glass of merlot, please."

"As you wish." He inclined his head and hurried to the bar.

A couple engrossed in quiet conversation sat at a nearby table. Across the room, another pair gazed into each other's eyes. *Romantic.*

Alone again, Laurie frowned and tried to forget how long she'd been alone.

When Iain returned, he set the wine on the table. "I understand you went walking on the grounds today. Did you enjoy our gardens?"

"They're beautiful," she said. "While I was out, I came across a stone cottage. Do you know who owns the place?"

"Aye, 'tis ours. We recently finished renovating it."

"Really?"

"Inside. The outside and grounds require a wee bit more sprucing up." His eyes twinkled. "Why do you ask?"

Playing with the napkin in her lap, she gave him a tentative smile. "Is it for rent?"

"Aye, lass, 'tis. Might you be interested?"

"Yes." She couldn't help but grin.

Iain glanced away when a college-aged girl approached. "Ah, here is your waitress. Let our Emily take your order. You can discuss the cottage with Mairi in the morning if you want."

He returned to the hostess station and said something to his wife. Mairi's gaze swiveled to the table and she pinned Laurie with a curious stare.

Four weeks later, after Laurie returned from settling her affairs in New York, she lay on her stomach across the enormous bed. The room seemed hazy. Had she drank too much wine? She stretched like a contented feline, the furs she lay on sensuous against bare skin.

She sensed his presence, then the mattress sank, and he moved over her, trapping her within strong arms and the pressure of a hard body. She trembled with a bit of fear.

Would she disappoint?

"Be still, sweetling. Let me pleasure you." His husky whisper curled around her heart, dispelling her silly fears.

This was a dream lover. With him, she could explore every fantasy. Her body thrummed with excitement as he rose slightly and feathered kisses along the nape of her neck, taking tiny nips. His lips slid ever so slowly down the arch of her back. Chills followed in the wake of his touch. Laurie shivered when his lips hit that sensitive spot at the base of her spine—the spot only he had kissed. His teeth grazed a hip, and then he explored farther. She tried to roll over, wanting to see her lover's face, kiss his lips. Gentle caresses kept her facedown and trembling with anticipation.

When she moaned, he eased open her legs and tenderly kissed the inside of one thigh. He held her firmly to the bed, nibbling sensitive skin. He was everything she wanted in a lover.

Once again, his body slid over hers. His erection rubbed against the cleft of her behind. He raised her hips, and with a quick thrust, entered her core. She clutched the sheets and cried out in pleasure. His movements were slow and teasing.

"More. Please," she begged.

"Aye, my love." He quickened the pace.

The pressure built. The fire burned. She soared among the stars.

Laurie woke, breathing in an exotic perfume clinging to the air. She curled into herself, trying to ease the slow burn at her core. Holy shit! Her first erotic dream. She muffled a groan of frustration into the pillow before flipping onto her back. She replayed the dream in her mind, wanting to hold onto the addictive heat. She tried to imagine what her lover looked like. She knew he bulged with muscle and made love with tenderness.

A floorboard outside her room creaked. She stiffened as footsteps moved down the hall. Had someone been at the door listening?

Embarrassment burned her cheeks.

She swung her legs over the side of the bed, rose to her feet and padded to the door. She opened it slowly and peeked out. The passageway was empty.

Shaking her head, she headed into the bathroom to take a cold shower. Two hours later, after breakfast in the inn's dining room, she met Mairi in the foyer.

"My dear, I was relieved when your furniture arrived. Iain didn't believe you would return after you left in a rush to visit your family."

"Sorry. I should've sent word from New York when I extended my trip. My cousin had problems with a couple of my old accounts. I couldn't leave until my replacement got up to speed."

She'd finally done the unthinkable, resigned from her high-profile business-consulting job. Never again would she allow anal executives who thought themselves superior merely because they were born male belittle her. Brussels was her final business trip for the family firm. She was finished with tiresome trips, living out of a suitcase, eating room service meals.

Her belly shimmied.

Just thinking about the way she marched into Finn's office and submitted her resignation left her giddy with relief and an incredible euphoria. The same soaring feeling she'd had when she flew in a hot air balloon over farmland while attending an air show in central New Jersey.

He could believe she wimped out if he wanted, but she was finally taking control of her life.

"I hope you straightened everything out so you don't have to go back," Mairi said, her gaze searching.

"Actually, I had a wonderful visit."

"Good. And you'll have plenty of time to relax here. Everything you sent from New York is in the cottage. I've set the day aside to help you unpack and get settled. I can hardly wait to discover what you have in all those boxes."

Taking Laurie's silver BMW, they drove down the long dirt drive toward the cottage. As they rounded the last curve, the meadow came into view.

"Look!" Laurie slammed on the brakes and pointed. "Those men are trying to kill each other."

Two huge men, dressed in kilts, bare chests bulging with muscle, metal flashing in bright sun, fought with extremely large swords. A terrifying sight, yet strangely thrilling.

She grabbed the door handle—

Mairi chuckled and grasped her arm, stopping her from getting out. "That is my Iain and Douglas MacKinnon rehearsing a battle reenactment for the society they belong to. I should have mentioned they practice here several mornings during the week. And some of the lads from town come to the meadow on Saturdays to train for the Highland Games at Grandfather Mountain. The gathering is quite the event come July. I hope they won't disturb you."

Laurie followed the graceful dance of the combatants, fascinated by their strength and agility. She flinched at a loud clang as one sword sliced down hard on the other, the vibration shrill.

"Laurie?"

"Oh, yeah. I mean, no. They won't bother me. My cousin Finn often attends the Highland games up north. I traveled most of the time and never had the opportunity." Laurie struggled to suppress a pang of resentment. Finn managed to make time for his personal pursuits, but expected her to be on the road, working, one hundred percent of the time.

She smiled, pleased with the changes she'd made in her life. She planned to do whatever she wanted, whenever she wanted. With her trust fund—if she were thrifty—she'd have the means to do just that, at least for a while.

"Watching the men practice will be interesting." Laurie pressed her tongue against the inside of her cheek to keep from smirking. "Besides, I'll get to ogle the muscular legs exposed by the sexy kilts they wear."

Oh, yeah, she'd enjoy watching the men.

"Are you Scot then?" Mairi arched a brow.

"My mother was a MacIntyre. I guess I'm half Scottish."

Mairi grinned and patted Laurie's knee. "A wee bit of Scot's blood makes you a Scot, lass." She leaned back against the leather seat. "By the way, that handsome devil, Douglas MacKinnon, owns the *Celtic Image* shop in the village. He carries lovely Scottish items. That is, if you've a mind to wear the plaid."

"I'll check out his shop the next time I go to the village."

When they entered the cottage, things were already in good order. They spent the next few hours unpacking and setting up housekeeping. Mairi carefully removed a bone china cup from one of the boxes. "Lovely tea service. I don't recognize the floral pattern. Where did you get it?"

"It's antique. The set belonged to my mother. She and my father passed away when I was a child."

"I am sorry."

"Was a long time ago." Laurie gazed at the beckoning garden beyond the kitchen window. "Let's take a break and go outside for some fresh air."

A few minutes later, she waved her arm over the messy beds. "Do you know anyone I might hire to help me? I have grand plans, but I can't refurbish the garden by myself."

Mairi considered for a moment. "You can borrow our garden pixie, Caitrina. She takes care of our gardens. I'm sure she could find time to help you."

"Shouldn't you ask me first?"

Laurie glanced around, then up. Above them, on the high wall, holding a picnic basket, sat Caitrina.

Great. She hadn't seen the rude woman since that day in the inn's garden. Would have preferred not to meet her again. Though maybe she should be thankful for the information about the cottage and garden.

Caitrina dropped from the wall to land gracefully on the soft soil.

It was quite a drop. How did she do that without twisting an ankle? Laurie eyed her with suspicion.

"And I'm not a pixie." Caitrina's chin jutted up and she sniffed indignantly.

15

"Of course not, dear. You are not nearly as mischievous," Mairi cajoled.

"I brought lunch. Emily thought you might be hungry."

The two women exchanged eye contact as if Mairi pleaded with Caitrina to be nice.

Caitrina graced Laurie with a half-smile. "Aye, I'll help. Do you ken anything about making gardens?"

"A little." Laurie knew plants. She'd spent many a flight thumbing through garden catalogs and magazines studying how to grow them and combine them to best effect. The fact she didn't have hands-on experience was insignificant. "I'm eager to learn."

"Are you now?" Caitrina wrinkled her nose. Do you think you'll be here long enough to make a difference?"

"Absolutely."

More than that, Laurie wanted to learn what it would take to start a garden business. Although she hadn't admitted it to her uncle, she would never return to corporate. Excitement she hadn't felt in ages swept over her.

Whoa. Take it easy. One day at a time.

She didn't care for the way Caitrina stared. Maybe she should find someone else to help with the garden.

"Well then, go to the library in the village and get some books for ideas. In a few days, we'll visit my favorite garden centers for plants. In the meantime, start the spring cleanup. Clear the dead growth and weed."

It seemed Caitrina intended to help. Perhaps it was for the best since she already worked for the inn.

"Mairi, are you positive you don't mind my borrowing Caitrina?"

"Of course not, dear. It will be to our benefit to have the garden beautiful again. And you will have a reason to stay with us." Mairi switched her gaze to Caitrina. "Now, lass, what did you bring us in that basket?"

❀ ❀ ❀

Later in the evening, the music from the stereo speakers

escalated to a crescendo. Laurie jerked her gaze away from where she stared at the wall. She stilled the rapid jouncing of her leg. God, a restless edge rode her tonight.

She fanned herself. Too warm from the fire, her living room became oppressive. She poured another glass of wine and walked into the garden. Mist embraced the night. Although the cottage windows cast filtered light, most of the garden lay in shadow. Lovely.

A tinkling noise startled her. The hairs on the back of her neck stood on end. An out-of-place exotic fragrance scented the air.

Sensing movement at the rear of the garden, she set her wine glass on the concrete bench and strode toward the gate.

The previously closed gate hung open.

An impressively tall, breathtakingly gorgeous man— wrapped in what could only be described as a large plaid blanket—stood in the woods just beyond the garden gate.

Laurie's gaze locked on the man's face. Her mouth went dry. Words lodged in a tight throat. Who was this man? He seemed familiar.

Impossible. He was fearsome. Built like a romance cover model.

"*Go to him*," a compulsion whispered within her mind. She stepped forward. No. This can't be right. Unable to resist, she took another small step, but stopped short. What is this? A barrier, invisible—seemingly made from some shrink-wrap like material, stretched taut—blocked the way through the gate.

She pressed a palm against the barrier. A vibrant pink light twirled around her tingling fingers and Laurie drew them away. The color dissipated.

What on earth was going on?

Laurie glanced through the gate.

Gazes colliding, the man's dark eyes pierced her soul. Every passion visible.

Unable to turn away, she stood motionless. A jolt of energy—as if shot with lightning—raced through her. Almost immediately, the energy seeped away. A boneless sensation buckled her knees. Laurie groped for something solid to hold onto and grabbed the gate.

The barrier had disappeared! So had the man.

Simply vanished.

This day was getting weirder by the minute. Behind her, the golden glow from the cottage windows seemed normal. She touched the cold metal grille again. Still no barrier. Still no man. A violent churning in her belly warned, "Run and lock the doors." Yet Laurie did neither. She stepped through the gate and walked to the edge of the woods where the path headed off into darkness.

"Hey, is anyone there?"

Silence.

She rubbed tingling fingers on her pant's legs and scanned the shadows.

The man was gone.

CHAPTER TWO

The Fir-wood, Scottish Highlands, 1509

*P*atrick stared at the spot where his father and stepmother had gone missing. Had his eyes deceived him? Had a petite woman stood there dressed in a lad's garments?

A strange light from a mysterious cottage had shone on the woman's pale cheek. Enchanted by expressive blue eyes, he'd frozen in fascination. Gold hair caressed her shoulders, making him want to stroke the silky tresses. He flexed his fingers. Was he a smitten fool? He shouldn't think about those lush pink lips and what he wanted to do with his mouth.

The cottage was gone now. A half-moon lit the mound where it had stood with an eerie glow. He hadn't meant to walk so far this night. But walking had become his evening ritual ever since he lost his parents. After three years, his pain had become a restless ache. Unlike others, he had faith one day he'd find them. He believed his parents were alive.

To assuage the ache in his heart, he walked.

Only on this foggy evening, he'd wandered farther than intended, ending up in the Fir-wood, standing before the retched faerie hill. He rubbed his tired eyes. The last thing he'd expected to see was a beautiful lass in the mist of a garden he knew didn't exist—a woman and a garden that both vanished from in front of him. He'd felt an odd oomph in his chest when their gazes met, then she was gone.

He was no simpleton. He wasn't imagining things. Something was seriously amiss. *Munn.* That had to be the explanation. The wee man was creating havoc again. Patrick wouldn't stand for it. He ran back through the wood toward the castle, determined to put an end to the mischief.

By the time he entered the courtyard, his chest burned from anger. Not watching where he walked, he tripped on a loose stone and collided with his cousin Stephen.

The blond warrior was his childhood friend, his henchman and personal guard. They had fostered together. No one knew him better, except perhaps for Patrick's young half-sister, Elspeth.

"Where have you been?" Stephen asked. "I was about to send out a search party."

"That would have been a damn fool thing to do in the dark."

"Would it now?" Stephen smiled. "Were you with a lass?"

"Never mind you that." Patrick tightened his lips and glared at his kinsman. "Where is Munn?"

That only served to broaden Stephen's grin. "I saw him earlier in the hall with Elspeth."

Whirling in the direction of the stairs, Patrick strode off.

Stephen's footsteps thudded behind him. "Whatever is the matter with you? You look as if you ate something spoilt."

Patrick took the narrow stairs two at a time, uncaring that his shoulders banged against stone. He burst into the hall and stilled.

The *Brunaidh*, whose duty it was to watch over Clan MacLachlan, sat on a stool near the fire, reciting rhymes for Elspeth. He waved his arms as he spoke. Dressed for foolery, the brownie wore baggy brown leather *trews* and a knee length *leine* of fine woolen cloth secured at the waist by a thick leather belt adorned with bronze. Around his shoulders, he wore a green *brat* held in place by a bronze brooch with a large clear crystal in the center. He tapped his feet in rhythm to the cadence of his voice. On those wee feet, he wore green boots with toes that pointed upward.

"Munn!" Patrick bellowed.

The little man twisted around, his whisker-covered face scrunched more than usual. Panic flashed in blue-green eyes, and he jumped to a full three-foot height. His bent nose twitched and he grasped hold of the funny-looking pointed green cap he always wore.

Anticipating the brownie's attempt to escape, Patrick took hold of him. "Not so fast, wee imp. What mischief have you been about this night?"

"*Nae.*" Munn's whole body shook. "Not I."

"Then what caused a strange lass to appear to me in the Fir-wood and to vanish as quick?"

The brownie's eyes grew big and round, his surprise obvious. Patrick had the sense to put him down and step back. Just in time. In a blink, the little man disappeared.

Patrick scrubbed a hand over his face. More questions plagued him than before.

Munn's essence flowed through the wood, searching for the taint of magic. Soft giggles sang along with the rustle of blowing leaves, alerting him to the lost *bairns* who lived in the trees.

He didn't have time to play their games tonight. He needed to find out what kind of spell caused the chief's vision. Why had it been cast? And who did the casting?

No one else could perform the task. It was up to him to discover the truth. Munn sucked in a chest full of air, pleased with his importance.

As he rushed along the trail, the sound of young voices faded behind him.

The night grew late. A dense fog crept across the moor and through the wood. No mortal man was about. No human saw him appear at the edge of the Fir-wood. He hid behind the old hut and waited. When sure no magic users lingered in the area, he approached the grassy mound.

He didn't know how the faerie knoll worked its magic. 'Twas a secret held dear by the *Sithichean*—the ancient faeries of the Highlands.

The vaporous mist wrapped around him, pressed against him, suffocated him. He inhaled deeply then recoiled, recognizing the exotic oriental scent, the fragrance of peony and freesia and sandalwood. That infuriating *sithiche* must have come out of hiding. She must be who spun the magic.

He searched for other traces, but found naught. The faerie did well to cover her trail.

Munn rubbed his aching temples. What trouble did she conjure this night?

He must warn the chief. Focusing on his destination, he summoned the travel spell, but anger blocked his magic. Munn kicked the dirt at his feet. He paced the knoll and cursed the fae.

Their interference would surely prove disastrous.

He concentrated on his breathing, spinning in frantic circles, until the pressure released and he melted into the mist.

Patrick stood before the fire in his chamber, sipping his finest claret. He swirled the ruby liquid in the cup, speculating the intent of the vision he'd seen in the Fir-wood. He didn't have visions. That was Elspeth's proclivity. His mind unsettled, he stared into the flames. Even the gold and blue dancing lights conspired against him, reminding him of the golden lass with the sparkling sapphire eyes.

Her expression of longing would haunt him through the night. The same need blazed within his chest. Would she have let him envelope her in a protective embrace? Kiss her fine lips?

The thought made him hard. "Ach, well…"

Who could she be? Where did she come from? She wasn't one of the villagers, that was for certain. Could she be one of their kin? Nae. That wouldn't explain the mysterious vanishing garden and cottage.

Seeing the woman where his parents disappeared gave him pause. Could she be a witch? One of the fae? He stilled, shivered, feeling as if a *banshee* walked through him.

A rustling sound disturbed his thoughts when Munn whirled into the chamber, hopping around, ranting unintelligibly. Patrick seized the little man by his tunic, and shook him until he ceased his tirade.

With an angry scowl on his weathered, brown face, the little man wagged his finger. "I ken who caused the mischief. 'Twas Caitrina."

"Witch?"

"*Nae* witch, *sithiche*. Mischievous female sprite set upon us by the old Earl of Argyll himself afore he died." Munn turned and spit on the stone floor. "Guardian of your father's lady-wife."

Patrick raised an eyebrow. "Why dinnae I ken who she is?"

"Ach, 'twas your father's wish to keep it secret." The brownie's voice lowered to a whisper. "When I learned about your stepmother's guardian, I grew angry. You were a *bairn*, too young to ken. We matched spells, Caitrina and me. Me more powerful." Munn puffed out his chest.

"Go on," Patrick urged.

"We created a terrible tempest, heavy rain, thunder and lightning over the mountains, we did. Tremendous rage escaped the otherworld. Your father and stepmother were rowing back from the village. They got caught in mayhem. Chief verra mad. Command us to stop. Nae more spell battles. Caitrina's comings and goings kept secret from all."

"Hmmm." Patrick drained the last of the wine in his cup and filled it again from the jug on the table. "What do you think this *sithiche* is about? Why would she conjure such a vision?"

Why now?

Crinkling his face, adding wrinkles upon wrinkles, Munn made a show of thinking. After several moments, he broke out in a puckish grin.

"You like bonnie lasses." He twirled around, spun in a circle, disappeared.

Damned brownie.

Patrick slumped into the chair beside the hearth and stared into the flames. The fire burned down until nothing remained but cold gray ash. Yet his musing hadn't produced the answers he sought. When he finally fell into bed, a restless sleep held him within its grasp, dreams filled with enchanting sapphire eyes, a petite curvy figure and silky golden-blond tresses.

In the middle of the night, he woke in a rush. Fear tightened his chest, and his heartbeat raced as if he'd run up a mountain trail with an enemy in pursuit.

After a tense moment, his surroundings came into focus. He sank back into the mattress. He needed to be more careful of what he consumed before retiring. Patrick swallowed, trying to ease the dread. In the terror dream, he failed to keep the woman safe from danger.

CHAPTER THREE

Present Day, North Carolina

*L*aurie rubbed the furrow lining her forehead and slumped into the sofa cushions. *Gah*, she must be going crazy. She poured herself another glass of wine and took several quick sips.

Was she hallucinating?

Even with the poor lighting, she found the man fabulously attractive. *Scrumptious*. He could have walked out of the steamiest romance novel. Intense, dark eyes—if only it had been light enough to see the color—set in a face only the Celtic gods could have molded. The sexy cleft in his chin made her mouth go instantly dry. The mere thought of him left her breathless and achy with need.

Had she really reached out to a stranger? How stupid. What if he was a nutcase?

She flicked her gaze to the dark windows then the locked front door. The house was secure.

A psycho? She hoped not. The man seemed familiar. She felt as though she'd met him before. Though where could that have been?

The adrenaline kick waned, taking her energy with it. She

yawned and finished the wine. Maybe there was no danger. The man might be one of Iain's unusual friends dressed in a reenactment costume.

Nothing more? Well, there was the pink light to consider and the weird barrier at the gate.

Imagination. Mentally shaking herself, she prepared for bed.

Unable to fall asleep, she lay beneath the covers and stared at the spinning ceiling fan, replaying the evening's events in her mind. The more she thought about it, the surer she was the whole affair was nothing more than a figment of a way-too-overactive imagination. With time, she succumbed to physical and emotional exhaustion.

A perfectly placed kiss at the nape of her neck caused her sex to clench. The cool, silky sheets did nothing to relieve the heat. He lay behind, her bare back pressed tight against a broad chest, each individual chest hair teasing sensitive skin, sending tiny shock waves along her spine.

"Ah, you've returned." She squirmed, and her dream lover groaned.

"Careful, lass. I wish to last the night." He laved a shoulder and nipped the skin.

He whispered words in a language she didn't know, yet understood in a place deep within her heart. Words of romance and promises of exquisite pleasure. Wave after wave of yearning spiraled through her, straight to the center of her soul.

Turning her to face him, he captured her in a tender embrace. His teeth toyed with an earlobe, and she dug her nails into the flesh on his back. He released a primal growl then continued kissing the way around her neck to the hollow of her throat. A velvety tongue played havoc with her senses. Every nerve ending tingled with pleasure.

With a shockingly rough touch, he caught a breast in his palm, and rubbed the tender nipple with a calloused thumb. Taking the hardened tip into his mouth, he sucked the flesh into a tight sensitized nub. My, God. All thought scattered.

"You're killing me."

"Nae. Loving you."

He placed his palm intimately against her. She inhaled his manly scent—pine and fresh air. No cologne could be as enticing. Repositioning their bodies, he pressed his erection against her softness and thrust. Her gasp was swallowed in an open-mouthed kiss.

More. She wanted more.

She grasped his hips and tugged, drawing him deeper into her body and into a rhythmic dance. He took her to places she'd never imagined. To heights—

The alarm pierced Laurie's fantasy. She reached over to the nightstand and slammed her hand against the off button. Urgh! Another sex dream and they hadn't finished.

Still hot. Still wet. She pinched a pebbled nipple with one hand and slid two fingers from the other between her thighs. She panted, arched her back, and rode her release with a scream.

When euphoria wore off and embarrassment settled in, she threw off the covers and jumped out of bed. She sniffed the air, catching a hint of that same exotic perfume from the room at the inn where she'd first dreamed of the man. *Strange.*

And another strange thing—her dream lover looked like the man in the woods last night. Had he really been there or had a vivid imagination created him after her earlier dream?

So many questions with no easy answers.

Two weeks passed, Laurie almost believed she hadn't seen a man. But...

Dammit there were other things to think about today.

She set aside the garden design she drew on graph paper the previous night and poured a mug of coffee. Dressed in an oversized t-shirt and a worn-out pair of jeans with a tear in one knee, she headed to the garden, wondering what new plant might be poking through the soil today. It seemed like every day something new showed its face to the sun. Today,

Caitrina was taking her to visit garden centers. Laurie couldn't wait.

Once she'd gotten to know Caitrina better, Laurie realized her initial gruff disposition was a facade. She was sweet underneath and they were becoming good friends.

Laurie savored the hazelnut-flavored coffee and the warmth it provided as she strolled along the paths and contemplated the garden's progress. Early morning fog drifted over the beds, adding a touch of charm.

It'd been the right decision to stay in North Carolina.

Though she couldn't ignore her dreams or the strange man no one at the inn seemed to know. Laurie pinched the bridge of her nose. Could he be a figment of her imagination? Was it possible he was nothing more than a manifestation of the stress she'd been under at her job?

Had she made him up because she was lonely? That didn't make sense, still…

With more time in the non-corporate world, would her life settle down, become normal?

She had to hope.

Morning sun burned through the mist. The emerging garden looked awesome. Maybe things had already begun to settle down and return to normal.

Lost in her thoughts, a tinkling noise near the rear gate startled her. A familiar hint of an exotic fragrance played on the breeze. As if in a trance, she rose and walked to the open gate.

Her dream man stood on a grassy knoll at the edge of the woods.

Laurie's pulse quickened and the muscles in her belly tightened as she tried to move toward him. Again, the invisible barrier at the gate held her back. Their gazes met. His deep blue eyes devoured her. The intensity sent a thrill through her system. He reached out his hand and time seemed to stand still. *His eyes are so blue.*

A bright white light arced between them, and he faded away.

She stared at the spot where he'd stood. When she turned around, she released a surprised scream.

"Sorry," Caitrina said. "I didn't mean to frighten you. Thought we might want to get an early start. Have breakfast in the village before visiting garden centers."

"It's okay, you startled me. Laurie pressed her palm against her chest in an attempt to still her racing heart. "I saw that man again."

"Really?"

"Yeah. I don't know what to think. Maybe I shouldn't stay in Anderson Creek. Maybe moving here was a mistake. Maybe I should go to New York and find a good shrink."

Patrick remained outside the walled garden, held in place by an unnatural force. The lass looked exquisite in the early morning light. Compelled to touch her, he reached for her, but a fierce jolt traveled up his arm and a bright light blinded him. Once his vision cleared, she was gone.

Strange. His visions of the lass only came to him in the Fir-wood, near the old hut and that cursed faerie knoll. And the woman, dressed in unusual garments, as if she were a lad. Odd, indeed. He was drawn to her. Not only was she beautiful, but he sensed a kinship between them. A longing to be loved.

Ach, he knew naught of the lass.

Patrick dropped his outstretched arm. What was he doing here, lurking, hoping to see her again? He should have given this place a wide berth instead of hanging about like a besotted fool. There were important activities requiring his attention—practicing sword skills, drilling his men, hunting.

The feud had been quiet of late, but that surely wouldn't continue.

He didn't have time to worry about the woman. Though Munn's insistence that the fae were involved with the lass and perhaps his parent's disappearance brought a disturbing thought. What had Patrick done to encourage their notice?

Why would the fae become involved in his life?

Frustration plunged him into a dark mood.

He trudged toward the castle, but as he got closer, he lengthened his stride determined not to waste the rest of the day. Not to think about the lass who stirred his loins. When he arrived at the stables, he yelled for Stephen to join him. Patrick needed a distraction. A strenuous ride through the forest would serve him well. A hunt would clear his head.

And one never knew what one would find while hunting.

CHAPTER FOUR

Caitrina rolled back and forth on the balls of her feet. "I ken what you need."

"Really?" Laurie braved a smile for her friend.

"You'll feel better after we go plant shopping." Caitrina gently touched Laurie's shoulder.

Laurie calmed, yet felt somewhat bewildered. It was as if the other woman's touch held some magical calming power. Sometimes Caitrina had a strange way about her.

"Shall we go?" She tugged the brim of her hat over her eyes.

"But what about the man?"

"Dinnae think about it."

Maybe Caitrina was right. Perhaps picking out plants for the garden would take her mind off what she thought she saw beyond the gate.

"All right. Let's go."

They drove into the nearby village of Anderson Creek, to the *Le Petit Café and Bakery*, entering to the tinkle of little silver bells hanging on the inside of the door.

"Hello." Caitrina waved to the owner.

The French woman signaled from behind the counter for them to seat themselves. They selected a cozy booth with a view of the creek.

"Did Mairi tell you about the *ceilidh* at the inn this coming Saturday night?" Caitrina asked. "It'll be a full moon, a wonderful reason to celebrate."

"No, she didn't. What is a *ceilidh*?"

"'Tis a wee house party with good food, storytelling, traditional music, dancing. Everyone dresses in Highland costume. You ken? Lots of tartan. 'Tis a grand time."

"Sounds like fun. Not sure what I'd wear though. I don't have anything tartan."

"We'll find something, even if we have to go to the *Celtic Image* shop."

As they finished their omelets, the bells on the door jingled again. A dapper older man sauntered in wearing dress slacks, a tweed jacket and cap, a walking cane at his side. His alert gaze spied Caitrina. Stepping up to their table, he removed his cap and bowed.

"Good day to you. 'Tis a pleasure to see such bonnie lasses." He grasped Caitrina's hand and brushed a kiss across the top of her knuckles. With a wink, he said, "Introduce me to your friend, lass."

"Hello to you, Mr. MacNaughton." Caitrina smiled playfully at him. "This is the lass living in the old cottage at the inn. Her name is Laurie Bernard."

"Hello, sir." Laurie produced a friendly smile for the handsome, elder gentleman.

His keen eyes measured her.

"Pleased to meet you, lass." He inclined his head. "Enchanting old place, the cottage. I hope you decide to remain among us."

"Thank you." Laurie squirmed in her seat, awkward, but needed to ask, "Do you know of anyone who might...hike the woods near my cottage?"

Caitrina stared out the window. Laurie frowned, wondering why she looked away.

"Why do you ask?" Mr. MacNaughton narrowed his eyes.

"I saw a man this morning outside my garden gate,"

Laurie said.

"Probably a guest from the inn out for a morning constitutional."

I doubt that. "You're likely right."

The stranger didn't dress like anyone she'd seen at the inn. The Scottish men at the inn wore modern kilts, not a blanket wrapped around pure muscle. Maybe she *had* imagined him.

"I see friends yonder, I must be off." Mr MacNaughton ambled over to the counter to chat with the women seated there.

"He's a terrible flirt," Caitrina whispered from behind her hand.

They paid the bill and left the café. They drove for a few miles until they glimpsed the sign for *May's Flowers*, apparently one of Caitrina's favorite garden centers.

After parking, they strolled among rows of plants and flowers, stopping often to discuss the merits of one plant or another. Halting at one of the display tables, Caitrina picked up a nursery pot with light green foliage.

"Foxgloves will be perfect in the semi-shade near the rear gate."

"I've seen them in catalogs. Digitalis *purpurea*. Am I correct?"

"Aye. They're biennial, and they'll self-sow each year." Caitrina tilted her head to the side. "Some say they attract faeries."

"Faeries, huh?" Laurie touched a soft green leaf and smiled over the fanciful idea. "What color will they bloom?"

"This variety is a mix. The flowers come in white and shades of pink or purple."

"Which color attracts faeries?" Laurie kept her grin to herself.

"All of them," Caitrina said with a straight face. "Especially the pink."

"Then I hope these plants produce pink flowers." Laurie selected several pots and placed them in their cart.

Before leaving May's, they crammed the small car with as

many perennials and annuals as would fit, and made arrangements for the delivery of more plants the next day.

After visiting two more garden centers, Laurie slid behind the wheel and sighed. The morning had been long and judging by the height of the sun, the afternoon was slipping by. She glanced sideways at Caitrina. "You are tireless, but I'm hungry. Could we stop for a bite to eat?"

"We probably should return to the cottage. We don't want the plants to dry out in the car. We can stop at the vegetarian restaurant in the village for a sandwich and soup to go. Teddy makes fabulous tomato, roasted-garlic soup."

Laurie's stomach growled. "You're making my mouth water. Let's hurry."

The *Baked Potato* was a storefront vegetarian café located next door to the *Celtic Image* shop on the main drag of Anderson Creek. Tantalizing aromas greeted them when they stepped into the crowded restaurant. Several customers waited in line at the counter in front of them.

One stood out among the others, not only due to his substantial height, but also for his mode of dress. His handsome six-foot-seven body was clothed in a cream fisherman's sweater, a red plaid kilt, and around his waist hung a fur sporran with a badger head.

He strode to them and gave Caitrina a cursory glance before smiling at Laurie. "Hello. You must be our new resident. Iain says nice things about you."

Laurie expected Caitrina to introduce them. When she glanced at her friend, she found her glaring at the guy.

"Douglas MacKinnon," Caitrina snapped. "Rude as usual."

His eyes turned cold. "Love, where were you last night? You were supposed to meet me."

"You assume much. I never agreed to meet you." Caitrina grabbed Laurie by the arm and pulled her past Douglas to the counter. He chuckled from behind her as she ordered sandwiches and soup from Teddy.

Douglas leaned close to Caitrina, and she stiffened.

"Ach, lass. Why do you fight it? You know we are meant to be together." Although he whispered the words near Caitrina's ear, Laurie overheard.

He stepped back and raised his chin. "Talk about rude, Caitrina. Wouldn't it be polite for you to introduce me to your friend?"

Visibly bristling, she turned to Laurie. "This horny toad owns the Celtic shop next door. Douglas, meet Laurie."

"Nice to meet you." Laurie shook his hand.

"My pleasure. As I said before this minx interrupted, Iain speaks highly of you."

Laurie couldn't help but notice the yearning in his tawny eyes when he gazed at Caitrina and felt a twinge of longing. Would be nice to have someone look at her that way.

The image of the man in the woods popped into her mind for the umpteenth time. What would it be like to have him desire her the way Douglas obviously wanted Caitrina?

"Come on." Caitrina took the bag of food from Teddy and again grabbed Laurie by the arm, dragging her out the door. Laurie glanced over her shoulder at Douglas and gave him a finger wave. His hearty laughter boomed as the door shut behind her.

When they returned to the cottage, she walked into the living room, and Caitrina followed with the bag of food.

"My new dining set hasn't arrived yet from the manufacturer. I hope you don't mind eating at the coffee table."

Putting the bag down, Caitrina sat cross-legged on the floor. "This is fine. Do you have any whisky? I could use a stiff drink."

Laurie chuckled. "I have wine. Would you care for a glass of pinot noir?"

"Most definitely."

After fetching glasses, the wine and a corkscrew from the kitchen, Laurie opened the bottle. She poured them both a glass and handed one to Caitrina.

"Douglas MacKinnon is attractive, don't you think?"

Caitrina accepted the wine and held it up in toast. "Let's drink to brawny men. May they be there when you want them, and disappear when you dinnae."

Laurie cringed. The toast made her think of the mysterious man. She chuckled at the idiocy and clicked her glass against Caitrina's.

They ate the tasty lunch, chatted and drank wine, more wine, and still more wine.

"I'll pick out something for you to wear to the *ceilidh*," Caitrina said.

Laurie followed her into the bedroom and into the walk-in closet. Caitrina selected a dark green skirt with a drawstring waist, adding a soft, cream-colored linen peasant blouse that tied at the neck.

She held up the blouse. "This will work with the skirt. It'll be comfortable, no zippers or buttons, only ties. You can go to the Celtic shop for a tartan shawl to wrap around your shoulders. If you pick a plaid that matches the skirt, you'll look perfect."

Laurie tried to remember having seen the clothes before. She couldn't. She tended to be impulsive when shopping. She'd probably purchased the items and never worn them.

Returning to the living room, she poured them both more wine while Caitrina pulled out the folder with the garden plan and made a note on the sketch.

Laurie set the wine glasses on the coffee table. "I was thinking there might be enough room at the south side for a greenhouse. I'm considering asking Iain if I can buy the cottage and some of the land around it."

"Really?" Caitrina's eyes took on a speculative tilt.

"Yeah. I think I'd like to live here permanently."

"Well, then, a greenhouse might fit."

"I wondered. Actually, I thought this might be a good setting for a garden center."

With the tip of a finger, Caitrina scratched her chin, studying Laurie. "It would."

Laurie cleared her throat. "I know there are already a few

garden centers in the area, but none with special services like workshops or design clinics."

"Interesting concepts."

"Yeah, I thought so. I'd like to open a garden center here. That is, if I can work out a deal with Iain and Mairi."

Caitrina's expression remained noncommittal. Maybe it was too much to hope that she might want to join Laurie in a new business. She would wait until her plans were more firm before asking Caitrina to be her partner.

"I don't mean to open a garden center right away." Laurie bit her bottom lip. "After I learn more about garden culture. I already have a lot of business experience." She picked up her glass and sipped the wine.

"In time, with my help, you might learn enough." Caitrina, too, took a sip of wine.

They talked about the garden, browsed flower catalogs, discussed Laurie's plans. They gossiped about who would attend the *ceilidh*. Time slid by. Day turned into night. A couple of empty bottles had rolled under the coffee table, and she opened another.

Her head pounded when she woke in the morning. Laurie lay on the bed, fully dressed, unable to recall how she'd gotten there. Oh, yeah, the wine.

God. What was she thinking?

While she'd slept, she had a bizarre dream. Now, when she tried to think about it, she couldn't remember anything. How weird was that? Oh, well. Not important.

She dragged dead weight to the shower and leaned against the tile wall under a spray of cool water. More awake, she dressed, made coffee, and drank a mug full. After forcing down toast, the woozy sensation faded. With a second mug of java in hand, Laurie walked outside.

The late morning sky threatened rain. She found Caitrina working in the garden. "This is a surprise. I wasn't expecting to find you here."

Caitrina stopped and looked up. "How are you feeling?"

"Like a Mack truck ran over me and thousands of foot

soldiers marched through my mouth. Other than that, fine. How about you?"

"Alcohol has no effect on me."

"Why not?"

Caitrina lowered her head and placed a root ball into a small hole. "It just doesn't."

That's odd. They'd both drank a lot of wine. Laurie shrugged. "Aren't you fortunate."

"Here. Start planting these as I've laid them out." Caitrina handed her a trowel and pointed to the trays of seedlings sitting on the freshly turned soil. "We're in luck. Drizzly weather is a good time for planting."

Laurie reached for one of the small fiber pots. A creepy sensation on her arm made her shudder and toss the plant aside with a curt scream. She brushed off a nasty-looking spider. "I hate the damn things." Caitrina laughed, and Laurie chuckled. "Foolish, I know."

They worked together until the middle of the afternoon. Laurie kept glancing toward the back gate. Would her dream man show up again? When—if—he came, did she want to see him? Her nipples hardened in answer, and she blew a stray hair out of her face. She needed to stop thinking about the stranger.

After Caitrina left, Laurie ate a sandwich, showered and dressed in clean clothes. Then she drove to the village. She passed the historic stone church and parked in front of the *Celtic Image* shop.

Inside, she scanned the merchandise. Racks of wool clothing—mostly tartan—lined the far wall. Other shelving contained linens and china and knick-knacks. Several glass-topped cases displayed jewelry and other novelties. Douglas MacKinnon stood at the front of the shop, behind a glass display counter full of knives, waiting on an older woman. He glanced up and waved.

Laurie strolled through the aisles, perusing the large selection of Scottish and Irish items. Welsh things also occupied the space. She stopped at one case to glance through CDs before moving on to a case filled with intricately crafted Celtic jewelry. Along with the modern, she found wonderful antique pieces. Her hands itched to touch the fine work.

"Hello." Douglas approached her. "How do you like my store?"

"Nice. This jewelry is precious."

"Aye, 'tis exquisite. I often get pieces from estate sales, pieces brought with emigrants when they came to America and passed down through the generations. The descendents don't always feel as strongly about tradition as their forefathers. Some prefer to sell their heritage, rather than hold on to it. 'Tis really a shame. Such pieces should stay within a clan." Douglas sighed. "Oh, well, my gain. Can I show you anything?"

"I came to purchase a shawl for the *ceilidh* at the inn tomorrow. I'd like to match this green wool skirt." She pulled the skirt out of her tote bag.

"Do you have a specific clan tartan in mind?"

She hadn't given it much thought. Shouldn't she wear her clan's plaid?

"Do you think the MacIntyre plaid might match?"

"I have a few different MacIntyre tartans." Douglas searched a shelf containing an assortment of plaid items in plastic covers. He laid several on the counter for her to consider.

One was predominately green and blue with red and white stripes. The green in the plaid matched the green in the skirt perfectly, as if made from the same dyed yarn.

"This one." Laurie pointed to the plaid she liked best.

"A nice match. 'Tis the MacIntyre hunting tartan. Now, would you like a *ruana*?" Douglas showed her a small poncho-like wrap, open in the front. "This is the long one. I also have a shorter version. Or, let's see…"

Laurie leaned forward.

He retrieved a couple more bags from the shelf. "I also have stoles and shawls."

Douglas laid them out for view.

She considered the stole, brushing her fingers over the soft wool fabric. This would be her first real piece of MacIntyre plaid. She'd been all over the world and bought all types of things, expensive and inexpensive. For some reason, buying this one simple item seemed a momentous occasion, as if she were committing herself to something. She gazed at Douglas through misty eyes.

"I like them all, but for the party the stole makes the most sense."

"Excellent choice. Shall I put the others aside for you?" he said with what she assumed his most winning salesman's smile.

She laughed. "Let me think about it and I'll let you know. By the way, will you be attending the party?"

"I never miss a *ceilidh*." His smile reached his eyes. "Will you spare a dance for me?"

"Sure, but if my guess is right, you'd rather spend time with Caitrina."

"Am I that transparent?" He walked toward the front of the store. "Shall I ring this up for you?"

"Yeah." Laurie followed him to the register at the front counter where a very large, very old sword secured to the wall above his head caught her gaze.

"Is that what you use when you practice with Iain?"

He chuckled. "Nae, 'tis for a client."

"Impressive." She took the bag from Douglas, her gaze lingering on the claymore. Rounding the counter, he gallantly offered his arm and escorted her to the door. Before she left, she gazed back at the sword and shivered.

Since the garden kept Laurie busy, she was surprised how quickly Saturday evening arrived. Although no one would see them, she put on her sexiest undergarments, a lacy sage green thong and matching under-wire bra with a front closure. They made her feel special. Feminine. She slipped on the peasant blouse Caitrina selected, allowing the string at the neckline to hang. The green skirt went on next, the hem grazing her ankles. Made of lightweight wool, it was perfect for the cool mountain air.

She wiggled her toes. What shoes to wear? She slipped into a pair of black hand-stitched China flats and wrapped the new MacIntyre stole around her shoulders. After clipping her hair up, she was ready to go. The reflection in the mirror proved the deep worry furrows had faded from her brow. She grinned, pleased.

Laurie hummed while walking to the inn, enjoying the short stroll through the meadow's wildflowers, through the woods, and across the flower-laden gardens.

The atmosphere at the inn struck her with wonder. Candles lit the foyer and the parlor off it, the effect a charming glow. A crowd had gathered in the parlor, everyone seated or standing huddled around the elder Mr. MacNaughton. He sat on a tall stool in the center of the room, telling a story, his audience enthralled.

She stepped closer to listen.

"The lass the prince sought ran across the meadow, stopping at the edge of the Fir-wood to catch her breath. She glanced over her shoulder and her gaze darted from place to place.

The clouds cleared the full moon and shimmering light washed over the wood, its silvery glow falling upon her beauty. Her thick, auburn hair hung loose down her slender back, to her waist, like a river of fiery flames. Her skin was as white as the purest Madonna lily, her lips the precious red of the holly berry, and she possessed sparkling green eyes more glorious than the purest emeralds.

For you ken…the lass was born a princess. The prince's unusually keen sight allowed him to see her from a great distance. He was not of human blood, but of the *Sithichean*. This in our ancient Gaelic tongue, the language of our Scottish fathers, means the faeries, although they go by many names in many other countries.

The prince found himself enchanted by the beautiful princess.

Hidden since childhood, she was the daughter of a beautiful mortal woman who captured the heart of Torguil, an ancient *sithiche* prince, a favorite of the high-queen. The immortal queen was a creature of great power, beyond the ken of mere humans, having descended from the gods who walked in ancient Scotia. Yet she was jealous of the princess.

Now, the halfling daughter of Torguil was unaware of the danger stalking her, not only from the young prince, but also from others...others more sinister.

Unmindful of the fate awaiting her, she ran through the Fir-wood, a place where the veil between the land of mortals and that of the fae was thin and where on full moons, there was an opening.

When the mist cleared, the princess found herself on a large knoll of rich green grass. She saw the prince pursuing her and stepped back, falling through space and time..."

"Hello."

Laurie jumped with a gasp, disturbing the people standing around her. They stared with disapproval, a finger to their lips, signaling for quiet. Caitrina rolled her eyes, inclined her head toward the foyer and walked out of the parlor. Laurie followed, somewhat disappointed to miss the rest of the tale.

"You startled me." She smiled. "Wow, you look wonderful."

Caitrina had traded her dirty work clothes for a gauzy, emerald green silk dress that molded to her tall, slender frame. Around her shoulders, she wore a sash of green and purple tartan with shimmering golden threads. Pinned at her shoulder was a gold brooch intricately crafted with thistle designs and amethyst gemstones. Her rich hair, usually hidden under her floppy garden hat, fell loose past her shoulders to her waist, the auburn strands on fire with highlights that glistened in the candlelight.

"You look like the princess Mr. MacNaughton describes in his story."

Caitrina shrugged. "You look nice too, but something's missing."

She opened her hand to show Laurie an exquisitely crafted Celtic brooch of silver, decorated with intertwining animals and spiral filigrees, adorned with six small moonstones. She pinned it to Laurie's stole at the shoulder. "There. Perfect."

Appreciating its fine artistry, Laurie brushed her fingers over the brooch. Moisture filled her eyes. "You are sweet, but I can't wear this. It must be a priceless antique."

"Douglas told me you were admiring the jewelry at his shop. He thought you might like to borrow the brooch for the evening."

"Must be worth a fortune. What if I lose it?"

Caitrina glanced away. "'Tis a mere reproduction."

Laurie didn't believe her. She knew jewelry and was positive this piece was very old and extremely valuable, but the last thing she wanted to do was insult her new friend. She'd wear the brooch for the evening and be extra careful not to lose it.

With a mischievous grin, Caitrina dragged her into the dining room where the furniture was pushed to the side. A fiddler played and couples danced. Someone handed her a glass of wine, only for Douglas MacKinnon to take it away and place it on a nearby table as he pulled her onto the dance floor where he taught her the intricate steps. After that, she danced with Iain until he handed her off to Teddy, who in turn handed her off to another fellow. She giggled with merriment as she whirled around the floor.

The evening flew and when the gathering ended, Douglas and Caitrina walked her home. It was a nice night for a stroll with the full moon shining bright in the clear sky. They took their time, enjoying each other's company.

At the cottage, Laurie offered them a nightcap, pouring them each a glass of port. They wandered into the garden to enjoy the beautiful evening.

"Do you feel the magic in the air?" Caitrina asked.

Douglas peered at the moonlit sky and chuckled. "Aye,

lass. Strong magic."

Laurie glanced around, feeling a sudden chill.

Caitrina grasped her hand. "Come. I want to show you the foxglove we planted. They've flowered. Pink."

"Pink?" Laurie squeaked.

"Aye, faerie pink."

Douglas's eyes narrowed. "What are you up to, Caitrina?"

"Nothing for you to worry about." She squeezed Laurie's fingers. "Come on."

Unease skittered along Laurie's spine as she walked with Caitrina to the back gate. She frowned when she smelled the now familiar exotic fragrance on her friend. "What the hell?"

A tinkling sound confirmed her fear.

The gate swung open.

He stood just beyond the garden gate. Her pulse jackrabbited. Pulling away from Caitrina, she stepped back in panic.

Caitrina pressed a hand against Laurie's back and shoved her forward. Terror forced the air from Laurie's lungs as she tripped through the gate opening.

Nothing held her back, no barrier. She fell forward...over a precipice into a swirling fog, down...down...down through a dark tunnel. The walls spun. She plunged faster and faster. In the distance, she couldn't tell how far, a blinding, bright light—just a white glow in a tunnel of blackness—showed. What was there? Death?

Oh God, what was happ—

All at once, she was sucked into the white brilliance. She choked on the scream in her throat, cringing against the intense whining assaulting her ears.

She spun, or everything around her was spinning, she wasn't sure which. Her sensitized skin tingled as if zapped by an electric charge. Laurie squeezed her eyes shut against the brightness. With her eyes closed, she felt lost, more frightened. She opened them just as the light exploded into a million fragments of brilliant color, a dazzling kaleidoscope. Then she was falling again.

Down...down...down, faster and faster. Water flowed below her, a stream. She plummeted toward it. Bracing herself, she thought she'd crash into the rushing water, only to propel across it. She hit the ground hard and saw nothing more.

CHAPTER FIVE

*L*aurie opened her eyes a crack. Her head pounded, her pulse raced. This wasn't good. Those couldn't be two, huge, leather-clad feet inches from her face.

She opened her eyes wider. Raised her gaze higher. Those feet—the ones that couldn't be there—was it possible they were attached to two muscular calves wrapped in soft napped animal skins?

Higher still. Bare knees. Plaid wool and saffron linen.

Farther up, she took in all of the man who towered over her. Piercing blue eyes blinked. Crinkles appeared in the corners. He was grinning. Not outwardly. The perfectly shaped lips remained tight and straight. But something within this gorgeous man was pleased.

She gasped with recognition. This was her man, the one from her heated dreams and visions. The man she didn't believe existed. The man who made her insides flip-flop.

Unsure what had just happened, she gave her head a firm shake. Mistake. Dizziness hit in waves. She swallowed hard. When the nausea passed, she pushed her palms against the ground and rose to her feet. Unsteady, she swayed. The stranger's image blurred.

Large calloused hands gripped her arms. A strange though

familiar jolt of energy coursed through her, causing her heart to beat too fast. He quickly released her.

He must have felt it too.

Again, she swayed. Laurie reached for his support at the same time he took hold of her upper arms.

She blinked to clear her vision and moistened dry lips. The flash of desire in his eyes made her shiver. He smiled for real this time, leaned forward, placed a hand behind her head, and brushed her lips with his. Gentle at first, then with vigor, his tongue delved into her mouth.

Instinct insisted she struggle. Holding her body rigid, she fisted her hands, which he'd trapped within his embrace. She forced her fingers open and pressed her palms against his hard chest—a vain attempt to push him away.

The current flowing between them became overpoweringly seductive. No man had made her feel this way before. For several moments, she wavered between fighting him—a familiar stranger—and succumbing to the delicious sensations swamping her. He deepened the kiss, and the internal battle ended. Desire won. She clasped hold of the front of his shirt with shaky hands and kissed him back with pent-up passion.

Satiny lips anchored her in a storm of unfamiliar sensation. Pleasure vibrated along her body. She opened her eyes a slit. The intensity of the man's shocking kiss matched the masculine power burning in his startling blue eyes.

His grip tightened. His fingers burned through her clothing, searing her skin. She closed her eyes and sank into the reality of her dream lover's embrace.

Patrick closed his eyes and growled deep in his throat as desire pooled in his groin. Their kiss, potent and deep, an intoxicating aphrodisiac, became more and more heated. At first, he'd been shocked by the arc of power, but he couldn't stop himself from claiming what he sensed belonged to him. What started as an unconscious display of dominance became a much more meaningful symbol of possession.

His forceful kiss demanded surrender.

She melted against him, and he savored his victory as her response matched his passion. He stroked and caressed her soft curves. Her well-rounded backside fit perfectly into his large hands as if God made her for him. He dragged his lips away from hers for only a moment, grasped a firm hold of her buttocks, and lifted her off the ground. The movement released her hands from the prison within his arms.

She curled her arms around his neck when he repositioned her against his length.

He held her tight against his chest, molding her to the contours of his body. A stranger—he'd never wanted anyone more. The proof of his unrestrained arousal was the hard pressure intimately pressed against the juncture of her thighs. Was she as shocked by his ardor as he? Rational thought disappeared when he rubbed against the lass.

She rubbed back, proving she enjoyed the connection too. A gasp escaped her soft lips. Patrick took her sweet breath into his mouth and released a moan of his own.

Tantalizing pleasure pulsed through his veins. His erection hardened. He wanted the lass in ways he couldn't comprehend. He felt her nipples tighten into hard buds through the linen of the *leine*. His need grew rock hard, almost painful, as he captured her mouth again, relishing her unique flavor, inhaling her intoxicating scent. Cinnamon and wine and roses.

A twig snapped nearby, and he jerked his eyes open to the sight of his cousin stepping from the trees. The warrior cleared his throat.

The lass came to herself at the same time, and froze. Patrick reluctantly ended the kiss, stepped back, but held her steady. For a moment, they stared into each other's eyes. Hers shone with confusion, fear and desire mingling with the passionate heat still flowing between them. He didn't want to acknowledge what his eyes must reveal.

Again, Stephen cleared his throat.

The powerful surge of energy dissolved, and Patrick

released the lass and took another step back. Although he refused to show it, the experience shook him. Somehow, in the deepest elemental part of his soul, he knew she belonged to him. He'd instinctively branded her with his bold kiss, staking his claim.

"You followed me. Why?" He glared at his cousin.

"To guard your back, you dolt. Elspeth is worried. You have been acting odd." A smirk curved his lips. "I see 'twas a lass that had you a wandering. Are you bewitched then?"

Patrick uttered a loud, "*Humph*," and glanced at the delectable lass.

Slower to recover, she raised a trembling hand to swollen lips. His blood ran heavy and his cock jerked within the folds of his *plaide*.

"The lass is a wee bit befuddled from your ardor, Patrick," Stephen said, still grinning. "Is this your vanishing lass then? The one from your visions?"

Her cheeks flushed a lovely crimson before she lowered her gaze to the ground. When she glanced at him again, Patrick ran an unsteady hand over his hair. With a great deal of effort, he forced a blank expression to his face. A beam of moonlight cast a glow over her curvaceous form. He studied her, raking her with his eyes. Starting with the glorious mass of golden hair pinned atop her head, moving downward, lingering for a moment on blue eyes filled with fear and perhaps a spark of defiance.

He slid his gaze farther downward until it reached her toes. He took in everything, missing naught, including the *plaide* wrapped around her shoulders clasped by a familiar brooch, the fabric clutched in a death grip by a delicate hand with elegant fingers, beautiful, unusual, enticing, each nail the color of oyster shells. He clearly imagined the sensual sensation of those fingernails grazing across his bare chest and other more sensitive skin.

He shivered and his breathing quickened. His heart thudded hard against his ribs as his body tightened more with desire. He fought for control. "*A bheil Gaidhlig agad?*"

The lass stared at him, opened her mouth as if to speak, and shut it again. He narrowed his eyes.

She blinked. "What did you say?"

Sassenach. She spoke the damn English tongue. And poorly. He tasted bitter disappointment. "Who are you, lass? What are you doing in this wood alone? Where is your escort?" He switched to the language of the Lowlands.

"Could this be a trap? Ambush?" Stephen pulled a knife from his boot, his gaze searching the surrounding area.

Patrick ignored him and returned his attention to the lass. Her eyes widened at the sight of the sharp-edged blade. He pushed her behind him while keeping hold of her arm and responded to Stephen in Gaelic. "Munn believes the lass not to be a threat."

Laurie's body thrummed, taut with desire not sated. She swallowed hard and tried to pull out of the man's grasp, but failed.

The now-familiar pressure of his grip no longer frightened her. She understood in the depth of her soul the man who kissed her with such tender passion would never physically harm her. Still, panic hovered too close for comfort. How had she gotten here?

No longer was she in the woods near her cottage and garden. Instead, she stood at the edge of a dark, dense forest near what appeared to be a one-room timber hut with a dilapidated thatched roof.

Who were these two men? Should she run? She didn't believe she could escape, and the last thing she wanted to do was enrage the men.

"This isn't Kansas," she whispered under her breath.

The man, whose name must be Patrick, yanked her in front of him. "What is Kansas? Speak, lass. I command it."

His aggressive attitude provoked her anger. She overcame her fear, pulled away and glared at him. Then turned to the other man. "Excuse me, sir, my name is Laurie Bernard. I'm confused, tired and frightened. I don't know where I am or how I got here. I just want to return home. Can you help me? Please."

She sneaked a peek at Patrick to gauge his reaction.

He clenched and unclenched his fingers, only to clench them again. He glared at the other man's grinning face. Patrick seemed angry. Although the other man's appearance unnerved her, she was glad he'd interrupted. How far would she have let things go had he not arrived? Her insides squirmed. She didn't want to think about that.

Patrick motioned for the other man to leave. Laurie held her breath, afraid to be left alone with the man who'd kissed her with such hunger. What if he tried to kiss her again? Could she resist? She stood straighter. Of course, she wouldn't permit it. He was a total stranger. She shouldn't have allowed him to kiss her the first time.

The other man swept his gaze around the area seeming reluctant to leave. Finally, he whirled on his heel and entered a trail in the woods.

Patrick faced her. He moved closer. She stepped back.

She flicked a glance toward the trail the other man took. Should she follow him? Maybe he would help her find her way home. Probably not. She peered at Patrick through her lashes.

His jaw tightened and he took another step forward.

She bit her bottom lip but held her ground. They silently contemplated each other.

"This way, Mistress Laurie." With his lips curved in a brittle smile, he grasped her by the elbow." We go to the hall where we will unravel this puzzle. And I assure you, we will."

Hall? She dug her heels in, pulling back. "Wait. I don't know who you are."

"Patrick MacLachlan of Clan MacLachlan, your humble servant." He bent at the waist in an old fashioned, formal bow.

She snorted, and his eyes widened in disbelief. Laurie sucked back the urge to grin. "I don't believe there's a humble bone in your body and you are definitely no one's servant."

"Quite true. And you are nae innocent," he taunted. "Do you throw yourself at every man you meet?"

Insulted, she opened her mouth to give him a good tongue-lashing, but he held up his hand, stopping her mid-breath. He ground his teeth, obviously working to suppress unwarranted irritation.

"There is something you need to understand, lass. I have claimed you as my own, with my cousin Stephen as my witness. I choose to believe you are an innocent and not a wanton. You belong to me now. If I ever find you with another man you will not enjoy the consequences."

"How dare you! You don't own me," Laurie sputtered. She couldn't believe the gall of the infuriating man.

"You became mine when you returned my kiss," Patrick said.

"Are you for real?"

"Aye. Come this way." He again took a firm hold on her elbow, daring her with hard eyes to ignore his command.

"*Phff.*" She exhaled and jumped from the man's grasp. "Why did you kiss me?"

His full lips slowly curved at the corners then widened into a devilish grin. Her mind turned to mush.

"I wanted to."

The rumble from his chest did enticing things; low, in the core of her sex. With effort, she ignored the seductive sensation. "Do you always do whatever you want?"

Still smiling, he nodded. "Aye. Now come."

"No." Laurie met the challenge in his eyes.

He glanced at the darkening sky. She followed his gaze. Clouds moved in fast, dimming the brightness of the moon. "Suit yourself, lass." He turned away and strode off into the woods.

Left alone in the dark was definitely *not* what she wanted. "Wait! I'm coming."

CHAPTER SIX

Caitrina hovered at the edge of the wood, cloaked in the glamour of invisibility. She raised her arms over head in a languid stretch until her spine aligned with a soft crack. It felt so good to have shed the gardener glamour. Posing as a human in the twenty-first century was taxing beyond measure.

She ran tactile fingers over her silk gown, relishing its soft luxury and drew in the fragrance of fir with bliss. Magic hummed. The verdant forest nearly crackled with her power. Her smile widened as sparks ignited and flashed between the intended couple.

The plan progressed as intended. She clapped her hands, more pleased than she'd been since forced to leave the shores of her beloved faerie paradise *Tir-nan-Óg* —land o' heart's desire—centuries ago. She would outwit the queen and win the first part of the challenge.

Easy as snapping her fingers. Almost.

When Laurie ran after the MacLachlan chief, Caitrina purred like a feline who'd caught its prey. Satisfaction shimmered within her mind, but then she thought about Oonagh and her stomach clenched. The High Queen of the Fae believed the challenge would force Caitrina into an eternity of servitude. She curled her hands into fists. No way would she let that happen.

A change in atmospheric pressure prickled over her skin. Sensing Munn nearby, she stilled, closed her eyes, and summoned her image with a mere thought. Without a whisper of sound, her form emerged and took shape. Inhaling sharply, she spun to face the meddlesome brownie.

The wee man slowly approached, even though his expression twisted into a portrait of fear. Stubborn *brùnaidh*.

"What mischief caused thee?" he demanded. "Where be the old chief? His lady?"

Caitrina stepped in close and frowned at the fool. She needed to get him out of the way before he endangered the completion of her tasks.

Although she smelled his terror, he held his ground and returned her glare. "Be gone! You dinnae belong here. Cease darkening MacLachlan lands.

"'Tis none of your concern."

"Aye, 'tis. You toy with the young chief."

"You'll not interfere." With a flick of her wrist, she cast him far away.

His image blinked out on a horrified scream.

Caitrina smiled, brushed some residual dust from her gown, dissolved into a passing plume of mist, and rode the breeze toward Castle Lachlan and her pawns.

CHAPTER SEVEN

Clouds moved swiftly across a starless sky, casting the land below in shadow. Every muscle in Patrick's body tightened with acute awareness of the woman who walked behind him along the wooded path. Although she dressed in the fine cloth of a highborn lady, when she stumbled over loose stones in her unsuitable shoes, she swore under her breath like a low-bred whore.

Had inattentive guardians allowed her too much freedom, and she'd lingered more than she should within hearing of stable lads or foul-mouthed warriors?

He would forgive her the minor failing, though suspected she'd require a heavy hand to guide her. Who cared so little for the lass they allowed her to wander about unescorted?

She grabbed hold of his arm and tugged hard. "Stop."

"What?" Patrick ignored the jolt from her touch, stopped in place and twisted around to glare at her.

"How much farther? We've been walking a long time." She puffed out a breath and brushed a stray hair from her face.

"Not far." He caught her frown and a glimmer of gold in the moonlight. Why did she wear his stepmother's brooch? He was tempted to question her, but he'd wait until he secured her in the castle.

Patrick whirled on his heel and started walking, expecting her to continue following. He squeezed his fist tight then uncurled his fingers. Too many questions rattled around in his head.

Was she involved with fae magic? Munn claimed the faerie, Caitrina, caused the visions. Was the lass in league with the faerie?

They left the trees, finding the sky had cleared. Patrick straightened his shoulders with pride at the sight of Castle Lachlan in the glow of the full moon. The lass would be impressed. He stopped and waited for her to catch up. Disappointment tweaked his pride when she didn't compliment the fortification of his home. When he grasped her elbow to guide her down the grassy slope, she trembled.

Maybe she wasn't of his station. Nae. Her garments were too fine not to be.

She stared toward the castle, took a step, hesitated, and almost tripped him. He urged her forward with light pressure. She stopped when they neared the beach across the water from the castle.

"Oh. My. God." Her trembling increased, and when she tried to pull away, he released her arm. "This can't be for real. Please, tell me that's not a medieval castle."

"Medieval? 'Tis my home."

She teetered and collapsed against him.

He shook her. Even with gentle slaps to her cheeks, she didn't respond.

For all the saints, what was he to do with her now? He lifted her and carried her to the water's edge. She weighed naught and was easy to carry.

Patrick placed her into the *currach* he'd left on the beach. She didn't stir, and a knot of alarm twisted in his stomach. He climbed in behind her and sat. The small boat, made of skins and wicker, pitched. He carefully settled himself and pulled the lass onto his lap—to balance the boat, not for any other reason.

Paddle in hand, he rowed toward the opposite shore.

He frowned at the limp woman. Women didn't swoon in his presence. There must be something wrong with the lass. At least her chest rose and fell with her breath. He hadn't scared her to death.

He shouldn't have kissed her, but hadn't been able to stop.

Feathery lashes graced smooth cheeks silvered in the moonlight. Patrick feasted on the sight like a starving man. His chest tightened for lack of air. This wouldn't do. He tore his gaze away. An ardent fondness for the lass would bring naught but trouble.

Though she belonged to him, it would be best to maintain a distance. He couldn't afford becoming attached. Not with the false betrothal hanging over his head. But damn, he desired the lass with every breath.

Arriving at the castle side of the small bay, he jumped into the shallow water. The boat scraped along the bottom when pulled onto the beach. Still, she didn't stir.

Patrick lifted the woman, held on tight, and strode across the shingle to the castle. Entering through the main gate, he made haste to the wheel stair. The tight space required caution to ensure the woman's head didn't bang against rough stone.

In the great hall, he found his cousin with Elspeth seated before the fire. His sister leapt from her chair and ran to him. "Stephen told me what happened in Fir-wood." Her gaze slid over the woman in his arms, and her eyes widened. "Did you hurt her?"

"Ach. She but swooned," he said. "You have nae faith in me, wee sister. I dinnae hurt lasses."

Elspeth gave him a sharp look. "I ken that verra well, yet these are unusual events. Bring her to my solar, she requires rest."

His sister hurried toward the far stair, signaling for him to follow. He did, until she entered the passageway. He continued past her, up another flight of steps, along the long corridor, to kick open the door to his bedchamber.

"Laurie." The unfamiliar name sounded pleasant as it rolled from his lips.

She didn't respond. He placed her on the bed and twisted to reach for a cover.

"Patrick, you cannae," Elspeth said softly. "'Tis not fitting for her to be in your bedchamber." His sister stood in the doorway, frowning at him.

"She is my responsibility."

"'Tis wrong."

"I have claimed her. 'Tis for me to decide what is right." His tone held unintended harshness, but he wanted his sister to understand the significance of his position. "Hear me, she stays locked in this chamber until I discover if she poses a threat."

Elspeth arched a feminine brow and he fought the urge to smile. His lips twitched slightly before he sighed and looked away.

The edge of the mattress sank when he sat beside Laurie. His fingers grazed soft skin as he covered her with a fur. Her feminine scent filled his nostrils, quickened his heartbeat, drove him to the edge of desire. She was comely with fine features. Allowing his gaze to roam freely, emotions, long dormant, surfaced.

Mine.

His chest tightened, and he found it hard to breathe. Who was this woman who'd stolen his breath?

He brushed his knuckles over her silky, golden hair before glancing at his sister. She worried overmuch. His honor insisted he protect the strange lass. He put a finger to his lips and went to stand beside Elspeth. "Return to the hall, Beth," he whispered. "I will ensure nae harm comes to her. But when she wakes, I will demand answers to my questions."

Elspeth left the chamber with a shake of her head. When she was gone, Patrick closed the door and strode to the fire. He placed his hand on the mantel and lowered his head to his arm. In his mind, he repeated the evening's events. He didn't care for the chaos the lass provoked.

Aye, he wanted her, but in his bed, not awakening emotions better left dead.

Damnable tangle.

Why was she wearing his stepmother's brooch? What did she have to do with his parents?

He wanted answers and he wanted them now.

Elspeth made her way along the passage to her bedchamber, musing over the evening's happenings. Her brother's heart shone in his eyes for all to see. An unusual occurrence. His out-of-character behavior took her by surprise and provoked concern.

First Patrick's visions. He didn't have the gift. His visions were an anomaly. Now the appearance of the lass. These were the only events her brother showed interest in since their parents disappeared.

He claimed the woman. Interesting, indeed.

Elspeth slid her palm over her chest where a pinching sensation stole her breath. She missed her parents, especially her mother. A deep inhale and exhale eased the ache.

Patrick took their parents disappearance particularly hard, having been out of the country, only to return after they'd vanished. He blamed himself for not coming home sooner. For not being there when their father needed him.

He claimed responsibility for the difficulty over Isobell Lamont and the ever-present feud. None of what happened should be blamed on Patrick, but Elspeth couldn't convince him of the fact.

Over the years since the disappearance, her brother had become more and more morose. She couldn't figure out how to help him. And their brother Archibald, Patrick's twin, still traveled with her betrothed for the king and was of no use with these strange happenings.

Elspeth entered her bedchamber and sat in her favorite chair before the fire. What good was her gift of visions when she'd received none to guide her? Even so, she recognized Patrick's desire for the woman.

She sensed no darkness from the stranger—only light.

The woman might be exactly what her brother needed to get him out of his black, brooding moods. His interactions with the lass warranted watching.

Waking to the comfort of warmth, Laurie slid a hand across fur covers, the unexpected sensual sensation somehow reassuring. The calm shattered, replaced with unease when she sensed someone else in the room. She opened her eyes to find Patrick standing by the fireplace, observing her through hooded eyes. Their gazes met. In that instant, reality crashed down on her.

She bolted upright. Adrenaline kicked in. She skittered back against the headboard. The man grumbled something harsh under his breath, and she swallowed hard.

"Dinnae fash yourself, lass. Nae one here will harm you."

Laurie peered at him, worried she was teetering on the verge of hysteria. "Where am I?"

"In my bedchamber at Castle Lachlan." He dragged a stool next to the bed and sat.

His gaze held hers. Heat crept into her cheeks. Unable to look away, she shivered, remembering what he said about her belonging to him. "Where is Castle Lachlan?" *And how did I get here?* She bit her lower lip. The same questions hovered beyond the grasp of her conscious mind before she fainted.

He stared, long and hard, before answering. "The Highlands."

She gulped and glanced at the furs spread across the bed. An extremely large four-poster bed with a canopy and heavy blue curtains pulled back at each corner post. The stone walls were covered in tapestries. Tapestries that looked much newer than any she'd seen at the Cloisters in New York or at any other museum for that matter. A huge fireplace took up most of one wall. A fire crackled, lending an ordinary air to a setting that was anything but.

Similar to antiques she'd seen in museums were several chairs and a table. Only these looked new. Excellent reproductions? Could they be originals?

With growing apprehension, she noted the lack of lamps. There were no light switches or outlets. Candles lit the room. Something was terribly wrong if what she was beginning to suspect was true. She flipped her gaze to Patrick. He sat like the king of his domain, exuding barely leashed power, stoically watching her.

She didn't imagine the Highlands he spoke of were in North Carolina. She'd once read a fantasy novel about a woman who'd been sucked into a book and traveled through space and time. Although she feared the answer, she had to ask.

"What year is this?"

"Are you addled?" The damned man looked at her as if she was crazy. "'Tis the year of Our Lord, 1509."

"Oh, God." She couldn't breathe, her chest burned and her eyes blurred.

A fiery sensation in her nostrils woke Laurie from her faint.

"What the—"

A young woman dressed in what looked to be a medieval gown stood over her, holding a horrible smelling container in front of her nose. Laurie waved her arm to push it away.

"You are back with us then." The young woman moved to the head of the bed, fluffed the pillows, and helped Laurie sit up.

"Who are you?" Laurie massaged the knot at the back of her neck. Her head pounded. The stupid girly fainting was giving her a migraine.

"Elspeth, Patrick's sister." The woman placed a calming hand on Laurie's shoulder. "I sent him away. You need rest. He can ask his questions of you on the morrow."

"Tomorrow? Is it still night?"

"Aye." Elspeth sat on the edge of the bed. "'Tis a lovely

brooch you wear."

"This?" Laurie touched the pin attached to her stole with shaky fingers. "A friend loaned it to me to wear to a *ceilidh*."

"'Tis quite beautiful." Elspeth accepted a cup from a plainly dressed older woman who stood behind her and handed it to Laurie. "Here, drink this. 'Twill help ease you."

"What is it?" Holding the cup, Laurie examined the contents suspiciously.

"Spiced wine with a wee bit of herbs."

The green scent of herbs smelled pleasant, like sitting in the garden on a sunny day. She took a small taste. Bitter, but tolerable. The liquid helped soothe her parched throat and she was glad for that.

She sipped the drink while observing Elspeth. The younger woman seemed sweetness personified, petite and feminine with strawberry blond hair woven into a long thick braid. Her light silver eyes peered at Laurie from within an angelic face, which glowed as if lit by a light from within.

"Thank you for your kindness," Laurie said softly.

"Aine will ready you for bed-going." Elspeth gestured toward the older woman. Then stood as if to leave, but hesitated. "Patrick ordered the chamber bolted. He placed a guard outside the door. If you are in need, call out and Duncan will summon Aine." She turned away and walked through the doorway, closing the roughhewn oak panel behind her.

"Why am I to be locked in? Am I a prisoner?"

"Nae worries, lass," Aine said in a soothing tone as she removed Laurie's China flats. "My name is Aine MacTamhais. I care for the needs of the chief's household." She unpinned the stole and placed the tartan and the brooch on a chest next to the bed.

"I'm Laurie, and I don't need you to undress me."

"Aye, Mistress Laurie." The woman pulled the blouse over Laurie's head anyway and gasped. "Tsk, tsk. You wear nae chemise. And what is this you wear that covers your bosom? Naught, but a wee piece of lace."

Laurie covered her breasts with both hands, horrified by the woman's shocked expression. Aine shook her head and handed the blouse back to Laurie. "You best keep this on, lass, till we find you proper garments."

As the older woman turned away and walked toward the door, Laurie pulled her peasant blouse on and sat on the edge of the bed. The door closed with a loud thud.

Trapped. Laurie's stomach clenched at the sound of the guard sliding the bolt. Breathing deeply several times, she tried to calm herself. She needed to clear her head and think. Alone in this strange place, she needed to carefully consider her options. Determine what happened to her and figure out how to get home.

A plan, she must make a plan.

This wasn't a fantasy come true. Being this frightened more than sucked. She didn't like the claims made by the Neanderthal man either. He might be gorgeous and kiss like a dream, but he had no rights to her. She didn't belong to him, or anyone else for that matter.

And she definitely didn't like the unaccustomed yearning he awakened within her body. She needed to be in control.

She wanted to go home.

Logical thought was required. If she used her reasoning skills, she could handle this situation. She could handle any situation if she put her mind to it. For God's sake, she'd earned a Wharton MBA.

Downing the remainder of the spiced wine, the warmth slid down her throat, spread through her chest and heated her belly. Suddenly groggy, Laurie attempted to rise, but fell back onto the bed.

Shit. What the hell was in the drink?

"I gave her a potion to ensure she sleeps through the night."

Patrick raised his gaze from the fire when his sister joined him in his work chamber. He made no effort to hide the deep sorrow surely shining in his moist eyes.

"Munn believes she has a connection to our parents, and she wears your lady-mother's brooch. How do you think she came to have it?"

"She says 'twas given by a friend to wear to a *ceilidh*. Do you think she wandered away from a gathering in the village and became lost?"

"Nae. Had there been a gathering, I would have heard of it. News of strangers travels fast." Patrick exhaled sharply, trying to rein in his chaotic emotions. "'Tis odd. First, she appeared in my visions and now she arrives on my land as if from nowhere. I dinnae ken what to think."

"I sense nae evil with her. I ken she is frightened, but not a threat."

"Munn said as much."

"Mayhap we can learn more on the morrow." His sister's smile was meant to reassure, but he wasn't reassured.

"Aye," he said. "The lass will explain much."

Her smile faded and a stern expression crossed his sweet sister's features. "Where will you sleep this night?"

Patrick raked a hand through his hair. He felt an unexpected protectiveness toward the lass. If he were honest with himself, he'd been intrigued since he first spied her. Not wanting any harm to come to her because of his unexpected lust, he didn't intend to dishonor her in front of his clan. He'd not sleep in his bedchamber this night.

Although the longing to do just that was near to maddening. "Though I have claimed her as mine, I will not shame her. I will sleep here in the laird's study. Duncan will guard her door until either I or Stephen relieves him." He gave Elspeth an unsteady smile. "Go and rest Beth. Nae harm will come to her while you slumber."

Tomorrow, he would have his answers.

CHAPTER EIGHT

*L*oud scraping woke Laurie from fitful dreams. The noise pounded at her temples. *Eeuw...* She felt awful, as if someone clobbered her over the head. She tried to open her eyes. They were glued shut. She rubbed them and finally managed to pry them open.

Darkness. Only darkness surrounded her and that annoying, grating noise. She massaged her temples, her mind filled with fuzz. She groaned.

She had to clear her head, get up, find out what was making the noise. What if someone had broken into the cottage?

Light assaulted her...

Laurie shrieked as bed curtains swept open. Memories from the previous night painfully flooded back. She hadn't been dreaming.

A smiling young woman stood next to the bed.

"Elspeth?" Laurie blinked several times. "You're real."

"You look as though you have seen a *banshee*." Elspeth chuckled. "Here, let me help you rise. Things will seem better after a warm bath."

Laurie blew out a puff of air and tugged her fingers through her snarled hair. She welcomed Elspeth's assistance to sit.

Several burly men stared at her as if she was crazy.

Maybe she was. She pulled the covers to her neck and glared at the men.

The men turned away and continued to tug a large wooden tub across the floor to position it before the fire burning in the hearth. They filled the tub with buckets of steaming water. When they finished, Aine bustled into the room, carrying several cloths, a small pot and a comb. She shooed the men out and shut the door.

After the men left, Laurie sighed, feeling out of her element, unsure how to act. The best approach, at least for now, was to go along with the madness. Elspeth and Aine seemed pleasant enough and probably didn't mean her harm.

Though something in the wine she'd drank the night before definitely knocked her out. Still, she would play along, but be wary. Very wary.

"I'd like a bath." She shot the women the smile she used to cajole executives.

She allowed Aine to help remove her blouse. Elspeth gasped at the sight of her thong and bra. "You wear unusual garments."

The young woman studied Laurie's underwear.

"'Tis improper." Aine wagged her finger at the younger woman. "I will go to your lady-mother's trunks and get a fresh chemise and gown for the poor lass."

"Aye," Elspeth said. "Bring the sapphire gown. She will look fetching in it. 'Twill accentuate her bonnie blue eyes and golden tresses."

"There's no need," Laurie said. "I can wear—"

"'Tis Patrick's favorite color." Elspeth inclined her head toward Laurie, a twinkle in her eyes and a smirk curving her lips.

Aine cackled and left the chamber.

Why should she wear the favorite color of that buffoon who'd dragged her here last night? Laurie chomped down on her molars. She loved the color too, but still, she didn't feel the need to get decked out to please him. Her fantasy of the man played better than the reality. He was a brute.

Laurie wanted a civilized man in her life. A man who understood the world she lived in. She wasn't about to become the property of some medieval lord.

Hell no.

Besides she wasn't staying. Although she doubted she'd wake from this bad dream any time soon. What she needed was to get back to the old hut where he'd found her and figure out how to get home. Maybe she could sneak out of the castle without laying eyes on the big jerk again.

For now, though, she'd take a bath. She took off her thong and bra and let Elspeth assist her into the tub. Being nude wasn't awkward. After all, the girls at the gym ran around the locker room in different stages of undress, many completely nude. The scent of herbs reached her nose and she swirled the leaves floating on the surface. Heat soothed her stiff muscles.

Elspeth handed her the pot and a small cloth. Laurie sniffed. Lavender.

"'Tis French soap. My brother Archie often travels to France with the Campbells for King Jamie. He brings back wonderful gifts."

"Thank you for sharing it with me."

Elspeth inclined her head, sat in a nearby chair and gazed away, giving Laurie the allusion of privacy. She washed herself, enjoying the moment while the young woman silently mended a piece of cloth.

After a few minutes passed, Elspeth glanced up from her mending. "Aine will wash your hair when she returns."

With the sound of heavy footfalls and loud voices approaching, they stared toward the door. The heavy panel crashed open and Patrick stood at the threshold gaping. A large man, his shoulders barely cleared the frame. His mouth twitched up into a crooked smile. "Ach, lass. You dinnae need a fine gown. You are bonnie in what God gave you." He strode into the room with Aine on his heels, making the large chamber suddenly seem quite small and overly warm.

Heat rose from the tip of her toes to singe the roots of her hair, Laurie tried to cover her breasts with her hands and with the tiny cloth, while glaring at the audacious man. "How dare you!" The rasp in her voice didn't produce the demand she'd hoped for. "Get out of here."

"I am Chief of Clan MacLachlan, Lord of Strathlachlan. I dare much, lass." His cocky grin made him even more attractive than she thought him the previous night.

Oh. Her blush must be brilliant.

He growled, whirled on his heel, and hurried from the room. Elspeth and Aine exchanged glances then stared at Laurie.

She slid down into the tub, relieved, yet not. She'd never been so mortified. He was big and overwhelming. She had to get out of this place and find her way home before she fell under the spell of that unbelievably gorgeous, brute of a man.

Aine cleared her throat. "I will be about the task of washing your hair then, lass."

"Yeah, fine, whatever," Laurie managed to choke out.

After using more of the lavender soap to clean Laurie's hair, the plump woman dumped buckets of water over her to rinse the soap away. When she finished, Aine helped her stand and patted her dry with a large soft cloth.

Unsure of proper etiquette and slow to understand their words, Laurie didn't speak. She allowed the two women to fuss over her while she mulled over the situation. There had to be a way to get home. All she needed do was get away from the confines of the castle and find the spot in the woods where she landed, so to speak.

Aine slid a soft linen chemise the color of ecru over her head and Laurie sat in front of the fire while the older woman combed out her hair and braided it. Elspeth left the room only to return a short while later with a tray containing something sloppy in a bowl, a small chunk of hard cheese, and a cup of liquid.

"I brought you a wee something to break your fast. After

you dress, I will show you the castle and grounds."

"I'm not to be locked in this room any longer?"

"Nae, Patrick reconsidered his order. He does not believe you can get into mischief. You cannae leave the castle grounds for the mainland."

"What do you mean?"

"You were in a swoon when Patrick brought you here so you did not see. Water surrounds Castle Lachlan. 'Tis impossible to leave, except by boat or during an unusually low tide."

Laurie didn't want to hear this. She needed to discover a way to escape, get back to the forest, and find her way home. Shit, she'd have to bide her time, try to sneak off and steal a boat. Not that she knew how to use one.

She'd earned an MBA. She could figure it out.

"Patrick commanded Duncan MacEwen to guard you."

More bad news. Escape would be difficult with a guard tagging along, but she'd figure out a way. She needed to believe she could or she'd lose her mind.

Determined, Laurie directed her attention to the tray of food. Sustenance first. The bowl contained some sort of oatmeal porridge. The gummy substance tasted bland, but the cheese and the ale were passable. Surprisingly, getting tossed through time hadn't destroyed her appetite. When she finished her meal, Elspeth and Aine helped her dress in the beautiful sapphire gown. She wrapped her plaid stole around her shoulders and secured it with the brooch from Caitrina. After putting on her China flats, she was ready.

For what, she wasn't sure. Laurie raised her head high. She would find her way home.

Following Elspeth down the wheel stair, she placed her hand against the cold stone to steady herself. The long gown made it difficult to navigate the steep, narrow confines of the twisting stairway. She relaxed when they entered the passage to the other side of the castle.

Elspeth pointed to the closed door they approached.

"'Tis the laird's study, Patrick's private work chamber. He

wishes to speak to you before I take you to the hall."

Something banged the door from the other side.

Elspeth glanced at Laurie, chuckled, and softly knocked on the door.

Patrick ran a hand over his face. He'd fled his bedchamber as if a *banshee* pursued him. Unbelievable, but necessary.

He escaped before doing something foolish like climb into the bath with her. He leaned his back against the heavy oak door in his private chamber and hung his head. What was the matter with him? Running from a mere lass? For Heaven's sake, he was the Chief of Clan MacLachlan—a fierce warrior.

How had he turned into a trembling imbecile?

When the lass made that funny little O-shape with her mouth, he'd nearly lost control.

God's teeth, he wanted to kiss her lips and every inch of her luscious body. After seeing moisture glistening along her fair skin, he'd realized he never should have gone to his chamber while she bathed. This night past, he publicly claimed her because it was the honorable thing to do after unleashing his lust upon her. During the night, while he fought the tension in his body, he decided he wanted her. Now he was determined to truly claim her.

And it would happen soon if he couldn't control the ache in his groin. He slammed his palms against the door at his sides. He should go to the village, find a wench, and relieve his desperate need. His chuckle sounded hollow, he wouldn't follow through on the thought. He'd not enjoyed the pleasure of a woman in over three years.

He'd sworn off marriage. And the gratification of the body hadn't been a temptation.

But now… There was a woman he wanted.

Patrick pushed away from the door at the sound of a soft knock. 'Twas certainly Elspeth with Mistress Laurie. *Damn*. How long had he stood inside the closed door with his blood thundering in his ears?

He strode to his worktable and sat before the pile of papers he'd worked on yesterday. He flexed his muscles, stretched, and reached within for the shrewd warrior.

"Enter."

After several moments of silence, Laurie jumped at the harsh voice bidding them enter. She'd hoped to avoid Patrick a while longer. Her hands trembled and she swallowed compulsively, not ready to face the man who haunted her dreams. Her reality.

She stiffened her spine. He wouldn't intimidate her. Few men made her nervous. She wasn't about to let this one unnerve her more than he already had. She took a couple of deep breaths and centered herself.

Laurie smoothed the front of her gown and followed Elspeth into the chamber where Patrick sat at a desk of sorts, reading. He glanced up. The light from the high window illuminated the papers on the table before him. Yet the play of shadow and light across his face made it difficult to read his expression.

"Mistress Laurie, sit." He tipped his head, motioning to the two chairs before the hearth.

She gave Elspeth a sideways glance, and the young woman nodded encouragement. Laurie marched over to where he indicated and sat in one of the chairs.

"Beth, leave us. I will bring her to you when we finish."

"Aye, you will find me in my solar." Elspeth left and closed the door behind her.

Patrick rose, striding across the room with smooth muscular grace to sit in the chair next to her. Instead of looking at her, he gazed into the fire.

The silence stretched and his expression remained blank. She fidgeted with the fabric of the gown, her palms damp. As the seconds ticked by, her stomach somersaulted with nervous anticipation. Nibbling at her bottom lip, she stared at her lap. The effort to remain silent killed her, but she refused to speak first.

Patrick finally cleared his throat and provided her with a close-up of his face. *God*, he was good-looking. His blue eyes were absolute stunners.

Those eyes stared at her mouth, and then they darkened. His chair creaked when he coughed and adjusted his weight. "Lass, I need you to answer some questions. Will you do that?"

"I'll try." Although it disgusted her to appear weak, she dropped her gaze unable to continue holding his stare. Why did this man make her more nervous than any other?

"Good," he said. "I understand your surname is Bernard. Are you French?"

She flipped her gaze to him relieved she could easily answer the question. "My father was of French descent."

"Was?"

"My parents were killed in a plane...ah, in an accident when I was a child."

"An accident on a plain?" A touch of humor threaded his voice.

"Yes," she said, relieved he hadn't caught her slip.

"A plain is rather large..."

She shrugged. His eyes narrowed.

"*Parlez-vous français, la langue de votre père?*"

"*Oui. Je parle couramment le français.*"

"Ach, well." Patrick chuckled. "Do you speak any other language?"

She was proud of her gift for languages, having spoken French fluently since childhood. She spoke Spanish, Italian and German good enough to converse with clients. She'd even picked up a small amount of Mandarin during her career. She wasn't about to tell all of that to a male chauvinist, medieval lord.

"I can read and write in Latin," she said.

"Unusual for a lass." He raised a skeptical brow.

"True. It's a dead language, but I studied it at school."

"Attending school is also unusual for a lass."

"Not where I come from."

"Aye, we will get to that," he said, an edge to his voice.

When would she learn to keep her mouth shut?

"You will find my household forward thinking. Living close to the Lowlands as we do, we speak both the Gaelic tongue and the language of the Lowlanders. Many of my men, including myself, speak French. And aye, lass, I read and write Latin, in addition to several other languages."

"Of course you do."

He stared at her for an uncomfortable moment.

"Your mother? She was French?"

How would he react to her answer to the question? Only one way to find out.

"My mother's surname was MacIntyre, of course, that was before she married my father."

Patrick's eyes narrowed. "Did you wander away from your MacIntyre escort and find yourself in our Fir-wood this past night?"

"No."

His jaw tightened. He worked to control annoyance.

"Then how did you come to be in our Fir-wood?"

Laurie sighed. This was all so complicated. She chose her words carefully, deciding to tell the truth no matter how absurd it sounded. "I was in my garden, outside of my cottage, in a place far away from here. I was with friends when I saw you outside the gate in the woods behind the cottage. It was the third time I'd seen you. I wanted to know who you were and why you were there. I was frightened, but a friend pushed me forward. As I stepped through the gate, I fell, and everything started spinning. There were flashes of light and color and the next thing I knew, I was on the ground at your feet. You might not believe me, but it is the truth."

Did he believe her? His features gave away little of his thoughts.

"What is the name of this faraway place? Kansas?"

"No, that is the name of a place in a mov...er, a play. I

live in the town of Anderson Creek, in a far distant land."

"On the Continent?" Patrick asked.

"On a continent? Yeah."

His gaze bored into her as he processed her answers. "One more question. Why did you ask me what year it was when we talked this past night?"

Afraid to answer, Laurie held her breath. Exhaling on a sigh, she sat straight. "My cottage and my garden exist in the twenty-first century." She braced herself, but the explosion she expected never came.

"You believe this outrageous tale?" His eyebrows nearly met his hairline.

His shocked expression caused her to shake her head. "I feared you wouldn't believe me." She looked directly into his eyes. His dark blue gaze mesmerized her. She swallowed. "It is the truth. You must believe me. I need your help to go back."

"How do you expect me to help you?" A flicker in his eyes gave her hope.

"Take me to the woods where you found me and help me find my way home."

He glanced away. "Impossible."

When he returned his gaze to her, his jaw set tight. "'Twill be for the best if you forget this strange tale. For your safety, you must never speak of it. Others might accuse you of delving in the dark arts."

Heat rose from her toes as dread filled her veins. She hadn't thought of that. They'd brand her a witch. Condemn her to death. She needed to get the hell out of here.

He gave a quick nod, reached over and patted her hand. "Aye. 'Twill be best to keep this our wee secret. I have claimed you and that puts you under my protection. Only Stephen, who you met in the wood, and Beth, my sister, ken what happened this past night. 'Twill be safest to keep it that way."

"But—"

He raised a hand. "For your protection I contrived an

explanation for your unexpected appearance. 'Twill be said you are the daughter of a deceased French noble. You shall be heralded as the Lady Laurie Bernard. My brother is in France with Beth's betrothed. We will make it known they sent you to us to be companion to Beth. In time, I will make you mine in truth. Nary a one will dare question you."

"What do you mean by *make you mine in truth?*"

"Aye, we will keep this secret between the four of us. Beth and Stephen can be trusted to do as I request." Patrick stood, avoiding eye contact.

She'd risked telling him the truth and he didn't believe her. What was she going to do? She couldn't stay—

Pulling her from her seat, he hurried her out of the room before she collected her thoughts and screamed at him. He grasped her by the elbow, led her through the passageway, and up a circular stair. He moved in such a rush, she could hardly keep up, never mind argue with the damn man.

Oh, but she would.

CHAPTER NINE

Sands of Time

*M*unn scanned the horizon. This place wasn't to his liking, not one bit. White sand covered the ground, a desert of sorts. The brutal yellow light from the sun blinded and made him sweat. He sat on the ground, running granules through his fingers, trying to think. The required magic remained hidden to him.

Without the correct chant, he'd never be free of this horrible place. He didn't deserve such a punishment. He forced himself to his feet and walked for what seemed like miles. The spread of the plain was endless, as far as his vision allowed.

Overcome with heat and thirst, he kicked at the sand. *Damn Caitrina.*

Damn faerie. She meant to cause terrible trouble or she wouldn't have flung him into the *Sands of Time*. Ach! What was he to do?

Hard consonants formed in his mind and he spat the related sounds from his lips. He conjured an oasis. A beautiful lush island sprang from the ocean of hot sand. In the center of the oasis, he fashioned a small pool shaded by tall tropical foliage with beautiful white flowers—a stunning flora display.

Sitting at the edge of the pool on a flat rock, he brought handfuls of pure water to his lips and drank deep. Water quenched his thirst and the fruit from a twirling vine satisfied his hunger.

Not enough. He needed to return to the earth realm.

He chanted, searching for the correct sounds and images to craft the magic required to set him free. His efforts were for naught. No matter how hard he tried, the proper sequence wouldn't come to him. He glared into the mirror-like water.

Caitrina would pay for her betrayal.

Munn continued stringing syllables together in a sing-song chant. He'd keep trying until claimed by exhaustion. He must get back to the castle to warn the MacLachlan, to warn his master about Caitrina, to warn him about her powerful fae magic.

CHAPTER TEN

Castle Lachlan

*P*atrick ground his teeth, annoyed to discover he stared out the window of his private work chamber like a besotted fool. The sun shined brightly to the east. He'd barely noticed the men fishing from the beach below, the rippling water of the small bay or the distant heather covered hills. Good Lord, the castle could have been under attack and he wouldn't have noticed.

Emotions he normally suppressed crippled him, making him uncertain how to proceed. Clenching his hands into fists, he reflected on his earlier conversation with *Lady* Laurie. She told an incredible tale, one most would not believe. He wasn't most, and unfortunately, he believed her. He knew, for certain, brownies and faeries existed. He'd even heard some of the fae possessed the ability to sift the sands of time.

Munn told him Caitrina, one of the *Sithichean*, was in some way involved with both the lass and with his missing parents. Could she sift time? Was it possible she was capable of such an extraordinary power? He hadn't yet questioned the lass about her connection to the faerie or about the brooch she wore, not wanting to warn her of his interest. He planned to bide his time until he gained her trust.

After seeing her in the bath, he knew how to accomplish that. He was determined to seduce Lady Laurie into sharing his bed.

Smiling at the mental image of her curvy, naked body stretched across the furs on his bed, he loosened his fists and turned away from the window. He paced the chamber. Concern replaced lust. No one had seen Munn since the lass appeared. With such unusual events happening, it was odd the clan brownie had gone missing. Munn's absence worried him more than he wanted to admit.

An unbidden thought pricked his mind. Could the lass be responsible for Munn's absence? Quite the riddle he needed to solve.

A heavy knock on the door pulled him from his thoughts. "Who dares disturb my peace?" he bellowed.

From the other side of the thick door came a masculine chuckle. "'Tis Stephen."

"Enter upon your own peril."

Stephen ambled into the room. Without invitation, he casually slouched in one of the chairs before the hearth, one leg hooked over the armrest. His focus on the arm of the chair, he rubbed his fingers across the fine wood grain.

"What?" Patrick glared at the back of his cousin's head.

"You seem to be of bad humor this morn." Stephen twisted to look at Patrick, meeting his gaze with a grin. "Might you want a challenge on the practice field?"

Patrick stilled. "What have you planned?"

"A *fine* Lamont warrior has brought a message from his chief, demanding a meeting to finalize your betrothal agreement. After providing victuals, I gave him leave to train with our lads. I thought you might enjoy a wee bit of sport."

There was no betrothal! When would Lamont accept that?

Patrick slammed his palm on the oak mantel. "Aye, I will show the Lamont dog how a good Highlander fights and send him back to his chief less than a man." He stormed from the chamber.

Stephen followed, keeping pace, first to the armory then to the practice field where Patrick planned to grind the Lamont warrior into the dirt.

Laurie lifted the skirt of the blue gown as she stepped over a raised threshold into the kitchen. She'd spent the morning touring the castle with Elspeth. The ginger-haired Duncan, her new shadow, always a step behind.

She learned from him that the MacLachlans were extremely proud of their home. Of a unique design, the castle was unusual for Scotland. From the outside, it appeared a great stone keep, but on the inside, it actually consisted of two separate wings along the east and west sides of a narrow courtyard. The wings connected at the north end by a small building and passageway, the building mainly used for storage and for housing the castle well.

The two wings contained both public rooms for the clan and private apartments for the chief's household. The chamber Laurie slept in the night before was on the third floor of the western wing, the top floor with a view of the sea loch in one direction and a small bay in the other. The largest bedchamber in the castle, it belonged to Patrick, the current Chief of Clan MacLachlan.

The knowledge he was the chief of a great Highland clan was somewhat daunting. Butterflies flew around in her belly as if caught in a whirling storm. She didn't want to think about him, especially not about the incredible kiss they shared. Not thinking about him wasn't an option. She couldn't seem to get his image out of her head.

When she did let her mind linger on him for any length of time, she felt a powerful longing to be near him, to touch him, to do incredibly sexual things with him.

"Argh," she actually growled out loud.

Cookie, the MacLachlan's rotund female cook, and Elspeth stopped their discussion of the midday meal preparations to stare at her.

"Lady Laurie, did you say something?" Elspeth asked.

"Nothing." Laurie's cheeks flamed. She hadn't meant for anyone to overhear her. "It's annoying to have Duncan following my every step." She glared in his direction.

He didn't take offense. He merely grinned and presented her with a formal bow.

Elspeth pulled her aside by the arm. "'Tis for your protection. You are new to the castle and dinnae ken the dangers that exist. When you are more accustomed to life here, I am sure Patrick will release Duncan from his duty. Jamie only guards me when my brother believes there is an extreme risk."

"What you mean to say is when Patrick decides he can trust me to obey his every command he might allow me modest freedom." She sounded petulant, but she couldn't help it. It had been bad enough over the years to be under her uncle's control and then her cousin Finn's. To be ordered about by a total stranger was more than infuriating.

"Aye." Elspeth cocked a brow. "He expects obedience. 'Tis for your protection. You dinnae understand our way of life. I am sure your life was much different in France." Her gaze darted with warning toward Cookie.

Laurie caught the subtle signal and dropped the subject. She lowered her head, covertly stole a glance at Duncan and suppressed a smile. He was one of those huge muscle-bound guys, the kind of guy born with an extra Y-chromosome. The kind of guy who intimidated most women and some men. The kind of guy you'd want at your back in a fight. And, after a few hours in his company, she'd learned he was a big, sweet, teddy bear. If she had to have a guard, at least she could deal with this one.

The muffled blare of a horn sounded from somewhere atop the walls. The kitchen staff stilled for a moment then switched gears to overdrive.

"'Tis time for the noon meal," Elspeth said.

They left the kitchen, allowing Cookie to complete her final preparations. They strolled into the courtyard and ascended the wheel stair to the hall.

On the first floor, the hall occupied the entire length of the western wing. A large hearth, tall enough for a man to stand in and wide enough to accommodate several men, was the prominent feature along one of the walls, although no fire burned today. Silence followed in their wake as she followed Elspeth across the stone floor toward the dais platform. When Laurie glanced at the staring people seated at the tables, they looked away. As soon as she sat next to Elspeth at the head table, whispers began.

Laurie inhaled a deep breath. She ignored the stares and took in the beauty of the castle. Until she escaped, she planned to immerse herself in the culture. Maybe she'd write a book when she returned home. It would need to be a work of fiction, who would believe the truth?

Duncan hovered over her like a nursemaid, but when friends hailed him, he joined a group of rowdy warriors at one of the lower tables.

She scanned the room, looking for Patrick, hoping he wouldn't make an appearance.

Not finding him among the men, she glanced at the light penetrating the smoky haze from the high windows. At least six feet off the floor, the windows contained leaded-glass fixed into the stone on the lower half, and wooden shutters on the upper half. Additional lighting and the annoying smoke came from candles atop tall iron stands positioned around the room. They cast a sickly yellow glow on the many tapestries covering the gray stone of the walls.

Elspeth tapped her arm and leaned in close. "We wait for Patrick."

Well, that settled it. He would be here soon enough. Part of her couldn't wait to see him. The other part determined to ignore him.

Chattering in the room escalated. Laurie inwardly cringed, certain the chatter was speculation about her arrival.

The door opened, and a man who resembled Duncan hurried in. Messy copper-red hair bobbed as he strode across the floor to the head table, stopping in front of Elspeth. A hush fell over the room.

"Lady Elspeth." He inclined his head. "The Chief, he instructed me to come directly to you. I am to inform you he will not be joining you for the midday meal. He wishes you to begin the serving."

Elspeth laughed. "Why Jamie MacEwen, what is keeping my brother from his meal this time?"

The man's gaze wandered around the room before landing back on Elspeth. "He is teaching a lesson to a Lamont on the training field."

Most of the men in the room jumped to their feet. Tables and chairs scuffed across the stone floor, some falling in the men's haste to rush from the hall. Jamie made a swift bow to Elspeth and ran out after them.

"What was that about?" Laurie asked.

"Naught for us to worry over." Elspeth calmly gestured to Cookie for the serving to begin.

Lunch was a hearty fish stew heavily seasoned with herbs. Smoked trout and spring greens followed, accompanied by wine. Wine, which had been watered to reduce its potency. Laurie would have much preferred a nice Californian pinot noir with the trout, but the food was surprisingly tasty and enjoyable. At least she wouldn't starve to death while she figured out how to return home.

Duncan remained behind when the other men ran out. With the meal finished, he approached the dais platform upon a signal from Elspeth.

"We go to the garden," she said. "Will you escort us?"

"Lady Elspeth, you ken gey fine 'tis my duty to guard the chief's new lady-love. You dinnae need to ask." He presented a broad grin, his eyes filled with merriment.

"I'm *not* his *lady-love*," Laurie blurted through clenched teeth in an overly loud voice.

The room fell quiet as the remaining folk stared at her. Heat raced to her cheeks. *Idiot.* She should be more careful. The last thing she needed was unwanted attention.

While she silently chastised herself, a ruckus came from outside the door and all heads turned in expectation. Patrick swaggered into the hall followed by his men. He wore a large grin on his dirt-smudged face and his chestnut hair stuck to the sides of his cheeks with sweat. His plaid was filthy and blood stained the front of his shirt.

Her chest tightened at the sight of the blood. Had he been injured?

He glared across the room at her. His dark eyes burned with anger. She cringed. He must have heard what she said. He sauntered to the dais, keeping his gaze locked on her. Jumping onto the platform, he strode directly to her, grasped her hand, and held her fingers in a tight grip. He yanked her from her seat, forced her to stand beside him, tucked tight against his side, held in place with one strong arm around her waist.

She tried to pull away, but he wouldn't allow it. Her nose twitched and she shrank back from him. He smelled worse than the men's locker room at her old athletic club after a rugby match.

With Lady Laurie's denial burning in his mind, Patrick was rougher with the lass than proper. Battle lust rode him hard. He wasn't about to be denied by a mere slip of a lass. He would teach her a lesson. A lesson he thoroughly planned to enjoy.

Facing the crowd, he held her tight, waiting for silence. In a thunderous voice, everyone in the room would be sure to hear, he said, "I have sent the Lamont dog back to his master with his tail betwixt his legs."

His clan cheered, stomping their feet and pounding their fists on the tables. Again, he waited for silence. Firmly holding onto Laurie, he ignored her struggles to escape his grip. When the crowd calmed, he cleared his throat.

All eyes riveted to the couple on the dais.

"I present to you the Lady Laurie Bernard." He held her hand out in front of them so the crowd was sure to see he clasped it. "She has come to us from France to be companion to my wee sister, Lady Elspeth. Hear me. She is under my protection and shall be treated as my honored guest."

Laurie subtly tried to free herself, but he easily held her in place. He flipped her hand palm up, bowed his head and placed a kiss in the center, licking her palm with the tip of his tongue.

Her gasp made him chuckle. He released her and boldly surveyed the room. Patrick grinned with satisfaction. Although there were a few grumbles, this public demonstration confirmed the castle rumors better than any other could. Those present knew, for certain, he claimed this woman as his own.

As his mistress, she'd be safe—provided she remained within the clan.

Still shivering from the sensation of his velvety tongue gliding over her palm, Laurie glanced around the hall. Everyone stared, many with smirks, while others harbored hostile expressions on their infuriated faces.

Mortified, she stepped down hard on the bridge of his foot. He chuckled at her lame attempt to hurt him. She wished she wore heels instead of soft China flats. Stilettos. Something that would do damage.

When he released her and stepped away, Elspeth leaned close to whisper. "Curtsy."

Laurie wanted to slap the grin off Patrick's arrogant face. Instead, she inhaled a bracing breath, swallowed her pride, executed a clumsy curtsy, and nearly fell to the floor.

He caught her arm in time to stop her from landing hard. "Now the whole clan kens you belong to me," he said in a quiet voice, thankfully only she heard.

He'd the nerve to laugh, the hearty sound echoing through the hall. She wanted to spit in his face or knee him in the gonads. Feeling her temper escalate, yet knowing she dare not make a scene, she glared at the jerk.

Proud of himself, he kept eye contact with her for several

long minutes, meeting her challenge with one of his own. Finally, his lips thinned and he released her arm, turning his attention to his sister. "I wish to have a bath sent to my bedchamber. I expect Lady Laurie to attend me. Will you see to it?"

Elspeth gave her brother a strange look before her usual serene smile returned to her lips. She rose from her seat and executed a perfect curtsy. "Lady Laurie, please come with me. I will explain what is expected."

Feeling as if she were tossing about in a gyrating washing machine, Laurie followed Elspeth from the hall. She worried her lower lip. What did Patrick plan? What would he expect of her? She was sure whatever he proposed she wouldn't like.

CHAPTER ELEVEN

*L*aurie felt the singe of Patrick's gaze as if he touched her skin with a lit match. Ignoring him was impossible. He leaned against a corner post of the large canopied bed, watching her through hawk-like eyes while she prepared his bath under the gentle guidance of Aine and Elspeth. Laurie squeezed the knobby cloth in her hand until her palms burned. If only she could strangle the arrogant jerk.

Aine bent over the tub, tested the water temperature with her elbow, and inclined her head to Elspeth. "Ready."

Elspeth clapped her hands then flicked them in front of her, shooing the servants from the room. Aine adjusted a pile of toweling and followed the men out.

"Duncan will remain in the passageway. If you are in need of anything, more hot water, drying cloths, anything, summon him and he will fetch whatever you require." Elspeth gave Laurie a reassuring nod before she left.

The heavy oak door shut with a loud thud, causing Laurie to jump. The tension thickened to an unbearable level. How had she gotten herself into this uncomfortable situation? Was this what a kidnap victim felt like? Totally out of control?

Only Laurie willingly followed Patrick home after sharing the most powerful kiss of her life. A stranger. God, what was she thinking?

She didn't believe he would harm her, at least not physically, but the domineering man did control her fate. Though only until she found a way home. She held out hope, if she went to the place where Patrick found her, she'd be able to return home.

He strode to the center of the room in silence. Silence that was more overwhelming than words would be. He towered over her by at least a foot. He stood still for several tense moments then removed his belt and the pouch at his waist, laying them aside on a wooden bench.

Laurie swallowed impulsively when his wool plaid fell to the floor at his feet. She wanted to dart for the door, but didn't dare. She glared at him, anger consuming her, making her dizzy.

How dare he force her into this awkward situation?

He had the nerve to flash a devilish grin. With a quick motion, he pulled his tunic over his head and dropped it too. Holy crap. He stood before her, tall and broad, displaying his magnificent male assets.

She lowered her gaze to the floor, but only after she enjoyed an eyeful of his athletically honed physique. Not just his ribbed six-pack—a major erection proudly jutted forward, reaching for her. She sucked in a shocked breath and froze in place.

Water splashed and Patrick sighed heavily. When Laurie retuned her gaze to him, he'd lowered into the tub. The wooden bathtub was large, but even so, he couldn't stretch his legs out. He sat with his knees drawn up, steamy water covering him to his waist.

She bit her lower lip. Even though he annoyed her, he was impressive to look at. Based on the smug smile he wore, he was well aware of his effect on her. The room was getting hot. She fanned herself, finding it hard to breathe. It wasn't only the temperature making her perspire, but the sensual way Patrick looked at her as if he desired more than help with his bath.

He leaned back against the tub, allowing time to drag. She bet he was taking pleasure from her discomfort.

Was this her predestined alpha-male?

She shrank from the thought. He was a barbarian. A medieval lord, for God's sake. Not for her. She needed to go home.

"Shall we begin?" His husky voice startled her, and a flush of heat prickled across Laurie's chest, up her neck, and burned her cheeks. "Have you never seen a naked man afore?"

She straightened to her full height and raised her chin. "I have, but he was my boyfriend."

Patrick's forehead puckered. "What is meant by this word... *boyfriend*?"

Whoa. Laurie wiped her clammy palms on the cloth she held. She needed to be more careful how she said things. But really, how could she be expected to carry on a conversation with him while he sat there, naked, knowing she was expected to wash his tempting body? How would she be able to wash all of that magnificently muscled nude man, touch all of his beautifully bronzed skin?

She was tempted to do a lot more than wash him, God help her. She was treading on dangerous ground. She shook her head, trying to remember his question.

Oh, yeah—boyfriend. How did one explain a boyfriend to a medieval warrior?

Caught by the deep blue of his eyes she hesitated, unsure how to answer. She ignored his nudity and stepped closer. His eyes widened and his nostrils flared.

She lowered her gaze and reigned in her scattered thoughts. "I'm not sure I can explain it properly."

"Try."

"A *boyfriend* is someone with whom you are romantically involved. Someone you think you might someday want to marry." She glanced at Patrick. The intensity of his gaze threw her off balance. She leaned against a nearby chair for support.

"Are you hand-fasted then?"

"No!" She was familiar with the meaning of that word from Finn and she didn't want Patrick to think she was married. Not that there could ever be anything between them. Still, she didn't want him to think she had a man of her own.

"Are you this *boy's* mistress?" Patrick quickly shot the question at her in a raised voice.

Laurie winced. "No, you misunderstand. I *was* just his girl-friend."

When Patrick splashed water over his chest, something in her gut fluttered as she watched the water trickle over his nipples, the nubs hardening. She moistened her lips, and stared at him. He held himself motionless, his gaze penetrating, his jaw tight.

"What happened to this *boy*?"

"I don't know. We went our separate ways a long time ago."

That one relationship, her only romantic relationship, had been the biggest mistake of her life.

Patrick grinned. "Good. Now attend to my bath, woman."

Laurie stiffened. She didn't particularly care for the tone of his voice or for his derogatory use of the word *woman*. She raised her arm to slap him, but a glance into the tub stopped her mid-swing. His cock jerked in the water, and rational thought flew from her mind. She gaped at him like an idiot.

"Lass, come here and wash my back." His tone was gentler this time.

Laurie blinked. *Okay, girl, get with the program.* She took the small cloth she still held and picked up the pot sitting near the tub. A whiff of the woodsy pine-scented soap made her smile. The fragrance was different from the one she'd used for her bath. Putting a generous amount on the cloth, she knelt on a towel on the floor behind the tub and rubbed the cloth over Patrick's back.

His muscles flexed and he made a rumbling sound from deep within his chest. Gooseflesh popped and danced across his slick skin. The depth of the sound of his voice surprised her as it resonated against her fingers, sending mini shock waves up her arm and along her spine. She shivered from the sensation, forgetting her earlier anger. A purr was the only word to describe the sensuous sound he made.

Emboldened by his obvious pleasure, she added more soap and rubbed the cloth across his shoulders, scraping her nails on his glistening skin. His muscles quivered with each pass.

"Ach, you make me feel as if I am drawn on a rack with each stroke." He sounded like he was in pain.

"Sorry." Laurie jerked her hand away.

"Nae, dinnae stop." Patrick twisted and grabbed her hand along with the cloth and brought them to rest on his chest. "I like your sweet caress. You set me afire."

A girl could get used to hearing that. Swallowing the remainder of her inhibitions, Laurie removed her hand from his body, stood before he grabbed it back, scurried to the other side of the tub and knelt. If he was enjoying this, so would she. This might be her only opportunity to experience a real man.

She touched his broad chest, hesitating only for a moment before swiping the cloth across his pecs. Her stomach tightened as she feasted on his masculinity. She boldly stroked him with her gaze, from chin to chest, to waist, and up again. A tremor raced through her. When she met his stormy eyes, she was lost.

She stilled, the cloth held in a tight grip, unable to move, unable to speak, unable to look away. Patrick reached for her hand and slid her palm, along with the cloth, over his heart. Each beat pulsed in rhythm with her own. Their gazes locked, and she dragged the cloth along with his hand over his nipples.

He sucked in his breath and released a guttural sound. "Use your nails on me."

Breathless, she searched his face. His eyes darkened with desire. Letting the cloth fall into the water, she scraped her nails gently across his chest. Each fine hair tickled, causing a pleasant pulsing sensation at her core. She drew circles around each of his nipples, brushing her fingertips across the hardened buds. Her breasts grew heavy and strained against the fabric of her gown.

He purred again, a purely sensuous sound. She could listen to the hum forever. A heated smile softened his lips, making him more breathtakingly handsome.

Blatant desire pooled down low, and she needed to touch more of him. Her sensitive fingers brushed across a rough ridge of skin below his right shoulder. A white scar ran from the side of his neck to just below his arm. Pulling her hand away, she winced.

"Do you find me so ugly you cannae bear to touch me?" He watched her through hooded eyes.

Ignoring his ill-hidden attempt to gain a compliment, Laurie ran a moist fingertip along the length of the scar. "How did you get this?"

Patrick shuddered with sensation. Laurie's gentle touch against his damaged skin drove him mad. "Ach, 'tis naught but a wee scrape."

She frowned. "Must've hurt like hell when you got it."

"Aye, that it did."

"Will you tell me how it happened?"

"I caught a cattle thief on MacLachlan land and he gave me the scar." He flashed a teasing grin. "A wee bit of blood-letting is a show of vigor, you ken."

She gaped at him.

"The thief received worse for it," he said, after glimpsing her horrified expression.

Again, she traced the length of the scar with her finger. "Does it hurt?"

"Nae." Patrick growled, reached over the side of the tub and pulled her in.

Laurie let out a curt scream as water splashed on the stone floor. He placed her between his raised knees, her back to his front, her soaking clothes clinging to all her luscious curves.

"What do you think you're doing?" She struggled to rise, but he held her in place.

"Lean against me, let me hold you." He wrapped his arms around her tiny waist.

"We mustn't."

Having seen desire simmering in her eyes, he ignored her protest. She wanted him as much as he needed her. Her wet skirt tangled around their legs when he pulled her against the hard ridge of his erection. He yanked her braid to the side and nuzzled her neck.

"Stop!" She batted at his hands.

"I beg you. Let me pleasure you," he murmured close to her ear.

She stilled.

"You ken you want me."

"You conceited bastard. How dare you?"

He laughed. "We have already established I dare much." He brushed his lips along the nape of her neck and whispered love words in Gaelic, knowing she wouldn't understand their promise. *Mine.*

She shivered. "Please, let me go." However, they both knew the words for what they were—an empty plea.

He took encouragement from that knowledge and slid the tip of his tongue along the edge of her ear, nibbled on the lobe, delved in. She squirmed, and his shaft stiffened to near pain.

She half-heartedly tried to break his hold, again. He held her gently in his embrace, and relaxing against him, she gave up the attempt. He took a soft bite at her nape and placed feather-light kisses along her hairline, desperate to possess all of her. The soft mewing sounds she made urged him onward. He kissed and nipped all of her wonderfully tender places.

Patrick cupped her firm breasts and toyed with the tight nipples through the now-wet cloth of her gown. He took his time, leisurely massaging each breast. Managing to fit his large hands inside the bodice of her gown, he pinched the hard tips between his thumbs and forefingers, drawing a moan from her lips.

Laurie arched against him. Her breath came in little pants as he continued to tease her flesh. When she rubbed her arse against his hard cock, he nearly lost his seed. Hard and throbbing, he clamped down on his jaw, seeking and then finding control.

The more he teased, the more she rocked against his erection, the more he teased.

"Have you changed your mind? Do you want to stay with me?"

"Mmm."

Laurie was fire, flaming hotter with each caress. Never before had he wanted a lass with such desperation. He reached below and cupped her precious mound through the cloth of her wet skirt, rubbing her most sensitive place. The thunder of her heart resonated in his chest. He stroked her slowly, faster, slower again, drawing out the pleasure. Her need. His need. Their need.

Her moans grew loader with every stroke. The sensations pulsing through her hit him hard. Hot. Burning hot.

She hummed with desire. He felt her need deep in the core of his being. She was ready for him. He rose and stood in the tub with her in his arms, water dripped from his body and Laurie's garments. He held her to his chest and gazed at her. She was lovely, soft and pliant in her state of intense arousal.

He lowered his head. "You please me, lass."

She smiled. "I want you." He growled and captured her lips in a sizzling kiss.

A sudden draft hit his wet skin as the chamber door jerked open.

"God's teeth. What in…" Patrick's words trailed off as he saw the group at the door.

Two male servants, holding buckets full of hot water, stood gaping. Aine, with her hands on her hips and a scowl on her plump red face, appeared ready to burst. Elspeth held a stack of drying cloths against her chest, her face a deep rose. And Duncan stood behind the lot, unable to hide his censure.

Laurie hid her face in Patrick's chest.

Shifting her weight, he concealed the evidence of his lusty desire within the folds of her sodden skirt. He placed her head against his shoulder, hiding her shamed face. She trembled in his arms. Hot tears against his skin left him with a pang of guilt.

Aine stepped forward. "Patrick MacLachlan, what are you about? Taking advantage of the sweet lass like that. Put her down. 'Tis highly improper. You should be ashamed."

"Out." His temper flared. "All of you. Get out."

As one, they leaped back, unwilling to deal with their chief's wrath.

"Elspeth, wait, bring those cloths here," he said. "Duncan, get everyone else out of here. Now. And shut that blasted door."

Elspeth stepped farther into the chamber while the servants scrambled to disappear.

Duncan followed the others and closed the door.

Patrick stepped from the tub, uncaring of the water dripping onto the floor. He carried Laurie to a chair by the fire and placed her in it. She sat quietly, her body trembling, her teeth chattering, staring forward.

He took the cloths from Elspeth, laying all but the largest on the floor. He squatted in front of Laurie and wrapped the soft cloth around her shoulders, pulling it snug. He leaned back on his heels. He'd made a muddle of things. He'd acted a fool.

He should have given her more time to grow accustomed to him.

"Beth, you may leave us now."

"Nae. I cannae leave you alone with her. Thank goodness Duncan summoned us." She placed her hands on her hips and tilted her chin defiantly. "Cover yourself."

Patrick raised his eyes toward heaven. Saints preserve him

from pushy women and gallant guardsman. He picked up one of the cloths, stood, and wrapped it around his torso. "I will not hurt her. Leave us."

Elspeth hesitated, but reluctantly left the chamber, passing Duncan on the way out. The man glanced in and when their gazes locked, Patrick saw anger in his man's eyes.

"Close the door," Patrick ordered.

Duncan inclined his head before shutting the door. Patrick would deal with him later.

"I owe you an apology." He once again squatted in front of Laurie. "'Twas wrong to encourage you as I did."

She shook her head though wouldn't look at him. "My fault too."

"Nae." He reached for the cloth at her shoulder. "We need to get you out of these wet garments."

She blocked him with her hand. "Please, go away."

"Aye, I will leave." She looked so miserable, he had to comply.

Rubbing the ache in his chest, he rose and strode to a trunk in the corner. After opening the lid, he removed a clean *leine* and *plaide*. He pulled the *leine* over his head, the cloth becoming damp from the moisture on his skin. If he thought too much about the way she'd felt against him, he wouldn't leave the chamber and he'd make a bigger mess of things.

From the bench, he picked up his belt and pouch, and placed them on the bed. He lay down and wrapped the *plaide* around his body, securing it with the belt. 'Twas obvious the Lady Laurie had a champion in his man Duncan. Patrick tightened his throat muscles to keep a possessive growl from escaping.

He attached his pouch as he went to another chest. From within, he retrieved a pair of deer hides. These he wrapped around his feet and legs, securing them with strips of leather. Then he pulled out a knife, attaching it to his thigh under his tunic with another strip of leather.

How should he deal with Duncan's intrusion? He had ordered the man to protect Laurie with his life. In a way, that was what the man did by stopping Patrick from taking the lass.

He'd need to tread carefully in handling his man.

Laurie's eyes widened when he grasped his claymore. Patrick swept his hand over the exquisite workmanship. He touched the large, sparkling sapphire in the crosspiece of the ornate hilt with reverence before he secured the weapon on his back.

With a terse nod to Laurie, he strode to the door. "You will stay in this chamber," he said with his back to her. "Nothing has changed." Under his breath, he added, "You belong to me."

He opened the door to leave but turned to her. Moisture pooled in her eyes. He'd meant to give her pleasure. Instead, he caused pain. He truly was a scoundrel. "I will send Elspeth to you."

Patrick slammed the door on his way out. Though it wasn't to Laurie he sought to demonstrate his anger.

Laurie heard Patrick's muffled voice through the door. She supposed he gave Duncan orders to guard her and not let her leave. Whatever. At the moment, she was too embarrassed to do anything but sit and seethe at her raging hormones.

She sniffled, but refused to cry. If a person could die from humiliation, she'd surely be dead. Her stupidity in the arms of Patrick made it more imperative to find a way to return home soon. She didn't dare get emotionally attached to the man. She needed to get back to her own time.

"Stop your bellyaching," a familiar female voice said from the direction of the bed. "He won't want you if you mope about and feel sorry for yourself."

Scrambling from the chair, Laurie dropped the drying cloth to the floor. She stared at the bed. No one was there.

She was losing it. Surely she was. She was starting to feel like Alice, lost in a medieval Wonderland. Laurie took a couple of steps closer to the bed. Had she too slipped through a rabbit hole, only to find her world turned inside out?

"Men dinnae like women who sulk," the voice said.

I'm not sulking," she said, talking to herself. She really was going crazy.

Laurie frowned, shook her head and walked toward the bed. It looked no different than when she first entered the room. Bed neatly made. Pillows neatly arranged. So where was the voice coming from?

She froze when Caitrina appeared in front of her, ever so slowly shimmering into solid form.

Laurie's mouth dropped open. What the hell? She should've realized Caitrina was near; the place reeked of her unique fragrance.

Caitrina moved forward, appearing to float over the floor, her silky green gown glistening in the late afternoon light. She looked beautiful and intimidating.

"How did you get here?" Laurie asked, her voice a tad shaky.

"I have been with you all along. Watching." A mischievous smile curved Caitrina's perfect lips. "You have made a mess of things, you have."

"What?" A forgotten memory came to Laurie. She'd had a conversation with Caitrina at the cottage after too many bottles of wine. Caitrina admitted to being a faerie. She'd said the man in Laurie's dreams and visions—Patrick—was her soul mate. That fate would bring them together. Until now, Laurie had thought the memory a delusional drunken dream.

Now she knew better.

Laurie curled fists to her hips and glared. "I've traveled through time to this barbaric place. A medieval, macho man has manhandled me. And you've been watching."

"Dinnae overreact."

"How could you?" Laurie wanted to pummel Caitrina. "Take me home, now."

Pursing her lips, Caitrina shook her head. "Cannae. Besides, you looked like you were enjoying the manhandling."

Laurie bristled. The remark came too close to the truth. "What do you mean, you can't? You're a faerie. Do your magic and send me home."

Caitrina had the nerve to grin. "I dinnae have the power to return you. Only you do."

"Please, spare me. Who do you think you are? The good witch in *The Wizard of Oz*, and all I need to do is tap the heels of my ruby slippers and quote *there's nowhere like home* and I'll find myself in my garden in Anderson Creek?"

"Of course not, dinnae be ridiculous."

"Then how do I get home?"

"You will figure it out."

"What do you mean?" Laurie asked. "I don't know how this happened. I don't know how I got here. Well, except for the part where you pushed me through the garden gate, and I found myself in medieval Scotland. I don't have any idea how to get home."

Caitrina lifted her arm in farewell and faded into a fine mist. "You'll find the way home when you fulfill your destiny."

CHAPTER TWELVE

When were guys in white jackets going to show up with a straitjacket and take her away? None of this could be real.

People didn't travel back in time. Faeries only existed in faerie tales.

Laurie's mind raced. She paced from the bed to the fireplace, back and forth across the chamber while mumbling her chaotic thoughts to the silent room.

Patrick's arms around her felt real. The memory grounded her. She shivered and wrapped one of the drying cloths around her shoulders. Picking up another cloth, she ran her fingers over the coarse fabric.

She needed to suspend long-held beliefs as to the workings of the natural world to accept the existence of faeries and time travel?

Well, duh, she traveled through time.

Caitrina spoke of destiny. Laurie rubbed her aching temples. Did her destiny truly involve Patrick? Her heartbeat spiked at the thought. He was a control freak and ordered her about, which she didn't like, but he made her feel wanted. Special.

Lost in her whirling thoughts, she tensed when the door creaked open behind her. When she spun around, Elspeth stood in the threshold, blushing.

"Come in," Laurie said in an effort to be friendly.

"Patrick sent me to assist you." The young woman warily stepped into the room. "I will help you to bed."

"Why? It's the middle of the afternoon, I'm not tired."

Elspeth winced. "Patrick thought you should rest."

"Sorry. I don't mean to offend you." Laurie sighed. "It's just that I need fresh air."

"I will open the shutters." Elspeth rushed to a window.

"No. I mean—"

"I am here to assist you." The young woman twisted around.

"Why are you being nice to me? I'm a stranger."

"You are a guest in my brother's home. Highlanders live by a strict code of hospitality. Besides, I like you."

"Listen, I have to get out of this room." Laurie flipped her wet braid over her shoulder. "You promised to show me your garden. Can we go now?"

"You cannae go outside in that damp gown. You will catch your death."

"Then help me change."

Elspeth assisted with removing the soggy dress, and Laurie slipped into her comfy twenty-first century clothes. As they walked out of the castle proper and into the courtyard, Laurie tightened her tartan stole around her shoulders and used the brooch Caitrina gave her to secure the wool fabric.

"'Tis unusually warm for late spring," Elspeth said.

"Is it?" Laurie hardly noticed the temperature, her emotions churned with too many conflicting and confusing feelings.

Images of Patrick's bath remained vivid in her mind. She still tasted him on her lips and felt his hands on her breasts. She tried hard to push the memory to the farthest corner of her mind, refusing to admit her desire for him.

She pretended nothing naughty happened between her and Patrick. Naughty—what a silly word to describe what happened. They'd almost had sex.

She shouldn't feel such a thrill.

With a sigh, she concentrated on putting one foot in front of the other without thinking too hard. The afternoon might be salvageable, if she didn't run into the irresistible man.

Laurie smiled at her guard and Elspeth as if she didn't have a care in the world. They strolled the short distance to the garden nestled within the security of the castle's outer fortifications. Enclosed within a high wall, the sanctuary offered both protection and solitude. She and Elspeth entered through the narrow stone archway, leaving Duncan outside to stand guard.

Laid out in a geometric grid, the castle garden provided a well at the center for irrigation. Heavy wooden planks held the soil in beds, most containing medicinal and culinary herbs and vegetables edged by lavender and white violets. Strawberry plants filled one bed and a large section dedicated to roses lay to the side. Though not yet in bloom, the roses' shiny new leaves glistened in the sunlight. At the center of the rose garden grew a bench of living plants.

"'Tis a turf bench of chamomile. 'Twill flower soon," Elspeth said with pride.

"I've never seen anything like it. Must be beautiful when in bloom." Laurie followed Elspeth as they meandered through the garden.

"Most of the seedlings are collected from local fields and woods then planted here. Other plants are brought to me by friends and travelers who visit the castle."

"What you've created here is amazing."

"Thank you. My love for the garden came from my mother." Elspeth's voice saddened. "We spent hours together tending the plants. Since she is gone, I nurture the garden in her memory."

"What happened to your mother?"

"My father and mother are missing—presumed dead by many—they disappeared three years ago while traveling across our land. After that, Patrick became chief of our clan."

"I'm sorry for your loss." Laurie's chest tightened with

sympathy.

"Aye, well." Elspeth stopped to pick a brown leaf from one of the rose bushes. "My brother Archie often brings me gifts of seeds and cuttings from the Continent when he returns from his travels."

"How many brothers and sisters do you have?"

"I am the only lass." A sweet pout plumped Elspeth's lips. "After Patrick, Archie is the eldest. He travels in France with my betrothed Alexander Campbell on embassage for the king. Suibne attends university in Glasgow while our wee brother, Iain the Younger, fosters with the Campbells of Glen Orchy." Elspeth's face glowed with love for her family.

"You must miss them."

"Aye, sure, but now you are here."

Laurie couldn't help but smile as she glanced around the verdant garden. She needed this diversion. She stood near the well and spun in a circle. Her mood lifted. The garden held a tranquil beauty, pleasing and calming. Both, she desperately required.

"Elspeth, the garden is wonderful."

The young woman gave Laurie an impetuous hug. "I hoped you would like it. As my companion you will be expected to help with the chores."

"At home, I was learning about gardening."

"Tell me about your home and how you came to be at Castle Lachlan. I would like verra much to ken where you came from. Patrick is secretive about your past."

Laurie cleared her throat and glanced around nervously. She wasn't sure where to begin or how much to share. And she definitely didn't want anyone to overhear her. Still, she needed to tell someone. She truly needed a friend.

Somehow, she sensed she could trust Elspeth. The younger woman seemed so young and innocent; she couldn't be much more than eighteen or nineteen. Yet an ageless wisdom shone in her silver eyes.

Elspeth seemed to understand Laurie's hesitation and took her by the hand, leading her into the rose garden, where they sat on the turf bench. "Laurie, dinnae fear telling me. You must have a special gift, as I do. I see things others dinnae."

Okay, this was awkward. Laurie seldom shared her personal life with anyone other than with her uncle David, who raised her, or her cousin Finn, when he wasn't acting her boss. There were no women Laurie felt close to, at least not close enough to confide in. She'd always been too busy dealing with her business life, where the competitive nature of the work made it difficult to trust. Caitrina was the first woman she considered a friend.

Look where that got her.

She liked Elspeth. She easily believed the young woman had a special gift. From her flowed a sense of serenity.

Cautiously, Laurie began her story. She told Elspeth she quit her job and went to North Carolina. How she found the cottage with its garden and decided to move there. The story unwound and she told her about the strange happenings. About her dreams and visions. How she traveled through time, ending up in sixteenth century Scotland.

Precious expressions crossed Elspeth's face while she listened. Wide-eyed through most of the story, she seemed to understand, though Laurie could tell at times Elspeth didn't comprehend specific words or phrases.

"How did you get the brooch you wear on your *plaide*?" Elspeth asked when Laurie finished.

"Caitrina, the woman who helped me with my garden, gave it to me the night I traveled here."

"Do you ken how she came to have it?"

"I think she might be a faerie," Laurie confided in a whisper, fearing the other woman's reaction.

Elspeth didn't appear the slightest bit shocked. She continued to smile as if discussing faeries a common occurrence. "May I see the brooch?"

Laurie unclasped the pin and handed it to Elspeth.

The young woman ran her fingertips across the delicate artistry, studying the brooch in deep concentration. Her brow furrowed and she gazed at Laurie with moisture in her bright eyes. "'Tis lovely. It belonged to my mother."

"The brooch belonged to your mother?"

"Aye. She was wearing it when she disappeared." Elspeth handed the pin to Laurie.

"That's incredible. Caitrina claimed the brooch was a reproduction, but I knew it had to be original. Here, you take it." Laurie held the brooch out to Elspeth. "It rightly belongs to you and your family."

"Nae." Elspeth sniffled. "'Tis yours now. Since it was given to you by one of the *Sithichean*, the brooch must be a key to your future. Besides, I feel you are the sister I never had. We will have such fun in the garden together." She hugged Laurie again.

"I'm sorry, I can't stay." Laurie glanced off across the garden. "I need to go home. I don't belong here."

"May I tell you what I believe?"

"Of course."

"Events often happen for reasons that are hard to understand at first. Dreams tell you things you need to know. Your visions of Patrick. Your traveling here. Neither happened by accident. There is a reason you cannae yet see." Elspeth's gaze penetrated. "You must stay until you find out why you were sent to us."

Why, indeed?

CHAPTER THIRTEEN

A fortnight later, Patrick held a tight rein on his temper, yet he was beyond furious. To his right at the high table, his uncle continued spouting words Patrick didn't wish to hear. He struggled to maintain restraint. He hoped the slight tic at his temple was the only outward sign of his escalating anger.

"I am truly sorry, but you ken the only way to end the strife is for you to marry the lass. 'Twas what your father intended all along. Let me go to the Lamont and negotiate the terms." How dare Donald lecture him on his responsibility to the clan. Did the man believe he didn't know his duty? A sense of duty had been drilled into Patrick since the cradle.

For nearly three years, his uncle argued his cause. On this morn, he ranted for over an hour. Patrick was sick to death with the quarrel.

"Are you listening to me, lad?"

"Aye." Patrick ground his teeth. He didn't trust the man's constant manipulations and political maneuvering. Donald forever caused problems for the clan. Especially with his unreasonable hatred of the Campbells.

"Tell me. What do you plan to do about the contract?"

"I would give my soul to Satan before I marry the

daughter of our enemy." Hands hidden beneath the table, Patrick clenched his fists, wishing he could pound his uncle senseless.

Movement at the doorway caught his attention. Elspeth and her new companion entered the hall followed closely by Duncan. *Lady* Laurie wore the blue gown again, her golden hair in a thick braid at her back. Even though a fortnight passed, he still remembered the wet gown clinging to her breasts, the tight nipples taut against his palms. Saints preserve him, the sight of those curvy hips hugged by the gown triggered lust to sizzle hot through his blood, tightening every muscle, pushing to the surface his frustration.

Ach! He felt crushed against a mountain by a boulder.

And lady Laurie would be caught there too if he wasn't careful. He regretted that each time they were in close proximity he'd lost his temper for one reason or another. She must think him an ogre.

Perhaps that was best.

"You must wed—"

Patrick swung his stare to his uncle. "Never!" He stood and smashed a closed fist on the table, catching Donald unawares. "Dinnae push me, old man."

"Dammit, lad—"

Patrick didn't wait to hear more swill. He stomped from the hall, the subsequent silence broken only by the thud of his boots as he descended the wheel stair. He would never wed.

My God! What caused Patrick's outburst of temper?

Laurie followed Elspeth farther into the great hall from the rear passage from where they'd witnessed Patrick's display of temper and thumping exit by way of the main stairs.

Although she'd occasionally crossed an executive or two with volatile temperaments, she wasn't accustomed to such violent displays of anger. And with each day she remained trapped at Castle Lachlan, his moods became more and more explosive.

Not that it mattered. He kept a respectful distance. He never entered his chamber when she was present and he slept either with his men or in his study since the castle's bedchambers were full. She lived in terror though, unable to trust him or herself if they found themselves alone.

She was drawn to him like a moth to a flame. As much as it didn't make sense, she couldn't stop herself from wanting a taste of what he would willingly give. Did she dare?

No. She needed to get out of here, return home before her desire overwhelmed her and she had sex with Patrick…and made the biggest mistake of her life.

She and Elspeth approached the dais with Duncan in tow. An older man sat at the head table, his gaze riveted on the doorway where the sound of Patrick's descent still echoed against stone.

He grabbed a cup of ale from the table and, sloshing some of the liquid onto his beard, drank deeply. As he wiped his mouth with the back of a hand, he caught their approach. He swiped the hand on his plaid while an unwavering blue stare—so similar to Patrick's—held her in place.

Duncan tensed and stepped in front of her, blocking the man's view. Was there a reason he felt compelled to protect her? The man couldn't mean her harm. She scooted around Duncan and continued forward.

"Greetings, niece." The older man stood and motioned for them to join him.

Laurie glanced at Elspeth and hesitated. Uncle? Would he suspect Laurie wasn't what Patrick claimed her to be? Elspeth stepped onto the dais, serene, smiling in her usual manner. Laurie startled when Duncan clasped her elbow.

"Thank you." She accepted his assistance onto the platform.

"Good morn, uncle." Elspeth sat to his right. She motioned for Laurie to take the next seat. Have you broken your fast?"

Elspeth's uncle glared at Duncan. The warrior glowered back then strode to the far end of the dais, and leaned against the wall respectful of the family's privacy. Why did the men of this time always scowl?

"Aye, I have eaten. Thank you," the uncle said to Elspeth. "I came at first light to report to your brother. My men have been patrolling the western border. Those cursed Lamonts have caused havoc raiding along the river. They stole several head of cattle and set huts afire."

Laurie gaped in horror. When she caught herself and closed her mouth, she noticed Elspeth's hand fluttered near her breast.

"Was anyone hurt?" Elspeth asked.

"Nae. Though several are left homeless." He patted her arm. "Dinnae worry yourself, lass. Your brother will see the people are relocated."

"I will see provisions sent."

"Good. Your parents would be proud of you." His gaze cut to Laurie. "Who might this comely lass be?"

"Lady Laurie Bernard. Alexander Campbell has sent her from France to attend me."

"Welcome," he said, though his tone held little warmth. Was he someone else she must win over?

"Thank you," she said, sweetly.

His eyes narrowed and he rubbed his chin, scrutinizing her. Great. Her manner of speech gave her away. What was he thinking? She swallowed uneasily. Would he cause trouble?

"This is my Uncle Donald," Elspeth said.

He held Laurie's gaze for longer than comfortable. Then, thank God, he returned his attention to his niece.

"Alexander will make you a good husband," he said. "Did he also send word informing when he an Archibald will return from the Continent?" He picked at a loose thread on his plaid.

"Nae, he only sent Lady Laurie to me."

"So they won't return home soon?"

"I dinnae think they will." Elspeth bit her lower lip and rose, motioning for Laurie to do the same. "I am glad you have been well fed, uncle. You must excuse us, we are for the garden."

Laurie followed Elspeth's lead. So much for having breakfast. Not that she minded. She doubted she'd have much of an appetite with Elspeth's uncle staring at her.

Elspeth hurried across the stone floor. Laurie in her wake with Duncan taking the rear.

Laurie glanced over her shoulder at the dais. Uncle Donald sported a cruel smile. For once, Laurie didn't mind Duncan guarding her back. Something didn't seem right with Patrick's uncle. She couldn't pinpoint what bothered her about the man, but he made her skin prickle with unease.

Chills along her spine made her shudder. She needed to find a way to escape. And soon.

Laurie walked through the bustling courtyard, pretending interest in the comings and goings but actually searching for hiding places in the shadows. Places she could use when she tried to sneak away some night after dark. She hadn't come up with a feasible plan yet, though she would escape.

They reached the kitchen without incident. Elspeth handed her one of the heavy aprons hanging on a hook near the doorway. The bulky garments were designed to protect their gowns from dirt or a wayward thorn while they worked in the garden.

Outside, an occasional puffy cloud drifted across the blue sky. Laurie inhaled a breath of fresh air. Even after two weeks, she still found it odd to look up at the expanse of clear blue and not see planes or contrails. It reminded her of the afternoon of 9-11 when no airplanes were permitted in US airspace. Fate touched her that day. With no college classes scheduled on that day, she had planned to assist her uncle. If it hadn't been for the cell phone call from his administrative assistant, canceling the client meeting at the towers, she would have been caught in the midst of the chaos.

Goosebumps prickled her arms, and she shivered.

As with her other visits to the garden, she found relief in the wonderfully heady scents. It was a retreat from the strong stench of the hall, the smell of unwashed flesh being one of the worst among the other unpleasant odors.

Kneeling close to Elspeth, Laurie helped weed the strawberry bed. She chuckled. "I always seem to be doing this. Weeds plagued my garden at home."

"In the twenty-first century?" Elspeth stopped and smiled at Laurie.

"Yes, the twenty-first century."

Elspeth pulled another weed and tossed it onto the growing pile. "Do you miss your home verra much?"

Not wanting to hurt her young friend's feelings, Laurie took a moment before answering. "It is nice here and you and Aine have been kind. But I don't belong at Castle Lachlan. I miss my little cottage and my garden. And, I would give anything to have a good cup of coffee."

"Coffee?"

"A hot, robust drink common where I live."

"Ah." Elspeth fixed her gaze on Laurie with eyebrows raised and mouth set in a slight curve. "What of Patrick?"

Laurie nervously coughed. "I don't know what you want me to say. He has been kind letting me stay with you. I guess he could have thrown me out."

"He would never be so inhospitable. But that is not what I am asking. He has claimed you as his own," Elspeth said. "Stephen told me you were…friendly, shall I say, at the Firwood. And we did find you verra wet and blushing from his bath."

"The only excuse I have is my emotions…my feelings… were running wild from traveling through the time gate. I wasn't myself. I was vulnerable."

Elspeth didn't press and continued weeding.

She had been vulnerable, but Patrick made Laurie feel things she'd never felt before. She'd never been with a man and he wanted her. Could she head home without exploring what might develop between them?

Yeah!

Staying here would be a mistake. Staying here would be insane. Staying here could prove fatal.

She'd heard storytellers glorify the Scottish clan's penchant for cattle raiding, but the tale she heard in the great hall was horrible. Huts burned. Had anyone been hurt? Patrick said he received his scar from a cattle thief. Laurie deplored violence.

She'd forgotten about the heightened potential for danger in this time and place.

Staying here was so not an option.

She wanted to go home. She didn't care what Caitrina said about destiny.

Laurie chewed on her bottom lip as Patrick's words jumped into her mind and she gripped Elspeth's arm. "What exactly is meant by…*claimed as his own?*"

"I am not as innocent as they believe. I ken the claiming has something to do with the…ah, relations between men and women. I think if you were verra nice to him, he would keep you." Elspeth blushed sweetly.

Patrick hadn't claimed anything from her. Well, nothing more than a couple of heated kisses. He wanted more. And so did she. But what you want isn't always good for you.

"These strawberries are thinly planted," Laurie said.

Elspeth giggled. "If you wish, we can talk about something else. I thought we might get Duncan to take us to the mainland to search for wild strawberry plants to add to these."

"When shall we go?" The outing might be the perfect opportunity to make a break for the Fir-wood and a chance to attempt to reverse whatever sent her back in time.

"I will need to ask Patrick for his consent for us to leave the castle grounds." Elspeth flicked another weed on the pile. "I will ask him after the evening meal."

Fat chance he'd let them go anywhere. Laurie sat back on her heels and watched a colorful butterfly flutter past. She shouldn't be pessimistic. Perhaps Elspeth would convince her brother.

Laurie needed to be more optimistic. She contemplated the possibility of returning to Fir-wood when she noticed color and movement out of the corner of her eye. She glanced at the archway and her breath caught in her throat.

Patrick was barefoot, dressed in a colorful plaid with a woolen tunic the color of saffron beneath. A plain brass brooch secured the fabric at his shoulder. He looked like he walked off the pages of a glossy coffee table volume titled *Highlander*, or better yet, *Celtic Gods*.

He leaned against the stone with his arms crossed against his massive chest, his height and width crowded against the archway. Laurie swallowed involuntarily over the way his startling blue eyes sparkled in the sunlight. She stifled the urge to go to him and touch his thick chestnut hair, which he wore loose. She put her hands behind her back to stop herself from even thinking about her desire to run her fingers along his handsome clean-shaven cheek. And she definitely wouldn't think about what she'd like to do with his bare legs.

Damn the man for looking so good.

Her mouth went dry. A tingly sensation tightened her skin. Dear God, he made her hot and wet and…

Why was he here?

Laurie's tentative smile did strange things to Patrick. He made an effort to clear his face, not wanting to expose the emotional upheaval she aroused. 'Twas bad enough he donned his best *plaide* and searched her out.

He strode through the garden, stopping beside her and offered his hand. She hesitated, her gaze wary. Doubt crept in. Would she accept his assistance?

She curled her fingers around his and he felt a kick to his gut. Her eyes flared. She must have experienced something similar. When her hand trembled within his grasp, there was satisfaction in knowing he wasn't alone in his uncertainty.

He forced a cocky grin. She bristled and snatched her

hand away.

Elspeth giggled, rose to her feet, and brushed dirt from her apron. "'Tis good to see you in the garden. 'Tis been a long time since you came to enjoy its tranquility."

"Aye, too long," he said. "Duncan has returned to the castle on an errand. I will watch after Lady Laurie. Beth, please return to the hall?"

"She doesn't need to leave," Laurie said in a rush.

Patrick raised a hand to silence her. "I wish to discuss an important matter with you, *Lady* Laurie."

Elspeth searched his face. "You are always sending me away to be alone with Laurie. 'Tis not proper."

"You will understand better when Alexander returns from the Continent." Patrick patted his sister's shoulder.

"Alexander is a good man." A wistful expression crossed her face. "He always does what is proper. I have never been alone with him."

"He fears my wrath." Patrick chuckled.

"Nae, he fears you not." Elspeth giggled merrily and squeezed his arm. "You will find me in my solar if you are in need of me." She skipped across the garden and through the archway.

Laurie watched him through wide eyes as if uncertain what to expect from him. Good. 'Twould be best if she remained off balance.

"Shall we sit?" He tilted his head toward the roses, grasped her elbow, and urged her in that direction.

They skirted the bushes, avoiding the thorny plants. When they arrived at the bench, he inclined his head, and Laurie sat. He waited until she arranged her skirt and apron before he joined her on the narrow seat. Her feminine fragrance teased his nostrils and he inhaled sharply.

She watched him through a fringe of golden lashes. 'Twas his undoing. He'd intended to keep her at a distance, calmly discuss their future. Instead, her sensual warmth drove him near to madness. He couldn't resist her. Patrick pulled her sideways onto his lap and roughly captured her mouth. He slid his tongue along the seam of her lips, forced her to open for him. Her breasts rose to meet his chest as she melted into him, her arms encircling his neck.

Mine. She belonged to him.

Their tongues danced, and his heart thundered louder than the sound of his favorite steed's hoof beats at a full-out gallop.

With regret, he seized control of his wayward body and ended the kiss. He didn't want to scare her off. He placed her back on the bench beside him, taking hold of both her graceful hands in one of his work-hardened ones, afraid she might flee if given the opportunity.

"Ach, lass. You are a tasty morsel," he said, his voice rough with desire.

Laurie lowered her gaze to her lap, embarrassed at how easily she fell into Patrick's arms. A mere glance from those blue peepers of his, and she succumbed to his charms. Had the damn man stolen her ability to think rationally along with her breath?

He frightened her and made her feel powerful at the same time.

Her leg brushed his and he made a groaning noise deep in his throat. She fought the smile that threatened. There was no way she could push him away. Heat radiated from him through the fabric of her gown and apron. He was incredibly hot and hard and wonderful.

She had the urge to fan herself.

"You wanted to speak with me?" She finally found enough air to ask.

Patrick cleared his throat. "I have decided 'tis time for me to sleep in my bedchamber."

Tilting her head back, she gazed into his eyes. He expected her to agree.

Just like that—not.

She blinked a couple of times. "Where shall I sleep?"

"Next to me. Where you belong, lass."

Laurie braced her feet and pulled away, managing to catch him off guard, and quickly jumped out of his reach. "Is this a marriage proposal?" She glared at him.

His eyes widened and he stared back. "Why are you being difficult? I will take care of you. You must ken that."

Difficult?

"Answer my question. Do you plan to marry me?"

Sure, she'd vacillated between wanting to have sex with him and pushing him away. In reality, in her heart, she knew the only way she could make love to him was if they were married.

"Nae, I cannae wed you."

Well, didn't that say it all? He was a tease.

That it mattered bothered her more than she wished to analyze. She didn't plan to stay in the past long enough to marry anyone. Even so, the fact that he wanted to have sex and not marry her, hurt—especially given what that would mean should she be forced to stay in this time period.

When she dated in college, Laurie insisted on waiting until marriage. The guys she went out with only wanted to have sex and never called for a second date. Then she met the boy she believed was different. They dated for six months and when he convinced her they'd get married the following year, she agreed to sleep with him. The almost-event turned into a nightmare.

She hadn't been able to take him into her body. The pain when he tried had brought her to tears. A visit to her doctor declared her normal. But when they tried again, it still didn't work.

After those two devastating nights, she never dated again.

For years, she thought there was something fundamentally wrong with her. After doing research, she learned she just hadn't been aroused. Not her fault. Another opportunity to make love never presented itself.

Patrick's eyes shone with regret. Still—she wouldn't be used.

"I wouldn't sleep with you unless we were married. And I

don't wish to marry you. I want to go home. I'll not join you in your bed for sex games. You may sleep there if you wish, I'll find somewhere else." She whirled on her heel and fled the garden, refusing to allow him a response.

A short time later, Elspeth found her on the beach throwing large pebbles into the loch.

"Patrick sent me to find you. He admitted to upsetting you."

Laurie continued searching the ground, selecting a handful of pebbles and pitching them one by one across the water.

"Lady Laurie?"

"What?" She spun and faced Elspeth.

"He is sorry."

"I am too, but I can't stay here any longer. I need to find my way home. Patrick wants me to sleep with him, to be his whore. I can't. I just can't." She attempted to swallow her anger. Elspeth didn't deserve it directed at her. "I can't stay here."

Elspeth sighed. "You dinnae understand. He wants you to be his mistress, not his whore. 'Tis an honor to be the mistress of a Highland chief. He will take good care of you. Give you everything you could possibly want."

"A mistress is the same thing as a whore. Don't try to color his insult rosy," Laurie snapped. "I'm sorry. It's not your fault."

Elspeth motioned the words away with a flick of a hand. "A man spends one night with a whore and pays her little. He spends many nights with his mistress and pays her handsomely with his love and gold."

"What of marriage? What about a wife?" Laurie demanded.

Elspeth sadly shook her head. "A wife is for begetting heirs, for creating strong political alliances and gaining additional territory. Patrick can never wed where his heart wishes. Since our father has disappeared and not been found, Patrick is the Chief of Clan MacLachlan. With that honor comes a heavy responsibility. He must make an advantageous match. Although he's fought it for many years, he is promised to the daughter of his enemy, Iain Lamont. 'Tis why he quarrels with our uncle. He cannae marry you."

"I don't want him to marry me. I want to go home." Laurie kicked a stone.

"Do you not care for him at all?"

Laurie inhaled a deep breath. "I care…a little. Not enough to be what he wants me to be, or enough to keep me at Castle Lachlan. I belong in the future, not here in Scotland."

"Very well, since you are determined, I will help you get home. When we go to the mainland to search for strawberry plants, I will persuade Duncan to take us to the Fir-wood, and you can try to go home." Her eyes filled with moisture.

"Thank you." Relief at having a conspirator allowed Laurie to breathe easier. With Elspeth's help, she'd be able to return home. She gave the young woman an impromptu hug.

Elspeth squeezed her back. "Convincing Patrick will not be easy."

After the evening's repast, Laurie sat beside the fire while Elspeth entertained their small group. Patrick, Stephen, Duncan and Jamie lounged nearby. Elspeth sang ballads in her sweet lilting voice, accompanying herself on the lute. Occasionally, the men joined in, their voices husky and deep. Laurie found contentment in sitting quietly and listening, enjoying the romantic melodies, although not understanding the Gaelic words.

She watched Patrick from under her lashes. She loved the sound of his voice. It washed over her, enchanting her. *Mmm.* A beautiful deep voice, delicious like rich, dark, Belgian chocolate.

Yeah, she definitely enjoyed listening to the man. And he was certainly a pleasure to gaze at, all virile masculinity. His long, thick, chestnut hair hung free around his shoulders, the red highlights gleaming in the candlelight. He looked wild and independent like the mountains beyond the castle. He'd make any woman sigh with desire. To watch him with his family and close friends was a revelation. He was well loved and he cared deeply for those around him.

He mostly ignored her. Though gracious when his duties as host required, he otherwise remained distant. She missed his attention, although she wasn't about to let it show. Just as well. She couldn't dally with her Highland warrior. She had to go home.

When time came for the women to retire, Elspeth sent for Aine. "Please see Lady Laurie to Patrick's bedchamber and ready her for bed-going."

"I will ride out this night to patrol the borders." Patrick's comment to his sister stopped the protest forming on Laurie's lips.

Elspeth sighed. "Is there trouble, then?"

"'Tis hard to say. Our uncle is patrolling the east and my men will patrol the south and west. Saint Columba willing, we will find nothing amiss."

Laurie rose and followed Aine across the hall. Her thoughts stayed with Patrick, though she didn't understand why she worried over his safety. At the doorway, she flipped a glance over her shoulder. He was staring, his expression difficult to read. Her stomach did a funny little flip.

From behind him, Elspeth mouthed to Laurie, "I will ask."

Normally, Elspeth left the men to their claret, but tonight she needed Patrick to agree to let her and Laurie leave the safety of the castle to go to the mainland. She wanted to provide her companion the opportunity to return home without interference from her brother.

She eyed Patrick warily. He'd been prickly of late.

"What is it Beth?"

At times, he seemed to read her mind, but only she possessed the true gift.

She flicked her gaze to the others. "I need to speak with you in private."

"Ah, then let us retire to my work chamber."

Taking a deep breath for courage, she followed him across the passageway and into the Laird's study.

"What is it? Are you concerned about the dreadful news of the cattle raid brought by our uncle?" he asked once they settled in chairs before the hearth.

"Nae. That is always of concern with Lamont on our border ready to force the marriage agreement." She played with a fold in her skirt unable to look directly at him. "It has nothing to do with that."

"Then what?"

"I request your consent to go to the mainland in search of strawberry plants for the garden. If you will grant permission, I wish for Lady Laurie to accompany me."

Patrick rubbed his jaw. "You will take Aine and Duncan and two additional guardsmen. And you will be cautious."

She released the breath she held. "Aye, Patrick, we will be well guarded. I thank thee." She jumped from her seat, kissed his cheek, and ran from the chamber showing little restraint.

Then she slowed to a disheartened walk. Would Lady Laurie truly return home?

CHAPTER FOURTEEN

Present day, Manhattan

Finn tossed a glance over his shoulder to make sure he'd ditched the woman who tailed him from the club, the fourth woman who'd propositioned him during his workout. He'd have to talk to management and find out what they served at the juice bar.

Whatever it was, they needed to stop.

He strode into the steel and glass high-rise office building where his family's prestigious consulting firm maintained their New York offices and with a nod to the security guard, rode the elevator to the executive level.

"Good afternoon, Mr. MacIntyre," The receptionist greeted him with a smile. "Your admin collected your mail and...your magazine."

"Magazine?"

"Yeah. Trendsetters."

"Okay. Thanks."

Trendsetters? He didn't subscribe to that gossip rag. He skirted his admin's empty desk, walked into his office and fell into his leather chair.

"Hey, boss." His admin strolled in carrying the mail.

"What've we got?"

She handed over the pile.

"What the hell is this?" He threw the recent issue of Trendsetters magazine onto the mahogany desk and shoved the other mail to the side.

His administrative assistant leaned against the doorjamb, sporting a snarky smile. He lowered his gaze and glared at his damn face staring back from the glossy cover along with the words Finn MacIntyre—Trendsetter's Best Catch of the Year in bold type.

"Shit. I didn't authorize this."

He dragged his hands through his hair. That explained the aggressive women. Crap. This wasn't something he wanted to deal with after the unsuccessful trip to Beijing. He had to get out of town until this blew over. "Get my cousin Laurie on the phone. Her new number is in contacts."

He thrummed his fingers on the desk.

"Pick up line two. They say she isn't there," the admin yelled from her desk a few minutes later.

Finn grabbed the receiver and pressed the line button. "Hello?" He listened intently to what the person on the other end relayed. "What do you mean she's been gone for a month?" More listening. More disbelieving. He leaned forward in his chair. "Just who the hell are Caitrina and Munn?"

Castle Lachlan

Morning dawned with the castle shrouded in thick mist, the air raw and damp. The little group, wrapped in heavy plaids, stood huddled on the shingle, waiting while a couple of men pulled two small, oared boats over the beach and into the water. The tide was high at this early hour and the tang of brine filled Laurie's nostrils.

Elspeth's gaze kept darting nervously to the opposite shore.

"Is something wrong?" Laurie whispered.

The young woman leaned in close. "I want to be on our way before Patrick returns from patrol."

Laurie suspected Elspeth didn't wish to lie to her brother or face him with half-truths that would provoke his suspicion. Laurie could imagine what Patrick would do if he learned what they planned. She feared he'd stop them and punish them both. After all, he forbade her to attempt to return home.

Would he miss her after she was gone?

It didn't matter. She couldn't allow herself to think about that.

Laurie eyed the small boats and worried her lower lip. She wasn't used to traveling by boat. Of course, that was the least of her concerns. More importantly, how would she get to Firwood once they landed on the mainland? And what would she do once she got to the forest?

Would Caitrina show up and try to prevent her from returning to the future?

Egads. So many things to worry about.

Elspeth gave her a reassuring smile as they climbed into the boats. Laurie, Duncan and a guardsman in one. Elspeth, Aine and the other guardsman in the second. The oarsmen made short work of rowing across to the mainland beach. They climbed out of the boats and onto the shore, Laurie relieved to be across. From there, they ascended a rise, passed the orchard, and on to the stable.

Young grooms brought out mares for the women. Attached to their flanks hung small leather panniers designed to carry refreshments for the day and the young plants on the return trip. No one seemed to find this odd for Elspeth was known for her excursions into the fields and woods in search of plants for the castle garden. Meanwhile, the men readied their larger stallions.

It took Laurie some time to get accustomed to riding in her long skirt with the heavy apron atop, and one of Patrick's large plaids wrapped around her for warmth. His scent lingered on the fabric, teasing her. She would never forget him. She clutched the wool near her heart and blinked away unexpected moisture from her eyes.

Elspeth had given her Patrick's plaid and lent her a pair of riding boots, but although they were both petite, the boots fit snug. Laurie half expected she'd have blisters before the day ended. She ran a hand along the horse's neck, thankful her uncle encouraged her to take riding lessons in her youth. They came in handy, even though she would surely be sore later. She wouldn't worry about that now. There was plenty of time to worry once she got home to her own little cottage and soaked her feet in the whirlpool tub.

The little group rode single file on a well-worn track that ran along the edge of a wooded tract. The fog was less dense here and the visibility better. They traveled above the loch and when the mist gradually cleared, beautiful views appeared off to the west. Hairy, large horned, black cattle and the occasional deer grazed on young green grass in nearby fields. Laurie hardly noticed the beauty, intent on finding a way home.

They'd ridden for about an hour when Elspeth stopped them and they dismounted. The mist had completely burned off. The sun hung low on the eastern sky with clouds blowing in from the north. Elspeth informed the group they would start their search here in this meadow at the edge of the wood.

The men split apart in a triangle around the women, keeping watch for danger.

On their hands and knees, the women searched among the grasses for the precious strawberry plants. When they found a young seedling, they used a small, short-handled spade to dig around the plant, keeping soil on the roots, wrapped them in moist cloths then carefully placed them into the panniers.

Two hours went by and the leather packs were filling. Laurie bit her lip and glanced toward the trail they'd followed earlier. How could she break away from the others and find her way to the forest where Patrick found her?

Elspeth knelt beside her. "After a short respite, I will ask Duncan to guide us to the Fir-wood on our return to the castle," she murmured close to Laurie's ear.

"Thank you." Laurie squeezed the young woman's hand.

They sat in the meadow on plaids to partake of oatcakes and ale from flasks. Laurie savored the sweet-tasting ale flavored with aromatic plants and herbs. The drink was one thing she might miss once she got home. A pinch near her heart made her breath hitch. She didn't want to think about other things she'd miss, certainly not a special clan chief.

"Please guide us to the old hut near Fir-wood, Duncan. We wish to seek plants there," Elspeth said when they'd finished their meal.

He looked at her as if she were insane. "Aye, lass." He grumbled under his breath as he made ready to leave.

They mounted the horses again and rode a narrow track through dense woodland, Duncan riding at the front of the party with the two guards following. Everyone kept an eye out and listened for wild boar that might spook the horses. Dim light filtered through branches. Thorny bushes snagged the fabric covering Laurie's legs.

Her anxiety increased with each step the horse took. Wound too tight, like a child's top, she felt like she might spin out of control at any moment. Finally, they arrived at the old hut. A breeze blew across the meadow. Laurie's sense of anticipation escalated. She was determined to get home.

They dismounted, and as before, Duncan and his guardsmen spanned out, guarding the perimeter of the area where the women worked to uncover the wild strawberry plants.

Meandering around the meadow, Laurie attempted to appear as if she searched for the tiny plants. She tried to remember exactly where Patrick found her. Maybe the knoll on the other side of the hut. She walked in that direction.

The mound seemed quite ordinary. Not a place of magic.

The only thing growing on the little hillock was rich green

grass and toadstools.

She strode to the center and stopped, positive she'd found the spot where she'd fallen at Patrick's feet. She shot a glance at each of her companions. Duncan held a rigid stance, staring into the trees at the edge of the knoll, guarding them against any potential danger.

Patrick shook his head. His man needed some additional training if he didn't spy Patrick hidden in the coppice of trees. He'd sat on the thick branch high up in the large oak since before daybreak. He'd predicted Laurie would sneak off to Fir-wood and try to return home to her own century, though he didn't believe she possessed the ability. Last night, he'd guessed what the two women were contriving when Elspeth made her request. So here he sat on his rump waiting.

Waiting for what? He didn't know.

He kneaded his stiff neck with his fingers, while holding on to an overhanging branch with the other hand for balance. He yawned. Patrolling the MacLachlan border through the night left him near to exhaustion. They'd been lucky, finding no trouble.

Clansmen slept soundly in their beds. Cattle grazed unmolested, guarded by few sleepy keepers. Lambkins sought their mother's tits while herders huddled by dwindling fires.

Before returning to the castle, Patrick rode to this spot to wait for Elspeth and Laurie. Frustrated he hadn't caught the perpetrators of the previous raid, yet glad all was quiet, he climbed the ancient oak and watched the sunrise. His tail, some of his best men, waited in a clearing not far away, close enough if he needed assistance.

The lass's movements caught his attention.

Laurie closed her eyes and said a silent prayer. She felt nothing. Spinning around in a circle, she still felt nothing.

Sitting down, there was nothing. No tinkling sound. Not even the mere hint of an exotic scent in the air. There was no impression of unnatural energy, nor unusual surge of power. No bright, white light, nor kaleidoscope colors.

There was absolutely nothing out of the ordinary.

Elspeth and Aine continued working, collecting plants a short distance away. The guardsmen paid little attention to Laurie, intent on watching for trouble.

Several hours passed with her sitting on Patrick's plaid in the center of the knoll with nothing happening, at least, nothing magical. She couldn't concentrate. Her thoughts strayed, her mind's eye seeing Patrick. She imagined him walking toward her, through a wildflower meadow, his gait determined. His chestnut hair pulled back in a tight queue. His hungry, dark eyes sought hers. As he neared, her heart raced. She wanted to reach out and touch him.

Then his image faded.

Stop it, her mind screamed. She glanced around the knoll, chills raced along her spine. It was imperative she stay focused on the task at hand, not dream about the man who made her heart throb erratically. She couldn't allow her purpose to cloud with her attraction to Patrick. Staying wasn't an option. She needed to go home.

Mid-afternoon, the rest of the group ate and drank the leftover food. Laurie refused to join them. If anyone thought this strange, they didn't comment.

Finally, the panniers were full of plants and the group readied to return to the castle. The others mounted their horses, except for Elspeth.

Laurie still sat in the center of the knoll, her hands folded in her lap. Elspeth approached. "Nothing has happened. You remain."

Tears burned the back of Laurie's eyes, but she refused to shed them. She held her head high while she gazed at Elspeth.

The young woman gave her a half smile. "We must return to the castle before darkness falls. Mayhap 'twill work another day."

"Yes, I'll return. Perhaps another time." Laurie's shoulders sagged. What did she think would happen? Was she foolish enough to believe by just standing there she'd miraculously return home?

She walked with Elspeth to the horses. They mounted while the rest of the group quietly watched. Then they rode in the direction of the castle.

Caitrina said she needed to find her destiny. Was Patrick truly her destiny?

Patrick sat in his treetop hideout grinning like a fool. The lass would stay. She couldn't leave! He had time to persuade her to become his mistress. Jubilant, he jumped to the ground and ran through the woods toward the spot where the men and horses waited.

As he rounded a thicket, a moaning noise caught his attention, a sound not of the wood. He stopped. Standing perfectly still and quiet, he listened. The noise came again. He pulled out his knife while peering into the thicket.

There it was again.

He moved with stealth, his body tense, alert to danger, movements calculated, ready for attack. Pushing aside some branches, he found a motionless form behind the undergrowth. Patrick eased closer. Reaching out with his foot, he nudged the body. It didn't move. He reached down and rolled the man over.

Ruari MacLachlan, a kinsman, a clan herdsman, moaned but didn't stir.

Patrick knelt next to the injured man and gently tried to rouse him. The young man was insensible but still breathed. Patrick ran his hands over the man. No blood. Nothing more than a bump on the lad's head.

"What befell you, Ruari?" he murmured.

Patrick shook his head and, with a sharp whistle, signaled for his lads to come to him.

Within a blink, the men who made up his tail surrounded

him. Big men, they were strongly built and well-armed. Stephen stepped from among the others and knelt on the ground next to Patrick, his gaze fixed on young Ruari. "What do you think happened?"

"I ken not. He is a long way from home. Have some of the men make a litter. Dispatch one of the ghillies with a message, our swiftest runner, to the castle. Send two scouts south, fast riders, to his dwelling to search for signs of trouble."

CHAPTER FIFTEEN

Sands of Time

Munn sat on a large flat rock at the side of the still pool. Leaning forward, his elbows resting on his knees, his chin on his hands, he gazed at his reflection in the turquoise water. Discouraged was he. He tried and tried to find the right string of sounds and images to release himself from this dreadful place.

But here he still was—a failure.

He'd let down his clan and his chief.

"Ach," he cried. "What to do?"

The tranquil water turned turbulent before his eyes. His reflection shattered and vanished. A whirlpool appeared where his image had been, foam swirling on the surface. He fell back in fear. However, his curiosity got the better of him. He leaned forward once again, to look into the water.

The pool calmed and turned an inky black.

Unable to see his likeness any longer, he thought to run away. Instead, he froze in place when the water again swirled. The murkiness cleared, the water became translucent. From the depths in the center of the pool appeared a bright white light. It spun, rising toward the surface, then expanded and changed. Soft blues and lavenders mixed with the white, slowly swirling, coalescing into the image of a woman.

Munn stared in awe at the most beautiful woman he'd ever seen. Her face shone bright with an iridescent glow, mesmerizing to behold. She rose from the water, her magnificent raiment clinging to her sumptuous form, clothed as she was in a spun silver diaphanous gown. She was superbly fashioned, tall and lissome, her skin a pale opalescence. Her glorious silky hair, a brilliant white gold, caressed her shapely curves, falling to her feet in glimmering curls. As she moved, her hair and skin glistened with a fine dusting of silver powder.

Entranced by her dazzling blue eyes, Munn couldn't glance away. "Who are you?" His words came out a croak.

"I am known as Oonagh," she said, her eloquent voice, a song to his ears.

Her music ran over him, soothed him, lulled as he was by her glamour.

Oonagh gazed upon him and slowly raised her arms to the sky. A searing breeze blew off the hot sand, disturbing the tranquility of the oasis.

Munn's trance broke. He shook his head, his daze clearing as he peered at the woman before him. His breath caught in his throat, his whole body trembled. He knew of her. She was the High-Queen of the *Sithichean*, her power absolute, as she took tribute from the lesser queens.

Fear seeped through his veins. What did she want of him?

"Little man, be calm," the queen said. "I am here to free you from the enchantment of Princess Caitrina."

He wanted to jump for joy. Oh, to be free. "She had nae right to send me to this horrid place. I must be off to warn the MacLachlan."

"Soon." Oonagh presented him a beguiling smile. "There is one thing, my little man, before I release you. You must pledge allegiance. You must perform a service to me."

Munn inhaled a quick breath, his delight vanishing. He was in serious trouble. She possessed the power to do unbearable things. What would she expect of him?

He wanted to run, to escape the enthrallment of her piercing blue eyes. He didn't dare. "Aye," he said in a whisper.

Oonagh narrowed her eyes. "You will vow to me, on your honor, and that of Clan MacLachlan? You will perform the task I name? Obey my command above all others?"

Again, Munn answered in a trembling voice.

"Aye."

"Kneel before me."

He fell to his knees at the dainty feet of the queen and bowed his head. After a suitable time had passed, he raised his gaze. A jeweled scepter had appeared in Oonagh's delicate hand. She pointed the golden instrument toward him.

"Here, little brownie. Place your hand on the *Scepter of Truth* and vow your troth to me."

Munn stared at the scepter. He didn't want to touch it. He didn't want to make a pledge of fidelity to the queen. But what else was he to do?

He placed his hand on the large round tip of the scepter. Pain shot up his arm as if lightning burned through his veins. He tried to pull his arm away, but couldn't.

"It is my will you keep the MacLachlan and his lady from the future apart. You will keep them from sharing the most intimate, ancient and carnal of dances. This you must pledge." Oonagh sang, using her fae power along with the persuasion of her melodious voice.

Bile burned in the pit of Munn's stomach. "Aye. I pledge," he said, relieved when the pain eased. He believed himself lucky to get off so easily. That was until the queen's expression changed, and he knew a terror like none other. Her sensual smile flashed pure evil.

"Failure will condemn you to an eternity trapped within the *Sands of Time*."

CHAPTER SIXTEEN

Strathlachan

She didn't mean to be a burden, but Laurie's dismal mood hung over the group like the dark clouds cluttering the sky. As the day grew short, the gentle breeze changed into a fierce howling wind, slowing the group's progress along the ridge.

"Lady Elspeth, a storm's coming. We might find protection from the wind in the forest," Duncan raised his voice above the din.

"Aye," Elspeth agreed.

Duncan led them into the shelter of the trees, following a game trail. The tight path weaved through dense undergrowth. Branches caught loose clothing and scratched exposed skin, forcing their pace to a slow walk. All was quiet, save for the wind whistling through the limbs overhead. There was no sign of animals or birds, as if the turbulence sent them seeking shelter.

Near dusk, the hushed group rode into the stable yard, wind whipping around them. Leaves and twigs, and blowing dust swirled in eddies, making it difficult to see.

The men dismounted and several grooms came running. The boys caught the stallions' reins and led them away. The men grabbed hold of the mares' reins and guided the horses into the protection of the stable where the women could dismount out of the biting wind.

One of the guardsmen assisted Laurie from her horse. She thought his name might be Dhughall, but she wasn't sure. A chill crept into her bones. Pulling Patrick's plaid close around her, she slipped out a hand and rubbed her mare's neck, wordlessly thanking the gentle beast for carrying her safely to shelter.

Bleak numbness pervaded her mind. She didn't want to face her failure, not yet.

She attempted a smile for the guardsman after he removed the pannier from her horse and slung the leather bag over his shoulder. He inclined his head and turned away. Duncan and the other guardsman also carried panniers over their shoulders, having taken them from Aine and Elspeth's horses.

The group left the calm of the stable, the men carefully assisting the women down the slippery slope toward the beach. The wind whipped at them, whirling around, tugging at their clothing.

When they reached the water's edge, Duncan signaled to the other shore for the oarsmen to row the boats across to the mainland. Laurie watched as they made their way through the choppy water. White caps splashed against the hulls, tossing the salty spray at the oarsmen, soaking them.

The Highlanders were well accustomed to these fierce conditions, but she wasn't. She pulled Patrick's plaid tighter, apprehension spurring her to say a silent prayer.

The boats beached and the men handed the women over to sit on the wooden benches. The small craft bobbed in the surf, forcing her to grip the gunwale. The three men jumped in.

With an order from Duncan, the oarsmen were pushing away from shore when a ghillie came running. "Wait!" he called, yelling over the crash of the waves and the screaming wind. He sprinted to the water's edge where he bent over, placed his hands on his knees and gulped air.

"Hold up," Duncan ordered the oarsmen as he jumped over the side of the boat and joined the lad on the shingle.

"The chief requests the castle folk make ready to receive the injured Ruari MacLachlan." Even though short of breath from his run, the ghillie still managed to get out his message in a loud, clear voice.

"Lad, do you ken what happened to Ruari?" Duncan shouted.

The ghillie inhaled a deep breath and yelled back, "Nae."

Elspeth faced Duncan, concern showing in her silver eyes. "The men will have to move slower to accommodate a litter. They may get caught in the storm."

"Dinnae fash yourself, lass. Your brother and Stephen will ensure they get through."

"I thank you for bringing the message," Elspeth said to the young man. "Ride across with us and partake of a meal."

"Aye. Thank you kindly." The ghillie climbed into the boat with Aine and Laurie and one of the guardsmen, making for a tight fit.

Duncan climbed into the boat with Elspeth and ordered the oarsmen to proceed. The boats moved through the rough water to the castle, salt spray misting everyone.

Upon reaching the castle's beach, they climbed from the boats and hiked up the slight hill to the gate. Once in the courtyard, one of the guardsmen and Aine took the panniers and headed to the kitchen, the ghillie following. The rest of the group ascended the wheel stair.

A hush fell over the room when they entered the hall, already crowded with men and a few women seated at the lower tables.

Miserable from the day's fiasco, Laurie dropped onto a bench at the first table she came to. She didn't know how to assist these people in the preparations for the injured man though she worried about his condition. She didn't think she could cope with the deficiencies of primitive medicine up close.

Her stomach rolled. Thank God, she hadn't eaten much.

She sat alone at the trestle table, Elspeth and Duncan having left the hall intent on their preparations for the injured man. Some of the men seated at a nearby table stared at her with open curiosity. Others ignored her. None of them sought conversation with her.

After a short time, Aine entered the hall and covered one of the tables near the hearth with a white cloth. A serving girl followed, placing a cauldron of water on a hook over the fire. Another appeared carrying a large earthenware ewer. A third brought a stack of clean cloths. The latter items they placed near the cloth-covered table.

Elspeth returned to the hall, having removed her damp clothing. She'd donned a long white linen *leine* that graced her ankles. Over top, she wore a striped wool *arisaid*, a cloak that fell to her heels, fastened at her breast by a beautiful silver and moonstone brooch and belted at her waist with leather and chain. Laurie learned shortly after her arrival the *arisaid* was the traditional dress of Highland women, though Elspeth, being nobility, most often wore gowns similar to those worn by women in France.

Elspeth carried two baskets, one contained bandages made from rags, a needle and thread, the other nearly overflowed with small pots and pouches. She placed these at the end of the table and joined Aine in a hushed conversation.

Laurie only heard a fragment of what they said—a word here and there.

She observed the activity in the hall as if watching a film. She found it appalling how useless she was in this time. On top of that, her failure to return home left her feeling inept and unsure. She was lost in a world not her own.

What if I'm stuck in this barbaric place? What if I can never go home?

Her stomach clenched and she found it hard to breathe. The old warning rang true. You needed to be careful of what you wished. She'd wanted a new life, but being stuck here was definitely *not* what she had in mind.

She was wallowing in self-pity. But who would blame her? She was damp and dirty. Hungry. Stuck in this world.

Her depression blinded her to most of the activity around her. Motion near the doorway at the other end of the great hall drew her gaze. Donald MacLachlan leaned against the passageway wall just outside the rear entrance. He was in an animated conversation—arms flailing—with a woman Laurie didn't recognize. More than likely a serving girl based on the way she was dressed.

Donald suddenly froze and stared into the hall to where the preparations for the injured man were taking place. He tilted his head and whispered something to his companion. The woman responded in a low voice and departed.

He strode to Elspeth. "What has happened, niece?"

She twisted to face him. "I did not ken you were in the castle."

"I returned after dawn from the southern border. What are these preparations?"

"We received a message from Patrick of an accident."

"Has your brother been wounded?"

"Nae, thank the Good Lord." Elspeth made the sign of the cross. "It's our herdsman Ruari. They bring him to the castle for tending."

"I told your brother there would be more trouble. He must resolve this quarrel with Lamont. If he agreed to the marriage with Isobell the conflict would cease."

Isobell? Marriage? Laurie's ears perked.

"We dinnae ken what happened. What makes you think Lamont was involved?"

Donald looked like he was about to retort when he stopped with his mouth half-open.

Laurie swiveled her head to the open window, where a noisy disturbance came from the courtyard below. The commotion moved up the stairs and the door to the hall slammed open. Patrick and Stephen entered, water dripping from their hair and plaids.

Behind them, two of Patrick's men carried a litter with the injured man up the awkward circular stone steps. Entering the hall with their burden, they set the litter beside the table where Aine indicated. They placed the man on his back atop the table while the rest of the men gathered round.

Aine examined the man, searching for injuries while she moved her hands over his body. The entire time, she shook her head and made tsking sounds.

Almost everyone in the hall moved to stand around the table. They were silent, waiting for Aine's assessment. Laurie moved with the group, though she watched as an outsider, not a participant.

Patrick's uncle stared at her. She used the corner of the plaid she wore to wipe some of the salt residue from her face. She must look a mess.

He gave a slight nod and looked away, relieving some of the tension in her shoulders.

"I cannae find any injury." Aine wiped her hands on a wet cloth. "Naught but this whappin' bump on his head. What has happened to the lad?"

Patrick shook his head. "We dinnae ken."

His uncle stepped forward. "I warned you, nephew. If you did not fulfill your father's wish and marry Isobell Lamont our people would pay the price."

Laurie tensed. That was the second time Donald said the name Isobell and the subject of marriage in the same sentence with reference to Patrick. She raised her tired eyes to Patrick. His gaze burned her, then he quickly turned away to glare at his uncle.

"Hold your tongue, old man," he bellowed.

His uncle's face contorted into a nasty grimace, but he remained silent, and stepped back from the crowd. His face reddened with anger.

"There's nothing for me to do for Ruari, but try to make him comfortable," Aine said.

"Naught?" Patrick's eyes shone with turbulent emotion. "Are you sure there is naught we can do for the lad?"

"Bide an' see," she said.

Duncan stepped forward from behind the others and peered at Ruari. "I have seen injuries like this afore. Some men never waken."

"We must rearrange sleeping quarters to accommodate the lad. Move Lady Laurie's things into Lady Elspeth's bedchamber and prepare mine for Ruari," Patrick ordered. "Someone is to be with him at all times."

Aine hurried from the hall.

"Beth, you will share your bedchamber with Lady Laurie until Ruari recovers."

"I dinnae mind. She is my sister."

"That is good." Patrick nodded. "Now run along and help Aine. And take Lady Laurie with you." Glancing at Laurie, he raised an eyebrow. "She appears to have had a disappointing day."

Laurie frowned. What did he mean by that remark? Their eyes met again and held. Did he know what she'd been up to? She shivered and broke the contact, glancing away, her unsettled emotions swirling.

The last thing she wanted was for Patrick to realize she planned to return home.

Later that evening, Patrick surveyed the hall, the tic throbbing beneath his eye, an annoyance. His rage bubbled below the surface.

The repast had been a quiet affair with only a small amount of stilted conversation. Lady Laurie sat at the high table at his left, looking much better than she had earlier. Healthy color had returned to her cheeks. Stephen sat on her other side while Elspeth took the place to Patrick's right with Uncle Donald next to her.

At the lower tables, a somber mood prevailed with his people concerned for Ruari. The clansmen bantered over much conjecture as to how the lad became injured. Most were ready to blame the Lamonts. As was he.

"Patrick, you must listen to reason," Donald said, breaking the silence at the high table with his thundering voice. "The Lamonts will continue to raid our land if you dinnae fulfill the promise of your father and marry the lass."

There was a collective intake of breath and all gazes shot to Patrick.

Stiffening, he slowly twisted his torso to look past his sister to his uncle, fury burned in his gut. "You ken there was never a promise. I will not bring the daughter of our enemy into this house to mother my sons."

"You must wed Isobell Lamont."

"Nae. That I will never do."

Before the argument could escalate, the two scouts who'd gone to Ruari's hut entered the hall and strode to the dais to report. They told a bloody tale of devastation, burned huts and torched fields, cattle gone. The other two herdsmen dead. Murdered.

Jumping from his seat, Donald slapped his hand hard on the table in front of Patrick. "I told you."

He ignored his uncle's outburst and stood before his clan. "This dishonorable deed was surely the work of the Lamonts. In that much, my uncle is correct. The time has come to retaliate. We must plan our strategy. To the council chamber."

Benches scraped across stone. Voices raised in debate as the men of the clan left the great hall to climb the wheel stair to the council hall above.

Before he left the dais, Patrick darted a glance at Laurie. Her alarmed expression tore at his heart. He didn't care for the pallid cast to her skin. The day's events must have upset her, but as much as he wished to ease her heartache, he couldn't coddle her.

Nor could he allow her to return to the future. Faerie magic was far too unpredictable. Too dangerous. Yanking his thoughts back to the problem with the Lamonts, he strode from the chamber with his men.

Laurie rose to follow, but Elspeth placed a hand on her arm to stay her. "'Tis a matter for the men."

"What do you mean? Oh, I forgot. Women aren't included in politics." She hadn't meant for her frustration to show in her tone of voice, yet it had.

Elspeth arched a brow. "Nae. Of course not."

"Well, where I come from women are involved in political affairs. Aren't you concerned about what the men will decide?"

"Aye. They will tell us after the council is concluded."

Laurie ground her teeth. "Don't you think they should include you in making a decision that will affect the future of your clan?"

"You have some unusual ideas. Let us go to my chamber and you can tell me about the women of your time." Elspeth's wary gaze shifted to those seated around them when she realized her slip. No one seemed to notice, too busy with personal speculation.

Laurie shook her head. She'd never get used to the role women played in this society. With a sigh, she followed Elspeth from the hall.

They ascended the circular stone steps. At this late hour, torches lit the stairs and passageways. Elspeth also carried a small lantern. When they reached the second level, Elspeth stopped and placed the lamp in a small niche in the wall. She put a finger to her lips, signaling for silence.

"Why so secretive?" Laurie asked in a whisper.

Elspeth shook her head and tapped the finger against her lips. She extended her arm and brushed her hand along the stone wall, and then pressed hard against one of the stones. A portion of the wall fell back, exposing an opening into darkness. What had moments before appeared as solid stone became the gloomy entrance to a secret passageway.

A chill of apprehension skittered along Laurie's spine. Elspeth clasped her hand again, shaking her head when Laurie opened her mouth to say something more. The young woman guided her into the darkness, stepping cautiously. The doorway closed behind them with a muffled thud.

Laurie gasped softly. Elspeth stopped and gave her damp hand a gentle squeeze. Her heart thumping hard, Laurie stood motionless, listening.

Muted voices came from nearby. It took willpower to trust Elspeth and stay quiet. Laurie couldn't catch her breath, claustrophobic in the confined space—in the darkness. She'd always been afraid of the dark. Fearing spiders waited in their webs ready to pounce on those who dared the shadowy places. Her skin prickled and she shivered.

After a moment, her eyes adjusted to the dimness. To the right she felt hard stone. To the left was an unusual wooden wall woven like a basket. Filtered light entered the hidden passageway from between slats.

Elspeth squeezed her hand again, and tugged her farther along the passage. Laurie took careful steps, brushing her free hand along the stones to her right. As they moved, the voices became more distinct. Soon she recognized Patrick's voice and realized where they were. She remembered the slatted wall from the other side.

When she'd first arrived, she'd toured the castle with Duncan and Elspeth and seen the council chamber.

She and Elspeth were at this moment hidden from the council by an elaborate wooden screen with slats weaved in a complicated Celtic design. The partition stood behind the large stone dais platform.

The reason they heard Patrick's voice clearly.

CHAPTER SEVENTEEN

*A*ngry voices reverberated round the council hall. Boisterous arguments erupted throughout the chamber. Patrick sat at the head table surrounded by his most loyal men. The exception his uncle, he didn't trust the man. Stephen, Duncan and Jamie debated the merits of making a raid during a full moon, whereas Patrick's uncle argued against retaliation of any kind.

If only Archibald had returned from the Continent and was here to lend his support. Patrick missed their shared confidences. Being twins, they'd always been close, but especially so after their elder brother died. Holding with tradition, their elder brother Donald was named for their grandfather, as was their uncle. Isobell Lamont should have been their brother's bride, not Patrick's.

Patrick drummed his fingers on the table, ignoring most of the discussion going on around him. His insides boiled. How dare Lamont take out the argument over the disputed marriage proposal on the MacLachlan clan?

He glanced at the men sitting at the two long tables stretched out in front of him and the others standing around the chamber. This was his family, and he'd failed them. His fervent denial of a marriage contract between himself and

Iain Lamont's daughter Isobell brought them to the precipice of this hostile confrontation. Yet a feud with the Lamonts had existed for generations. The recent raid was only the most current act of treachery.

His gaze drifted to the ceiling, his thoughts on the chamber above. The chamber his precious Laurie slept in, his bedchamber, the one where Ruari now lay unconscious.

Patrick took full responsibility for what happened to his herdsmen. If only he'd agreed to Iain Lamont's demands—married Isobell—Ruari wouldn't be lying in the bedchamber above, insensible from a bang on the head. And the others wouldn't be dead.

Lamont had prodded him ever since Patrick lost his father. This time the man pushed too far. Patrick would have to retaliate. It was an issue of honor. This latest infringement couldn't be left unpunished. It was a matter of his clan's survival.

Was he wrong? Should he break his oath, marry Isobell, and hope in doing so, he'd end the feud? It wasn't that Isobel was undesirable. She'd make someone a good wife. She possessed a fine dowry and was comely. But he felt nothing when she was near. Certainly not the burning fire he experienced with Laurie. Isobell had no warmth. She was like cold stone. He'd never even had the desire to steal a kiss.

Archibald thought him daft. Repeatedly, he reminded Patrick of her value. After all, she was the co-heir of Iain Lamont. Now, that was the problem. How could he be expected to marry her? He believed her father responsible for his parent's disappearance.

And possible death? No, he wouldn't consider the possibility.

When he learned his parents had gone missing while chased by Lamont clansmen, he swore from that day forward Iain Lamont was his enemy. He vowed never to agree to a marriage between the two clans.

He raked his fingers through his hair. What of Laurie? What was he to do about his lass from the future?

Stephen poked his arm, interrupting his contemplation. "The full moon is two days next. 'Tis the best time to raid."

"Aye. A good time for a raid," Jamie agreed, a brutal grin spreading across his face.

"'Tis not the time to raid." Donald pinned Patrick with his gaze. "Marry Isobell. End the dispute."

Patrick glared at his uncle. "I will agree to marry the lass on the day my father stands afore me and requests it of me."

An anxious hush fell across the chamber.

"You cannae yet believe your father alive. If he were, he would be here with us now."

"For all I ken, he and my sweet stepmother suffer in Lamont's pit," Patrick said, his tone sharp.

Across the chamber, Aine's husband Angus stood, slamming his palms flat on the table. All gazes shot to him. "Leave off, Donald. 'Tis time we seek revenge for the insults wrought by the Lamonts. I say we raid."

Most of the men roared in agreement, raising fists and shouting. Donald glowered. His gaze circled the chamber from man to man. "Decided, is it? You will rue this day."

"'Tis a matter of honor." With his fists clenched and his knuckles white, Patrick struggled to maintain control over his temper. "I am a warrior fighting to maintain my honor and that of my clan."

"And what of King Jamie? What do you think will happen when he hears of this?" Donald demanded.

Loud voices erupted again in the chamber. "Quiet!" Patrick bellowed. "He will not interfere with a mere skirmish."

They were well aware of King James IV's policies. He sought to do in the Highlands what had been effective amongst his Lowland lords. The king's strategy to play one clan against the other, perpetuate ancient feuds and generate renewed bitterness ensured his control in the Highlands.

Patrick believed King Jamie wouldn't bother to get involved unless it came to all-out clan war. Another matter altogether. He was determined not to let that happen.

His uncle scowled. "You will regret your decision." He stomped from the chamber. Several men standing near the doorway followed.

Let the man go. Patrick couldn't trust him at his back anyway.

Laurie held a lungful of air, listening to the discussion from the opposite side of the screen. She released her breath in a rush after Elspeth squeezed her hand again. So much anger, so much hate, so much violence, and centuries hadn't changed that. The world remained much the same.

The women made their way back along the screen. Elspeth slid her hand along the wall, hit the trigger stone and the opening emerged in front of them. They stepped through the doorway into the outer passage, and Laurie blinked in the brighter light. With another stone pressed, the wall swung back into place.

Once again, Elspeth made the sign for silence. The women ascended the steps to the upper floor, crossing over to the eastern wing to Elspeth's bedchamber. The young woman plopped into one of the chairs before the hearth and Laurie sat in another. Neither spoke.

The bedchamber was tiny in comparison to Patrick's, yet seemed well suited to Elspeth. Laurie swirled slippered toes in a circle on the woven rush mat beneath her feet. She eyed the canopied bed. Though smaller than Patrick's, the intricately carved bed had beautiful spring-green velvet drapes. Several luxurious furs lay across the matching coverlet. A large wooden trunk with decorative brass hardware sat at the bed's foot.

Laurie scanned the rest of the room. A small window seat with a green velvet cushion matching the bed's adornment softened the stark gray stone at the only window in the room. Her few possessions sat atop a small wooden chest nearby. Patrick's borrowed plaid lay folded on top along with her tartan stole. Across the wool draped her skirt and blouse and a sleeping gown. Not much to call her own.

The day's events, the long ride on horseback, the digging of plants, the disappointment at Fir-wood, and the excitement over Ruari and the proposed retaliation, took their toll. Exhaustion swamped her. She brushed her hand across her gown, still damp from the boat ride across the bay. She'd be lucky if she didn't get sick.

Scooting closer to the fire, she rolled her neck on her shoulders and attempted to assimilate what she'd heard while hidden in the secret passage.

"What will happen now?" she asked after several long minutes.

"The men will stay up most the night planning and drinking. Then they will stumble to their beds."

"Is there anything we can do to change their course?"

"Nae. 'Tis foolhardy to get in their way," Elspeth said. "Shall we ready ourselves for bed? I told Aine she could spend this eve in the village."

"Sure." Although worn out, Laurie doubted she'd fall asleep.

After an hour passed, she lay on the bed next to the silently sleeping Elspeth, listening to the night wind wailing outside the castle walls. The occasional clap of thunder rumbled in the distance as the storm moved away. Wide-awake, she tensed at each noise, every creaking sound in the castle.

Unable to remain still, she rose and tiptoed to the chest in the corner. Pulling Patrick's plaid around her, she opened the door and looked into the torch-lit passageway. No one was there. Not even Duncan skulked outside the door. When her eyes adjusted to the dim light, she made her way along the passage to the foul-smelling garderobe. She took a deep breath and pinched her nose before entering the privy.

Instead of returning to the bedchamber when finished, she found herself wandering near the wheel stair. She crept down the steps, two levels down, still not seeing anyone. Stopping outside Patrick's study, she listened. All was quiet.

She pushed the door open a crack. No one stirred. She edged the door farther open and peered in. The chamber was dark, except for a golden glow coming from a partly open doorway across the room.

She wasn't sure why she'd come. *Why she sought Patrick.*

Sneaking into the chamber, she warily made her way to the far door. Her bare feet made little noise as she crossed the cold stone floor. She peeked around the edge of the door and gaped in awe at the unexpected chapel with its one worshiper. Brilliant candles bathed the chapel in a radiant glow. Golden light jumped and flickered while shadows danced on the walls. Patrick knelt before the altar, his head bowed in prayer. His chestnut hair hung about his shoulders, deep red highlights ablaze, creating a halo effect around his head. The ethereal scene sent a thrill down her spine.

Not wanting to intrude, she stepped back into his private chamber to leave, bumping into the corner of a table as she went. Something crashed to the floor, hitting her foot. She cried out. Before she realized what happened, Patrick's arm encircled her chest and the edge of his knife pressed against her throat.

He exhaled sharply, let go of her, and quickly replaced his knife in the sheath on his thigh. "Lass, you are going to get yourself killed if you insist on sneaking up on a man."

She shrank back against his desk, her heart pounding a staccato beat.

"Stay here. Dinnae move." He strode into the chapel, returning a moment later with a lantern, which he set on the table. "What are you doing here?"

Patrick's worried frown caused her to nervously cough. What to say?

"I understand you are going after the raiding party. I couldn't let you go without—"

"Tell me."

She hesitated, surprised by the softening of his features. "I wish you well."

"We will not go until just before the full moon."

"When the time comes...stay safe." The thought of Patrick being injured made her crazy.

Patrick barely resisted reaching out and touching Laurie. She was a sight, his beautiful angel. She wore a flowing white bed gown that was sheer in the soft light. His borrowed *plaide* hung loose over her arms providing a glimpse of her peachy skin through the gossamer fabric of the gown. Silky golden hair flowed around her shoulders and down her back. Expressive blue eyes entrapped him, stirring his blood.

"Ach, lass. You are fetching." He stepped closer. Unable to stop, he pulled her into his arms. He hugged her close and gently kissed the top of her head.

She raised her gaze and leaned back to look at him. Questions simmered in the depths of her eyes.

"Lass?" He needed to know what she was thinking.

"Will you wed as your uncle suggests?"

"Nae." He shook his head. "I cannae wed the daughter of my enemy. Besides, you are the one I want."

A furrow creased her forehead. "How do you know?"

He rubbed the ache in his chest. "I felt you here in my heart since first we met."

"Do you believe in love at first sight?"

His lips twitched into a grin. "Lust at first sight?"

"So you lust after me."

"All I ken is I want you as I have never wanted another. Is that not enough?" He tightened his grip on her arms. "Can we not take time to learn to care for one another?"

"Sometimes you are sweet." Her features grew wistful.

Not wanting her to think too much, he scooped her up and cradled her in his arms. He moved to one of the chairs before the hearth, sat, held her on his lap, and hugged her.

"Mmm." She snuggled against him.

Neither spoke, Patrick savored the closeness.

After a short time, he repositioned her on his lap to view her expressive face. He lifted her chin and gazed into her eyes. They glistened in the lantern light. Brilliant flecks of gold swam within sapphire. He bent his head, gently kissing her lips. Pulling her plump bottom lip into his mouth, he tasted her essence.

She kissed him back, as if she needed and wanted him.

His manhood stirred, and her eyes popped open. She nipped his lip and leaned slightly back. A precious smile graced her face as she nestled her side against his cock. "To state the obvious, you've risen to the occasion."

"Aye." Patrick shifted uncomfortably in the chair. He desired her more than he dared admit. "Though, I will not take you before riding out on a raid."

"I didn't offer."

"Impertinent wench." He cupped the back of her head and brought her mouth close to his.

He used his lips to tease her mouth and pressed for entrance. Their tongues whirled in a dueling dance.

His blood burned hot. He could lose himself to this woman. Shocked at the thought, he pulled back. "You planned to leave me."

CHAPTER EIGHTEEN

*E*ngulfed in a sensual haze, Laurie's pulse hummed. She sighed, disappointed Patrick stopped kissing her and wanted to talk more. Then she realized what he said. She sat straighter and leaned her head back to see into his eyes. "You know?"

"Aye. I saw you at Fir-wood. You must never go there again." He tried to hide his emotions, but she glimpsed hurt.

She frowned. How was she to explain her confused feelings?

"It wasn't you I tried to leave. I just wanted to go home, back to the future. But I couldn't find my way." Moisture pooled in the corners of her eyes. She blinked to stop the tears, but one slipped.

He gently wiped the escaped drop from her cheek with the tip of a finger. "Ach, lass. Dinnae cry. I cannae bear it." He pulled her close again and touched her lips with his, a gentle, tender kiss lasting an eternity.

She lost sense of time and place. A cool current of air swirled over her arms bringing goosebumps to her flesh. She heard papers flutter on the table. Patrick deepened the kiss, and the exquisite sensation reached her toes. Nothing else mattered, only the erotic feel of his mouth and tongue and the warmth of his body.

Chilly air swept over the back of her neck, annoying her.

The draft grew in intensity, becoming a strong, cold breeze.

No longer able to ignore the drop in temperature, Laurie shivered and pulled away from Patrick's talented touch. Papers flew from the desk and were caught in a whirlwind in the corner of the chamber. A chill raced along her spine that had nothing to do with the dropping temperature but everything to do with magic. Was Caitrina about to make another appearance? Laurie jerked her gaze to Patrick. If Caitrina appeared, would he think Laurie a witch as he warned her others might think of her?

He stared at the swirl of papers, his jaw tight. "Munn, what are you about? Make yourself visible."

Munn? "Who are you talking to?" Laurie asked, confused.

Patrick wrapped his arms around her, holding her in place on his lap. A stool fell over while another chilly gust rushed through the room, knocking his personal seal matrix to the floor with a metallic thud.

"Enough!" he shouted.

"What the—"

"Show yourself, wee man."

Laurie stiffened in his arms. Had Patrick lost his mind?

An odd little man with weathered, brown skin materialized in front of them, his green tunic and brown leather leggings covered in white sand. He leapt up and down darting to and fro, mumbling words that didn't make sense.

With a heavy sigh, Patrick released his hold on her. She shook her head, hardly able to believe her eyes.

"Stop," Patrick commanded.

The strange man twirled around in a circle. Then the frenzy ended abruptly. He stood in front of the fireplace, brushing sand from his tunic onto the stone floor. He pointed a crooked finger at Laurie.

"'Tis your fault. Caitrina sent me to that horrid place. Hot. Sand everywhere." His gaze pierced her while his words tumbled forth.

"Slow down," Patrick said. "Tell me where you have been. What has happened?"

"Caitrina dropped me into the *Sands of Time*. She didn't want me to warn you about the lass. About Caitrina. The meddling *sithiche* causes trouble."

"If Caitrina trapped you, how did you get away?" Patrick asked.

My God. This was another creature like Caitrina. Well, sort of. He was much smaller and grumpier and angry with Caitrina. Laurie's gaze bounced from the little man to Patrick and back to the man.

"The High Queen of the Fae released me." Munn wagged his finger at Laurie. "You dinnae belong here. Leave. Go away. Be gone."

Losing her balance, she slipped from Patrick's lap and hit her butt hard on the stone floor. Should she laugh or scream at the maddening creature?

"Cease," Patrick demanded as he assisted her to another chair. His lips thinned and he turned back to the man. "Lady Laurie is under my protection. You will leave her alone. Do you hear me?"

The little being hung his head.

"Promise," Patrick ordered.

"Aye." With a frown etched into his wrinkled face, the annoying creature nodded.

"Give me your vow."

"I promise," Munn said.

Behind his back, Laurie spied chubby fingers crossed.

Great. She'd landed in a loony bin. The insanity took root in North Carolina and was now fully entrenched.

"You are a wee bit pallid." Patrick grasped her hand. "Will you swoon?"

"That man appeared out of thin air."

"Aye, he's a *Brunaidh*, the MacLachlan Clan brownie."

"Well that explains it." She glared at Patrick. The man was *not* her friend.

Although Patrick wanted to discover where the wee man had been, he wished Munn choose a different time and place to return. Laurie looked as if she'd seen a *banshee*.

Patrick released her hand and rubbed his chin. Munn's antics didn't amuse him. Odd of the fae queen to interfere in a squabble between a faerie and a mere brownie. Patrick feared the events his man described forebode trouble.

He sensed Munn hadn't revealed everything. There might be a clue, hidden somewhere in the tale—to his parents' disappearance, and to Laurie's sudden appearance. A puzzle he needed to solve. And soon.

"Come, Lady Laurie." He offered his hand. "The hour is late."

"Yes, I should return to Elspeth's chamber."

The tentative touch of her fingers had Patrick tightening his lips. He wanted to believe she was as she appeared—a beautiful woman lost.

He would return her to his sister's bedchamber where she belonged. Later, he'd question Munn more thoroughly in privacy and get answers. He may have relieved Duncan of his guard duty too soon.

Patrick didn't believe Laurie posed a threat, but he needed to be certain.

The next day, Laurie joined Elspeth in the garden, hoping to forget her dilemma. The castle garden received a good soaking from the previous night's storm. Moving among the planting beds, she lifted her skirt to keep the hem off the wet ground. She marveled over the beautiful plantings, brilliant green with tiny crystal droplets shimmering in the sun.

The heavy apron protected her skirt from the moist earth when she knelt beside Elspeth in front of the strawberry bed. Laurie reached for the small spade and dug a hole in the rich soil. Picking up one of the young strawberry plants, she carefully placed the tiny root ball into the prepared spot.

After covering the roots with fresh soil, she patted around the stem, creating a well with the dirt for catching water. When she finished, she poured water around the transplant from a small wooden bucket.

They worked for a good portion of the early morning, transplanting the plants collected the previous day. The pleasant trills and warbling of a lark serenaded them as they worked in silence, intent on their own thoughts. Laurie's often strayed to her fears. What would be her future?

When they finished with the strawberries, she touched Elspeth's arm. "Shall we tidy the rose garden?"

"Aye. We will be less likely to spread any sickness that may exist from one plant to another now the leaves have dried in the sun." Elspeth stood and stretched, rubbing her lower back.

They walked to the rose garden to survey the planting. The budded plants of pink and white delighted the senses. The curved beds formed a semicircle around the flowering turf bench where one could sit and enjoy the garden's heady scents. The plants needed little work, only the removal of some yellowing foliage.

"What happened during the night?" Elspeth gave Laurie a sideways glance. "I woke to find you gone. When you returned, I pretended to sleep, but I saw you in the lantern light. You kissed Patrick?"

Laurie reached down to remove a dead leaf from a bush, her eyes averted from Elspeth. "I wished him goodnight."

She kissed him in the bedchamber's doorway after he walked her to the room she shared with Elspeth, had initiated the kiss. Earlier, they'd been close, Patrick gentle and loving. Of course, that was before the nasty little man appeared. Then Patrick became aloof, almost curt. She'd kissed him again, trying to regain their earlier warmth. She sighed, reaching for another brown leaf. He didn't pull away, but his kiss had been…dispassionate.

"But why were you with him?" Elspeth continued to needle.

"Darn, I pricked myself." Laurie sucked on the puncture wound at the tip of her finger.

Why had she gone to Patrick's private chamber? Good question.

An impulse. She hadn't expected to find him in the chapel and she definitely hadn't meant to disturb him at prayer. Yet she had and she was glad. When he held her in his arms, the world felt right again.

Until the strange creature arrived.

What was it with this place? People appeared out of thin air. They popped in and out, startling a person, like Caitrina and the ugly man.

"You have tender feelings for him. You do," Elspeth continued to tease.

Laurie sighed heavily. "Something strange happened last night. Can we sit for a moment and talk?"

"What is it?" Elspeth grasped Laurie's hand and pulled her to the bench, where they sat amidst the flowering chamomile. "What happened to distress you so?"

"Last night a strange little man appeared in Patrick's private chamber. He babbled about Caitrina zapping him to a desert, to a place where he said time doesn't exist. Caitrina is the faerie I told you about. The man said a faerie queen saved him and returned him here." Laurie inhaled a deep breath. "This is all too unreal. Who is he? What is he?"

"Munn's come back, then?" Elspeth smiled.

"I guess he has. What is he? Why can he appear out of thin air?" This place made Laurie crazy.

Elspeth chuckled. "He's a brownie, one of the *Brunaidh*. One of the wee people. You ken?"

"Patrick said the same, but I don't understand. Brownie's are make-believe." Now that she believed in faeries could she not believe that brownies existed too?

"Munn was my father's wee man, and his father's afore him. Now he is Patrick's man. He watches over our clan."

Okay, paradigm shift, faeries and brownies exist.

"Is a brownie the same as a faerie? Like Caitrina?"

"Similar, but not the same. If Caitrina is a faerie, as you believe, she holds more power than Munn. He has his limitations."

Laurie shook her head. This was all too unbelievable. A horn sounded from the castle.

"'Tis time for the mid-day meal." Elspeth stood and brushed dirt from her apron.

"I guess we better go." Laurie also rose from the bench.

They swiftly moved around the garden, collected the tools and put them into a large leather satchel. When they walked through the archway, they found Duncan on the other side, leaning against the garden's outer wall, a blade of grass between his lips.

Laurie frowned. "What are you doing here? Don't you have better things to do than follow us around?"

"Nae, Lady Laurie. The chief ordered me to watch over you. Make sure you stay out of trouble."

She bristled. Patrick placed a guard on her again. Well damn, he still didn't trust her. His lack of faith hurt. Though it shouldn't, she had tried to leave without telling him.

Such a tangled web.

"Make yourself useful and carry this to the kitchen for us." She thrust the leather bag at Duncan.

He accepted the weight without complaint, an idiotic, adoring smile spreading across his face.

Laurie pursed her lips. *Oh, great, the big brute has a crush on me.* Just what she needed.

Linking arms with her, Elspeth giggled, distracting Laurie. They walked, arm in arm, toward the castle, Duncan following, whistling a merry tune.

"I ken." Elspeth grinned. "You fancy Patrick," she whispered into Laurie's ear.

Laurie growled, pulling away. She rubbed her eyes, sighing softly. "I do like him. However, he is an overbearing, autocratic, arrogant, irritating man, and I shouldn't bother with him."

"We will be sisters." Elspeth smiled brightly. "Come. Let

us go to the hall."

The younger woman's gaiety was infectious. Laurie couldn't help but smile, although she wanted to steer the conversation in a different direction.

"Do you think it will rain again?" she asked as they walked along the path to the castle. "A shower would be good for the young strawberry plants. Would help them get established."

Elspeth glanced at the sky. "We will have to bide an' see. 'Tis clear now. Yet the weather, like my brother, can be unpredictable."

Seeing Laurie and Elspeth together as they entered the courtyard lightened Patrick's heart. But he must be careful. Munn's return and the tale he told implicated Laurie through Caitrina. Although the lass seemed innocent of any wrongdoing, he still didn't know why she appeared or how she was involved with his parents.

When the two women moved out of sight to enter the wheel stair, he turned back from the window to the bed where Ruari sat against the bed-head, eating a bowl of porridge.

Aine summoned Patrick to the chamber earlier when Ruari woke. Now, she fussed over the lad in her customary motherly fashion. At first, he seemed confused, ranting and raving about the attack, not making much sense. He grumbled about the ache in his head. As his mind cleared, he complained of hunger.

Patrick waited, arms crossed, leaning against the wall of his bedchamber. He was a patient man. He'd wait until Ruari finished his meal, and then he'd question him about the attack.

Ruari slurped the last bit of porridge with gusto. Sitting the bowl on the tray at his side, he beamed.

"Good lad." Aine smiled and patted his cheek. She collected the tray and left.

Dragging a stool next to the bed, Patrick sat. "Tell me again how you got the bump on your noggin."

Ruari scratched his head. "A hooded warrior rode from the wood with two other mounted men. I think one was a Lamont. The other…he may have been a Maclay."

Patrick scowled.

Clearing his throat, Ruari continued. "The hooded one went after my brother Ewen and the Lamont rider chased down Gil, the other herdsman. The big Maclay lad chased me to the edge of the wood. He hit me on the head and knocked me down. He must have thought me dead for he left me there and rode off to take part in the looting and burning with the other men who arrived by foot, as many as I can count on my fingers and toes."

He coughed. Patrick patted his shoulder, offering encouragement.

"They set the huts on fire. The fields too. Drove off the cattle. A fine herd of twenty cattle, gone."

Ruari gazed into the distance, horror contorting his features. "After the raiders left, I crawled to Gil and Ewen. They lay dead where they dropped." His sad eyes searched out Patrick. "I tried to make it to the castle, but only made it to the Fir-wood before the pain became too great. The next thing I remember is waking up in this bedchamber."

"Here." Patrick handed him a mug of ale. "Quench your thirst."

After taking a large gulp, Ruari set the cup down. He rubbed the large bump on his head and winced. "I am sorry, Chief. I failed you."

"Nae, lad. 'Tis I who have failed. Failed to protect you. Failed to protect our property. Failed to protect the clan." Patrick rose, paced to the fireplace. "We retaliate on the full moon."

On the night before the full moon, Patrick hesitated. With Ruari up and about, Laurie moved back into his bedchamber.

She slept there now. He crept to the door, struggling with himself. Several times during the night, he made his way up the stairs, planning to enter the chamber and take the lass. Each time he returned to his study frustrated and riddled with guilt.

This time he wouldn't stop.

Entering his bedchamber, he glanced toward a window and noticed sunlight beginning to peek over the horizon. Morn approached and he hadn't slept. His time grew short. He stepped to the bed, making as little noise as possible. He set the lantern he carried on the chest before pulling open the bed curtain. His breath caught. The sheets tangled round her ankles and her sleeping gown rose high on her thighs. His gaze roamed freely over her form. She was lovely in slumber, his precious angel. He marveled at her beauty. The morning light enhanced her skin and hair. Her plump lips begged to be kissed.

When she didn't stir, he bent and placed a feather-light peck on her smooth cheek. Laurie woke with a jerk. He hadn't meant to frighten her.

"How dare you?" she growled, eyeing him with mistrust.

He grinned. "You ask me that quite often, yet you ken the answer."

"Why are you here?"

"I leave soon." Patrick sat on the edge of the bed. "Send me off with a kiss." Bowing his head, he made ready to kiss her when something cold and wet hit his back. A dripping cloth soaked his *leine*, having appeared out of nowhere.

He stood and grabbed the intrusive rag from his back. He stared at the damn cloth, first in surprise, then anger.

Laurie eyed the cloth and snickered. "Where did that come from?"

"Munn," he grumbled.

The lass covered her mouth with her hand and tried unsuccessfully to conceal her grin. He snarled at her. But the glee dancing in her eyes snapped something inside him, and he threw back his head and roared with laughter, tears stinging his eyes.

"That pesky wee imp finds humor in pestering me," he said once he contained his merriment. He winked at Laurie. "Wish me well."

With a brief nod of his head, he turned and strode from the chamber.

Laurie sat in bed for quite some time, wishing Patrick finished kissing her. His smile stole her breath. She'd never seen him laugh like that. Marvelous. Made him appear young and carefree, much more pleasant than his usual scowls.

The shouts of men broke her train of thought and she remembered the raid. He was leaving. She padded to the window on bare feet in time to watch Patrick and his men leave through the courtyard entrance.

Elspeth stood at the side of the path to the water's edge, waving farewell.

Laurie hadn't said goodbye. She'd let him leave without saying the words. Her chest clenched. What if he got hurt? Or worse?

She was beginning to care for the fool man. She prayed he'd survive unhurt.

CHAPTER NINETEEN

*S*et high in the sky, the moon cast its silvery light over the earth below. Shadows danced with every movement. Animals would easily spook, making raiding more difficult.

Patrick stood beside Stephen in the shadow of a massive oak. Most of his men spread out, slinking noiselessly from tree to tree to surround the meadow. Finding cover where available, they waited for his signal.

Duncan and Jamie hid nearby in the darkness provided by another large tree. In the low land, on the other side of the rise, a sizable herd of shaggy, longhorn cattle grazed. The scouts, who stalked the herd, reported two herdsmen. They counted at least sixty-five head. Mostly cows with calves. Patrick's twenty were certainly part of the herd.

The men were in place, but something didn't feel quite right. Seemed strange Lamont would leave the animals with no more than a light guard, after bothering to steal them. Patrick rubbed the prickle at the back of his neck before tapping Stephen on the shoulder.

"'Tis too quiet. I dinnae like it. Something is wrong, but I cannae figure what," he whispered close to his cousin's ear.

"Aye. The eerie glow of the moon 'tis unsettling."

They fell back to where their horses waited content to

chew grass. Mounting his horse, Stephen signaled to Duncan and Jamie to do the same. Patrick scanned the wood around them. "Be on guard. Remember, kill no one unless necessary."

"Aye," Stephen murmured.

Without sound, hand signals given, the four walked their horses into position, keeping to shadows, staying out of sight.

A whistled birdcall signaled the MacLachlan men to commence the raid.

Two of Patrick's lads silently crept from their hiding places, each stalked one of the warrior-herdsmen. They took them by surprise, knocking them out with a bash to the head.

The rest of the men ran from their hiding places. Encircling the agitated cattle, they shouted, running, driving them toward the river.

The chosen crossing site was near. They reached the edge of the shallows, the best place to wade to the other shore. Jamie and Duncan rode across first. Next, the men crossed, coaxing the cattle to swim to the opposite shore.

Patrick and Stephen watched from the water's edge, guarding the rear. Unease ran along Patrick's spine with an unearthly tingle. Something was definitely wrong. He scanned the area around them, searching for anything out of place.

A flash of metal glittered in the moonlight.

From the wood charged a band of Lamont warriors led by Malcolm Maclay, Iain Lamont's henchman. The same warrior Patrick bested on the training field, not a fortnight ago. He counted five mounted men, and many more on foot.

Patrick didn't hesitate. He reined his stallion around. At the same time, he pulled his sword from its sheath. Stephen did the same. They held their ground as the first two riders reached them. Patrick made short work of knocking his man from his horse, disabling him. Before he'd time to think, a second warrior charged. He fought the attacker off, cutting with his sword.

He yanked his horse about. The cattle had made it across the river. Jamie and Duncan battled with a couple of Lamont warriors who had followed. Patrick's men maintained the upper hand.

He reined his horse about again. Maclay attacked Stephen with a battle-axe. Patrick maneuvered his horse between them, only to take a hit to the shoulder. The blade cut through his leather hauberk, drawing blood, yet even with blinding pain, he managed to keep his seat. Reaching out, he slashed at Maclay, drawing his blade across the man's face, breaking his nose and gashing his cheek. Blood spewed in every direction and Maclay fell from his horse.

Patrick and Stephen jumped from their horses, defensively fighting, back to back, to ward off several more men.

When the skirmish ended, two men lay dead at their feet. The rest blended into the wood. Damn the man to hell, Maclay was gone.

Someone betrayed them. How else would Lamont have known to lay a trap?

"We need to go," Stephen said.

They found their horses and mounted. Fording the river, they caught up with the rest of their party.

Gritting his teeth, Patrick held tight to the horse's reins. His shoulder burned like Satan's hell. The going would be slow with many calves within the herd. He clenched his mount with his thighs and prayed he wouldn't fall.

When dawn approached, they found themselves nearing MacLachlan lands. Stephen kept glancing at him, aware of the difficulty Patrick had keeping his seat. He grimaced from the pain piercing his side, though each time Stephen suggested they stop to rest, he waved his cousin off.

They rode farther. He slumped over in his saddle, barely holding on to the reins of the gray. Stephen rode his horse alongside, the horses running neck to neck. Snatching the reins from Patrick, Stephen used the body of the gray, in addition to his stallion, to keep Patrick from falling to the ground.

Duncan rode forward to the other side of the gray and helped slow the animal to a walk. Jamie trotted to the other side of Stephen and took the reins from him.

Managing to jump from his horse to Patrick's, Stephen sat behind, holding him in place with the bulk of his body and strong arms. When Patrick went limp against him, Stephen stiffened.

"You are more injured than I realized."

"Aye," Patrick managed the one word before he passed out.

Laurie tried to hide her agitation while she sat with Elspeth in the solar. Patrick, his tail of men, plus several other heavily-armed men left several days before for the raid against the Lamonts. No messages arrived since.

The evening meal came and went and still no word of the men. Elspeth serenely sat at a bench in front of a large tapestry frame deftly working colorful silk thread into a fanciful dragon design.

Laurie chewed on her lower lip while her gaze darted about the room without landing on any particular item. When she again glanced at Elspeth, the young woman stared straight ahead with unseeing eyes, as if caught in a trance. She swayed and slumped over the frame, holding her hand to her belly with pain marring her fine features.

Laurie leapt from her chair, ran to Elspeth and knelt at her side.

When the glaze cleared from Elspeth's silver eyes, they filled with tears.

"'Tis Patrick. He is injured," she said in a faint voice.

"How can you know this?"

The young woman struggled to catch her breath. "Vision."

"What?"

Elspeth inhaled several deep gulps of air. "My gift. I see things others dinnae see. Sometimes, with a touch, I ken a person's inner thoughts. Other times, I glimpse the future."

Laurie's heart kicked into overdrive. "How seriously is he hurt?"

"That, I cannae see." Elspeth rose slowly, almost stumbling.

"Should we send someone after him?" Laurie's concern nearly choked her words.

"His men will tend to him until they reach the castle." Elspeth staggered to the door. "I must prepare for his return."

Laurie stared at the empty doorway after the young woman left. She didn't want to believe Patrick was injured. A virile man, it didn't seem possible he could be hurt.

Another day passed without word. Laurie's body buzzed with a frantic edginess. During a sleepless night, she came to a realization. She'd fallen for Patrick. Fallen hard. He was like a piece of hard candy with a soft center. Tough on the outside, soft and sweet on the inside.

Glancing at Elspeth, she frowned. The younger woman sat quietly, mending sheets, her eyes glistening with unshed tears.

Unable to contain her agitation any longer, Laurie stood. She couldn't sit there doing nothing. She circled the room before returning to her seat. Where were they?

Raucous noise and loud voices rose from the courtyard below. She and Elspeth jumped in unison and ran to the window. The men had returned. Laurie followed Elspeth as they rushed through the passage to the northern wheel stair, careful not to fall in her haste.

They ran into the great hall in search of Patrick. The men drudged in dirty and tired. They straggled into the hall and collapsed onto benches. Patrick wasn't among them.

"Where is my brother?" Elspeth questioned the first man she came to.

The warrior pointed to the doorway. She ran to the threshold, Laurie on her heels. They stopped abruptly. Two men carried Patrick into the hall. He attempted a smile, but it was short lived. A spasm of pain wracked his body.

He was sweaty and dirty, his leather hauberk covered with dried blood. Laurie swayed and gripped a nearby chair for support. He looked bad. With effort, she regained her composure and followed the men carrying Patrick.

They sat him on a bench near the wall. He leaned against the stone and closed his pain-filled eyes. Elspeth hollered for Aine. The older woman hurried to them carrying the two healing baskets.

Stephen handed Patrick a cup filled with a golden liquid. "Here, drink this."

Laurie couldn't help herself. She stayed his hand, stopping him from drinking. "What are you giving him?" She couldn't bare the possibility they might unintentionally give him a concoction of poison.

Stephen lifted a brow, obviously annoyed she interfered. "*Uisge-beatha*—water of life."

"'Tis whisky, lass," Aine said.

With a curt nod, Laurie stepped away, letting Patrick drink. Taking a swig, he coughed. He tried to speak, but the words came out incoherent. She stood back, allowing the others to work, watching fearfully.

Stephen removed Patrick's hauberk. The once saffron-colored tunic beneath was now a brownish-red. With a swipe of his dagger, Stephen cut away the fabric.

Laurie held a hand over her mouth. Fresh blood oozed from fine wool strips wrapping Patrick's chest. Stephen carefully unwrapped the binding, revealing a jagged laceration.

Using a wet cloth, Aine carefully removed stray fabric sticking to the wound. Then she splashed some of the whisky onto the gash. Patrick's intake of breath was audible. He gripped the edge of the bench with his hands, digging his nails into the wood.

Elspeth threaded a large needle and handed it to Aine to begin the gruesome process of sewing the wound closed.

"*Ortha casgadh fala*," Aine chanted in a melodic voice.

Patrick grimaced. Someone gave him a piece of leather to bite. He gritted his teeth against the pain. Laurie could hardly bear to watch, yet refused to look away. The pain etched in

Patrick's handsome features caused her physical discomfort. She placed her hand over her stomach, forcing herself to continue watching.

"*Ortha casgadh fala.*"

Laurie leaned close to Elspeth. "What is she saying?"

"Aine recites the prayer for staunching blood flow."

When the older woman finished, she applied a generous amount of smelly salve from one of the pots that made Laurie's nose twitch. Then Aine placed clean bandages over the wound and with help from Stephen bound Patrick's chest. After returning her supplies to the baskets, she ordered him removed to his bedchamber.

By the time several of his lads carried Patrick up through the confines of the circular steps, two levels up, he was near to losing consciousness.

Moisture crept into Laurie's eyes as she followed them and came to stand beside his bed. He reached for her hand. She laced her fingers with his, holding his hand gently. He gave her a shaky smile, closed his eyes, and drifted off into oblivion. Duncan dragged a bench over and she gladly sat, but continued to hang onto Patrick.

She raised her gaze to Aine. "Will he be all right?"

"We will have to bide and see, lass." The older woman patted Laurie's shoulder and shooed everyone from the room, leaving Laurie alone with her wounded Highland warrior.

She refused to leave his side. She stayed in the chamber with him night and day. She wet his brow and lips while he fought fever. She bathed his splendid form with cool damp cloths.

He fought demons in his delirium. He cried out as if confronting an unknown foe. He made little sense during these outbursts. Several times, she called for Duncan to hold him down, until Patrick's fits subsided.

Elspeth and Aine brought her food and drink along with potions for Patrick. Laurie barely ate enough to sustain herself. She realized she loved him and was determined not to lose him to a damn fever. Laurie needed him to wake up so she could tell him. She even decided it would be tolerable to stay in the past as long as she could be with Patrick.

Elspeth sat with her often, the young woman's voice always calm and comforting even though she must be worried sick about her brother. She tried to get Laurie to leave and take her own rest. Each time, Laurie refused.

Duncan brought a pallet for her. Instead of using the crude mattress, she climbed into the big bed and lay next to Patrick, holding him close when the spasms of chills racked his body. She wished with all her heart they were in the twenty-first century and she had antibiotics to give him.

Laurie prayed, begging for his life.

At times, the hair on her arms prickled, a sure sign Munn watched. Although he kept well hidden, she suspected he observed her every move to ensure she didn't harm Patrick.

As if, she ever would.

Early one morning, she lay dozing next to him. She woke to startling blue eyes peering at her. Clear blue eyes free of fever.

"Thank God!" Tears of relief blurred her vision.

Within moments, his arms encircled her, drawing her to him. He sucked in his breath and held her tight. Laurie cuddled against him, holding him with trembling arms, afraid to let go.

When she finally leaned back, he touched her cheek with the tip of a finger and brushed a tear away. Her smile faltered.

"What is it, lass?" His voice sounded coarse from lack of use.

"Oh, Patrick. I thought you'd never wake. There is so much I need to tell you. I—"

Stephen appeared in the doorway and cleared his throat. "I am afraid I interrupt the two of you, yet again." He strode to the bed. "We feared we would lose you, cousin."

"I'll summon Aine." Laurie jumped from the bed and straightened her gown. She must be a sight, not having bathed or changed clothes in days. "I'll ask her to bring broth." She nearly ran from the chamber. She wanted to make herself more presentable.

Though she hastened a quick glance at Patrick before she left. She needed to take the image of his clear blue eyes with her to assure herself he was well.

Patrick stretched his sore muscles. He was glad to see Stephen, but disappointed Laurie hurried off. Although, Patrick felt as weak as a wee *bairn*, he'd enjoyed her body pressed against his. He was lucky to be alive.

"How long have I been with fever?"

"Several days. Lady Laurie has not left you in all that time." Stephen sat on the bench next to the bed.

The thought of Laurie caring for him brought Patrick a bone deep warmth. She was a good lass. He kept his smile to himself, not in the mood for his cousin's teasing.

"Anything from Lamont?"

"Nary a word. And your uncle has not been heard from since he left the council."

Patrick didn't care for the sound of that. But he couldn't worry about it now. He needed to get his strength back before he dealt with his wayward uncle.

Aine entered the chamber carrying a tray with Elspeth right behind her. They fussed over Patrick, making him drink every drop of broth and ale.

Disappointed Laurie hadn't returned he kept glancing to the door.

When he finished his meal, his eyesight became fuzzy. From the gleam in Elspeth's eyes, he suspected she added one of her potions to the ale to ease his aches and help him sleep.

With stealth, he moved through the dense, dark forest. Branches slapped at him, scratching his skin. Hearing the screech of an owl and the flutter of wings, he peered into the darkness. He searched, had been searching for so long.

But he couldn't find what he searched for.

What was it?

Nae? He shook his head wanting to be free of his confusion. Who was it?

His lass!

Moving forward, he feared if he didn't find her soon, she would be lost forever.

Patrick twisted and turned, became ensnared.

A trap. They dragged him down…held him there…forced him to watch.

He screamed.

A blood-curdling sound woke Patrick. His heart raced in his chest as if he'd run a great distance. He opened his eyes.

Duncan and Stephen burst into the chamber, swords ready, searching for a threat.

Entangled in his sheets, Patrick struggled. Sweat covered his body. Had he made that horrific sound?

Laurie, Elspeth and Aine came running. Jamie behind. Duncan shooed them away. "'Twas nothing but a terror dream. All is well."

Stephen helped Patrick detangle from the sheets. He gave him a mug of ale and stared into his eyes. "What was it?"

Patrick looked away. "As Duncan said, 'twas nothing but a terror dream."

Though he wasn't so sure. The dream seemed real. He couldn't save his woman from danger.

Forced to stay abed by his guardians, Patrick strummed his fingers on the edge of the mattress. When would Laurie return and tell him the rest of her outrageous tale?

Over the past couple of days, she'd shared wonderful stories with him. He especially liked the yarn she started this morning, a tale about a lass who, after being caught in a tempest, found herself in an enchanted land of wee people and other magical beings. Laurie had just gotten to the part where the lass, her dog and three companions had escaped capture by a wicked witch and found themselves before the gates of a city built with emeralds when she stopped and insisted he take a nap.

He'd blustered and glowered and complained, but she'd have none of it. She told him she wouldn't tell the rest of the tale if he didn't sleep for a wee.

The only thing that kept him from leaping from the bed and likely ripping open his wound was this unhurried time he spent with Laurie. She visited him often and usually joined him for meals. She filled the empty place within his heart.

Even so, frustration rode him.

When the door creaked and opened, he sat up straight with his arms crossed over his chest and glared at Laurie. She rolled her eyes and sighed in the same manner his sister often did. She strolled into the chamber and smiled, ignoring his foul disposition. "How are you feeling this afternoon?"

"Well enough to be up and about," he grumbled.

"Maybe in a few days if you follow directions and rest."

He grunted though she didn't deserve his scowls and ill humor. Wasn't her fault boredom drove him mad.

She raised a brow and plopped into the chair beside the bed. "Would you like me to finish Dorothy's story?"

He nodded, keeping the smile tempting his lips to himself. The more time they spent together, the more he wanted her. Wanted her in a way he shouldn't. He wanted her as his wife.

"Let's see, where were we? Oh, yeah. Our heroine and her companions are greeted at the gate by a horse of another color. As they travel through the city in a grand carriage, the horse's coat changed from blue to green to yellow to orange to red."

Patrick leaned against the pillows and allowed her sultry voice to flow over him, into him, to heal him. He'd nearly fallen into a doze when he noticed a change in her tone.

"She clicked the heels of her ruby slippers together and said the magic words and woke in her room at home as if from a dream."

Laurie's words cut deep. "Is that what you hope will happen? That you will wake and all of this..." Patrick waved his arm, "was nothing more than a dream?"

"No, I—"

"I am sorry, lass. You dinnae deserve my rancor." Of course, she still wished to go home. He hadn't given her a reason to want to stay.

"No worries. Most men make bad patients."

He cleared the lump from his throat. "Have you tended many men?"

"Just you."

What would make her want to remain with him? The answer stole his breath. He needed a distraction, unnerved with the path of his thoughts. "Tell me another story."

"I think not. It's time for you to rest." She leaned in and pulled the covers over his chest.

Her warmth embraced him. He wanted to kiss her, to pull her close and hold her within his arms. Protect her from a world full of danger.

Laurie patted his arm. "I'll be back in a couple of hours with your supper."

He grasped her hand and gently squeezed before releasing her fingers. "I thank you for caring for me."

Her eyes misted and held his gaze.

"Be off with you and let me take my rest," his voice cracked.

He watched her walk across the chamber. She stopped at the doorway, turned and waved her fingers before leaving. Patrick dragged his hand over his face. He hadn't let her finish what she was about to say. What would she have said if he hadn't interrupted her? He should have asked before she departed.

After several days passed, he still hadn't asked Laurie, but his strength returned. He couldn't stay in bed any longer. He rose, dressed and went in search of his lady. Aye, she was *his* lady.

He found her alone in the garden, humming softly while weeding. Sunbeams played with the golden highlights of her hair. His chest tightened with a sensation he was becoming far too accustomed to. He wanted her more than he believed possible. Life was too short. Easily stolen by the slice of a blade. His decision firmed in his mind—she would be his forever.

His footfalls were silent as he navigated the garden paths and stopped behind Laurie.

"Lass, you take my breath away."

Startled by the unexpected voice behind her, Laurie fell backwards onto the ground. She narrowed her eyes at Patrick. "You frightened me."

"Forgive me." He offered a hand to help her to her feet.

Happiness twirled around her heart at the sight of him outside, away from the sick room. The tender expression on his face made her stomach flutter, and she found herself staring at him.

"Speechless?"

What could she say, mesmerized as she was by his smile and the smoldering intensity in his alluring blue eyes?

"Come." He took her hand, escorting her to a wood bench near one of the walls. Recently bloomed yarrow surrounded them. They sat and gazed at each other. Everything else faded away. There was nothing in the world but them.

They started to speak at the same instant, stopped, and smiled at each other. "You've something to tell me," Patrick said.

"Yes, but it seems you wish to say something also. You go first."

"You began saying something the other day, but I interrupted. Tell me now."

"Okay. I've been thinking." Laurie swallowed. "Since I can't go home. And, since you said you wanted me. Blast it. I don't know how to say this."

Patrick stared at her intently, waiting.

Taking a deep, shaky breath, she plunged in. "If you still want me… That is, if you still want me as your mistress… Well, then…"

Confusion clouded Patrick's features.

"I'll be your mistress. That is…if you still want me," she blurted the words.

Patrick's jaw tightened, his expression sour. "You will be my mistress?"

She winced. Confused by his sharp tone, she warily nodded.

"Let me understand. This is because you cannae go home?"

Laurie frowned. "That's not what I meant. I have feelings for you."

"But, you dinnae love me?"

Shit. She'd messed this up. Why couldn't she just come out with it?

"All right. If you must know—I love you. You overbearing goon." She shoved her hands against his chest. Even after the fever, she wasn't strong enough to push him off the bench.

Patrick grinned. He reached for her hand and squeezed. "I dinnae want you for a mistress."

Tears burned the back of her eyes. "You don't?"

He didn't want her. She'd opened her heart to him, and he didn't want her. Disappointment and embarrassment collided, singeing her cheeks.

"Nae, sweetling. I wish to wed with you." He shifted his weight on the bench. "That is, if you will have me."

"What did you say?" Had she heard him right? "Say it again."

He squeezed her hand. "Lady Laurie, will you wed with me?"

Happiness effervesced within her chest until she remembered what his uncle said and Elspeth confirmed. Patrick was already betrothed.

The play of emotions crossing Laurie's face concerned Patrick. She seemed confused then angry. He didn't like it. She was supposed to fall into his arms. She'd said she loved him.

She pulled her hand from his and placed balled fists on her hips. "What of Isobell Lamont and the betrothal agreement your uncle is constantly sniping about?"

"Ach, lass." He understood where her fear lay. "There was never an agreement. My father never would have agreed to the marriage without my goodwill. He was verra much in love with my mother before she died, and later was blessed to find love with Elspeth's mother. He never would have condemned me to a loveless marriage."

"But your uncle claims there is a contract."

"Aye. He wishes it thus. When I was a child, my father negotiated for a marriage contract between my elder brother Donald and Isobell Lamont. When Donald died, there was talk of my wedding the lass. However, they never finalized an agreement. My da gave me the choice. I could not wed the lass, not without love. Now, her father and I are sworn enemies."

"But weeks ago, you said you couldn't marry me."

"True." Patrick smiled. "I determined I would not wed anyone in order to keep the peace. I believed in time Lamont would give up and wed Isobell to another."

"What changed?"

"I don't believe Lamont will relinquish and allow Isobell to wed another. I make matters worse by staying unwed. Besides, I want you. I cannae live without you." Reaching down, he grasped her hand again, caressing the palm with a gentle touch. "I ask you again. Will you wed with me?"

"Yes." Laurie bestowed upon him a brilliant smile, which glowed bright as the sun.

He took her face into his hands, bent his head and brushed a sweet, gentle kiss across her lips. He pulled his head back and gazed into misty, blue eyes and saw their shared future.

He would make a family with the love of his life.

"In a fortnight, we will journey to the fair in Glasgow, where I will procure your betrothal ring." Hopefully, they could sail past Lamont territory unmolested.

Caitrina stood in the shadow of the garden wall, unseen by the lovers. If she possessed a one-hundred-percent mortal heart, she'd be gushing over the scene playing out before her eyes. As it was, with a halfling heart, she remained merely amused.

She believed from the beginning, she'd win this round, the next, and the next. The only requirement remaining to complete this match was for the MacLachlan chief to plant his seed. Considering the testosterone he threw off, the carnal joining would happen soon.

Caitrina tasted freedom on the wind. It wouldn't be long. Her royal status would be restored along with the right to return to *Tir-nan-Óg*.

Suddenly, an unexpected tingling skittered across her skin, warning of fae activity. Something was wrong. She held motionless, sensing a power surge surround her. One second, she watched Patrick kiss Laurie. The next, she was in the queen's antechamber.

The disoriented sensation from the unexpected realm-hop passed quickly and the nausea subsided, but trepidation built. Many human centuries had trudged by since she visited the palace. The last had been the awful day of her banishment. Now she found herself summoned by the High Faerie Queen.

The large room was much the same as she remembered. Silver columns and crystal walls, brilliant sapphire gemstones in cut-glass bowls, luxuriant royal blue velvets and silks draped about, all to enhance the silvery splendor of the high-queen.

In the center of the chamber lay the white brocade chaise on which Oonagh lounged in comfort, a smug smile playing on sensuous lips.

"So good of you to attend me," she purred.

"What do you want?" Caitrina demanded as she hid

trembling hands within the folds of her gown. They didn't shake from fear but from resentment. Oonagh must know of her progress. The queen wouldn't play fair. She'd interfere with the mating.

Whatever the queen intended meant trouble.

Caitrina couldn't allow it. She'd need to think of a way to stop the queen. Perhaps she could find an ally.

CHAPTER TWENTY

Castle Lachlan

A sennight later, Munn pinched the bridge of his nose and tried desperately to think.

Something he preferred not do.

He sat in one of the crenels on the battlements, unseen by the guards. They tramped to and fro, striding from corner post to corner post, eyes directed beyond the castle walls.

Bored with their repeated motion, Munn gazed out across the loch. The water was calm tonight, a contrast to his circling thoughts.

"What was he to do?" he grumbled, forgetting to mute his voice.

One of the warriors shot a look in Munn's direction, furrowed his brow, and returned his gaze to the shadows beyond the walls. At any other time, Munn would have fun and spook the guard. Tonight he had a dilemma. The MacLachlan planned to wed the woman from the future.

Munn couldn't allow it to happen. Although she seemed to care for the chief, he must stop the match. But how? If they consummated their marriage, his vow to Oonagh would be broken. The queen would condemn him to an eternity entrapped within the *Sands of Time*.

A punishment far worse than the most tortured death.

Torn between his loyalty to Patrick and to his vow to the queen, Munn sadly shook his head. He needed to do something soon, betray his chief or break his vow.

He didn't wish to do either, but knew which would cause the most damage to him. With a shudder, he dissolved into the breeze.

Laurie could barely contain the joy radiating from her heart. She wanted to whirl around the room and dance a jig. Instead, she sat in front of the fireless hearth in Elspeth's solar, pretending to concentrate on the embroidery hoop in her hand. She glanced at her future sister-in-law seated beside her.

The young woman glowed with energy. Overjoyed by the news of the upcoming wedding, Elspeth swept Laurie through a whirlwind of activity during the past week.

Patrick scheduled the wedding to follow their return from Glasgow on the eve of *Lunasdàl,* the first harvest festival. Aine worked magic with a fine gown of midnight blue for her to wear. Elspeth designed a pearl and sapphire adornment they planned to weave through her hair.

Though much remained to do in preparation for their journey to the fair, the wedding remained foremost in the women's discussions.

Although Patrick's steward, Lachlan, traveled ahead to procure housing for the family for the duration of the event, Elspeth instructed him to purchase special provisions, including exotic spices and fruits for the wedding. She had an elaborate celebration planned.

Laurie drew a lavender thread through the cloth. She wouldn't have the big wedding in Saint Pat's she'd always dreamed of, but she'd have her very own Patrick as groom.

The dear man romanced her. He trained with his men during the day, working to regain his strength. In the twilight hours, he belonged to her. They spent their evenings alone in his study, eating meals in privacy. Patrick charmed her with his deep seductive voice as he sang gallant ballads filled with heroic deeds. He told her about his childhood and youth, about his parents and his brothers. She, in turn, shared stories about her life, describing for him the wonders of the twenty-first century.

Her only disappointment was the ever-present, annoying brownie. Munn appeared at the most inopportune moments. Each time Patrick made a move to take her into his arms, the darn brownie showed up to cause havoc. Chaste kisses were all she'd received from her fiancé during this entire week.

And she wasn't happy about the lack of snuggling.

"You are not listening to me." Elspeth nudged her arm.

"Sorry. What were you saying?"

Elspeth rolled her eyes in the same manner as a modern teenager. "'Twill be such fun. There will be all kinds of merchants at the fair, selling everything for which you could possibly wish. Some come from far distant places with all matter of luxury. At the last fair, Patrick allowed me to purchase new riding boots and a pair of fancy slippers. I am sure he will indulge you as well, now that you are to be his lady-wife."

Glancing away to hide her smile, Laurie noticed Patrick standing in the doorway. Feet apart, hands on hips, he listened to his sister chatter on. The sides of his mouth twitched when he tried to restrain his amusement. He couldn't do it. His lips slowly bloomed into a full grin, making the sexy cleft in his chin more prominent.

Laurie took a deep breath, reining in the sudden rush of sweet desire that shot through her veins.

Patrick inclined his head and sauntered into the room, stopping next to her chair. He leaned against the hearth and chuckled. "I will not indulge either of you, if you are not prepared to leave at dawn."

"We will be ready." Elspeth laughed, the sound a musical note of delight.

Laurie locked gazes with Patrick. He wore a suggestive, seductive expression. His powerful presence washed over her, bathing her in sensual heat. Could the man be any more alluring than when he smiled, his deep blue eyes twinkling? He stole her breath.

Holy shit. She would soon marry her Highland warrior.

"My sweet lass, I came to fetch you. Aine is about to serve our evening meal." He flicked his eyebrows, a naughty glint sparking in the depth of his hungry eyes.

What did her future husband plan?

Certain she would enjoy whatever he proposed, she laid her needlework aside.

Grasping her hand, he kissed the back of her fingers, sending tingles up her arm. She shivered, and he gave her a knowing look, his eyes darkening even more with seduction. Heat burned her cheeks and she batted at his arm.

"Shall we?" He assisted her to her feet, placing his hand on her elbow to escort her from the solar.

Glancing over her shoulder with a pang of guilt, Laurie caught Elspeth's smirk. She'd been neglecting her young friend. "Elspeth, would you care to dine with us?"

Patrick stiffened, but when Laurie checked the expression on his face, he appeared indifferent.

"Nae. I think my brother would prefer to have you to himself." Elspeth grinned.

The hand on Laurie's elbow relaxed and Patrick whisked her from the solar. "I have plans for us that require privacy," he whispered, his breath teasing her ear, his voice deep and sensuous.

They hurried along the passage. Patrick placed his hand on her lower back and a thrill climbed her spine. Heat spiraled through her with hot anticipation. He helped her descend the stairs and they practically ran to his private chamber.

When they arrived, they found their meal set on his worktable, Aine having already left.

Patrick assisted Laurie to a seat and sat across from her.

She met his fiery gaze. He looked as if he'd leap across the table and devour her. His passion thrilled her. Her nipples tightened and her breasts grew heavy.

"I was thinking." Hesitating, she toyed with the creamed fish on the plate in front of her. Would he think her too forward?

"Aye?"

She licked her dry lips.

Patrick shifted in his chair. "You kill me, lass."

"Well, I've been thinking."

"Aye, so you said." Patrick's smile took on a predatory tilt.

Laurie glanced away. She swallowed and settled her gaze on the tapestry hanging on the wall beyond his shoulder. "Since we plan to wed…"

She lost her nerve. She hated having to be the one to ask. She didn't understand why he hadn't come to her room before now. She moistened her lower lip.

Patrick groaned. "What do you wish to say, m'sweet?"

"Will you join me in your bedchamber tonight?" She blurted the words without finesse.

Within a heartbeat, Patrick jumped from his chair as if scorched. He stood over her and tilted her chin so she had to look at him. Grasping both her hands, he knelt before her.

His expression sizzled. The intensity was thrilling.

"'Twould be my pleasure to spend the night with you." He swept her into his hold and strode to the stairs.

Laurie twined her arms around his neck. Enamored by his strength, she leaned into his hard body and nuzzled her face into his neck to capture his masculine scent. The earthy smell of forest and wind intoxicated her. She nipped the exposed skin, playfully kissing and teasing him with her teeth.

He held her close, his chest rumbling. When he reached the bedchamber, Patrick kicked open the door and gently laid her on his huge bed. He left her for a moment, only to close the door and put the wooden bar in place, securing them against intrusion.

She lifted up onto her elbows. For his large size, he moved in a lithe and sensual way, like the lion king he reminded her of. She swallowed a nervous giggle before the silly sound escaped. She'd never been loved before, but she'd never wanted anything more than she did at this moment—for this man to make passionate love to her.

He twisted to stare with eyes ablaze. Strutting across the room to stand before her, his gaze never left hers. He stripped. A slow dance of masculine beauty.

First, he removed the countless knives hidden in various places on his person. Then he dropped his belt to the floor along with his pouch and his sheathed knife. His plaid came next.

He stood before her in his linen shirt.

Her mouth went dry. God, he was magnificent.

He yanked the leather strip from his hair and allowed the reddish-brown strands to fall freely around his shoulders, making him look even more the wild cat.

His rock hard thighs, corded with muscle, flexed as he ever so slowly lifted the tunic up and over his head, pulling the shirt free.

When the garment hit the floor, she hissed on an intake of breath.

Chippendale dancers, eat your hearts out.

His arousal jutted out. Grew larger.

Pain from her first sexual experience jarred her memory, and her boyfriend hadn't been hung like Patrick.

Fear replaced lust. *Shit.* There was no way she'd be able to do this. Patrick was too big. She sat up and scooted back on the bed, crossing her arms over her chest.

"I can't."

Patrick winced. Fear was not something he wanted marring Laurie's precious face when she gazed upon him. She looked like an ensnared animal, her eyes, big and bright. The lad she'd called a *boyfriend* must not have been very manly.

A twinge of jealousy rushed through his veins. He didn't like the idea of anyone having come before him. Still, he'd have her. And he'd ensure no man came after him.

"Dinnae be alarmed. I will not hurt you."

"You're too—big."

He refrained from flashing a cocky grin. With quick strides, he crossed to the bed, sat next to her, and gently stroked her silky hair, hoping to alleviate her fear.

"We will fit perfectly." His rough tone voiced his desire. "Let me show you. I promise we will both enjoy our mating."

Laurie searched his face. When she finally lowered her arms and smiled, he sighed with relief.

He placed his hands on either side of her waist and pulled her close. She reached out her arms. He carefully removed her gown and tossed it onto the floor to mingle with his discarded clothing. Caressing with a gentle touch, he swept his fingers along her bare shoulders, along her neck, along the edge of her chemise. He grazed her cheek, bent his head and kissed her lips.

A kiss that was soft. Persuasive. Filled with love.

She kissed him back. Tentatively at first. Then with abandon.

When they were both breathing hard, he pulled away to remove her shoes. Those, too, landed on the growing pile of garments. He swept the chemise over her head and slid his gaze over her nude form.

A lovely crimson blush colored her exposed flesh.

"You are beautiful."

"Thank you," she murmured, her voice a husky whisper.

Muscles coiled tight in anticipation, he lowered his head, used his teeth to slide a stocking over her knee and down her shapely calf, and tossed it aside. He kissed the arch of her foot, and she squirmed. Then he repeated the teasing play with the other stocking. Gooseflesh prickled her skin.

She brought light to the shadows within his soul.

With her golden hair draped across his sheets, her eyes soft and alluring, her lips puffy from his kisses, she was everything he desired. The woman he wanted at his side while he led his people through these turbulent times.

Patrick inhaled her feminine scent and prayed for control.

He planned to go slow. He wanted this first time to be special. A memory they would share.

He rolled on top of her, holding himself up by his arms, not wanting to press his weight into her. He placed kisses along her neck. Slow and sweet. Lingering. Drawing his tongue across the hollow of her throat, he nibbled his way over her skin to her left breast and drew the nipple into his mouth, ran his tongue over the tip, swirling it in the moist recesses of his mouth.

She gasped and held him to her breast. She cradled his head, her fingers laced in his hair. Encouraged, he used his teeth to drive her harder.

Her moan skirred over his skin, drawing him tight. Her breath whizzed in and out in soft, needy pants. God, he wanted her. Wanted to taste every exposed inch of her skin. He drew her unique fragrance into his lungs with each breath and moved his mouth to her other breast to lave the nipple. His cock hardened more with each pull of his lips.

Exquisite torture.

She pressed her mound against his shaft, soft mewling sounds escaping her lips. He released her breast, breathing hard.

"Easy." He wasn't sure if he meant to convince her or himself. "If we go too fast, I will be spent afore we begin."

"Patrick. I need…"

"I ken."

If he didn't claim her soon and relieve the pressure in his groin, he surely would burst and die. Soon she'd be his completely. She'd give herself to him willingly. Later, she'd become his lady-wife. He couldn't wait.

It killed him to go slow. He was heavy and hard, his body demanding release. But he wanted to draw out the pleasure for her—for him. He lowered his lips to a rosy nipple, sucked the puckered tip into his mouth, savored the pleasure he gave his lady.

A chill breeze blew across his arse. He raised his head, glanced around and found naught out of place. Yet a shiver slid across his shoulders. The warmth of the woman in his arms beckoned.

Placing his knees on either side of her hips, he knelt over her. He leaned in low and licked her stomach, sweeping her belly button with the tip of his tongue, moving his moist touch ever lower, to the edge of her golden curls.

"Please," she begged.

He spread her thighs and the tender folds hiding her secret place. He licked his lips and was almost unmanned by the glory of her womanhood. He dove in. Suckled. Tasted her desire.

Ambrosia.

He relished every lick, every nibble, and the essence that was his precious Laurie. Patrick continued to tease her flesh, glorying in the moment, marveling at the pure pleasure. Sensations he'd never imagined flooded him.

Laurie thrashed on the bed. Tugged his hair, twisted her fingers in the heavy mass and yanked. He growled against her moist folds and continued to lap up her liquid desire. She arched her back, searching for release. Her head rolled from side to side. Her hands gripped the bedding. The sounds coming from her mouth drove him harder.

"Patrick, please."

"Please what, m'sweet?" he teased.

"I want—"

The horn blew long and loud, several times. Patrick's heart thudded hard against the wall of his chest and he raised his head to listen. Releasing Laurie, he jumped from the bed and grabbed for his garments.

"What's wrong?" Her husky voice weakened his resolve. He hated to leave her.

He threw a sheet over her naked body. "The castle is under attack."

CHAPTER TWENTY-ONE

*P*atrick dashed up the steps to the wall-walk two at a time. Men shouted. Others ran from every direction, up the circular stairs to the battlements. He made his way through the chaos of warriors to the watchtower only to find his man Dunall insensible on the floor, the now-silent horn lying next to him.

Stephen squatted over the man, shaking his head and chuckling.

"What is happening?" Patrick yelled above the din.

Eyeing his disheveled appearance, Stephen arched an eyebrow.

Patrick ignored the look. "Why was the horn blown?"

"Before he swooned like a lass, Dunall claimed the horn to be enchanted. Said the damn thing flew out of his hand and blew on its own. I guess 'twas Munn."

"Curse the wee man if it was." Patrick growled, low and deep. Damn the meddlesome brownie. "We must ensure there is nae threat. Assemble a search party. Prepare the men and meet me at the beach within the quarter hour."

He returned to his bedchamber and found Duncan standing guard outside the door. "I leave shortly. Guard my lady well."

"With my life." The lad placed a hand over his heart and inclined his head.

"See to it the women are ready to leave at sunrise," Patrick said as an afterthought.

"Aye." Duncan stepped aside.

Patrick entered the chamber, closing the door behind him. This time he didn't bother to secure the bolt. Laurie sat on the edge of the bed her legs bent and drawn against her body. His *plaide* draped around her, yet exposed to his view were two smooth, milky-white knees. The muscles in his gut tightened.

She was a sight, his precious lady. His cock twitched, but he couldn't have her now, not with potential danger lurking beyond the castle walls. "What's happening?" she asked.

"False alarm." He crossed the chamber to the bed. "Yet I must ride out and search the area to be sure."

"Must you go?" She swept teasing fingers along his arm, raising gooseflesh.

"Aye."

"Can't you send someone else?"

The seductive glint in her eyes made his blood run hot. He wanted to stay yet couldn't set an irresponsible precedent. He hardened his resolve and stepped from her reach. "I lead my men."

"Of course." She glanced away. Before she did, he noted her lip tremble. He hadn't meant to hurt her feelings. He should reassure her, but he wasn't good at that sort of thing.

"I expect you to be ready to leave for Glasgow when I return in the morning." He brushed a light kiss across her brow and left the chamber, his thoughts consumed by the impending search.

A loud rapping woke Laurie before daybreak. She cracked the heavy oak door and peeked out.

"'Tis time," Duncan said.

"Give me a couple of minutes."

He nodded, and she shut the door. She swept her hair into a knot and pinned the unruly mass on top of her head. Using water from the ewer, she washed the sleepers from her eyes. During the night, she'd waffled between understanding and anger.

In the early morning-light things made better sense. Her anger was misplaced. Patrick couldn't change the way he lived because she worried about his safety. Agreeing to wed a Highland lord meant accepting his life.

But would she ever get used to him running off into danger? Especially in the heat of the moment.

Probably not.

Her core throbbed when she thought about where his mouth had teased when the horn blew. She'd gotten herself off after he left, but still...her emotions teetered on edge and her sex drive hummed. She was more than a little cranky.

After dressing in her own clothes, she prepared for travel. She wrapped her extra dress—the sapphire blue gown Patrick liked—and her undergarments in a soft cloth and packed them into the *creel* he gave her along with a few toiletries she'd gotten from Aine. The basket woven from heather didn't weigh much. Laurie slipped the straps over her shoulders like a backpack.

She followed Duncan through the dim passages. Meeting Jamie and Elspeth in the courtyard, they hurried to the edge of the water where Patrick and his search party waited.

The sun peeked over the hills lightening the sky.

"'Tis time you arrived." Patrick sounded cross. His features displayed a combination of annoyance and fatigue.

Well, that made two of them. She wanted to snap at him, but held her tongue. Women of this place and time were demure. Laurie didn't quite fit the bill. She growled under her breath. She'd try to make him a good wife. But right now, she wanted to smack him upside the head.

"Did you find anything while you searched?" she asked, ignoring her annoyance.

Patrick shook his head. "Naught."

"Maybe we shouldn't leave."

"Why not?"

"Well, if you think there is a threat."

"Dhughall and the other lads will take good care of our interests here."

He grasped her elbow, and she noticed dark smudges beneath his eyes. He must be tired. If it were possible, the shadows made him look even sexier. Maybe it was the memories from last night embedded on her mind making him so damn irresistible. Heat flooded her cheeks and she glanced away unable to hold his gaze.

Geez, he made her crazy.

"This way." He guided her to the first of three *birlinns* floating in the surf ready for their journey. Patrick lifted her, assisting her into the boat. Stepping in himself, he helped her to a seat on one of the wooden benches where cushions were placed for comfort. He took her *creel* and stashed it. Elspeth sat beside her while Patrick sat behind. Stephen joined them along with a group of well-armed warriors—swords, axes and shields in-hand.

"Why so many men?" *Way too much pumped up testosterone.*

Patrick glanced around as if he hadn't noticed. "We will travel near the Lamont controlled coastline as we sail out of Loch Fyne and then again when we head *up the watter* past Toward Point. We prepare for every possibility. There is always the risk of an attack, a challenge from either Lamont galleys or freebooters."

"Freebooters?"

"Thiefs upon the *watter*."

"Pirates?"

"Aye, lass."

Laurie swallowed hard. Perhaps the journey wouldn't be so pleasant.

"Trust me to keep you safe." Patrick reached around her waist and placed his hand over hers.

She twisted her head and gave him a wobbly smile over her shoulder.

"'Tis thrilling. Aye?" Elspeth leaned close and whispered in her ear.

The young woman's enthusiasm was hard to ignore. Laurie settled down, attempting to relax, trusting Patrick with her life.

Patrick inhaled the briny air and stared at Laurie's exposed neck. He liked the way she'd pinned her golden locks on top of her head, leaving her silky flesh exposed to his greedy gaze. The memory of her taste on his lips and tongue had him heavy with need. He pulled his hand away from hers, fearing she'd feel the desire thundering in his veins.

Patrick shifted his weight on the wooden bench to ease his discomfort. There was no relief for his groin and many days before he could love her properly or release the effects of his leashed passion on the practice field. He was hopelessly doomed for the duration of the journey.

Although he didn't admit it to Laurie, he was concerned about leaving the castle for the duration of the fair. He glanced back at his home. The wee brownie must have been the one who blew the horn. What was Munn up to?

And his uncle? What intrigue did Donald plot?

Patrick massaged the back of his neck. Time would tell on both accounts.

With a tight jaw, he set his mind to their voyage.

The three *birlinns* of twelve oars, each with his armed lads and provisions, set off across Loch Fyne. They would sail the length of the western shore. He hoped to avoid unfriendly galleys. Once they reached Dumbarton by boat, the danger would decrease and they could journey overland on foot the remainder of the way to Glasgow without too much risk.

He scanned the horizon before returning his gaze to Laurie. Maybe finding some trouble would be good. He could fight off the edge of his frustration.

Munn sat in the aft of the lead *birlinn*, unnoticed. He hated to travel by boat. Wave motion made him turn green. Ach, the things expected of him. He twisted his lips into an angry scowl. The lass from the future caused this misery. If she'd not appeared, he wouldn't need to attend the chief in Glasgow.

The boat pitched, forcing him to clutch the gunwale with one hand and his belly with the other as a wave of nausea ripped through him. He steadied his weight and glowered at the wench. He could push her over the side and she'd drown in the deep water.

Munn mulled the idea over in his mind, a grin stretching his lips, until he remembered—

He couldn't do that. There were covenants he couldn't break. The rules mandated he not cause death. What to do? What to do? The heck with Oonagh and her demands. Performing his duty to the clan didn't include leaving MacLachlan land. He would remain at Castle Lachlan. That's what he'd do. In a huff, he vanished into the air.

Laurie observed the men at the oars strain with effort, muscles bulging, as the boats left Castle Lachlan and set out across Loch Fyne.

Once the boats were away from shore, the men stopped rowing and raised the sail. At first, the speckled sail flapped in the breeze. Then the wind filled the cloth and the boats moved smoothly. She'd never seen a square sail before, especially not one made of wool fabric. Higher up on the mast, a pennon bearing the MacLachlan device billowed in the wind. The flag clearly identified to whom the boats belonged.

After an initial bout with queasiness, she enjoyed sailing over the water. Lucky for her, the weather remained clear— unusual for the Highlands or so she'd heard.

The dramatic scenery was beautiful and pristine, unspoiled by development. The *birlinns* passed headlands, some covered with thigh-high heather and others scarred by rock gullies. Waves washed spume onto the shores of pebbly beaches.

Laurie grinned, scooting forward to sit on the edge of her seat.

The bays and inlets filled with imagined secrets and tiny islands with a magic all their own delighted her imagination. Beyond the beaches, she glimpsed wetlands of reeds and bracken and beyond that, heather covered moors and forests rising up into hills and mountains.

Seabirds soared over the waves, rose on updrafts then plummeted to the water to catch their prey. Laurie inhaled the pungent, salty air, tasting it on her tongue. Loose hair blown free from her bun tickled her neck.

She caught Patrick's eye, and he winked.

When the sun sat high in the sky, the men lowered the sails and rowed to shore. Her rubbery legs wobbled when she walked across the pebbles to the low grassy bank beyond. Angus and Aine, along with several servants spread plaids on the ground for a picnic.

Afterwards the party continued sailing on its way.

The prevailing wind changed to little more than a mild breeze and the men took to the oars.

Far behind us, Castle Lachlan,
Soon before us, the Glasgow fair,
And ye ken, lads, trinkets gleam, lads,
In the wee stalls at Glasgow fair.

The helmsman chanted a verse of song.

Heel ye ho, lads, let 'er go, lads,
Keep her head 'round, row together;
Heel ye ho, lads, let 'er go, lads,
Sailing onward to Glasgow fair.

Oarsmen responded with the chorus.

Laurie wrapped her arms around herself, finding pleasure in the poetic meter of the song. Singing and rowing continued for twenty minutes longer until the wind picked up again, and the men put down the oars.

Patrick tapped her shoulder. "Look yonder."

They sailed near a protected harbor where a large castle stood.

"That is the royal residence of Tarbert," he said.

"Do we need to fear attack?" Laurie twisted on her seat to search his features.

"Nae. The guards will allow us to sail past without challenge. They are our allies. The keepers of the castle are Campbells and our wee Elspeth is betrothed to one of their own."

"The castle is impressive."

"Aye, that it is. In the time of Robert the Bruce, the castle and nearby fort were mostly rebuilt. And King Jamie has recently fortified both." Patrick's pride in his heritage shone in the gleam of his eyes.

After they passed, the men whispered and threw anxious glances toward the eastern shore. Elspeth's usual serene expression became agitated and the young woman chewed on her lower lip.

"What is it? What's happening?" Laurie whispered to the younger woman.

"We near Asgog Castle, a heavily fortified stronghold of the Lamonts."

"Nae worries, lass, my lads and I will keep you safe." Patrick squeezed her upper arm.

The men rowed, adding their strength to the power of the sail, increasing the boats' speed. The boats continued to hug the western coastline, the *birlinns* staying close together, until they sailed beyond what Patrick called Ardlamont Point and out of Loch Fyne. Those aboard exhaled a sigh of relief when they entered the relative safety of the sound. The men put down the oars and allowed the sails to do the work.

"Look there, lass, Arran," Patrick said and pointed to a far distant island.

Laurie sat straighter. During her business travels, she'd been to Scotland on several occasions, working in either Glasgow or Edinburgh, but never once ventured from the cities.

She wrapped her arms in a self-hug. *All of this beauty is part of my new home.*

She couldn't keep the grin from her face.

They sailed past a small island, south along the coastline, around a headland and into what Patrick called the Firth of Clyde. The sails came down and the men rowed into shore to beach in a large bay surrounded by red sandstone cliffs.

"Where are we now?" Laurie asked as Patrick helped her from the boat.

"The Isle of Bute," he said. "Your cheeks are rosy, sweetling."

She attempted to spin in a circle, but wobbled and he caught her against his side. Heat flared and they both pulled away as if singed. "I'm happy, Patrick."

"Good." He scanned the beach. "All is quiet."

"Where will we stay the night?" Laurie cupped her hand over her eyes to cut the glare from the late afternoon sun.

"Most of the warriors will remain with the boats while we and a few others hike a short distance to a cave where we'll make camp."

"Sounds like exercise."

Patrick smiled and pivoted to face his cousin. "Send a fast running ghillie to Rothesay Castle to pay homage and to request the permission of the Stewart keepers for us to set camp."

"Aye. And I will send a hunting party ahead."

Patrick nodded, and Stephen set off across the beach.

"Are we on private property?" Laurie asked. "Are you sure we should be here?"

"I have nae doubt we will receive consent to camp from the sheriff who keeps these lands in the name of our king. MacLachlan's come here often. But protocol requires I seek permission."

Laurie watched the men remove the sails and drape them over the boats, making a sort of tent for protection against the elements.

"'Tis time to find our camp. We will bed before a bonfire

in a clearing near a small cave where we can seek refuge should the weather turn fickle." Patrick took Laurie by the hand and they started the trek up the path, climbing above the shore through rough grassland.

The rest of their small group followed. The path partly hugged the side of steep cliffs and Laurie fought the urge to glance down. At one point, a prominent outcrop of red stone seemed to teeter over their heads. She sucked in her breath, not releasing it until they were clear.

The track climbed to higher ground and around a curving hillside where they made for another hill at the top of a ridge. At the summit, Laurie gasped. Below was a small loch, the surface green with lilies and bulrushes. The sight was so beautiful, her chest tightened.

Flocks of birds fed among lush foliage, the flapping of wings and cries creating a noisy, chaotic orchestration. Even though it was noisy, she loved it.

The group descended the hill. At the lowest part of the ridge, a small cave overlooked the loch. Stephen and his men waited in the clearing at the mouth. They were fortunate the days were long at this time of year and they would have ample time to set camp before nightfall.

Angus and Aine spread out several plaids in front of the fire Stephen's men had set. Patrick handed Laurie onto one of the blankets.

"Rest, lass."

Elspeth sat on another plaid nearby. Laurie uttered a heavy sigh as she parked herself on the wool-covered ground. She took off the tight boots Elspeth lent her and rubbed her sore feet.

One of the hunters returned with a small deer and a ghillie butchered the poor thing. She'd eaten venison before, but seeing the animal cut up made her stomach roil.

Aine selected pieces of meat and placed them into a pot she hung on a spit over the fire along with turnips, carrots and some greens she'd collected from the woods. From a flask, she added ale. While the stew cooked, she used a long handled wooden spoon to give the contents an occasional stir. Laurie's stomach gurgled when she caught a whiff of the flavorful aroma and her hunger returned.

The ghillie who'd gone to Rothesay Castle arrived, and Patrick stepped away to speak to the lad in private.

Stretching out on the plaid, Laurie dozed. She woke to Patrick's gentle touch as he joined her on the blanket. "Here." He handed her a flask of wine. "Quench your thirst."

She accepted what he offered and savored the sweet taste.

Although the middle of summer, nights were chilly. She cuddled against Patrick, cradled in the comfort of his strong arms, and dozed once more. He woke her after a while, encouraging her to eat a hearty portion of the stew and bannocks. The venison stew and the griddlecakes made from oats tasted delicious and filled her empty stomach.

Afterward, Patrick made a place for them to sleep near the fire atop a heavy plaid and wrapped a second one around them, warming her with the heat of his body.

Laurie glanced across the fire to where Elspeth cuddled against Stephen sound asleep. "Is there something between Elspeth and Stephen?" She cringed at the unintended accusation. "I mean…"

"Nae. They make use of their shared body heat. 'Tis all," he whispered. "Elspeth is promised to another."

Leaning back, she snuggled against his chest and fell into a contented slumber.

Sleep didn't come easily to Patrick. Laurie's backside nuzzled his shaft in the most pleasing way. He'd lain awake for hours, suffering the tension in his body, fighting the urge to have her right there in front of the fire in the midst of everyone. But there was no way he'd shame her in such a way.

Nor could he push her away.

The chilly night air didn't cool his lust. The lass pressed intimately against him fired his blood through the long, long night.

One of the ghillies stayed awake through the hours of darkness, keeping the fire ablaze. Patrick thought to relieve him, but didn't wish to give up the painful pleasure provided by the precious angel in his arms. He gritted his teeth and inhaled her intoxicating fragrance. Counted the stars in the sky. Counted his blessings.

Did he dare hope his good fortune would continue?

CHAPTER TWENTY-TWO

*L*aurie woke before light; she found herself wrapped in Patrick's embrace, warm and protected. Snuggling back against him, she encountered the hard pressure of his arousal and gave a soft moan.

"Shh," he whispered. He kissed the nape of her neck. "We will wed soon and I will make you mine. Have patience."

He was the one who should be patient. She gulped, remembering the size of his erection. She never thought she'd be the nervous bride type. Now she knew better. Would that one unpleasant encounter during college ruin her first time with Patrick? She hoped not.

Patrick pressed light kisses along the arch of her neck, and her negative thoughts scattered. His tongue swept the lobe of her ear. She shivered.

"I wish to show you something. Stay quiet and come with me." He helped her to her feet and they linked hands. He put a finger to his lips for silence and guided her to the mouth of the cave. An uncomfortable chill ran down her spine when he pulled her into the cavern.

Laurie pulled back, embarrassed to confess, "I'm afraid of the dark." She hated spiders and other creepy crawlies found in dank places.

"Dinnae fret. I dinnae think less of you."

Laurie squeezed his fingers.

"I promise nae harm will come to you."

She believed he would always protect her. Patrick wrapped an arm around her waist and coaxed her deeper into the murky opening. She reluctantly allowed him to pull her forward. After several steps, he stopped and wrapped his arms around her in a comforting hug. He ravished her mouth in a kiss that seared her soul. Her heartbeat quickened as their tongues waltzed.

Ending the kiss, he took one step back, his breath ragged in the silence. "Lass, you tempt me."

"It is you who tempt me." She held onto his arms, breathless.

He leaned in close and kissed her again. A mating of lips so sweet her heart twisted. When he pulled away, she attempted to tug him back to her.

"Nae, we must return to camp."

"I thought you had something to show me."

"Ach, I wanted a moment alone with you. Privacy will be hard to come by on the remainder of our journey."

She rolled onto the balls of her feet and kissed him again. His response curled her toes. Left her wanting.

"Come, 'tis time." He dragged her forward.

Laurie reluctantly stepped with Patrick into the early light of dawn. She blinked. He moved a bit stiffly as they joined the others.

The group came to life. They broke their fast, packed up camp, and headed for the boats.

As they descended the ridge, Laurie raised her hand to shade her eyes from the bright sun. Her breath caught. The sight before her stole the air from her lungs. Cormorants flew over the water, dipping and diving, plunging into the sea in search of fish, surfacing moments later nearby. She even glimpsed a seal poking its whiskered nose out of the water for air.

"Oh, Patrick. Everything is lovely. Thank you for bringing

me here."

This was everything she wanted and more. Patrick being the more. Maybe she owed Caitrina thanks. Maybe there was such a thing as destiny.

"'Tis my pleasure, sweetling." Patrick gazed at her with such tenderness, her eyes misted.

As they continued the descent, he held her hand firmly, ensuring she didn't fall. They reached the beach to discover a small group of men waiting for them along with the MacLachlan warriors.

"We have company," Stephen said from behind them.

Among the newcomers stood a finely dressed gentleman about the same age as Patrick, similarly built, but less muscular. To her mind, he looked like a peacock, his mannerisms almost feminine.

The multi-colors of his costume where anything but masculine. The tight queue holding back his black hair made his features hawk-like. His dark, calculating eyes narrowed when he caught her gaze and a chill slid along her spine.

Patrick grumbled something harsh under his breath she couldn't make out. Must have been a Gaelic curse based on his sour expression. "I hoped to avoid this," he whispered for only her ears and then strode forward and shook the man's hand, signaling for Laurie and Elspeth to join him. "May I present my betrothed, Lady Laurie Bernard."

She dipped into the curtsy she'd practiced after her first miserable attempt upon arriving at Castle Lachlan.

Patrick tucked her close to his side when she rose. "M'lady, I present Ninian Stewart, Sheriff of Bute, Keeper of Rothesay Castle and our host."

The man's eyes narrowed as he grasped Laurie's hand. "'Tis a pleasure to greet you." He grazed her knuckles with cold lips before releasing her hand, though continued to study her.

"My pleasure, sir." Her skin crawled.

"Intriguing creature, MacLachlan. I congratulate you on your good fortune." He kept his gaze on her overlong.

The man's regard made her uncomfortable and she glanced at Patrick.

Patrick didn't like the way the sheriff leered at Laurie. He draped his arm about her waist, plainly staking his claim. She was *his* betrothed. "You ken my wee sister, Lady Elspeth," he said, his voice tight.

Ninian seemed to take the hint and turned his attention to Elspeth.

"Good morn to you, sir," she said as she curtsied.

"Lady Elspeth, a pleasure as always." He kissed her extended hand. "My sister, Lady Jonet, will be disappointed she missed you."

"Will she be at the fair?"

"Nae, lass. She is in France, visiting."

"Our brother Archibald is in France with Alexander Campbell," Elspeth said.

"I did not realize they were still on the Continent."

"They are, and they sent Lady Laurie to me as a companion. Patrick fell in love with her and they are going to be wed when we return from the fair." She smiled brightly.

Patrick ground his teeth. He wished he could silence his sister.

"So you are to wed." Ninian's smile didn't quite reach his eyes. He slapped Patrick on the back. "Congratulations. Though I expected you to wed the Lamont lass."

Extending an arm around his shoulder, he drew Patrick away from Laurie before he could retort. "Had I kenned you were traveling with such bonnie lasses, I would have insisted you stay at the castle this past eve."

That was exactly what Patrick hoped to avoid by sleeping in the greenwood. He hadn't wanted his future wife too near the scoundrel sheriff. He walked off to converse with Ninian, but kept his lady in sight.

"We did not wish to impose on your hospitality," Laurie overheard Patrick say before his voice faded.

Elspeth giggled, leaned close and cupped her hand over her mouth as if to share a secret. "The old folk say Rothesay Castle is haunted by the ghost of a lady."

"Really?"

"Aye. They say she stabbed herself after Norseman slaughtered her family, preferring death rather than submitting to a forced marriage with a barbarian."

"Horrible story." Laurie feigned revulsion. *She'd decided to marry her barbarian.*

"Aye 'tis. I heard the lady's apparition often is seen on the stairs behind the chapel. And Jonet told me one time they found fresh blood on the stairs that couldn't be explained." Elspeth made a disgusted face. Then taking Laurie by the arm, she smiled broadly as if she hadn't been talking about ghosts and blood and suicide.

They linked arms and strolled to the boats, chatting about the absurdity of the tale.

Laurie kept glancing to where Patrick and Ninian conversed. Finally, the peacock mounted his steed and trotted off with his men.

When Patrick returned to the boats, worry lines furrowed his forehead.

"Is anything wrong?"

"Naught to concern you."

His tone set her teeth on edge. She lifted her chin. "Did I do something to displease you?"

"Nae." He shook his head.

"Can you not share your troubles with me?"

"We still have Lamont country to pass." He sighed. "'Tis always a worry."

She wrapped her arms around his waist and gave him a squeeze, pressed her face to his chest, listened to the even beat of his heart. He stiffened at first then hugged her in return, holding her tight before they broke apart.

Still, the morning's events left her uneasy. Meeting Ninian made her realize she'd be required to meet more of Patrick's contemporaries and pretend she really was from France, circa early sixteenth century. Too bad she hadn't been an actress rather than a business consultant in her prior life.

The men quickly loaded the boats. Everyone boarded and the group pushed off from shore, the oarsmen rowing out into the Firth. They would make their way to Dunoon Castle where they planned to spend the night. Elspeth's grandfather, Sir Robert Campbell, was in residence there, the Campbells being hereditary keepers of the royal castle.

Raising the sails, they made their way east, past the Isles of Cumbrae. Hugging the eastern shoreline of the Clyde, they managed to pass Toward Point and Lamont country without incident. They ate their mid-day meal while en route, a light meal of oatcakes and ale. The time was near to twilight when the three boats sailed west again.

Even in the dim light, the imposing shape of the stronghold perched on the rocky promontory inspired awe. They had arrived at Dunoon Castle.

Laurie held Patrick's hand while Robert Campbell greeted them in the great hall. A gracious man of stature with graying hair and beard, he congratulated them on their betrothal and promised to attend the wedding.

The staff served a main course of freshly caught salmon from the nearby river for dinner. Afterward, Elspeth commanded her grandfather's attention with animated anecdotes of everything that happened since her visit the previous year.

Finding it difficult to suppress her yawns, Laurie was glad to join Elspeth in a bedchamber on the second level though she would miss Patrick's warm embrace during the chilly night. Morning arrived too quickly. After farewells, they headed to the boats. A steady drizzle fell, the kind that saturated clothing and left one feeling miserable. Laurie huddled on the bench next to Elspeth, wishing for the sun to appear.

It wasn't to happen.

The rain still fell when they sighted their destination. Despite the wet weather, the small burgh bustled with many travelers stopping over on their way to the fair. Towering above the town—over two-hundred feet high on a massive twin-peaked hunk of volcanic rock above the River Leven where it merged with the Clyde—stood Dumbarton Castle. Unease settled on Laurie's shoulders. The sight of the stronghold brought home the fact she was living in another time and place.

The oppressive, miserable gray day made her more susceptible to doubts. Had she made the right decision to stay in the past and marry Patrick? He must've noticed her agitation, for he gave her fingers a gentle squeeze.

"You'll feel better after we arrive at the house I rented."

"Of course." She straightened her shoulders. How could she resist his gorgeous blue peepers, especially when he graced her with such a tender smile? Of course, she wanted to stay with him.

And she couldn't wait to attend the fair.

CHAPTER TWENTY-THREE

*P*atrick shouted orders as the *birlinns* grounded on a stony beach where the boats would remain guarded by a few MacLachlan warriors until the return trip to Strathlachan.

The retinue that set forth for Glasgow was large, fifty-five in all. Stephen, as captain of the *Lèine-chneas*, led Patrick's elite bodyguard—his tail of fifteen proven warriors personally selected from the most trusted and loyal of MacLachlan and MacEwen men. Jamie, Duncan, the clan historian and the chief's mouthpiece belonged to this esteemed group. Several young ghillies traveled with them. One of whom held the coveted honor of sword bearer, responsible for Patrick's great claymore with its sparkling sapphire gemstone.

For additional safety, he brought an extra contingent of well-armed warriors, lads who were chosen for their battle skills from the *buannachan*—the ranks of MacLachlan professional fighting men. He planned for some of the lads to escort his steward, Lachlan, and the provisions back to the castle overland after the fair, while others would sail back in the *birlinns*. He wanted Laurie and Elspeth to remain safe.

A gentle rain fell throughout the day. The muddy track slowed their progress. Concern plagued him. He wanted to reach Glasgow before dark. As the day waned, he hurried them along, yelled orders up and down the line, prodded everyone to continue walking.

For a short time, he walked alongside Laurie, doubting she was accustomed to walking such great distances. She must be tired and cold, yet she didn't complain. She plodded on, making him proud. "How do you fare?"

"I'll be fine once I find a bed to fall into." She flicked a stray hair from her face. He would ensure her comfort when they reached their destination.

At gloaming, they neared the outskirts of the burgh. When Patrick feared Laurie would drop from exhaustion, she picked up the pace and followed the others through the darkening streets.

His people were weary and soaked to the skin when they finally reached the house Lachlan procured. Located on one of the nicer lanes, he'd hired this same lodging for the eight days of the fair for the past two years. Although the timber house was small, it met his needs. Each of the two floors consisted of three rooms, and with the additional space provided by the garret in the big barn, there was room enough for his entire party. Behind the residence, off the courtyard, several outbuildings and a cookhouse provided more space.

Lachlan greeted him when he banged on the heavy oak door. Patrick grasped Laurie's cold hand and tugged her into the small hall where a crackling fire burned in the hearth against the far wall. His servants had prepared well. The cozy room was warm, clean and neat. Settling her on a bench before the fire he spoke briefly with Lachlan while his people settled. Stephen, Duncan and Jamie found a spot to huddle near the hearth, warming their hands and allowing their clothes to dry. Laurie stretched, moving her feet closer to the flames.

Laurie's pale face concerned him. During a light meal, her eyes drifted shut on and off. He prayed she wouldn't become ill from the wet or the chill of the day. When her eyelids finally closed, he gathered her in his arms and carried her up the stairs to the chamber she would share with Elspeth.

As much as he desired taking Laurie to his bed, he needed to keep up appearances. Some of the staff were not of his clan and might be prone to whispering rumors he didn't wish spread. He didn't want Lamont to catch wind of this betrothal.

Twining her arms around his neck, she gazed at him through sleepy eyes, filled with what he hoped was true love. Her soft, pink lips parted into the most glorious smile. His heartbeat sped and he gave her a quick peck on the cheek before depositing her on the bed and escaping the chamber. He needed to put some distance between them. She enticed him beyond his control.

Patrick returned to the hall and mused on the woman upstairs. His life had changed in many ways in the short time since he'd found her. He could almost say he was happy.

Yet doubts nagged.

There was much he didn't know about her, or understand about her sudden appearance. Too many mysteries remained yet to solve.

She had wound her way around his heart, his passion for her overwhelming. He didn't like his blindness to all else when his blood burned with fire, thinking only of his need for her. His burgeoning desire left him vulnerable.

He remained in the hall when the others went to find their beds. Staring into the flames, he thought of his father and stepmother, and his brother Archibald. He wished Archie had returned from the Continent. Patrick was in need of his brother's quick mind.

Stephen joined him after a short while with two goblets. "Lachlan procured a delicious French wine to serve at your wedding celebration. Might you wish to sample it?"

"Aye."

His cousin handed him one of the goblets full of the dark ruby liquid. "For a man who is about to wed the lass of his dreams, you look a wee bit glum."

Patrick swirled the wine in his cup, taking only a tiny sip.

He raised his head to glare at Stephen. His cousin but laughed.

"Care to unburden your soul?"

"I want the lass more than I should, yet I am unsure of where she came from, or the why of it. And I dinnae ken what happened to my parents."

"Do you believe Lady Laurie is involved in your parent's disappearance?"

"Nae. Yet I dinnae like the meddling of the faeries. And I am yet to learn more about my stepmother's faerie Munn warned me of. He has been silent on the matter of late. That is, beyond warning me of dire consequences if I wed Laurie."

"Mayhap you should bed the lass and forget the wedding." Stephen's lips curved into a wary smile.

"I made a promise. 'Tis only right I wed her. I am the only one who can protect her." He massaged the back of his neck.

"Well, then, I will be at your back, protecting you."

Patrick stared at his cousin for a long moment. "For that, I thank you."

They sat quietly, comfortable with the silence, and with each other's company.

Stephen finished his wine and left him to his thoughts. Several long hours passed before he went to find his own bed. Sleep wouldn't come.

Hours passed before he drifted off, only to waken with his heart pounding against his ribs, fear twisting his gut, and a scream burning his throat.

❀ ❀ ❀

Laurie stretched, enjoying the warmth of the sun shining on her face from the window. They'd arrived in Glasgow a day early. Although the bishop would proclaim the festival this evening, the fair wasn't to begin until tomorrow.

Small as the town seemed, Elspeth assured her there were wondrous places to visit.

Stephen assembled the men, and Patrick's tail encircled them. Laurie wasn't used to bodyguards. Remembering an incident that happened to her in New York City, she laughed.

She'd been rushing home from the office one evening when she rounded a corner onto Fifth Avenue and collided with a famous celebrity's personal guards, six big men surrounding the much shorter actor. One of the guys actually picked her up as if she weighed nothing and moved her to the side. She'd been insulted and furious for days.

She sized up the men who now surrounded her. They were definitely bigger and much fiercer than the actor's bodyguards had appeared. It hadn't been clear whether the twenty-first century guards carried concealed weapons. Her current escort did, along with large swords strapped to their backs.

They made their way up the High Street, above which towered a lofty stone spire.

"May we go to the cathedral?" she asked.

"Aye, we will go there now, if you wish, before we visit my wee brother." Patrick placed her hand on his arm.

"Please." Elspeth clapped her hands. "You will love the cathedral and the bishop's house."

Patrick chuckled. Thank goodness. Earlier he'd admitted to having a nightmare, which had left him unsettled.

Laurie loved the gothic architecture of the magnificent cathedral. It stood majestically over the burgh. They visited the nave and the choir. What she loved most was the lower church and the series of chapels. The beautiful vaulted space inspired awe. She dropped to her knees on a padded cushion and prayed, thanking God for the marvelous man standing beside her.

The grandeur of the bishop's tower house with its high wall and fortified gatehouse was equally impressive. Finding oneself surrounded by history had a sobering effect.

Many historians and authors would sell their soul to have this experience.

After spending the morning in and around the cathedral,

they strolled back down the street and stopped before a large stone building. Patrick banged upon the wooden door and waited. Laurie knew he was impatient to see how his young brother fared.

A hunched over, elderly man in black robes answered the door and directed them inside. Patrick along with Laurie and Elspeth entered the small, sparsely furnished chamber. He explained to the man the reason for their visit. The man inclined his head then left the chamber through a darkened doorway.

A few short minutes passed before a solemn man appeared. Tall and thin, with a homely face, and gnarled long fingers.

"Edward Erskine, principal regent," Patrick said softly.

"Laird MacLachlan." The man crossed the room with a lanky gait and shook Patrick's outstretched hand.

"Good day, Erskine." Patrick waved his arm to Laurie. "My betrothed, Lady Bernard, and my sister."

"M'ladies." The man bowed.

They curtsied in-sync. Laurie wanted to crack-up. She was finally getting the knack of the etiquette bullshit.

The two men moved away from the women and spoke in hushed tones.

Laurie scanned the room, a musty, dark and dreary chamber. The odor reminded her of some of the shops she once frequented in Paris, the establishments dealing in books of antiquity.

Elspeth leaned toward Laurie and whispered, "I cannae wait to see my brother."

The regent left, and Patrick returned to Laurie's side. "Master Erskine has gone to retrieve Suibhne."

After a few minutes, Patrick's younger brother appeared in the doorway, his head held high, proudly wearing his university scholar's black gown. Clutched in his stiff arms was a leather bound book.

Suibhne hesitated. He seemed to brace himself before walking forward to join his family.

Laurie sympathized with the boy's discomfort. Patrick had told her the boy was a bookworm. Suibhne preferred his studies to the *manly* pursuits his older brothers reveled in. She could relate. She'd always preferred reading to the uncomfortable social gatherings expected of a debutante.

Her foolish husband-to-be had assured her his brother wasn't a lass. The lad had the ability to fight and hunt, Patrick had said. Being the son of a Highland chief, Suibhne had trained in fighting with the sword, shooting with bow and arrows, and seamanship. Yet the boy chose instead to study the arts. She suspected Patrick and his brother Archibald intimidated Suibhne. And the young man's timid ways certainly rankled her fiancé.

Suibhne nodded to Elspeth before his eyes widened at the sight of Patrick's arm draped around Laurie. The boy recovered quickly and awkwardly kissed his sister's cheek. Then he turned to Patrick and greeted him with a formal bow. Patrick wasn't so formal. He grabbed his brother, wrapped his arms around the lad, and pounded him hard on the back several times.

Red in the face, Suibhne stiffened in Patrick's embrace, clearly embarrassed by his older brother's display of familial affection. Patrick didn't seem to notice the young man's restraint. He released him and pulled her to his side. "Brother, this is the Lady Laurie Bernard, my betrothed."

A tingling thrill rushed through Laurie when he introduced her as his betrothed. Curiosity burned in Suibhne's blue eyes—eyes so similar to Patrick's. Reminding her of someone else. But who? She couldn't remember.

The boy bowed to her.

After exchanging more pleasantries, Suibhne excused himself to return to his lessons, having agreed to meet them later for the evening meal.

Patrick, Laurie and Elspeth left the university building, joined the guard waiting outside, and returned to their lodging for their mid-day meal. Afterward, Patrick requested the women spend the afternoon resting. He explained there would be much excitement over the next sennight and didn't want them to overtire or become ill.

Laurie wasn't so sure she liked the way he dictated her actions. What would Patrick think if she defied him and went out to explore?

During the evening meal, Patrick observed Laurie and Suibhne from his seat at the head of the table. His brother sat next to Laurie and seemed comfortable speaking with her.

"What do you study at University?" she asked.

"Robert Leslie is the regent. He instructs us in the works of Aristotle, among other subjects."

"In Latin, I presume."

"Aye." Suibhne smiled. "Do you understand Latin?"

"I do."

"I kenned you would." His smile widened. "The university's program covers many other fields of study— logic, rhetoric, mathematics, physics, ethics, politics, psychology and even metaphysics." His voice rose with excitement.

"So many topics." Laurie inclined her head to the book on the table next to Suibhne's plate. "You must enjoy reading."

Suibhne glanced at Patrick then lowered his eyes. "A bit too much, I fear."

"Never too much." She patted the book.

Hopefully, with Laurie's encouragement, Suibhne would feel a sense of achievement. The lad was most often too reserved and lacked confidence. Especially on the field. Patrick inhaled a disappointed breath. At least, the lad excelled at his studies.

Laurie was good with his family. Patrick was well pleased yet the terror-filled dream he'd had during the night left him uneasy.

Come morning, the small group moved with the flow of

people along the High Street. Laurie gawked at the other fairgoers. Some finely dressed attended by guards, while others wore no more than rags. Patrick's lads kept the throng back, ensuring no one jostled them.

Laurie hadn't seen crowds like this since she'd attended the San Gennaro Festival in Little Italy many years before. Years that had taken place in the twenty-first century. Now here she was, observing history, up close and personal. Goosebumps prickled her arms when she thought about her time traveling experience.

The entourage made its way along the street toward the Market Cross, the marketplace downhill from the cathedral.

If the crowds of people weren't interesting enough, surely the colorful stalls full of all kinds of merchandise were. She tried to see everything, look in all directions at once.

Stalls and carts were set up along the course of the street. Displayed before her was every medieval item she could imagine. There were food stalls, some with baked goods, and others with produce and cheese, some with fruits, nuts and honey, and still others with spices. There were fishmongers and butchers. Even a merchant from France selling fine wines.

The calls of the merchants hawking their wares added to the chatter of the excited crowds. Patrick stopped before a cart of sweets and purchased treats for her and Elspeth.

As the candied fruit melted on Laurie's tongue, she closed her eyes in pure ecstasy. When she opened her eyes, Patrick studied her, his eyes dark with desire. Her heartbeat quickened in response. Their marriage couldn't come soon enough.

The MacLachlans moved on.

They passed booths containing cloth and other textiles. Stalls with leather. Others with animal skins and still others with goods made from leather. They passed booths with high quality metalwork—swords, knives and armor—while others displayed more domestic items. With so much to see, Laurie couldn't decide where to visit first.

Elspeth stopped before a goldsmith's booth and rummaged through the displayed goods.

"Show us your finest blue sapphires," Patrick ordered of the smith.

The man laid a selection of gems on a black velvet cloth before him. The quality was suburb. Patrick picked up a large, clear stone and presented it to her. "Do you like this one?"

"Lovely." The sapphire he chose was the most beautiful gem she'd ever seen.

Patrick held out his hand and she placed the stone on his palm. Then he returned it to the smith. "Make this into a betrothal ring."

"No!" The gemstone would cost Patrick a small fortune. She'd studied enough history to know times in the Highlands had been difficult. She couldn't allow him to squander his gold on her. "A plain gold band will be enough."

"You refuse my gift?" A peeved expression clouded his features.

"I don't want you to spend too much money on me."

His features iced over, and Laurie's stomach dropped. "We return to the house for the mid-day repast," Patrick bellowed, ignoring her.

She couldn't believe she pissed him off. He didn't even bother looking at what else the smith had to offer. She bit her lip. Had he changed his mind about marrying her?

He glowered throughout the meal then stormed off after ordering her and Elspeth to stay at the house. His domineering manners were beginning to piss her off. She was tempted to go out, just to spite him. The rebellious impulse made her smile and she returned her attention to her embroidery. He'd get over his huff and so would she.

As she'd anticipated, Patrick recovered from his grouchy mood, and the remaining days of the fair were full of fun and merriment. They shopped and sampled the marvelous foods, often stopping along the way to view jugglers and tumblers or singers and dancers.

Late one afternoon, they watched a puppeteer and laughed

aloud with the children. When the show ended, they walked along the thoroughfare. Laurie smiled, looking this way and that, her hand poised on Patrick's arm.

He stiffened and stopped short, the entire entourage coming to a halt. In front of them, a group of armed warriors blocked their way.

Patrick wore a cold expression. Chills ran down her spine as she stared into the face of a fearless warrior.

"Patrick—"

"Whist!" He shoved her behind him. "'Tis Lamont."

Stephen stepped close to Patrick's side.

Laurie peeked from behind his broad back, peering between the two huge men. The warriors who stood before them looked more ruthless than the MacLachlans. She shuddered. Then she glimpsed the girl.

In the midst of the warriors stood a beautiful young girl, a woman-child, with hair the color of ebony, skin like fine ivory porcelain, and almond-shaped eyes, the deep blue color almost violet. She looked to be about sixteen, possibly younger, yet striking. An unwanted pang of jealousy surprised Laurie when the girl's identity dawned on her. *The infamous Isobell.*

The girl was a teenager, for God's sake.

Two men stepped forward from the group of Lamonts. The short, stout man with gray stringy hair, heavy eyebrows and a heavy beard, must be Iain Lamont. Laurie guessed the other, who stood to his right, was his henchman. The man was huge, tall and broad, cruel looking, ugly with horrible scars on his face. One scar—pink and puffy—stretched jagged from his lip to his right ear. Both men wore mean expressions.

"Ninian Stewart told the truth," the older man shouted. "You have broken the agreement and plan to wed the outlander." His voice dripped insult.

Laurie tensed. This was about her.

"There was never an agreement," Patrick retorted. "And well you ken it."

Both groups of warriors pressed forward. Patrick thrust Laurie at Duncan and Jamie grabbed hold of Elspeth. They rushed the women to the back of the guard.

"Thus you have said. Yet your father agreed to the match." Though the MacLachlan warriors blocked Laurie's view, she still heard Lamont's angry voice.

"I have not seen an agreement. You cannae show me proof." Patrick's tone was strong and impassioned. Shoving and jostling broke out among the warriors.

"Is your father's promise not enough?" Lamont snarled.

"Again. I say, I have nae proof. And 'tis not your business to whom I chose to wed."

Swords were unsheathed. The clink of steel against steel rang out as Duncan and Jamie hurried Laurie and Elspeth down an alleyway toward their hired residence and safety.

"Stop." Laurie stubbornly held onto Duncan's arm, trying to halt him. "We can't leave them. What if Patrick gets hurt?"

"Go!" Duncan pushed her along. "I will be the one hurt if we get caught in the fray and the chief does not find you and Lady Elspeth safe at the house when he returns."

"I don't want to leave him," Laurie shouted.

CHAPTER TWENTY-FOUR

*P*acing from one end of the hall to the other, Laurie worried her bottom lip.

"Sit," Elspeth said. "Nae harm will come to my brother."

Laurie stopped and frowned at her companion. "That child with the Lamont warriors, was she Isobell?"

"Aye. Though she is not a child. She is eight and ten summers."

Laurie gaped. Catching herself, she closed her mouth. She walked away, then back. "Too young, I think, to be expected to wed Patrick."

"I am the same age and am betrothed to Alexander."

"Different." Laurie waved her hand, dismissing the comparison. "You're not to wed until your twenty-first birthday."

"'Tis unusual and only because we must wait until Alexander receives keepership of Skipness."

"So what of Isobell?"

"She was meant for our elder brother Donald. They were to wed when Isobell turned four and ten, but he died five summers ago. That is when her father claimed Patrick should wed her since he was next in line as our father's heir. My brother refused, and my father agreed. Patrick went to the

Continent and did not return until he received word from our father that trouble brewed. By the time Patrick returned, our parents had disappeared. Only their horses were found near the faerie knoll at Fir-wood. You have heard most of the rest of the tale."

"Does she wish to wed Patrick?"

"That I dinnae ken. She lost her mother when she was verra young. Her father dotes upon her." Elspeth shook her head. "She is verra spoiled and not pleasant to be with."

Laurie contemplated that bit of information as she resumed pacing.

After what seemed like an eternity, a loud disturbance came from the street. Laurie bolted to the window to peer out.

Patrick burst into the room with Stephen on his heels. Stepping backward until she hit the table, she rushed her gaze over both men. They appeared to be fine, only a few cuts and bruises.

Patrick barked out orders, sending Aine scurrying out to the barn to care for a couple of men who'd been injured. Angus came in from the back and handed Patrick a mug of ale, which he accepted. Their gazes met over the lip of the mug.

Patrick took a long pull of ale. Laurie stood with her back against the table, watching him, her soft, blue eyes filled with concern, her lips plump and inviting. Battle lust rode him hard. He strode to her and slammed the mug down beside her, splashing liquid on the table. Hauling her into a bear hug of an embrace, his lips claimed hers, hard and rough until he tasted her sweetness, and softened the kiss.

Wild with his yearning for her, he wanted to throw her across the table, toss up her skirt, bury his shaft within her, and end his torment.

He inhaled a deep breath. Although he craved her beyond all reason, he wouldn't shame her. He ended the kiss.

She stiffened in his arms and looked away. "Maybe we

shouldn't wed."

"Why?" With a growl, he released her and strode across the chamber, keeping his back to her. Anger clawed the walls of his stomach. He didn't want her to see his snarling grimace.

"I don't want to be the reason your men are injured fighting with Lamont warriors."

He spun and faced her. "We will wed as planned." He'd accept no argument. Without another word, he left the house with Stephen chasing after him.

The flicker of defiance he'd seen in Laurie's eyes bothered him for the remainder of the day. He'd need to smother that spark. Then he'd soften her resentment with a special surprise.

The next day, Laurie waved goodbye to Patrick.

He strode away with several of his men to trade for cattle and horses. Elspeth left earlier, having talked Jamie into taking her to a merchant stall where she'd seen some pretty hair ribbons. Laurie was stuck in the little house alone.

She fanned herself. The hall was stifling. Patrick told her not to leave the house, but surely, he wouldn't mind if she got a bit of fresh air. In the courtyard, she found little in the way of relief, the air muggy and still. The stench of rotting garbage making her want to cover her nose and mouth. The burgh smelled worse than the castle.

Duncan stood near the barn conversing with some of the other men. None of them paid any notice when she crossed the courtyard and rounded the side of the house, slipped down the alley and into the street, hoping to find a sweet breeze.

Strolling along the narrow way, heading toward the water, Laurie hummed, glad to be free of the confines of the house. Though after a short distance, the hair on the back of her neck tingled. She glanced around.

Nothing seemed out of the ordinary. The street was quiet

with most of the residents still attending the fair. Ignoring her apprehension as foolish, she walked farther. Around the corner, the air should be fresher.

Without warning, an arm wrapped around her waist from behind while a dirty hand clamped over her mouth, muffling her scream. Her hair fell from its knot into her face, blinding her. The attacker dragged her from the street into the shadows of a narrow, dark alley.

Her breath left her lungs when he slammed her hard against a stone wall. Adrenaline and fear raced through her veins. Fighting her assailant, she tugged on the dark hood covering his face, but it held in place. She scratched him. Kicked.

He used his massive body to press her hard against the wall where he grabbed her arms and held them over her head in one of his large hands. "You are a wild one." His foul breath burned her nostrils. "I will enjoy taming you."

Laurie screamed until his wet mouth crushed hers, silencing her. She tried to break the contact. His teeth bit into her flesh. Pain sent her into a frenzy. She bucked. Tried to throw him off.

Heavy footfalls came from the street, people running. A battle cry pierced her ears.

Her attacker abruptly dropped her to the ground and disappeared into the shadows. She pushed the hair from her eyes. Patrick ran toward her, sword in hand, his face contorted in a snarl.

Patrick's heart slammed against his ribs and his blood raged. Laurie huddled on the ground, her beautiful blue gown gaping open to the waist. Dirt streaked her face. He picked her up and held her against his chest. His fear and anger combined, simmered just below the surface. He couldn't remember having been this frightened or this furious.

Some of his men ran farther along the alley, searching for the attacker, but returned empty handed.

"Who did this?" he demanded. "Who attacked you?" His

voice sounded harsh from the terror in his gut.

Laurie hung like a child's rag doll, limp in his arms.

He shook her. "Answer me!"

Her head fell back. She stared at him through moisture-filled eyes. "I don't know."

"Was it one of Lamont's men? One of those we met in the street yestereve?"

"I don't know. I couldn't see his face. He was big and strong. That's all I could discern."

"Why were you in the streets alone?"

"I wanted fresh air."

She tucked her face into the folds of his *leine*. He held her gently as he carried her to the house, but his chest remained tight. Although he didn't want to, he'd have to punish her for disobeying him.

"Foolish lass! Had I not forgotten my pouch and returned..."

He didn't want to think about what could have happened. She needed to learn his word must be obeyed.

Later that night, Laurie entered the hall and gingerly sat on the edge of a bench, refusing to look at Patrick. He sat in the large ornate chair at the head of the table all superior-like as if he were the CEO of a large corporation above reproach. She tapped her foot on the floor, livid, enraged with anger and humiliation she barely contained. He not only scolded her when they returned to the house, he put her over his knees and spanked her. Her backside still smarted from his not so tender lesson.

He'd called her a stubborn wench when after one smack she refused to beg his forgiveness. As if, she forced him to hit her. When she finally gave in and screamed at him to stop, he made her promise to never again go anywhere without an escort.

How could I have thought I wanted to marry him? Forgotten he was a barbarian?

She raised her chin. Her pride stung. He treated her like a disobedient child. She wasn't used to being manhandled. Her uncle never once spanked her as a child.

Patrick's abuse outraged her. She deserved a scolding. Nothing more. When they returned to Castle Lachlan, she would try again to return home.

"Lass, I did not want to hurt you." He frowned and ran a hand through his hair. "How else am I to make you understand the risks you take?"

Laurie glanced at the others in the room to make sure no one listened. "A simple lecture would have been sufficient." She glared at him, daring him to disagree.

Before he could respond, the others joined them at the table and the evening meal was served.

Apparently, he wasn't only angry with her. He gave Duncan a pointed look and the poor man lowered his head, his ears turning bright red. What punishment had he received? The festival-goers probably heard Patrick's bellows earlier when he yelled at Duncan for allowing her to leave the house unguarded. She'd be lucky if in the future she could use the loo without Duncan following her in.

She toyed with the food on her trencher unable to eat. She didn't feel like participating in the lively conversations around her. Patrick watched her with an unfathomable intensity that served to piss her off more.

Working herself into a fine tizzy, she wanted to hit something—someone. *Patrick.* "Excuse me. I'm not feeling well." She stood.

Patrick raised an eyebrow. She glared at him, hurried to her chamber and threw herself onto the bed, pounding her fists in frustration. She threw a pillow at the wall. God, she hated him.

In the bright light of morning, things appeared different, became clearer. He was partly right. She'd made a judgment error. She never should have left the safety of the house and grounds on her own. Not being used to such restrictions, she hadn't thought it through. Hadn't thought taking a walk a big deal.

She'd been wrong. Patrick was a barbarian. But she loved the darn barbarian.

He'd only done what he thought necessary to make her understand. His customs were different from those of the twenty-first century. His only wish to keep her safe.

Oh, but she'd find a way to make him pay for the brutal treatment. She'd teach him that although his motives were pure his methods needed adjusting.

She wanted him to prove he could be gentle. That he wasn't a brute. She wanted to believe their marriage would be full of unconditional love and mutual understanding.

Until then, she would devise a way to make him suffer.

On the morning they were to leave Glasgow, Patrick personally saw to the loading of the packhorses. He sent Lachlan on his way with the cattle and horses, well-guarded by a heavily armed escort. Then he gathered the rest of his entourage and they left the burgh for Dumbarton and home.

The return trip was, for the most part, uneventful, yet progressed slower with fewer men to operate the oars. They spent three nights sleeping in the greenwood, avoiding the sheriff of Bute's land. The first night passed in an oak wood near Greenock, the second at the edge of a secluded bay on the small isle of Cumbrae and finally the last night near Tarbert Castle. Once again, they managed to sail past Lamont country without challenge.

A deep chasm developed between he and Laurie while they sailed from Dumbarton. She remained sullen and uncommunicative, still harboring ill feelings over what she believed to be his heavy-handed treatment of her. The silence between them became unbearable.

He left her to sleep alone the first two nights.

On the last night, he lay behind her and despite her chilly reception pulled her back against his chest. She stiffened.

"You must get over this huff of yours and forgive me. I

merely did what I had to do to make you see your folly." Patrick kissed the nape of her neck. She shivered and melted against him. Pulling her closer, he molded her to his hard body and tenderly held her.

"I haven't forgiven you."

"I ken, but you must."

Several tense minutes passed, and Patrick didn't believe Laurie would respond. He shut his eyes and counted backward from one hundred.

The previous two nights, Laurie had been cold and miserable and lonely. She missed Patrick's embrace. She couldn't hold on to her anger. "You could've just given me a lecture, you know," she said.

By his even breathing, she knew she wouldn't get a response so she elbowed him.

"What?"

"I want you to promise you'll never hit me again."

"I cannae. If you refuse to follow my dictates, I will be forced to punish you."

"In my time, we've learned hitting doesn't change behavior. It only increases hostility."

He sighed so heavily she felt his breath on her neck. "You dinnae understand the dangers."

"And you don't trust me," she accused.

He held her and was quiet for a long time.

When she'd given up on him, he responded, "I will agree to try to have words with you only. But you must promise to never wander off alone again."

Maybe he could be taught. Laurie crossed her fingers. "I promise."

"Do you forgive me?"

"I forgive you."

"Good." His lips moved against her neck. She felt his grin as she relaxed against him.

Afternoon sunshine brightened the stone of Castle Lachlan as the oarsman brought them closer to shore. Laurie shifted restlessly on her seat, eager to be home.

Home. Castle Lachlan had really become her home.

Dhughall, who'd been left in charge of the castle while they were gone, hurried to greet them as they beached. Patrick jumped over the side and onto shore. The two men walked away to confer, their heads close together.

Laurie's gaze followed Patrick. A deep frown burrowed into his face. Whatever news Dhughall reported must be bad.

The *birlinn* swayed and Duncan offered his hand, assisting her from the boat. The ground seemed to waver under her feet and he held her arm until she gained her balance. Then she waited for Elspeth to join her.

"'Tis good to be home," the young woman said.

"Oh, yeah." Laurie rolled her neck.

Then Patrick distracted her with an obscene gesture.

"What has my brother in a lather?"

"I'm not sure. But it must be bad."

"What's wrong?" she asked when he returned to escort her to the castle.

"'Tis naught." He held his jaw tight.

"Why don't you trust me?"

"'Tis nothing." A forced smile curled his lips. "Shall we go?"

She knew the lie for what it was. Something was terribly wrong.

Patrick placed her hand on his arm and escorted her toward the castle.

She couldn't understand why he refused to share his troubles. Without trust, their marriage was doomed. Should she reconsider staying?

"I wish a moment to myself. If you don't mind, I'd like to take a walk on the beach and get my land legs back."

"Duncan will join you."

"Of course."

As she strolled near the water's edge, she remembered the

night she traveled through time. A full moon had glowed over the garden gate. Had Caitrina not pushed her, Laurie would have moved through the gate drawn by the glimmering moonlight. A revelation caught her by surprise—the moon. She knew how the magic worked; she felt the rightness of it in every fiber of her being. Should she try the faerie knoll again or talk some sense into her stupid man?

A glorious sunset glimmered over the mauve-colored hills. She walked along the pebbly beach, gazing across the loch, marveling at such beauty. As the last trace of vermillion faded from sight, she wrapped her arms around her chest and made a decision. She would stay and work things out with Patrick. She would teach him how to confide in her. How to give her his trust.

She dragged her gaze over the water, one last time, ready to return to the castle. The silhouette of a galley approached from the west.

Warning horns sounded from the watchtower.

Before she moved, Duncan ran to her from where he'd been standing at the edge of the beach, grabbed her hand and dragged her at a run toward the castle gate.

CHAPTER TWENTY-FIVE

Tir-nan-Óg

*M*ost of Caitrina's endless life, she performed impossibly difficult tasks at the dictate of the faerie queen with the hope of regaining her royal status. To once again live and play amongst the other faeries in paradise, in *Tir-nan-Óg*, was her heart's greatest desire.

Dammit, she'd been so close with Laurie and the MacLachlan.

Once they mated, she could move on to the second match of the queen's three-match challenge. Then the third. Too bad Oonagh interfered.

Caitrina skimmed a hand along the length of a rich velvet curtain. Here she was, ensconced in luxury at the palace within *Tir-nan-Óg*, on the whim of the queen.

But as a prisoner.

At least she was alone. Oonagh had left the palace to meet her consort for merrymaking at a distant faerie pageant. Had the queen not realized Caitrina would plot escape?

Caitrina paced the confines of the chamber, indifferent to its splendor. Lost in thought, she stopped before a crystal table and ran her fingers through the collection of sapphires displayed in a cut glass bowl. Outside, on the veranda, one of Oonagh's boy toys strutted across the tile to the pool— nude—and dove in. He emerged to his waist a few steps from Caitrina, wet muscles on his packed chest glistening in golden sunlight. Her mind whirled furiously and she settled on a cunning plan.

With a thought, she changed her glamour to that of a veiled harem girl and stepped from the queen's boudoir, through the curtains, onto the warm tile. She smiled with her eyes to entice the lesser faerie. She wouldn't think of Douglas while she seduced her prey.

"Gabriel," she purred.

Desire flashed in her quarry's green eyes and with feline grace, he leapt from the water. She read his intention to dry himself with a thought and shook her head.

"I like you wet." Her tone was a husky come-hither invitation.

Gabriel didn't disappoint. His cock grew into a splendid erection.

Caitrina hesitated. How could she betray Douglas? She had to. Besides, they didn't really have a relationship. He only thought so because he was human. She needed to use Gabriel and one of his woman to escape.

Before she lost her nerve, she swung her hips in an erotic belly dance, ripping the gauzy, lavender strips of her gossamer garments one by, ever so slowly, one. When the last piece of fabric fell, Gabriel reeled her into his body, lifted her, and carried her to the poolside, chaise lounge.

When his fingers caressed her inner thigh, she pretended he was Douglas.

She couldn't do this. She stayed his hand.

"Perhaps we could enjoy a threesome." Caitrina placed a persuasion spell on the words.

His eyes flared. "I will summon Briganna."

The beautiful lesser faerie, trained to sexually please, appeared beside Gabriel and they both joined Caitrina on the wide chase. With a kiss to each of their lips, Caitrina planted a sleep spell and slipped from the palace using Briganna's glamour. As much as she wanted to stay in *Tir-nan-Óg*, she couldn't.

She needed to complete the match quickly, before the queen became aware of her escape. It was essential for Caitrina to find and silence that meddling MacLachlan brownie. Stop him before he exerted more harm.

Cloaked in Scottish glamour, she stilled her mind and sought Munn. She inhaled a deep breath, seeking composure, and sent her feelings into the mortal realm. Where would be the most likely place to find Munn?

When she sensed his whereabouts, she dissolved into tiny particles, moving through the gray mist unseen, through the veil of time and space.

She swept into the MacLachlan stables on the lightest of breezes and slowly coalesced into solid form, appearing in the loft. She found Munn there, perched in the rafters, watching the young lads groom Patrick's favorite horse.

Munn faced her. He stuttered, his ramblings becoming nonsensical, on and on he blathered, accusing her of every imaginable heinous misdeed.

"Whist, wee man. You shall not reveal anything to anyone."

The queen wasn't here to protect him. He spun, ready to escape, but wasn't fast enough. Caitirna raised her arms over her head in an arc and seized his voice.

Munn attempted to speak. Nothing passed his lips.

No words. No sound.

No anything. His voice was gone.

Caitrina grinned then vanished, heading through time to the future.

CHAPTER TWENTY-SIX

*P*atrick couldn't believe the audacity of the Lamont. To have an unfriendly galley anchored in his bay. To have Lamont and his men at his gates demanding entry—requesting hospitality—the possible significance greatly troubled him.

His uncle, who had taken up residence in the castle while Patrick was in Glasgow, compounded his unease. The man claimed to have reconsidered his outburst during the council meeting prior to the raid and now spouted the need for unity. Could the union be not of the family but that of his uncle with the Lamont?

Pondering his next move, Patrick slammed his fist on the worktable. He glanced at Stephen and met his cousin's worried gaze. "Meet Lamont and offer our hospitality in my name. Have Dhughall see to Lamont's lads and make sure our men watch them. After Lamont has refreshed himself, bring him to my private chamber."

"We could bar the gates." Stephen's lips formed a grim line.

"Aye, if only I could. I will not risk war. Offer our hospitality. But keep your weapons at the ready."

Stephen left him to his troubled thoughts. Patrick walked

to a window and peered out. Rubbing his forehead with a tense hand, he tried to relieve the pressure building there.

What are the wily old rascals about?

A tapping sound startled Elspeth when Munn appeared in her solar. He danced around the chamber, whirling in circles at a dizzying pace. In the glow of the candles, his shadow spun on the walls.

"Where have you been, my wee man? I have missed you."

Munn made frantic motions with his arms, silently imploring her with stark eyes, gesturing for her to follow him.

"What game is this?" she asked. "Do tell."

He remained mute, continuing to gesture, beckoning her to come with him.

"If I must, I will come. But I dinnae ken what you are about." She laughed at his antics.

Taking the lantern from atop a chest, she lit the wick and followed him through the castle.

No one else seemed to notice Munn as she followed him. She suspected he used a cloaking glamour to hide from the others' view.

What could he possibly be up to?

He made his way down the stairs and through the courtyard and out the gate. Munn paused in front of one of the larger planting beds. The one herb bed that was special, almost sacred, to Elspeth. Her mother planted it several years prior, before she disappeared with Elspeth's father. Munn dug in the soil with his hands.

Elspeth knelt beside him, holding the lantern to see what he was doing.

"Stop! You mustn't dig here. My lady-mother planted these herbs," she scolded, annoyed by his disregard for the precious little plants he uprooted in his haste.

He ignored her and continued to dig, breathing heavy as he did so. He tugged at something, putting a considerable amount of exertion into the effort, and then fell backward across the path onto his arse, landing in a patch of strawberries.

Elspeth's annoyance turned into delight. Munn held an intricately carved box. "What is this?" she asked, reaching for the small wooden chest. "What did you find?"

The wee man leapt away, shaking his head. He shoved a stubby hand into the pouch hanging from his belt and retrieved a tiny brass key, which he handed to her.

She wrinkled her brow.

His gaze darted around the garden then with relaxed shoulders, he returned his attention to Elspeth and handed over the box. Before she could question him further, he disappeared into the fine mist that shrouded the garden, leaving her puzzled.

What is inside that made the brownie act so strange? She examined the box then inserted the key into the small lock and twisted it. The lock fell open. She lifted the lid and gasped in shock.

Elspeth sat next to the herb bed heedless of her fine gown. She rummaged through the contents of the box. After examining everything, she replaced the lock with unsteady hands and turned the key, once again locking away the dreadful contents.

She stood and slowly walked out of the garden. Then she ran to the castle to find her brother.

Elspeth found him in his study. She hated being the one to bring the mysterious box's contents to his attention. She could only imagine the possible consequences. Holding the chest tightly to her breast, she took a deep breath and rapped lightly on the door.

He bid her enter.

She hesitated, gathering her courage, trying to smooth her expression. Then she walked into the chamber, stopping inside the door. "Patrick."

"What is it, Beth?" He glanced up from where he sat at his worktable.

She walked across the room to stand next to him. Their

eyes met, and he seemed to sense her apprehension.

He glanced at the box in her arms and raised an eyebrow. "Why so mysterious, lass?"

She held the carved box out to him.

"What is this?" He took both the chest and the key from her, placed them on the table, and waited for an explanation.

Patrick stared at the box with a sense of foreboding.

"I found this buried in mother's herb garden. Munn showed it to me." She twisted her fingers in the fabric of her skirt.

Placing the small key into the lock, he twisted it. The lock easily fell open. He raised the lid. Documents. Jewels. Coins.

"What is this? Where did it come from?" He thumbed through the papers then raised his gaze to his sister, desperate for her to deny his fear.

She sighed. "Da's papers. Your betrothal agreement is among them."

He shuffled through the pages, searching for that all-important one. Finding the document bearing his father's signature and seal, he narrowed his eyes. He wanted to deny what he saw. It couldn't be. It wasn't possible. His father wouldn't have signed an agreement without first discussing the consequences with him.

Patrick swallowed hard. He'd been away for a long time, only returning after his parents' disappearance. Still, his father wouldn't have been this calculating or this manipulative or this devious.

Patrick continued to stare at the parchment in disbelief. His chest burned. "Please leave me. I need to consider this," he said in a voice rough with emotion.

Elspeth gave him a tremulous smile and left him alone.

He paced the floor, unable to believe the unwelcome turn of events. He returned to the worktable and picked up the condemning paper. Holding the document in unsteady hands, he glared at the offensive sheet.

"Patrick!"

He startled and shot an angry glower at his uncle. How dare the man intrude on his privacy, barging into the chamber without knocking?

Donald glanced from Patrick's face to the parchment in his hand. "What have you there?" He grabbed the document. "You have found the agreement. Now you ken your duty. You will wed Isobell Lamont. Give up this notion of yours to wed the outlander." His voice rose, charged with excitement.

Commotion outside the door caused Patrick to pivot and stare. Lamont pushed past a startled Duncan, Maclay with him, and burst into the chamber. Lamont gloated, his lips curved in a victorious grin. "You have found the agreement, have you?"

Patrick smoothed his features and impassively gazed at the man. "Aye. The agreement, if 'tis real, has been found."

"He kens his duty." Donald handed the document to Lamont. "Sit. 'Tis time to discuss the final terms of this betrothal." He smiled broadly.

Duncan and Stephen stood outside the door, mouths agape, knives in hand, ready for a fight. Patrick inclined his head, and Duncan closed his mouth and the door. He would remain outside with the somber Stephen to stand guard while awaiting Patrick's next command. At least he knew he could trust his men.

Patrick didn't dare show a hint of weakness. He forced his expression to remain blank though he seethed on the inside, and turned to his *guests*. "Please sit and find comfort."

The three other men sat.

"Sit, lad," Donald said, his voice laced with triumph.

"I prefer to stand." Patrick loomed over his uncle, hoping to make the man uncomfortable.

Donald remained unfazed and addressed the financial details. Patrick grunted at the appropriate times but refused to actively participate.

Trapped. His mind whirled. There must be a way out of this mess. He should refuse to uphold the agreement.

Nae. He couldn't dishonor his father's wishes. If in fact, it was his father's signature on the document. How could it be? Ach! He couldn't risk war. He didn't want any more of the clan's deaths on his conscience.

Deep in thought, he barely caught the insanity Lamont spewed.

"Repeat that," Patrick demanded.

"Malcolm has graciously offered to take the outlander whore off your hands and forget the affronts you've inflicted upon him. He is even willing to marry the wench."

"Over my dead body!"

"That can be arranged." Malcolm lunged from his seat.

Lamont grabbed Malcolm, and Donald caught Patrick in a bear hug from behind. Lamont cleared his throat. "We'll leave you to consider our proposal."

"Release me." Patrick struggled against his uncle's hold.

"Take control of yourself, lad," Donald whispered near his ear before easing his grip.

Patrick shrugged from his hold and opened the door. Duncan and Stephen jerked to attention from where they leaned against the wall. "Are you in need?"

"See to the comfort of our guests." Patrick kept his voice even, but anger clawed at his insides.

"Aye, chief." Duncan shared a sharp look with Stephen. His men knew what to do. They'd escort Lamont and his henchman to a bedchamber on the upper floor and keep a keen eye on both men for the remainder of their stay at Castle Lachlan.

Lamont pushed Maclay past Patrick and into the passageway.

Patrick turned his scowl on his uncle as soon as the other two men were gone. "You could not leave it alone, could you, old man? You had to forge this agreement."

Not offended in the least, his uncle shrugged. He brushed a piece of lint from his *plaide*.

"You cannae prove 'tis not real." Donald stepped toward the door and paused, his face split by a smile of victory. "You can believe what you wish, but you cannae prove the document false."

Patrick slumped into the nearest chair as soon as his uncle left. Being forced into marriage with Isobell made him impotent. He rubbed an ache near his heart. They'd successfully maneuvered him into an impossible position. He had no choice but to acquiesce to Lamont's demands.

However, he refused, in no uncertain terms, to the proposed betrothal between Laurie and Malcolm Maclay. That bastard sat through the entire negotiations, watching Patrick with a smug expression on his repulsive, scarred face. The man's audacity made Patrick's temper boil.

Saint Columba help him, he wouldn't allow Laurie to wed Maclay. He'd never agree to such a match for the woman he wanted for his own. The thought of her with another man was more than he could bear.

And the thought of her with Maclay sickened him.

He'd go to her. Explain things. Persuade her to stay and be his mistress. She'd have to understand. He'd make her understand it was the only way for him to protect her.

With the agreement in hand, he left the study. His pace was slow as he climbed the stairs to his bedchamber. He dreaded telling Laurie he was to break his pledge. His honor was offended, as was his heart.

When he arrived, he found the door ajar.

Duncan stood guard outside Elspeth's solar, a short way from the suite of rooms Lamont and Maclay shared. Stephen was in position in an alcove near the stairs.

As Duncan expected, it wasn't long before the suite door opened and Maclay stepped out into the passageway. He glanced in both directions. Seeing Duncan, he grinned. Then he turned the other way and headed for the stairs.

Duncan fell in behind him. "Maclay. Where are you off to?"

Maclay stopped and glanced over his shoulder. Taking in Duncan's threatening pose, he stiffened and placed his hand on the hilt of his sword. "My chief wishes to send a messenger to fetch the Lady Isobell and her guard. I go to see to it." He tilted his head toward the door he'd come from. "Or are we prisoners in that chamber?"

"Nae. You enjoy the hospitality of the MacLachlan Chief." Duncan didn't try to hide his contempt.

"Then I will continue on my way. I am sure MacLachlan would want his future bride secured within his keep." He laughed and walked along the corridor. He stopped short when Stephen stepped from the alcove in front of him.

"MacEwen." Maclay inclined his head in acknowledgement.

"Maclay," Stephen returned.

They faced off. Stephen raised a brow, smiled crookedly, and stepped back, allowing Maclay to pass.

The cur briskly brushed by and hurried down the stairs. Duncan followed and gave Stephen a nod as he passed. He and Stephen agreed earlier that Stephen would keep watch on Lamont and Duncan would track Maclay should the need arise.

The great hall was crowded and noisy with the addition of the Lamont lads. Maclay made his way through the crush of warriors to a table where some of his men drank ale.

Duncan sidestepped a serving maid.

Donald MacLachlan, along with some of his drunken lads, waylaid him. "Where you off to, lad?"

Duncan tried to brush past.

"Here, here, dinnae run off," Donald said. "Have a tankard of ale with us. We celebrate my nephew's upcoming nuptials."

One of the warriors handed Duncan a tankard and shoved him into the center of the group. Declining would be interpreted as an act of disrespect to his chief.

He drank several toasts while trying to keep track of Maclay.

By the time Duncan pulled free of the merrymakers, Maclay slipped out of view. Duncan searched the hall.

Maclay was gone.

Sunlight from the un-shuttered window touched Laurie yet didn't warm her. She'd fled to Patrick's bedchamber earlier, after Lamont and his men gained entrance to the castle. Patrick thought it best, fearing for her safety. They never learned who attacked her in Glasgow.

Lamont's men were suspect.

She shivered and glanced up from her needlework. Patrick stood in the open doorway, his expression grim. Her insides twisted. Something must be wrong.

He moved swiftly across the room to kneel at her feet. Wrapping his arms around her waist, he laid his head on her lap.

"What is it? Whatever is the matter?" She stroked his thick hair, loving the silky feel of the chestnut strands as they slipped through her fingers.

He raised his head to gaze at her through darkened eyes, a forlorn expression on his features. "I have come from a council with Iain Lamont and my Uncle Donald. A betrothal agreement between my father and Lamont has been found. I dinnae believe 'tis my da's signature, yet his seal is on the document."

She tensed. "What are you saying?"

"They are forcing me to wed Isobell and break my promise to you."

Laurie swallowed uneasily, a multitude of unpleasant emotions rushing through her.

Patrick stood and paced across the chamber then faced her. "I ken my duty, but I cannae give you up. I came here to tell you and beg you stay as my mistress, but I cannae bear burdening you as such. I cannae marry Isobell."

"I…" She didn't know what to say.

"Pack some things. We leave. We shall sneak away and wed. Then 'twill be too late for them to stop us."

Laurie bit her lip. An awkward silence made time seem to

stand still. Finally, she shook her head. "I won't be the cause of a war or permit you to dishonor yourself. I can't allow you to marry me and risk the welfare of your clan. You must agree to the terms of the betrothal agreement with Iain Lamont. You'll have to marry his daughter, Isobell. Not me." Her voice cracked. Tears burned the back of her eyes, but she refused to shed them.

Patrick came to kneel before her again. He gazed at her with the saddest expression she'd ever seen. She hated the anguish in his gorgeous blue eyes. It matched the ache in her heart.

"It's for the best," she lied. "I don't belong here. I'll return to the future."

"Nae, you must not."

She needed to convince him.

She loved him. She must protect him.

"I believe I've guessed the secret to the time travel gateway. I think it has something to do with the phases of the moon. On the night I traveled here, a full moon glowed overhead. I believe if I'm on the faerie knoll on the full moon, I'll go forward in time."

"I will not allow you to take such a risk." Patrick gave her upper arms a quick squeeze.

"There's to be a full moon tomorrow night. I must go to the Fir-wood and try to return to my own time." She wiped a single teardrop from her cheek with the back of her hand. "And you must wed Isobell."

"I cannae let you go." Moisture glistened in his eyes and his voice strained. "I beg you to stay with me and be my mistress. I vow to be good to you, to ensure you want for naught." His lips curved as he tried to smile with little success. "You once offered to be my mistress."

"I was wrong when I made the offer. I could never be any man's mistress, especially not yours."

Patrick's eyes widened, as if she'd slapped him.

"Please understand. It would kill me to watch with Isobell, knowing she was the mother of your children. That I was nothing more than your whore. Besides, it's a sin."

She gently placed her hand on his cheek. He didn't pull away. He just stared at her. As if he tried to see into the core of her being.

Laurie inhaled his masculine pine scent. She closed her eyes, making a memory. The way he felt in her arms and the taste of his kiss. The midnight blue of his eyes and his smile and the alluring cleft in his chin. She opened her eyes again and gazed into the depths of his. If she continued along this path, she'd be lost.

She glanced away and mentally shook herself. "Don't misunderstand. I shall always love you. But I need to go home to my own time and place, to the world that I understand. Where I'm safe."

"Nae. Please, dinnae leave me. I'll be the man you want me to be."

She placed a finger against his lips to silence him. "Then marry Isobell."

Patrick pulled away. He ran his fingers through his thick hair, getting them caught in snarls. Ripping them free, he said, "My mind understands your logic, but not my heart. Is there nary a way I can persuade you to stay by my side?"

Laurie shook her head again. "I must go. Please, have Duncan take me to the Fir-wood tomorrow evening."

Patrick stood and once again strode across the chamber, stopping at the window to stare out. "I cannae allow it," he said, his voice firm. "'Tis too dangerous. Faerie magic can be perilous. You dinnae ken where you would find yourself. There would be nary a soul to protect you."

He hesitated for a moment, as if he reined in his emotions. When he faced her again, his features hardened.

What would be the best argument? Getting to the Fir-wood would be a hell of a lot easier with Patrick's help.

"There is another solution, little I like it. I will find you a husband and see that you are well cared for. Someone I can trust to be good to you."

Laurie felt like she'd been gut punched. He wanted to find

her a husband? Her shock morphed into red-hot anger. "How dare you?"

"I dare much, as you ken." Patrick strode from the room, his hands in tight fists.

"Get back here," Laurie called after him. "Don't you dare walk out on me."

No way in hell was she wedding someone chosen by Patrick MacLachlan. She threw her needlework across the room. Damn the man.

If she couldn't have Patrick then she was going home.

Laurie jumped from her chair and ran into the passageway after him, but he was gone. She stormed through the corridor toward the east wing, talking to herself. "How dare he, the arrogant jerk."

Someone roughly grabbed her from behind and slapped a filthy hand over her mouth. *Not again.* Her spine tingled with fear.

CHAPTER TWENTY-SEVEN

*P*atrick made his way to his private chamber, feeling as if he carried a heavy rock within his chest. He found it difficult to breath. How would he give Laurie to another man?

Jamie waited by the door with a lad whose garments still carried the dust of travel. "This is Peter. The Glasgow goldsmith sent him."

"Have you my wee jewels?" Patrick asked, no longer caring.

"Aye." The lad patted the large purse he wore at his waist and followed Patrick into the chamber while Jamie remained outside the door to stand guard.

Patrick sat at his worktable. Peter placed two small leather pouches on the table before him. Picking up the first pouch, Patrick tugged on the strings and dropped the cloth-covered contents onto the surface. He unraveled the soft linen with hands that trembled much more than he'd have liked. He inhaled sharply and hardened his heart for what was to come.

Patrick smoothed the cloth on the table. The beautiful sapphire ring sat in the center, glistening in the flickering candlelight. He held his breath.

The betrothal token would have been lovely on Laurie's dainty finger.

With a sigh, he reached for the second pouch, opened it slowly, and removed its cloth-wrapped contents. He placed the small package on the table and pushed aside the cloth. Picking up the delicate piece of jewelry, he reverently held it in the palm of his large work-hardened hand. A pain like none he'd ever experienced tightened his chest as his heart splintered into tiny pieces.

"Thank your master for sending these. They are exquisite," he said, the words thick in his throat. He rewrapped the piece in its cloth and placed it in the pouch. Then he reached for the purse at his belt, removed a sum of coins and handed them to the messenger.

"Jamie," Patrick yelled. "Take the lad to the kitchen for a meal before you send him on his way." Dismissing the two men from his thoughts, he fingered the ring. Patrick dreaded the day he'd place Laurie's ring on the finger of cold Isobell.

"How could Elspeth have been wrong?" he demanded of the silence.

Donald lay on the floor atop the young woman's crumpled clothing, hidden behind the storage barrels cluttering the room. Dim light from a small window above allowed him to watch her at her labors. Blood rushed through his veins and throbbed in his cock.

Pressure built. He thrust, his hands pressed against the back of her head. She took him deeper. Good. The whore was good, very good. He rode the crest of release.

His heart thundered. His blood raged. He shot his seed with an explosion of intense pleasure.

Pushing her away, he grinned with satisfaction. She swallowed, wiping her mouth with the back of her hand. The wench smiled seductively. Believed she held him by the balls. She was naught but a pawn.

The door burst open, banging heavily against the wall.

Donald grabbed the whore and hauled her back against him. He slapped his hand over her mouth, warning her to silence.

Laurie was dragged into the semi-darkness of a storage room. She clawed at the large hand clamped over her mouth, but was quickly subdued when he used his body to force her roughly against the wall. *Not again. Oh God, not again.*

It was the same man. She knew it instinctively. She tried to fight him, the attempt futile. His weight pressed hard against her, the ridge of his sex stabbing at her belly.

She gasped at the cold steel blade skimming her face.

"I will scar your tender cheek. Make it look like mine if you struggle or make a sound," he said in a low, harsh voice.

Blinking, she went perfectly still. She recognized her captor, his ugly face close to hers in the dim light provided by the small window high on the back wall.

She nodded several times.

"Wise lass, you are." The knife disappeared.

Her breath came in and out, hard and fast, her heart beating furiously against her chest. Yet she remained perfectly still. A cold chill ran down her spine and bile burned her throat.

He pulled her peasant blouse down over her shoulders exposing her breasts, barely hidden beneath the thin linen of her chemise. He stared at her in the dim light, pressing against her. Her terror thrilled the bastard. His twisted smile depicted pure evil.

She cringed. Though it might be foolish and even dangerous to try to stop him, her mind raced. How could she escape without getting cut?

She inhaled a deep breath, trying to take a firm hold on her fear.

He cupped a large rough hand over one of her breasts, squeezing it painfully as he took her mouth, thrusting his tongue between her lips, forcing entry. She shuddered with revulsion.

He ravaged her mouth, his possession choking her,

bruising her. He tasted foul. Unable to pull away from his tight grip, her panic mounted. *Oh God, this can't be happening, not to me.*

Abruptly, he released her and the sharp blade was at her throat with enough pressure to cause a tiny puncture. She felt a trickle of blood slide down her neck. She tried to scream, but no sound came from her dry throat.

He lessened the pressure on the blade. "You will agree to the marriage proposal Lamont offers for you. You will wed with me or your lover will die." He released her suddenly.

She tried for his balls, but missed and slammed her knee into his upper thigh.

He slapped her hard, and her head hit the wall, stunning her. "Feisty wench. I look forward to breaking you." He grinned then backed out of the storage room.

Laurie slumped against the wall and slid to the floor. Tremors wracked her body. *Oh God, what will I do?*

She swallowed hard. Straightening her clothing, she inhaled several breaths to calm herself. She stood on shaky legs, made her way to the door and peeked into the passageway. No one was there. She darted to her room on rubbery legs.

She needed to go home.

Donald and his woman lay silent for several minutes. "Get dressed." He pushed the whore away.

He watched her shimmy into her gown, her movements meant to entice. Her voluptuous assets no longer made him hard. He'd more important matters on his mind.

"I have another task for you." She smiled wickedly and slid the gown from her shoulder. "Cover yourself. I refer to your other skills."

She pouted, but when he said no more, her eyes narrowed. "What will you give me?"

"Are you not satisfied with what I have already given you?"

"Bah."

Donald jiggled the purse at his waist and the whore smiled. She wet her lips. "What do you want me to do?"

He leaned close and told her.

She nodded, eager to do whatever he requested. Surely, she already felt his coins in her pocket.

Dirty. Violated.

Laurie sat on the large bed in Patrick's bedchamber.

Pushing up from the mattress, she walked to the mantel and poured wine from a flagon into a mug that sat there. She rinsed her mouth with the sweet liquid and spit it into the washing bowl. With a shudder, she poured water from the pitcher on the washstand onto a cloth and carefully scrubbed the dried blood from her neck. She applied more pressure to the cloth, scrubbing her chest until the skin became raw. Could she ever scrub hard enough to wash the filth of Maclay's evil touch from her skin?

Laurie paced the length of the room. She must leave. Make her own way to Fir-wood and try to return home. She had to get away from these barbarians.

Deep in her heart, she understood she'd never be the same again. She would never love another man as she did Patrick. But she couldn't stay in this dangerous place. And she certainly couldn't risk what might happen to Patrick if she told him about Maclay.

Fear fueled her anger. She hated being a victim, making her all-the-more determined to escape. She'd find a way to get to Fir-wood and attempt to return to the twenty-first century on her own.

What would she do if the time gate didn't work this time?

She couldn't worry about failure now. If she did, she'd fall apart. She'd worry about it later, if and when the time came.

A soft tapping sounded. Swallowing her anxiety, Laurie scooted across the room. "Who's there?" she asked.

"M'lady, may I speak with you." Laurie hesitated at the

unfamiliar voice. She chewed on the edge of her lip, uncertain. "What do you want?"

"I must speak with you. Please."

Laurie opened the door a crack. A young serving woman stood in the passageway. Laurie narrowed her eyes, having seen this woman before. She was the buxom brunette, who the other evening sat on Donald MacLachlan's lap, giggling, while he fondled her breasts in front of everyone in the hall.

The woman darted nervous looks up and down the passageway and then back at Laurie. "Please, m'lady, I am Moira. Mayhap I could come in? I need to speak to you in private."

Laurie stepped back from the door, and waved the young woman in. Moira again peered in both directions before entering the chamber and closing the door behind her.

Several shocking minutes later, Moira left. Laurie sank to the bed, staring blankly at the stone wall.

Later in the evening, Patrick sent a meal to her with orders she was not to leave the bedchamber. He thought it best she dine alone, hidden away while Lamont and his warriors were in the castle. At least that was the message she received from the lad who delivered the food.

How considerate.

All she had to do was glance at the food and her stomach rolled. She stepped away from the table and peered out the window into the gloom.

After several minutes, she walked to the door and tried the lever, even though she was sure she'd find it barred from the outside. To her amazement, the heavy oak door opened. She peered out and looked both ways along the passage.

No one lingered. No one guarded her chamber. Where was Duncan?

Well, there was probably no longer any need for her to have a guard since Patrick would soon wed Isobell. Laurie would miss Duncan, the big, burly teddy bear, when she was gone.

She waited for what seemed like hours for Moira to

return. Pacing and sitting. Pacing again. The castle was eerily quiet. Eventually, she heard what she waited for, the soft tap at her door.

Laurie greeted Moira. The young woman carried a coarse, dark-colored cape, similar to the one she wore herself, which she helped Laurie don over her traveling clothes. They pulled hoods up over their heads, hiding their faces within the folds of heavy material.

"We must hurry, m'lady," Moira whispered, taking her by the hand. They crept down the passage to the circular stairs.

The usually well-lit passageway was dim. How had the girl managed to find her way? Laurie tried to tread as softly as possible. Moira was as quiet as a mouse, sneaking along the shadows in silence, leading her back to the storage room, the place of the attack. Laurie trembled as she followed the girl into the room. Was she out of her mind to trust her?

Moira showed Laurie a hidden trap door.

"Outside is a stair, which will take you to the beach."

Laurie stood motionless, her hand pressed against the wooden door. Fear tightened her gut. She didn't want to leave, hated the idea of never seeing Patrick again. The thought almost paralyzed her. She couldn't allow the weakness to rule her though. She had to go.

When she finally managed to push the door open and step through, a cold, damp breeze hit her face. Shutting the door, she leaned back against the rough wood, her heart pounding so fast she thought she'd have a panic attack.

In reality, only dread twisted her gut. She waited another moment, unsure if she were doing the right thing. Swallowing her fear, she descended the stairs, crossed the grassy bank, and slipped into the shadowy thicket along the edge of the beach.

Duncan spent the better part of the evening searching the castle and grounds, trying to find Maclay. To his dismay, he always seemed to miss the man. He heard from others that

Maclay sent the messenger to Toward Keep. Since then, no one had seen him.

Where was he?

Duncan made his way to the suite Lamont and Maclay shared. Shadows slid across the stone wall. Two short, furtive figures crept along the passageway. He hid until they passed then stealthily followed them to the storage room. Leaning against the opposite wall, arms crossed over his chest, he guarded the door they'd entered. Pursing his lips, he waited, expecting to catch a couple of servants thieving.

The wait wasn't long. One of the cloaked figures emerged.

Duncan reached out his hand and grabbed the individual by the shoulder. Her softness gave her away. He held a woman.

She trembled. "Please sir, dinnae hurt me. He forced me."

Duncan shook the woman and the hood of her cape fell, revealing her face. Moira. Donald's whore. "What mischief are you about? Are you thieving or whoring this night? Where is your other wee friend?"

She stared at him, eyes wide.

"Who forced you to do what? Tell me," he demanded, shaking her again.

"To…to send the Lady Laurie away."

"Cursed wench." Duncan tossed the woman aside. "I will deal with you later." He entered the dark storage room. The trap door hung open. He stepped out, bracing against the chill breeze.

At the water's edge, three bulky figures huddled near a *currach*. One hurried away.

Duncan had descended several steps when a petite figure joined the two remaining near the boat.

Lady Laurie? He leapt the remaining steps and ran for the beach.

Dense clouds covered the moon tonight. Laurie needed to reach the faerie knoll before tomorrow night's full moon. She stood perfectly still, allowing her eyes to adjust. She shivered from the cold and pulled the heavy cloak tighter, cautiously making her way through the dark and dreary night to the beach.

Two short men, heavily muscled, with lots of straggly hair covering their heads and faces waited for her. She didn't recognize them from among Patrick's fighting men. They must be his uncle's men.

She hesitated, wishing she could turn back.

This was the only way. She had to go with the men even though they gave her the creeps.

Laurie had accepted Uncle Donald's assistance and told Moira she wanted escort to the Fir-wood. Moira said the men would escort her across the bay and provide her with a horse. After she reached Fir-wood, she'd be on her own. She only needed to be in their presence for a short time.

She wouldn't be able to find the wood without their guidance.

The men did little more than grunt at her. Laurie inhaled a deep breath, reining in her anxiety and allowed one of the men to assist her into the small boat. She cringed and rubbed her palm on her cloak, repulsed by the scabby feel of his hand. She swallowed her distaste and sat on the bench he indicated.

The two men jumped aboard and busied themselves. Talk about claustrophobia. And they smelled raunchy. She buried her nose within the fabric of her hood.

They pushed away from shore and into the bay. Laurie glanced back at the castle, at the light shining in Patrick's study. She wiped away the single tear that slipped from a stinging eye. Her heart was breaking. She wished she could have at least said goodbye.

Apprehension pulsed through Laurie's veins, her heart pounding a rapid beat. The two hulking men remained silent, the slapping of the oars against the water the only sound. The rhythmic repetition grated on her nerves.

She stared into the darkness, her anxiety growing. It was

taking much longer than it should. The clouds cleared the moon, creating a silver glow on the water, but she still couldn't see the shore. She was sure they should have reached the mainland beach by now.

Panic set in. She twisted to question one of the men and something hard struck the back of her head. She fell to the side. The boat swayed. Her world went fuzzy.

"You fool! Why did you do that?"

"The lass moved about, agitated like. The laird paid good coin for her. He would nae want her to fall overboard. At least not afore he has his way with her."

"He will likely drown her hisself afterward."

Both men guffawed, continuing to row. Laurie fought the darkness enveloping her. She needed to get away from these men. They weren't here to help her get away. She got her hands under her, but couldn't lift her weight. The gray at the edges of her vision crept closer.

Patrick, what have I done?

Gray turned to black.

CHAPTER TWENTY-EIGHT

Present Day, Anderson Creek, North Carolina

Finn stared, fixated on the antique claymore hanging on the wall over the checkout counter. Fine hairs at the nape of his neck hummed with static electricity. No matter where he stood in the *Celtic Image* shop, the sword grabbed his attention and held on like a tenacious nuclear-altered vine from a classic B-movie, pulling him ever closer.

"Can I help you?"

When he tried to tear his gaze from the blade to respond, Finn's pulse sped up and he panted as if he worked through reps at the gym. He couldn't look away from the large moonstone in the center of the cross. He took a step forward and reached for it.

"Sir?" The sharp voice snapped Finn out of the hypnotic fugue and he let his arm drop.

"I want to buy that claymore," he said before realizing his intention.

"Who says it's for sale?" The kilted, big guy—at least five inches taller than Finn's six-foot-two height and slightly broader built—quirked a brow and gave Finn the one-two with a long glance.

"I must have it."

"Do you know how to use a sword?"

"I did a bit of fencing in the military, but I've never handled a claymore."

The man silently studied Finn. Minutes passed. "Here's the deal. I'll consider selling the piece to you if you hire me to instruct you on how to fight with the weapon."

"When can we start?"

Something akin to approval flashed in the man's eyes and his lips curled slightly up on one side. He strode to the door, locked the handle, and flipped the cardboard sign hanging in the window from open to closed. When he returned to Finn, he held out a hand. "Douglas McKinnon."

"Finn MacIntyre." He grasped the man's hand—firm handshake coupled with solid eye contact. Good man. You could judge a lot about a man from his handshake.

Douglas took the sword from its rack and two-handed it over. "Shall we step outside?"

Finn followed him through a storeroom full of Scottish weaponry—claymores, broadswords and targes, dirks, and a Lochaber axe or two—into a large dirt courtyard behind the *Celtic Image* and *Baked Potato* shops fitted out like medieval lists. Or what Finn believed medieval lists would look like.

"Give me the sword. I'll show you two ways to grip it. Which is your stronger hand?"

"Right." Finn hesitated not wanting to give up possession of the two-handed sword, but finally relinquished his hold on the weapon. He rubbed his chest, feeling angst he didn't understand. He wanted to grab the sword back. He hated seeing it in the other man's hands.

Douglas narrowed his eyes then started the lesson without commenting on Finn's reluctance. "Space your hands as you would on an axe handle with your right hand under the cross guard and the left just above the pommel like so." Douglas demonstrated. "With the second grip, the forefinger of your right hand will be locked over the cross guard thusly."

Douglas returned the sword, and the moonstone in its center winked in the sunlight. Finn inhaled deeply surprised by the intensity of relief he felt with the claymore's cold steel in his hands again.

"Once you practice the grips we'll move on to the guards. I'll teach you where to place your body and feet for the best footwork execution. Then we'll discuss the positioning of the weapon to facilitate successful attacks and defense."

"Sounds good."

"What the—" The man's eyes widened and he spun on his heel and stared into the narrow alley between the two shops to the street.

"Is something wrong?" Finn asked.

"No. Let's continue." Douglas turned back, gripped the sword, and moved one of Finn's hands to a better position. Then his gaze slid back to the alley and he frowned.

Caitrina tensed. Douglas couldn't possibly know she was hidden in the alley watching. She'd covered herself in an extra thick cloak of invisibility. There was no way he could sense her presence. Mortals didn't have such a gift.

Then why was he staring right at her?

To make matters worse, she felt a tremor of fae energy charge the air.

Caitrina grabbed her head over her ears as pain pierced her skull.

"I forbid you to use the MacIntyre warrior before his training is complete."

The queen's words bored a hole in her forehead and Caitrina nearly lost hold of her glamour. Douglas narrowed his eyes and took a couple of steps into the alley. Caitrina concentrated hard, caught a wisp of a breeze, and vanished through time.

CHAPTER TWENTY-NINE

Strathlachlan

"Lady Laurie!"

She heard her name through the thick fog clouding her brain. She made a halfhearted effort to open her eyes, but it was too difficult. It was easier to stay as she was—half asleep.

The man's voice sounded far away, yet she sensed he was near.

"Lady Laurie, wake up," demanded the harsh, masculine voice.

Someone shook her. Why would anyone do such a thing? And why did her head hurt so much? She made a soft moaning noise, annoyed the voice added to her misery, magnifying the pain already thumping in her head.

"Lass, wake."

The insistent tone of the voice finally penetrated her fuzzy mind. She forced her eyes open, only to find Duncan hovering over her, his facial features taut.

"I'm awake." She tried to swat him away. "Leave me alone."

He forced her to sit against a nearby tree. "How badly are you hurt?"

"Hurt?" Laurie squeezed her eyes shut against the bright light assaulting her. "Oh…my head, I think. What are you doing here? Why are you in my room?"

She opened her eyes a slit while gingerly rubbing the bump on the back of her head with a trembling hand. The feel of sand in her hair surprised her. Bringing her hand around to the front of her face, she stared at it. Moist sand covered her fingers.

"Your room? Dinnae you ken you were kidnapped by two men and dumped on this beach?" Duncan's voice grew sharper with each word. He scanned the area. "I fear someone may be watching us. I dinnae ken why those men left you here. I have a feeling they will come back for you."

"What are you talking about?"

"This might be part of an elaborate trap. We need to get you to the safety of the castle."

Bright morning sunlight pierced Laurie's eyes. She groaned and shut them tight. Then it hit her. The men were supposed to take her across the bay to where horses waited. Then they were to escort her to the hut near the Fir-wood. They must have knocked her out instead and deserted her here. But why?

"How did you find me? Donald's men were to take me away so I could go to Fir-wood and find my way home. Why did they hit me? Why did they leave me here?"

"To France? From Fir-wood? Your injury must be verra serious if you think you can get to France from the Fir-wood. On a horse, nae less. And those men, they were nae MacLachlans, at least none loyal to the chief. Why were you with them to begin with?"

The fierceness of his voice made Laurie cringe. She sat a little straighter and took a good look around. They were at the edge of a beach somewhere, but she didn't recognize any of the landmarks. Somewhat embarrassed she'd gotten herself into this mess, she nervously looked at Duncan. "Where are we?"

"At the head of the loch. Took me the whole of the night

to find you. 'Twill take us the whole of the day to return to Castle Lachlan."

"How did you find me?" Laurie asked.

He gave her a severe scowl. "I was walking along the passageway when I saw two wee shadowy figures enter the storage room and only one come out. I confronted Moira and she told me you ran away. Why would that be, lass?"

"You know as well as everyone else at the castle. Patrick will wed Isobell Lamont. I must leave."

"Nae, lass, you belong to the chief. Nae matter what happens, you are one of us now."

If only that were the truth, but it wasn't. She was right to leave. Now she must convince Duncan to take her to the Firwood before the full moon set this evening and she lost this chance to return home. She didn't want to contemplate what would happen if she had to wait for the next full moon.

Laurie fluttered her eyelashes, giving him her best smile. Then she winced from the pain throbbing at her temples.

He shook his head. "You are a handful."

Shrugging, she gazed off over the hills. "How far are we from Fir-wood?"

He thought for a moment. "Not far. Less than a day's walk, nae more. Why do you ask? You are not thinking of going there?"

Slowly, Laurie stood. She stumbled at first, but caught her balance. The sand itched and she brushed it from her skin and straightened to her full height. "We'd best get started."

"Nae, we will not go to Fir-wood. We will return to the castle in yonder *currach*." Duncan glared. "And the chief can put you over his knee again and beat some sense into you."

"Now Duncan, you know Patrick will marry Isobell. Where will that leave me?" She raised her hands.

"You are one of us now. The chief will see to you."

"No, he won't. Point me in the right direction. I'll go to Fir-wood on my own. I need to arrive there before the moon sets." Laurie glanced toward the tree line, where several paths entered the woods. Which way was the right direction?

"Lady Laurie—"

She spun to face Duncan. "Tell me!"

He gaped. Closing his mouth, he tightened his lips into a taut line and gave her a hard look. "Do you plan to go to the faerie knoll again?"

"Yeah. I need to go there in order to return to my home." She gave him her best smile, pleading with her eyes and lips, hoping to coax him. She'd no qualms about using feminine charm.

He narrowed his eyes then his mouth fell open again. "You sprouted wings!" His eyes widened. "Are you one of the faeries?"

"What?" She glanced over her shoulder. "What are you talking about?"

"I saw golden wings." He frowned. "Now they are gone. Are you a faerie?"

She should tell him he was crazy. But...

She hated to deceive him, to play on his ignorance, on his superstition. However, this was an emergency. She crossed her fingers behind her back. "Yes, I am. I've lost my way. I need your help to return to the faerie knoll to find my way again."

He stepped back and shook his head.

"Will you help me? Please." She smiled and bated her eyelashes.

He scanned the beach with a fierce frown. "This is deeply troubling. The faeries are a power to reckon with."

An understatement. She prayed Caitrina didn't catch wind of what she planned and stop her.

"If I dinnae help you, your brethren will likely cause havoc and devastate MacLachlan lands," he continued.

Laurie lowered her head and gazed at him through her lashes.

"Where is Munn when trouble is afoot?" he mumbled.

She kept smiling at him, hoping he would cave.

With hands on hips, he glared at her. "I will take you. But I dinnae like it."

He glanced toward the water, and back at Laurie. "Wait here." He walked to the shore's edge and pulled the *currach* up higher onto the beach and into the woods, covering it with brush to hide it. He returned to her, still mumbling to himself under his breath. "I ken I will regret this decision to get mixed up in matters of the *Sithichean*."

Laurie hid her triumphant smile behind her hand. He truly was a sweet teddy bear.

She'd miss him once she was safe at home.

Munn applauded himself. He'd frightened off the northern men, and spent the whole of the night guiding Duncan's small boat without the lad being the wiser. Munn grinned, relieved to see the pair on their way. For if they dallied, Maclay's men would surely find the two.

He snickered. The warriors from the northern clan would be angry when they learned they lost their prize.

The chief won't like it, but Munn needed to make certain the lady from the future returned to the future, to where she belonged. That was the only way he could ensure she and the chief stayed apart, enabling Munn to keep his vow to the faerie queen. He just needed to make sure Duncan got her to the Fir-wood before the full moon set. Until then, he'd keep Maclay's men from finding her. Then she'd be gone.

And he'd be free once again to serve his chief.

Setting off to foil the Maclay men's pursuit, he lost control of his body, pulled by an incredibly strong force in another direction. He fought the unknown power with all his strength, but it was too much for him. He spun out of control, whirling through the veil of time and space.

Laurie and Duncan walked for most of the morning, only stopping briefly for water at a narrow burn, a small crystal-clear stream bubbling through the rocks. They'd just set off again and were cutting across a field when the sound of galloping horses thundered.

A hooded horseman rode from a trail in the woods in front of them, swinging a battle-axe. Another rider followed the first. Others on foot came from behind, carrying wooden staffs and other makeshift weapons.

"Maclays!" Duncan pulled her behind him, his claymore at the ready. He never got a chance to swing his large sword. The first horse charged him, knocking him to the ground where his head hit against a rock.

Laurie screamed as she barely fell out of the way of the horse's hoofs. She managed to get back on her feet and ran in terror.

Her attempt to escape was useless. The men quickly surrounded her. She screamed, and screamed, and screamed. It didn't matter. No friend would hear her. Duncan lay unconscious, or possibly dead.

The leering men encircled her, playing a game of cat and mouse. They taunted and teased, poked at her with their staffs, grabbed at her hair and clothing. She twirled around kicking out.

One large man caught her. She wildly fought him off, using her arms and legs until something hard hit the side of her head. Blinded by a bright explosion of light, she fell.

Munn managed to break away from the force that controlled him, materializing atop a limb of a tall oak. He watched the scene play out with disbelief. He failed again. Gripping his hands into tight fists, he grimaced. He was too late. He wasn't strong enough to interfere. He was helpless to stop the flow of events.

He'd have to go to the queen and inform her. How would he explain this debacle?

Not only might she condemn him to an eternity in the *Sands of Time*. He'd heard stories. She might choose to torture him, causing unbearable pain and then imprison his soul in a jar, leaving him a shell of a body.

He sat for a while fretting over what he'd tell Oonagh. Completely self-absorbed, he was unaware of Caitrina's presence until she shimmered, emerging into solid form to sit beside him on the thick limb.

He tensed.

"What have you done, you foolish meddling brownie?" Caitrina demanded before he said or did anything.

How dare the halfling question him?

"Naught!" he said. "I did only good. I brought Duncan to watch over the lass from the future."

"And look what happened."

"You can fix everything. Send her back where she came from. She does not belong here."

Caitrina tried to control her nasty fae temper. He could see it in her stubborn eyes. "Why didn't you stop this from happening?" she asked in a deceptively calm, cool voice.

"I couldn't. You used your power against me." He fisted his hands at his waist. "You pulled me away. You ken I floated in endless time before you released me."

"Not I."

"Then who?"

"Oonagh," they said in unison.

They glared at one another for several minutes before they both dissolved into fine dust and scattered with the wind.

Patrick woke, uttering a groan. His head throbbed and his tongue felt thick. He lifted his head from where it had fallen against the hard wood of his worktable and raised his hands to rub his temples. He glared at the empty cask. He'd drunk himself into a fine stupor during the dark hours of the night and must have passed out here in his private chamber.

Loud banging came from outside the door. Squinting against the bright light assaulting him from the un-shuttered window, he groaned again.

"Enter," he thundered, wincing from the pain his own voice caused in his head.

Jamie stepped into the chamber, his eyes darting about.

"What is it?" Patrick growled, grimacing in misery.

"Duncan is missing. We cannae find him anywhere within the castle nor without. I have searched as have several other lads."

"Perhaps he has hidden away with a willing lass," Patrick offered, annoyed he'd been disturbed from his stupor for such foolishness.

"Nae. He was to keep an eye on Malcolm Maclay. Stephen ordered him to do so."

An uncomfortable sensation burned in the pit of Patrick's stomach. "And where is Maclay?"

"Gone."

"Gone?" Patrick held an unsteady hand to his forehead.

"Aye. Lamont swears he doesn't ken where."

Cursing under his breath, Patrick rose from his chair. He ignored the aches and pains racking his body and strode toward Jamie. Then a terrible notion occurred to him. What if Laurie were missing too? He didn't wish to consider that. The thought made him ill. But what if Maclay took her and Duncan had gone after them?

He charged past Jamie, out the door, across the passageway and up two levels to his bedchamber. Jamie's footsteps echoed behind. When Patrick reached the chamber, he forced open the door. The wood slammed hard against the inner wall with an echoing thud.

There was no one there. No one slept in the bed. She was gone.

He raced to Elspeth's solar. His sister glanced up from her needlework and blanched. "What is wrong?"

"Where is Laurie?"

"In her room."

His roar was that of a wounded wild cat, a horrible sound filled with tormented anguish. "Damn them. She is gone." He pushed past Jamie and headed for the stairs. He stopped and looked over his shoulder. "Where is Lamont?"

"Greeting his daughter in the great hall. She arrived with

her maid and her guard."

Patrick thought he'd burst. "Isobell has arrived?" He shouted the question.

"Aye."

Standing motionless, Patrick tried to guess at what was going on. He needed to find out. Had Laurie run from him or did Maclay have her? If Maclay had her, what would the bastard do to her? Patrick didn't want to dwell on that horrifying contemplation.

His anger merged with his fear, forcing his temper to the surface. He bolted for the stairs ready to confront Lamont.

The man had manipulated Patrick and he didn't like it. Not in the least.

He stopped short. He couldn't make accusations without more information. He needed to be careful. Reaching deep inside himself, he sought calm, fought for a warrior's control.

The only way to approach Lamont was with caution.

"Form a search party and see what you can discover. Find Duncan." Patrick ran his hand through his disheveled hair. "And find the Lady Laurie. I beg you."

"We will."

"And, Jamie."

"Aye."

"You might try searching the Fir-wood. The Lady Laurie has a fondness for that eerie place."

Patrick thought he best make himself presentable. He would meet his future bride, be civil to her father, and pretend all was well.

Pretend the woman he loved more than life wasn't missing. Perhaps dead.

The castle wasn't as awful as Isobell expected. The great hall was actually quite lovely. She gazed around the fine chamber, taking in its rich tapestries and carved furniture. The large stone hearth was beautiful, the fire inviting.

Several warriors sat at the lower tables, drinking from

mugs. The MacLachlan men stared at her with ill-disguised contempt.

How dare they? She didn't want to be here anymore than they wanted her to be.

In the past, her father always gave into her demands. Given her whatever she asked for. This time, he refused to even consider her desires. He was determined to wed her to the heartless enemy, her clan's enemy, her enemy.

Patrick MacLachlan. His name alone made her shudder. There had been a time when she believed...

No. She shook her head. That was a long time ago. She'd been a mere child then. Now, she was a full-grown women and betrothed to the much-hated Patrick MacLachlan.

She cast an angry look at her father. She didn't understand how he could be so cruel. MacLachlan would probably kill her. Poison her or do something else dreadful.

The sound of heavy footfalls brought her gaze to the stairs. There he was. She stiffened, her hands balled into tight fists at her side. He might be a fine looking man on the outside, might make many a lass swoon, but she knew he was a horrible monster on the inside with a glaciated heart.

Isobell stood at her father's side, watching MacLachlan stride across the hall toward them, his steps long and sure. He appeared the cold warrior. She felt the blue ice of his dark eyes for a brief moment, and then they dismissed her as if she was insignificant. The MacLachlan directed the chill at her father.

"Lamont, I did not realize your lovely daughter would join us so soon. Our Aine is making ready a chamber in the east wing near that of the Lady Elspeth's as we speak." His frigid stare once again fell upon her.

She couldn't help the shiver creeping down her spine when he took her hand, barely grazing the knuckles with his lips. His touch was like frost skimming across her skin. His lips like ice.

Her heart burned with hatred.

Pulling her hand from his grasp, she glared at her father.

"I will not wed him!"

She moved to leave, but her father grabbed her arm in a painfully tight grip and twisted her back. "Aye, you will, lass. And you will remain here at Castle Lachlan and be Lady MacLachlan."

"If she does not wish to wed with me, there is nae need to force her."

He would let her out of the contract? Hope flared in her heart.

Her father's gaze flew to the MacLachlan. "You will wed as we agreed. She kens my will." He jerked her arm and swung her afore him. "You will do what you are told or you will suffer for your stubbornness."

Her father's gaze was unrelenting. When he released her, she pulled away from him and rubbed her arm where his fingers bruised her. This was so unfair. She glared at the two men.

"Aye, I will do as you say, Father. But I will not wear the ring made for another woman. Nor, will I abide having her living under the same roof." She turned her gaze to MacLachlan. "Your *leman* must go. You will put her aside and remove her from this castle. And I want a ring adorned with rubies."

He met her gaze. "I dinnae have a *leman.*" The words were spoken calmly though his voice held an edge.

Heat flamed Isobell's cheeks. "Dinnae make a fool of me, sir. Everyone kens you keep a French whore. And they ken you spent good gold on a sapphire ring at the fair."

"You have been misinformed, lass. If you intend to malign the character of my wee sister's noble companion, I will not abide it. The Lady Laurie Bernard is a guest in my home and I expect you to offer her the hospitality due a highborn noblewoman." His glare matched a frightening smile.

How dare he? Isobell sucked in a sudden breath and stared at him in stunned silence. She dug her nails into the soft flesh of her palms as her fists tightened more. She forced her chin up. "Father, you cannae allow—"

"Enough. I have made the arrangements. You will wed. Such matters as a *leman* will be between you and your husband."

Isobell moved her balled fists to her hips, glaring at MacLachlan and her father.

MacLachlan raised his hand, stopping her retort before it left her lips. "I will grant your one request. I will send to Glasgow for a goldsmith and will purchase a ruby ring for you."

She realized she'd made a mistake. He'd demean her by giving the sapphire ring to the French whore. Everyone would laugh at her. "Sir—"

The MacLachlan's serving woman rushed into the hall. "Lady Isobell's chamber is ready," she said after catching her breath.

"Indeed. Please, show the lady to her chamber." MacLachlan smiled at the old woman.

He dismissed Isobell without a glance, addressing her father. "You will excuse me. I have urgent business to attend." With that, the frigid devil turned on his heel, strode across the hall, and out the door.

She stared after him. Never had she ever been so insulted, or so angry. Never in her entire life.

She'd take matters into her own hands and find a way to remove the French whore from the castle. Then Isobell would make Patrick's life hell.

Hours later, Patrick headed to the great hall for the evening meal. He dreaded the thought of the evening to come. The only good thing to happen during the entire lengthy day was Iain Lamont left, taking with him all his warriors.

When he thought of Isobell, his rage surfaced. Like hell, he would give Isobell Laurie's sapphire ring. Perhaps if he were lucky, the time required to procure a new ring for the selfish wench would buy him the time needed to prove the betrothal agreement a forgery.

He entered the already-crowded and noisy hall. Everyone fell silent. He strode across the chamber; all eyes were on him. When he joined Elspeth and Stephen at the head table, whispers sounded. He sighed heavily and took his seat between the pair. This would be a long night.

Elspeth greeted him with a sweet smile. "Good eve to you, brother. The Lady Isobell's maid brought the lady's regrets. She will take her meal alone in her chamber this eve. I am afraid she suffers a pain in her head." Elspeth rolled her eyes as she lightly banged her forehead with her hand.

Relief washed over Patrick and he gave his sister a small, crooked smile. He raised his mug in salute. "We can only hope this will become her custom."

After taking a long swig, he set the mug on the table and turned his gaze on Stephen. "Is there any word from Jamie?"

His cousin shook his head. "Nae. I would have brought you the news directly if a messenger arrived. 'Tis too soon for them to have found anything." He patted Patrick on the shoulder. "Give them time. They will find the lass and Duncan."

"I dinnae have time. Tonight is the full moon." He turned back to Elspeth. "Beth, do you sense anything?"

Elspeth lowered her eyes. "She is verra afeared."

Patrick jumped up, but Stephen pushed him back into his seat. "There is naught you can do this night. Give Jamie and the lads time to find her."

"What of Duncan? Beth, do you sense anything of him?"

"Naught...naught but a void." She moistened her lips and glanced away. A tear slid along her check and she swiped at it. "I can't find him at all."

She drank deeply from her cup of wine as if she braced herself. Did she hide something from him? What?

Danger? Was Laurie in terrible, terrible danger?

CHAPTER THIRTY

*L*aurie woke to a foul taste. She choked on a rag stuffed in her mouth.

She jerked her eyes open. Her scream died against the gag. Her vision fuzzy, the oppressive dark night closed in. Her head throbbed. Her numb fingers tingled. The dirty cloth in her mouth made her nauseous.

She sat on the hard ground, her arms tied around a large tree behind her. An awkward position. She tugged against the restraint, hoping to loosen the knots and wiggle her hands free. The leather dug deeper into her skin, causing her to whimper in pain.

Laurie leaned back against the tree, discouraged. Where was Duncan? She had no answer. If only she could get the gag out of her mouth, she might breathe more easily.

A disturbing sensation skittered across her flesh. She glanced at her ankles with unease. A scream caught in her mouth. Dozens of creepy little spiders crawled across her skin. She kicked her legs out, trying to dislodge the nasty things.

One bit her and she bucked against her bindings. *Oh God.* She prayed they weren't poisonous. The sensitized skin started to itch. If only she could brush them away. Scratch her ankle.

Oh God. If only she could get free from the restraints. Laurie tugged at the bindings again and pain shot up her arms.

Mentally shaking herself, she tried to get a handle on her fear. She needed to figure a way out of this mess. Laurie closed her eyes briefly, wanting to cry. Instead, she opened them again with determination. As her vision focused, she saw an ugly, dirty man squatting several feet away. A torch held in one hand, he stared at her with unkind eyes.

He smiled wickedly before saying something guttural under his breath. He stood and walked away.

Suddenly, spiders were the least of her worries. A small fire burned nearby. Scattered around were torches. They lent an eerie glow to the surroundings. She attempted to make out images in the dim light, but the ugly man returned with two other big, heavily built men dressed in filthy rags.

The two cruel-looking newcomers stepped behind the tree. One untied her wrists. Then each man took hold of an arm and pulled them away from her body. She kicked at them. The effort was hopeless. The men were too strong.

The third man brought an iron ring with two chains attached. At the end of each chain was a thick leather strap. She'd seen an apparatus like that at a museum in London. She fought harder, yanked on her arms, tried to break free. She struggled through the pain in her armpits and shoulders and neck. Her efforts were to no avail.

They easily restrained her and pulled her arms in front of her. They tied each hand to one of the chains with the straps, making the leather tight.

Ouch! Her wrists burned from the chafing and open cuts from her previous ill treatment. She squirmed, swinging her body awkwardly in an attempt to break away. She thrashed, kicked at them. Their legs were like tree trunks. In the end, she only gained more pain.

Forcing her to the ground, the first man spoke harsh words she didn't understand. He slapped her face. She curled her body protectively. He stepped back and glared at her. Grabbing the iron ring, he pulled, yanking her to her knees. *Urgh.* Pain shot up her thighs, burned in her belly.

He tugged on the tether. She lurched forward. He dragged her toward the fire. Her skirt snagged and tore on rocks and twigs as she scraped across the ground. The skin on her arms and legs became bruised and raw.

Beyond the fire, the limb of a large tree stretched straight out. A heavy rope hung from the branch. The men dragged her to the tree and tied the ring to the rope, pulling the line taut, jerking her to her toes, her arms stretched painfully above her head. The tip of her toes barely skimmed the ground.

The men left her alone. Tears burned her eyes. The pain in her arms became a terrible ache that made her want to scream. Soon, her arms went numb.

Terror lodged in her throat. Never in her life had she been more frightened. To the left was the opening of a cave. The image of another cave came to mind. The one where she'd kissed Patrick on the way to Glasgow. This cave was much different. This experience horribly different. Out of the darkness walked her worst nightmare.

Malcolm Maclay. He stood before her, his legs braced apart, his hands on his hips, a smug grin on his ugly scarred face.

Laurie cringed at the sight of him, her heart pounding furiously.

"Whore. We meet again." He touched her cheek with his dirty, calloused fingers. She flinched and he chuckled. Obviously, he relished the terror in her eyes. He reached around her, untying the rag from her head. Then he pulled the gag out of her mouth.

Laurie screamed. The high-pitched sound shrill against the silence of the night.

He threw his head back and roared with laughter. "There is nary a soul to hear you." He reached out and slapped her hard across the face.

Her head snapped back from the impact, and she swung

on her tether. Her cheek stung, instantly raw where he'd struck. Tears fell freely, burning sensitive flesh. She opened her mouth to scream again, but before a sound came out, he cruelly struck her again, splitting her lip. Blood oozed along her chin.

He continued to hit her several more times. With a final stroke, he struck one of her eyes.

"Agh."

"Look at me, whore." He grabbed hold of her braid and yanked.

Laurie tried to see him through her swelling eye, his image fuzzy. She sought to moisten her swollen lips with her parched tongue. She tasted the metallic tang of blood. Fear became a living thing within her, batting against her insides.

Maclay's eyes burned with a wild lust. He grabbed the front of her blouse and tore it to the waist. Her breasts freed to the breeze, her nipples hardened from the cold. Pinching one of the buds, her torturer twisted it between two fingers.

Agony scorched her flesh.

"Stop," Laurie cried, unable to pull away. This couldn't be happening.

Maclay continued his torment. He squeezed her other breast, digging his nails into her tender flesh, inflicting more agony. She recoiled, the pain blinding, the humiliation burning in her chest. Yet she feared her suffering had only begun.

He released her breasts and stood back, staring at her with feral eyes. "I was willing to wed you. Now I will take you like the whore you are."

Laurie bit her lower lip to hold back her screams. She feared if she screamed, he'd continue to beat her. It would be better to conserve her strength. It would be the only way to survive the ordeal.

"Come all. Come hither. Look at the whore of Castle Lachlan," Maclay taunted. He leaned in close, his foul breath on her face. He grabbed her chin, forcing her to look at him. "I will enjoy taking every inch of your *precious* body, lady-whore, in front of these fine warriors." Spittle hit her cheek. He waved his other hand toward the men who hovered in the background, snickering and hooting. "When I have finished, each and every man here will have their turn."

More softly, so only she heard, he said, "You ken he will never want you back."

The men who ogled the scene cheered. They moved closer out of the darkness, grabbing at her clothing, touching her flesh with dirty hands, scratching and bruising her skin.

Maclay released her chin and pushed the others away. He snatched a willow switch from one of them. He walked behind her and tore what was left of her blouse. He brought the switch down across her back.

"Stop. Oh, God, please stop."

He whipped her again. She gritted her teeth against the spasm of pain.

He struck another blow.

"Have mercy," she pleaded.

"Aye. You will learn to beg. You will learn to obey. I will break your spirit, lass. You will crawl to me and beg for my attentions. You will, so help me." He brought the switch against her raw skin again.

The agonizing pain raced across her nerve endings. She no longer screamed, instead she prayed. Prayed she'd faint. That the misery would end. Maclay stopped his assault and slowly walked around her several times, glaring as he moved. When he stopped to stand in front of her, an unholy hatred glowed deep in the depths of his eyes replacing the lust she'd seen in his stare.

Laurie prayed she'd pass out.

She was fading into unconsciousness when someone tossed a bucket of cold water over her. She convulsed from the shock.

Maclay threw the willow switch to the ground, pulled his knife from the sheath on his belt, and brought the blade close to her face. His smile was ugly and cruel. He moved the knife downward, placing the blade to the side of her right breast.

At the touch of cold steel, Laurie jerked, her heart hammering painfully in her chest.

"I will punish you each time you dinnae please me." He dragged the knife along the edge of her breast, deep enough to flow blood.

She choked on a scream, the sound gurgling in her throat. Whimpering, she wished she'd die, anything to block out the dreadful torture.

Maclay bent his head, placed his lips over the wound, and sucked the blood. As he did, he made a moaning sound that made Laurie's skin crawl.

This was much worse than spiders. *The man is insane. He must be.*

He rested his blade on her cheek, all the while laughing sadistically.

Laurie screamed and screamed and screamed.

Patrick paced, his emotions in turmoil, his bedchamber a lonely place. He tortured himself by remaining, but couldn't leave.

Laurie's presence remained all around him. The chamber still held her scent along with some of her things. He picked up the silver brush she'd used to tame her beautiful golden locks. A silky strand remained in the bristles. He wrapped the precious thread around his fingers until his chest tightened with pain.

How would he live without her?

He paced well into the night.

When he finally slept, his fears took hold and twisted his dreams. He tossed and turned, caught in the sheets. He woke, a scream burning his throat.

Laurie was in danger. And he did nothing.

He played the proper bridegroom to the wrong bride. He hated feeling so utterly helpless. His fear gnawed at his gut. He hadn't felt this miserable since his parents disappeared. He'd been helpless then as well.

No more!

Stephen burst into the room, sword at the ready. "I heard you scream. What is wrong?"

"We go after Lady Laurie." Patrick threw the bed coverings to the side and padded butt-naked to his chest. He quickly dressed and secured his weapons on his person.

He'd find her himself. He didn't care what Isobell or her father thought. He'd find a way to make things right.

Determination stiffened his spine as he strode from the chamber with Stephen at his heel. They gathered some men and rode out before first light.

Laurie sensed someone's presence in the cave. She didn't dare move. If the intruder was Maclay and he realized she was conscious, he'd come for her, and the pain and degradation would begin anew.

How long had she been here? Several days? An hour? She couldn't be sure.

The madman beat her often. When she was no longer responsive to his insults, he left her in the damp cave, where a stranger with gentle hands came to her, tending to her battered body. She'd become numb to the cold and the pain. Her only solace was she hadn't yet been raped, though he persistently threatened he would take her in the most unpleasant way.

Laurie listened, trying to detect who approached.

Duncan was in the cave too. Somewhere. She overheard them talking when they'd thought her unconscious. He was a prisoner also, still insensible, or so they said.

The only thing that kept her from losing her mind completely was the single thread of hope someone would come searching for them. If not for her, certainly they'd come for Duncan. And they'd both be set free of this horrible lunatic.

Laurie lay on her belly across a dirty pallet. Painful oozing sores covered her back. The bastard had tied her arms and legs, but she had grown numb to that discomfort.

Muffled footsteps approached her corner of the cave. A gentle hand smoothed her hair, and she felt relief from her fears.

The old woman hovered over her, softly crooning in the lilting language of the Highlanders. Laurie almost smiled. Thank God, it wasn't Maclay. The strange woman resembled the wicked old hag that brought Snow White the poisoned apple in the animated classic tale. Only this woman eased Laurie with compassion.

Ancient, her leathery skin folded into baggy wrinkles and a large ugly wart protruded from the tip of her pointed nose. But her eyes were the green of emeralds and sparkled within her withered face...eyes that were somehow familiar.

The woman gently applied a healing salve to the sores on Laurie's back. Her pain lessened, and once again, she sank into blessed oblivion.

Much later, the woman chanted over her. Words she didn't understand, that sounded ancient, but she found calming.

"Ugly crone, get out of my way." Maclay pushed the woman aside and grabbed hold of Laurie, dragging her from the pallet.

The torture began again. Only this time he seemed different. More intense. Laurie feared this time he'd surely commit rape.

CHAPTER THIRTY-ONE

*T*he horses stomped the ground, frightened by the eerie, soul-wrenching screams echoing through the hills. With the land covered in heavy fog, Archibald MacLachlan couldn't tell from whence the sound came.

He leaned close to his companion. "Something is amiss in the hills this night."

"Aye. But, where?" Alexander Campbell said as he stared into the thick, gray haze.

Seeing more than a short distance was impossible.

Abruptly the screaming stopped.

With a whistled signal from Alexander, the small group of men who journeyed for King James IV moved forward. Having been away on the Continent for a lengthy stay, they traveled this night in an attempt to make up for lost time, eager to reach Castle Lachlan.

When they cleared the forest and road into the glen, a mysterious woman galloped out of the mist. Tinkling music filled the air. She raced toward them across the moor, her flaming red hair flying behind her like a pennon billowing in the wind. She rode a handsome white steed with a golden bridle and with golden bells plaited in his mane. The stallion was a fine beast, fast as wind, with an arched neck and broad chest. His nostrils flared; his ears laid back.

The woman rode headlong into the midst of the traveling party.

Her approach brought a bold grin to Alexander's mouth and Archibald found himself grinning too, forgetting his unease. She rode with more skill than most men. A stunning display of horsemanship, the most beautiful woman he'd ever seen, her emerald gown and green mantle enhancing her fiery beauty.

"Who is she?" Archibald asked.

"I dinnae ken. But I recognize the *plaide* she wears. I am certain it is the work of my father's weaver," Alexander replied in an awed voice.

The guardsmen moved apart, falling back, making way for her. Most of the men's jaws dropped open and they stared at her enchanting beauty. Stopping in front of Archibald and Alexander, she spoke directly to Archibald, her green eyes sparkling, alight with an uncanny glow.

"I am known as Caitrina. You must come with me, now, to the caves of the gray women. There is no time to waste. We must save your brother's betrothed, for she has been abducted and is held prisoner."

She gracefully turned her horse about and rode back into the misty night. Her horse flew across the moor as if with wings. Did she expect them to follow?

Archibald glanced at Alexander. He shrugged, then smiled and nodded. Archibald spurred his horse and gave chase. Alexander stayed close, followed by the rest of the men.

After following a strange green light through the fog, they approached the mouth of a large cave. Men ran from the opening, escaping into shadows and mist before they reached them.

The sight of so many king's men must have frightened them away.

Archibald headed into the cave while Alexander and some of his men pursued those who fled.

A battered woman lay naked on the floor in a slimy corner

of the dank cavern. Covered in filth, her dirty, stringy hair matted around her head and shoulders. Her wrenching sobs yanked at Archibald's heartstrings.

Reaching down, he touched her shoulder. She flinched, curling tighter into herself. He gently spoke to her in Gaelic. She didn't respond to his words. Her weeping continued, her shoulders heaving.

After placing a *plaide* over her bloodied and beaten form, he lifted her, careful of her injuries. She hung limp, her slender form trembling in his embrace.

As he carried her from the cave, he found himself staring at her marred face. Who was she? What was he to do with her? He didn't even consider leaving the responsibility to Alexander or the others. Whether, in truth, she was his brother's betrothed or not, he'd take care of her.

His gut clenched. What had been done to the lass disgusted him. How could anyone so abuse a woman? If, in fact, she belonged to Patrick, who could hate him so much they would torture a young woman in such a horrible manner? Lamont?

Iain was a hard man, but the chief of Clan Lamont wouldn't stoop so low.

Archibald carried the woman to where his lads waited with the horses. He handed her into the arms of one of the other men. He mounted then reached down and took her into his arms again. He placed her sideways in front of him.

The wee woman leaned into him, slid her arms around his waist, and placed her head below his shoulder as if she realized she was safe. He wrapped his arms around her, tenderly holding her. He softly murmured calming words, trying to soothe her.

She tilted her head back to look at him. The small effort must have been painful, for she closed her eyes and again leaned into him.

Having seen the pain in her blackened eyes, he patted her gently to reassure her. Her hand reached out from under the *plaide* she now wore and grasped his *leine* with surprising strength.

"Patrick?" she said before she thankfully swooned.

Archibald groaned. Another female mistaking him for his twin.

He didn't know for sure if the lass belonged to his brother, but she obviously knew Patrick. His parents raised him and his brothers to believe all women precious. Gazing at the small hand on his chest, he made a heartfelt vow to protect her with his life.

Luck blessed Patrick this eve. After several days of dense fog, the murky vapor finally dissipated and the waning moon shone bright, making tracking easier. He and his lads rode north to the head of the loch where they met up with Jamie's search party. Jamie reported finding a *currach* hidden in the brush at the edge of the wood near the beach. After conferring, the two groups of warriors split again, Jamie taking his group farther north.

Even though he assured Patrick he'd seen no sign of Laurie or Duncan near the forest, Patrick's party headed east anyway, toward the Fir-wood.

Although it might be unwarranted arrogance, he refused to believe Laurie managed to return to her own time. He'd convinced himself they'd come together for a purpose, that they were matched souls. Together they had to fulfill their destiny.

He couldn't marry Isobell.

Patrick and his men searched through the night directed by the shimmering light of the moon. Morning dawned to crystal-clear weather. With the rising sun, Patrick's frustration grew beyond bearing.

He and Stephen climbed a high crag just beyond the wood. From this vantage point, on the cliff above the tree line, they could see to the west as far as the bay, the castle beyond, and the sea loch. Patrick noted the huge cloud of dust at the edge of the bay. A large party of riders swiftly approached the crossing to the castle.

Patrick pointed outward. "Stephen, what do you make of that? Can you see who draws near the castle with those keen eyes of yours?"

"Might be Campbells. Perhaps Archibald returns with Alexander."

"Aye, Campbells. Mayhap Archie." Patrick frowned. "Even if we hurry, we will not make it in time to greet them." He ran a hand through his snarled hair. He didn't want to stop the search for Laurie. But if his brother were with the travelers...

Patrick would return to the castle before resuming his search. He couldn't leave it to Elspeth to explain the chaos his life had become.

They watched the progress of the riders for several more minutes before they scrambled down. Their descent required caution as they crawled over steep and slippery rocks, using exposed roots as handholds. Carefully moving over the scree at the base of the incline, they made their way to the clearing where the others waited with the horses.

"We make haste to the castle!" Patrick shouted as he mounted.

The trail rose and fell as they made their trek downward. At times, Patrick caught a good view of the loch and the castle, and saw the visitors take boats across to Castle Lachlan. At other times, the trees hemmed in the view.

The men carefully worked their way through the thick stands of fir.

Once they were out of the trees, they quickened their pace. Over the heather-clad slopes, they galloped to the stable where they saw the Campbell device. Archibald had returned. Patrick and Stephen wasted no time and ran to the water's edge where a boat waited with oarsmen ready to take them across.

Patrick glanced at the purple tinted hills. He'd speak to his twin and resume the search.

His jaw tight, Patrick stood next to his brother at Laurie's bedside.

"She was tortured. Beaten. Cut with a knife," Archibald said.

Pain coiled in Patrick's chest. He felt as if he was experiencing Laurie's torture. He barely remained in control, feeling incredible guilt.

He clenched his fists. Her black and blue body enraged him. Welts and oozing sores covered her back and arms where she'd been whipped. *Damn Maclay.* Patrick pressed his lips together, damning himself as the biggest fool. He'd seen the cut on Laurie's breast when Aine cleaned and tended her wounds. He could only imagine the other horrors she'd faced because of him.

How many times had the bastard taken what belonged to him? How many times had he taken her? Maclay would pay. He'd suffer before he died. He'd learn the meaning of pain.

His brother watched him through wary eyes. "Who is she? When we were told your lady had been taken and held captive, I expected to rescue Isobell. Instead I find this woman, a stranger to us."

Patrick turned away from his brother to gaze at Laurie. "'Tis a long tale. She is mine. I must take care of her now. However, Isobell is also in the castle." He ran a hand through his hair. "'Tis complicated." He faced Archibald once again. "Please, dinnae speak of this to anyone until we talk more. See that Alexander keeps silent as well. I beg this of you."

His brother nodded, his lips held in a grim line.

Laurie opened her eyes. She shook her head. Grimaced. Then closed her eyes for a moment and inhaled a deep breath before opening them again.

She attempted a smile and winced. "Patrick, there are two of you," she muttered.

He stepped forward and grasped her hand, holding it protectively in his much larger one. "Nae, lass. There are, in truth, two of us. 'Tis my brother Archie you see. He found you and brought you home."

Laurie moistened her split lip with her tongue. "You…" She had difficulty speaking and ground her throat. "Have a twin?"

Patrick watched Archibald leave the chamber, thankful for the privacy. "Aye, I have a twin. We shared our mother's womb." He helped Laurie to sit against the pillows.

Pain flared in her eyes, yet she didn't cry out, enduring the agony in silence.

"You must rest now. Aine will give you something to ease your hurts."

Laurie's fingers fluttered near her throat.

"Aine!" She came quickly at his summons, bringing with her a potion for Laurie.

"Here, lass." Aine held the cup to Laurie's lips, forcing her to drink the bitter liquid by pinching her nose. When she'd taken most of it, Patrick helped her lie back against the feather pillows.

The old woman left the chamber, but Patrick stayed. Seated at his lady's side, he held her hand while her eyes fluttered closed and she drifted into a potion-induced sleep. When he was sure she slept soundly, he called for Aine to return and watch over her. Then he went in search of his brother.

Annoyed he hadn't been the one to find Laurie and vexed Archibald rescued her, Patrick swallowed hard, pushing his frustration deep within him. He unfairly directed his anger at his brother. He owed his twin an apology.

He found Archibald in the great hall. "Join me in my private chamber. I wish for us to speak."

"Why are you keeping both your mistress and betrothed under the same roof? You had better have a good excuse for your heartless behavior."

Patrick pursed his lips. "I do."

"Then explain."

"Not here. Join me in my private chamber." Patrick was

well aware that at times, the hall had ears. None should overhear this conversation.

Archibald glanced around before nodding his agreement and silently followed Patrick to his study.

"How is Duncan?" Patrick asked.

"He will come around. Though he will be sore for quite some time, recovering from the beatings he suffered."

Patrick paced the chamber while Archibald leaned against the wall watching him. Finally, he stopped and faced his twin. "How did you find them? I had several parties out searching. I searched myself. We found nary a trace. Nary a trail."

"A mysterious woman came to us." Archibald smiled. "She was enchanting. The most beautiful woman I have had the pleasure to gaze upon. She rode a white steed with golden trappings. Alexander recognized her cloak as the work of the Campbell weaver or we never would have followed her. We took a chance, never considering she may lead us into a trap."

"I thank Our Lord that you did. Follow her, that is."

"Aye. Thank the good Lord," Archibald agreed. "She told us your lady had been abducted and held captive. She said we would find the lass near the caves of the gray women. When we found your lady, she lay naked, broken and bleeding in the filth of one of those dank caverns. Who would do such a thing?"

"Maclay. You did not capture him?" Patrick's voice strained.

Archibald glanced away. "If 'twas he, he escaped into the fog. As did the beautiful woman, I fear."

Patrick roared his frustration, the sound bouncing off the stone walls.

Days passed before Patrick could question Duncan thoroughly.

Much improved, the lad whined and complained and argued, claiming he was well enough to get up from bed. Aine wouldn't stand for such nonsense. She practically kept him prisoner in one of the bedchambers.

Learning Laurie's abduction was part of his uncle's intrigues made Patrick heartsick. Donald MacLachlan and his whore Moira both had gone missing from the castle. Donald had left a message he was off to another of Patrick's holdings, one that was under the stewardship of Patrick's father and uncle's cousin, Allain of Dunadd. Everyone in the castle assumed Moira snuck away to follow Donald. However, Patrick had his doubts. More than likely, Donald cast her aside, forcing her to run on her own. The wench feared his wrath, having played an integral part in Laurie's abduction.

Donald, on the other hand, remained a problem. His political maneuverings and interference in Patrick's life was something Patrick could no longer tolerate.

He would need to deal with his uncle, and soon.

As for Maclay, Patrick sent a small party of warriors to hunt him down. Once found, they would bring him in to stand trial. Patrick would like nothing more than to kill the bastard, slowly, inflicting an incredible amount of pain.

However, Patrick was a man of the law and he'd see justice served.

There was still the problem of Isobell and their upcoming nuptials to deal with. For now though, he had an immediate crisis. Laurie remained fevered and incoherent. He feared she fought for her life.

CHAPTER THIRTY-TWO

*I*sobell inhaled sharply, horrified at the sight of the fevered woman's abused face. She found it difficult to look at her, to see her as a victim instead of Patrick's whore. She didn't want to feel sympathy for the woman. In reality though, they were both merely pawns in the game the men played.

She could well believe Malcolm Maclay had done this. More than once, she'd witnessed his brutal treatment of serving women at her home. When she interceded, the man glared, though retreated. Why didn't her father better control his henchman?

Patrick's woman's eyes opened slightly. The fever held her in its grip. Glancing around, Isobell located an ewer of water on a nearby table. She poured some into a cup and tried to get the woman to drink a wee bit.

A small amount passed her lips. The rest dribbled down her chin and onto her chest to soak her linen nightrail. Isobell turned to leave the chamber, planning to slip out unseen.

Too late. Patrick and Archibald stood in the doorway.

Rage radiated from Patrick, freezing her in place. He moved across the chamber with long, quick steps and grabbed Isobell by the wrist. "You poison her."

She franticly tried to pull away, but he held her in a tight, painful grip. She winced, tears coming to her eyes. "Nae. Nae. I but gave her water to quench her thirst."

Archibald strode across the room. He sniffed near the sick woman's mouth then tasted the liquid in the cup. "Release Isobell. 'Twas but water."

With a frigid glare, Patrick freed her from his hold and tossed her away. "What are you doing in Lady Laurie's chamber? Where is Aine?"

Isobell wiped at the few tears on her cheek with the back of a shaky hand. "I came to see what your whore looked like," she said before she thought better of sounding so mean.

"Get out." Patrick stared at her with icy hatred. "Get out before I strike you."

He went to the French woman's bed and swept her hair away from her bruised face. Sitting on the bench at her side, he grasped her hand and murmured to her.

Isobell couldn't believe how gently he handled the woman. He'd never been kind to her. She caught Archibald's eye before she fled the chamber.

"Isobell wait. I must have words with you," Archibald called.

If only it was he whom she was to wed.

Laurie leaned against the down pillows and raised her hand a few inches before the effort became too much and she dropped it back to the mattress. Her fever had broken, but she remained weaker than a newborn kitten, and when she moved too quickly, felt twinges of uncomfortable pain.

Time passed slowly. Nightmares haunted her. She often feared Maclay would sneak into the castle and abduct her again. For weeks, she'd remained in bed dependent on Aine and Elspeth to care for her. They forced bitter tasting potions on her to relieve the pain and to help build her strength, cajoling her with soothing words and praise. Patrick sat with her often, holding her hand and whispering gentle words of encouragement.

She wanted to scream.

At times when she gazed into his dark eyes, she caught a glimpse of guilt reflected there. It was there now.

"You're not to blame. None of what happened is your fault." Laurie took full responsibility for her actions and the consequences. She'd been at fault, not he.

"How can I not be to blame? You were harmed in my home. I should have done a better job watching over you. You are my responsibility."

She clutched his hand. "I left of my own free will. You are not accountable."

He shook his head and glanced away.

"Look at me." She squeezed his fingers. "Thank you for sitting with me."

A sheen coated his eyes when their gazes collided. Their time together was bittersweet. Patrick's wedding to Isobell loomed in the too-near future.

Oh, no. Isobell dashed into a curtained niche and waited for Patrick to pass. While he locked himself away with Lady Laurie, she sought out Archibald's company.

Isobell scurried along the passageway in the opposite direction and slipped into Archie's bedchamber to wait for his return. She plopped into a chair and leaned her chin on her hands. At first, she'd been angry. After all, they planned to force her to wed a man who loved another, and worse yet, disliked her. She'd become another of his possessions, one he didn't care for, possibly even hated.

She'd resigned herself to her fate, but didn't truly accept it. What was she to do? She had no recourse. Her father was adamant.

While Patrick spent time with his mistress, Archibald made her laugh with entertaining tales of his journeys. They'd become friends. She wished it were he, not Patrick, to whom she was betrothed. Even when she was younger and betrothed to Donald, she'd wished it Archie to whom she would wed.

Archibald exemplified everything a husband should be. Kind and gentle. A strong warrior and a courtier.

When Donald died, her father had betrothed her to Patrick. How awful to be given to the wrong brother. She thrummed her nails on the wooden arm of the chair.

She eyed the big bed. If she gave her virginity to Archie, Patrick would refuse to wed her. Archibald was honorable. She'd have to seduce him.

Isobell dropped her gown and chemise to the floor and climbed into the bed. A chill prickled her skin. Archie better hurry, before she lost her nerve.

Several minutes later, she shivered. The room was cold without a fire. She covered herself. The fur tickled and she giggled. *Archibald will be surprised to find me in his bed?*

Excitement made her smile. Then she lost her smile.

She waited hours, but he didn't come.

Fine. She'd search him out. She'd refuse to wed Patrick.

"Read these. Tell me how I can get out of it." Patrick handed Archibald the pages from the forged contract.

The door to his private chamber flew open. They shot to their feet, ready to defend themselves. In the doorway stood Isobell, her violet eyes sparked fire.

"What now?" Patrick demanded, arching a brow.

Isobell stepped into the chamber, her arms at her sides, her small hands clenched into tight fists. Her lips pursed, she boldly stared at him.

He rounded the worktable and leaned against the front of it. He crossed his arms over his chest and stoically returned her stare. Would he ever get used to her temper tantrums?

Archibald stood before the hearth. Isobell's gaze darted to him. He returned her look, shook his head, and quickly glanced away.

Patrick rubbed his chin. What did his brother have to do with this?

Isobell's facade crumbled. Her eyes turned a deep shade of cool purple, the color of a stormy sea. She appeared vulnerable. Yet she straightened her back, raised her chin defiantly and held his stare.

"I will not wed with you." A tear fell from her eye to drip upon her pale cheek.

He wanted to scream at her, to rant and rave, to tell her he didn't want to wed her either. Instead, he glowered, his patience close to its limit. They faced an impossible situation.

"You have nae choice, lass. Your father demands it," he bellowed. Tamping down on his frustration, he lowered his voice. "Little as I like it."

"I cannae marry you."

"Perhaps you should persuade your father to dissolve the contract."

Isobell glanced at Archibald, beseeching him with her eyes, imploring him to intercede. His gaze sad, he shook his head once again before lowering his stare to his hands.

"You fools!" Patrick sighed heavily. "What a fine mess."

"'Tis not Isobell's fault. You should not take your anger out on her. You ken her father is determined she marry you," Archibald said, frustrated anger burning in his eyes.

"Who then should I take my anger out on? You?" Twisting away, Patrick dragged both his hands through his hair, trying to compose himself before turning back. When he did, he caught another visual exchange between Isobell and Archibald.

He shook his head and fell into the chair at his worktable. "Isobell, you will leave us and return to your chamber."

"Nae—"

"I have something to say and would have Lady Isobell stay to hear it." Archibald stepped forward and straightened his shoulders. Isobell gave him a tremulous smile. He cleared his throat. "I wish to wed Lady Isobell."

Patrick blinked several times, staring at his brother. "Do

you ken what you are saying?"

"Aye, I do."

Isobell's demeanor bloomed and she broke out into a radiant smile. She glided across the floor to stand next to Archibald. They gazed into each other's eyes for a moment. Archie took her small hand into his and they turned in unison to face Patrick.

"And you, Isobell, let me guess, you wish to wed Archie."

She nodded. "Aye. With all my heart."

This was the answer! Relief and joy slammed into him. But he needed to tread carefully. Lamont must be handled.

Patrick rose, paced across the chamber, and stopped. He stood erect with his back to them, his hands clasped behind his back. After several minutes, he turned to face them.

"I will consider your desires. Now, Isobell, return to your chamber until it is time for the evening meal."

Both Isobell and Archibald moved to leave.

"Nae. Archie, you remain."

Isobell gave Archibald a final glance and left.

"You want the lass?" Patrick faced his twin.

"Aye. We have become close."

"Are you doing this for me, so I might wed Laurie?"

"Nae, I want Isobell for my wife."

"So be it. You have my blessing to wed. And I will wed my lass as soon as I can make arrangements."

"What of Lamont? Isobell's father may not agree. I am not a chief, only second in line and not even that when your *bairns* are born. He may go to King Jamie and request your marriage to Lady Laurie be set aside."

"Not if we wed before a priest. He has nae friends in Rome. 'Twill be impossible to set our marriage aside. Besides, Lamont should be happy to acquire you for a son. You are a MacLachlan. You are a good man, Archie. And well he kens it."

Patrick clapped his hands. Now to share the news with his lady.

Laurie worried her bottom lip. She'd spent the afternoon in the great hall with only Alexander Campbell as companion. They sat before a glowing fire in chairs with soft sapphire cushions. Patrick left her in the other man's care after placing a fur across her lap for warmth. He'd given her a kiss and went off to find the priest.

She shifted her weight on the cushion. Although Patrick corroborated her story, she doubted Alexander believed she came from France. Elspeth's fiancé made her nervous. He had the tendency to ask probing questions she couldn't answer.

Whenever Alexander was alone with her, he watched her with his all-too-knowing stare. "You ken there are many legends about the caves of the gray women." He stared at her as a scientist would an insect under a microscope. As if, he wanted to learn her every secret.

"I'm sure," she said softly.

"Countless tales of witches and strange happenings."

Laurie frowned. The caves were eerie. "There was an old, gnarled woman in the cave with me. Did you find her when you rescued me?"

That was stupid. When would she learn to keep her mouth shut? Each time she spoke, she encouraged him.

"Nae. Nary a soul was there besides you. Everyone else disappeared into the blasted fog."

Laurie rubbed her hand along the fur in her lap, the sensation comforting. "The old woman came often to tend my wounds. Although there was something unusual about her, she treated me kindly."

"Mayhap she was one of the infamous gray women—the witches of the caves." Alexander's eyes twinkled as if he teased. Still Laurie sensed something else, something unnerving.

She continued to stroke the fur. "No, I don't think so. Yet it was quite odd, actually. There was something very queer about her. She had the most intense green eyes. I'd the strangest sense I knew her before, but in a different form, as someone else. The idea was disconcerting."

Alexander had a knack for getting her to say things she didn't want to say, confide her deepest thoughts, voice her fears.

"The woman who came to enlist us in aiding you was verra beautiful with exquisite green eyes." He watched Laurie closely. "She told us her name was Caitrina."

"Caitrina?" Laurie gasped, unable to conceal her shock.

"Aye. You ken her?"

"No." She shook her head. She couldn't admit it. How would she explain Caitrina? She couldn't tell a medieval man she believed in faeries. Or that Caitrina was a faerie from the twenty-first century.

Could it be possible?

Was Caitrina one and the same with the old woman? Had she been with her all that time, taking care of her? If so, why would she have let such a horrible thing happen in the first place? More questions with no easy answers.

Alexander continued to stare at her with that annoying penetrating look. He evaluated what she said, analyzing every word. He grinned devilishly.

"What?" she asked.

"You are a witch," Alexander said with a chuckle.

"No. I—"

He raised a hand. "Many occurrences in this world are difficult to explain. Although, I dinnae believe witches exist, I find the concept of such superstition fascinating. Most who are accused are either a product of political revenge or illiterate prejudice."

"I'm not a witch."

"Nor is Elspeth, yet there are those who would accuse her because of her special gift."

"You know about her visions?" Laurie inhaled sharply. She shouldn't have said that. The family tried to keep Elspeth's sixth sense a secret.

"Aye. 'Tis what makes her so desirable."

"What do you mean?"

The sound of approaching footsteps distracted her from the grilling she wanted to give him.

Patrick strode across the hall, stopping beside her, a broad smile on his handsome face. "I am returned from the old priest. We will wed on the morrow, before Lamont hears of it. For that reason, 'twill be a small gathering, only our clansman who are already here at Castle Lachlan. I hope that won't disappoint."

"I couldn't be happier."

Patrick crouched in front of her and kissed her sweetly. She hung on him wanting more.

She would wed her Highland warrior.

The gilded chapel glowed with candlelight. Laurie's gaze circled the small interior, filled with her new friends.

With a twinge of regret, she thought of her family. She would never take the long walk down the aisle at St. Patrick's Cathedral on Uncle David's arm. Nor would she see the expected smirk on her cousin Finn's face as she passed him on her way to meet her intended at the altar. She wholeheartedly wished they both could be here with her now, to share her happiness.

Lost in her thoughts, she startled when the chapel quieted.

Laurie raised her gaze to Patrick, forgetting all else. Only him, the man of her dreams. The man she desired for her own, the man with whom she wanted to spend the rest of her life.

Even if it meant staying in the past.

Her heart swelled and she smiled at him with love.

Patrick strode past those gathered, eyes only for her. His heated gaze scorched her. Her nipples puckered in response. Oh, how she wanted this man.

He came to stand before her. Their eyes locked in communion. Time and space no longer existed, they were alone, two souls united.

The old priest cleared his throat, breaking the spell. Directing them to stand together in front of him, he joined their hands and bade them kneel. He motioned for Elspeth and Archibald to step forward, for they were to witness this union before God and their clansmen.

Patrick squeezed Laurie's fingers. The mass and ceremony buzzed by in a blur. She hardly remembered saying her vows.

Laurie accepted Patrick's assistance to stand. With his hands on her shoulders, he twisted her to face him. He placed his fingers on her cheeks and lowered his head. His eyes smoldered.

His lips were warm and persistent. The kiss shot to her toes.

Everyone cheered, and her cheeks burned.

Patrick stepped back. "Wife."

She stifled a giggle. "Husband."

They left the chapel and crossed the passageway to the council chamber where they would celebrate their union with a wedding feast. Patrick's warriors, some with their wives, and some with their sons and daughters filled the chamber when they arrived.

The cheer echoed from the rafters.

Laurie toyed with the large sapphire ring on her finger, the beautiful token of Patrick's love. This was the happiest day of her life. Yet it was as if she walked within a dream.

Could this be real?

She sighted Patrick across the chamber, standing with some of his men. Jamie slapped his back with some jest and they laughed. Catching her eye, Patrick raised his cup to her, and she smiled.

The crowd moved in waves and she lost sight of him.

Her stomach clenched when Munn approached. He made odd sounds as if he couldn't form words and handed her a beautiful bejeweled goblet.

Elspeth joined them. "He presents you with an offering of peace."

The little man made a choking sound, but vigorously nodded.

"Thank you." Laurie accepted his token and sipped the sweet wine. The ruby drink tasted delicious, fruity flavor burst on her tongue. More wonderful than any wine she'd ever tasted before.

Strolling around the hall, she accepted the best wishes from Patrick's clansmen. She sipped from her goblet. The cup never emptied. Each taste was more luscious than the last.

She danced with Patrick, ate from the savory assortment of foods, and drank from the goblet given to her by Munn.

Later, she whirled around the floor with Stephen. When they danced past the trestle table where her goblet sat, she stopped to take more of the sweet wine. *Delicious.*

Laurie enjoyed the minstrels and more dancing. She moved to the side of the hall to rest her aching toes and sipped from the goblet. *Whew.* She blew out a puff of air. A feverish heat flushed her chest and neck, making her desperate for Patrick's embrace. She wanted to consummate her marriage. She'd been waiting forever and didn't want to wait any longer.

Taking another sip of wine, she spied him at the edge of the hall. She rushed across the oak flooring toward him. Everyone else faded away. She giggled as she stumbled into him. He caught her by the arms. He was so sexy, and tonight, finally, all of that glorious man would be hers. She wrapped her arms around him and breathed in his earthy scent.

He smelled different. Felt different. His eyes were different.

It gave her pause, but only for a moment. They were married now.

Everything was different.

She leaned into him. When she hit his hard chest with her sensitized breasts, she pressed even tighter to him. She kissed his neck, slid her tongue along his jaw.

"Lass, what are you about?" He chuckled, the sound

rough against her throat.

Why was he trying to push her away?

Laurie wouldn't allow it. She wrapped one leg around his hip, laced her fingers in his hair and shimmied up his body. Without losing her stride, she sucked his bottom lip into her mouth.

He let out a tormented groan.

CHAPTER THIRTY-THREE

When Patrick caught sight of Laurie on the other side of the hall, an intense, hot fury boiled within him. Her arms draped his brother's neck and she smiled adoringly at Archibald as if he were her one true love. Couldn't she tell them apart?

Did she prefer Archibald?

A red haze clouded Patrick's eyes and angry words choked his throat. He strode across the chamber, his steps long and sure. Somehow, he managed to gain some control, forcing himself to swallow his rage before he made a public display of his disgust.

Archibald wrestled with her. She was an unruly vine, clinging to him.

"Archie, take my lady-wife to our bedchamber. I will follow," Patrick ordered through clenched teeth.

His brother had the audacity to chuckle. He practically manhandled Laurie to move her. He lifted her through the doorway and up the stairs before anyone noticed. She attached herself to Archibald, wrapping her legs and arms around his body, kissing him with sloppy, wet kisses. He struggled with her. Finally, managing to get her to the bedchamber and off him, he dropped her onto the big bed.

"I am not Patrick. He is over there." Archibald pointed to where Patrick watched the scene from the threshold, fury smoldering inside his chest.

"You're mine." She jumped up, reaching for Archibald once more.

Moving quickly, Patrick lunged across the chamber and grabbed her around the waist, pulled her away from his brother and dumped her back on the bed.

She laughed and swayed as she tried once again to rise. "Wow. Everything is spinning. Hey, there are two of you." She giggled and fell back against the mattress like a heavy boulder.

"I never thought the day would come when you would covet my bride." Patrick glowered at his twin.

Archibald raised his hands, palms forward. "I stand before you, falsely accused. Your lady-wife is in her cups. She is not herself."

"How did she get that way? I saw her take but one goblet of wine. Nary enough to confuse us. She is a trifler, playing with us." Patrick continued to glare at his twin, his disappointment and anger consuming him. "'Tis too late. I have wed the wench. I will have to teach her I am her only master."

"You make too much of this. She is but drunk."

"Leave. Before I forget you are my brother."

Archibald pivoted on his heel and left the chamber without uttering another word. Patrick stared at his new wife in disgust. She laid on the bed, insensible, as intoxicated as a drunken warrior. Since he first found the lass, she'd been naught but trouble. Not in his thirty summers had he ever been this angry.

He reached for her and as if he held a rag doll, shook her. She didn't stir. Cursing harshly, he dropped her onto the feather mattress.

Divesting her of her gown and chemise, he folded them over the chest at the foot of the bed. She wore some lacy thing over her breasts and her female mound. He ground his teeth in frustration. His hands shook with anger, with desire, as he slid the tiny piece of lace down her legs. He glared at her, almost hating her. She was completely bare, except for the fragile lace on her breasts, which he couldn't figure out how to remove, and the betrothal ring on her finger, the symbol of their disastrous marriage.

If she loved him, she should be able to tell them apart.

His desire sickened him. Even in his anger, he wanted her with soul deep yearning. Patrick removed his knife from its sheath at his waist. Cutting his palm, he drew blood. He moved his hand over the bed, letting the dark, red blood drip onto the sheet, and across her thighs. Only enough to make it appear that the marriage had been consummated. He didn't want gossip, or anyone to doubt she belonged to him.

Leaving her lying there alone on their wedding bed, he walked across the chamber to sit facing away, far from her, in one of the chairs before the hearth. He stared into the fire, contemplating the future. Even the flames mocked him. The blue of her eyes and the gold of her hair burned his vision, haunting him.

She didn't love him enough to realize she was with the wrong man. Patrick rubbed the ache near his heart.

What was he to do? The question plagued him. He wanted to get away from her, as far as possible, leave her here where he wouldn't have to see her.

Maybe if he visited his father's Cousin Allain at his castle near the ruins of the ancient fort in Glasrie, he could forget the image of Laurie twined around Archibald. Patrick meant to visit his lands there for many a fortnight. Needed to handle the problems created by his Uncle Donald, who'd gone there. By going now, he could give himself time. Time to come to terms with a wife who didn't love him as much as he loved her.

He'd rather deal with his traitorous uncle than his disappointment.

Patrick stared into the fire, waiting for the night to pass, planning his departure.

Atop the battlements, Munn performed an intricate jig. Precariously close to the edge, he skipped on tiptoe from one crenel to the next, his joy effervescent.

He won!

The coupling never took place. The marriage wasn't consummated.

The chief would never forgive his new wife's betrayal. He'd have the marriage annulled.

Munn must apprise the queen of his success.

He rubbed his hands together in glee. What would the queen give him for a reward?

Jewels? He'd always wanted a jewel-encrusted dirk. Not that he had need of one. Still, he wanted one.

So relieved was he that he'd soon be free of his vow to the queen, he continued to dance throughout the misty night. Thankfully, the guise of invisibility masked him, for had it been otherwise, the wall guards would surely faint like silly lasses.

He chuckled over the image in his mind.

Before the sunrays kissed the land, Munn melted into the fog and drifted off to the realm of the faerie queen.

Laurie woke, her mind fuzzy. She stretched to remove the kinks from her muscles. Sensing the lateness of the hour, she yanked one of the bed curtains back. The sun pierced her retinas and her memory flashed. She'd married Patrick the night before.

Where was he?

She grimaced. Her head pounded. Nausea pooled in her belly. Weird. She'd no memory of going to bed the previous night. The last thing she remembered was that nasty little man giving her a goblet of wine.

For God's sake, she still wore her bra.

The blood on her thighs proved she'd truly wed. She was

no longer a virgin and she didn't even remember doing the deed. How had she gotten so drunk she couldn't remember having sex with the sexiest man in the world?

She'd done it again, made a mess of things.

This was all Patrick's fault. Since she'd fallen in love with the gorgeous man, she'd been doing brainless things. Now this. Getting drunk on her wedding night was the epitome of stupidity.

She slipped out of bed and shuffled to the washstand where she found a cloth. With a shaking hand, she wet the washcloth and used it to clean away the blood. Her chest ached with self-anger. She couldn't believe she'd ruined the most important day of her life.

But she hadn't drunk more than one goblet of wine, just one, the one Munn gave her as a peace offering. The wine must have contained something, which thoroughly intoxicated her. The little bastard.

As she climbed back onto the bed, Patrick entered the chamber. She gave him a coy smile, knowing her cheeks were flushed. He shot her a look that clenched her heart. His eyes were cold and empty, his blue gaze dispassionate.

"I am leaving. I have ordered Duncan to watch over you. You are not to stray from this chamber without him at your side. And stay away from my brother and every other man that strokes your fancy." His voice, void of emotion, sent a chill through her.

What? "Patrick, what happened? Why are you leaving?" Her voice quivered. "Tell me what is wrong."

He stared at her, a frigid glare filled with ice. "Your behavior last night was intolerable." He turned away and walked to the chamber door.

"What the hell are you talking about?" Needing to stop him, she pulled a sheet from the bed and wrapped it around her body, toga style, then chased after him. "Don't walk out on me."

Patrick stopped before opening the door. Laurie's fists

pounded against his back. Spinning around, he grabbed hold of both her wrists. He managed to pick her up, carry her to the bed and drop her atop the mattress.

She grabbed hold of his *leine*. A piece of the fine saffron fabric tore in her hand. Her eyes—large and glowing with shock—held his gaze for several heartbeats.

Her chest rose and fell with quick intakes of breath, her nipples taut against the thin sheet. Patrick's control broke. The emotions ripping through him were sudden and powerful, and he seized Laurie, dragged her against his chest, and roughly captured her mouth with his lips. The kiss was harsh and punishing, born of anger. She kissed him back with as much ferocity, biting his lip with pearly white teeth. He growled, slanted his mouth, deepened the kiss.

He forced her to submit. Anger didn't douse the desire burning between them. It stoked the flame. Hotter. And hotter.

Patrick pushed her back, pressed her shoulders into the mattress. He stripped off his *leine* and *plaide* and mounted her, pushing her into the soft bedding with his weight. He ripped away the sheet she wore and forced her legs apart. Positioning himself between her thighs, he thrust, burying himself deep.

She screamed.

Damnation. With that one violent stroke, he broke through her maidenhead. Tears rolled over Laurie's cheeks and she pressed her palms against his chest, trying to push him away.

Patrick froze. He panted with the effort to remain motionless. He dropped his forehead onto hers. He couldn't believe what he'd done. She was a virgin and he'd taken her in the roughest manner, his possession, swift and fierce.

"Sweetling, look at me," he demanded.

Her moist eyelashes fluttered open. He winced at the distrust in her eyes.

"I ken I hurt you. The pain will soon ease." Guilt clawed the inside of his chest. "Do you wish me to stop?" He offered her the option, though restraint would surely kill him.

"No." She gave him a tremulous smile. "I'm your wife."

"Aye. In both word and deed."

She touched his cheek. "Why are you leaving?"

"I-I was angry, because..."

"Because I got drunk last night?"

He closed his eyes. "Because I am a fool."

"Don't leave." Her kiss slid from sweet to flame, and made him realize how much he wanted her love. With time, maybe she would feel for him what he felt for her.

Patrick slowly moved within Laurie's velvet embrace.

"Are you all right?"

"Aww, yes. Fine." Her facial features had softened. "This is nice, but I think faster would be better."

Patrick quickened the pace. She seemed instinctively to follow his lead. Her body moved with his, stroke for urgent stroke. They were as close as two people could possibly be. He reveled at the feel of her, the intimate slide of thrust and withdrawal.

Her nails dug into the muscles on his forearms as he rocked against her. His rhythm quick and sure. Moist skin slapped against moist skin. Flames of fire raced through his veins, driving him harder, deeper, faster. Yet he wanted more. Needed more.

"More," she begged.

He gave their lovemaking everything from within him. Heart and soul.

She inhaled sharply and screamed his name.

The sound of his name on her lips while in the throes of ecstasy pushed him over the edge. A shudder ran over him, and he growled. The world exploded into a million, beautifully colored, bright lights.

When his breathing returned to normal, Laurie gazed at him with wonder in her eyes.

He held her tight for a moment, still panting. Then he rose onto his forearms and stared down at her. "Did I hurt you overmuch?"

"Only at the start."

Guilt burned within his chest. He silently cursed. What had he done? He was a fool. The sticky evidence of her innocence scorched his thigh. She'd been a virgin. She'd never been with that boy from the future. Maclay hadn't raped her. She'd not betrayed him.

He'd not needed to use his blood to prove her virginity. Possessiveness, so forceful, the feeling nearly consumed him, emerged to the surface. She was his and he'd never let her go.

He'd hurt her. If he only realized she'd never lain with a man before, he could have eased her first experience. He regretted having taken her in anger, having treated her no better than a whore.

"What happened last night?" She blushed profusely and didn't look at him.

"This past night, I left you alone. You were verra drunk and quick to sleep." He didn't add that she had clung to his brother, that she couldn't differentiate between he and Archibald.

"But the blood." Again, her cheeks glowed with hot color.

"'Twas mine. I did not want anyone to suspect our vows had not been consummated. I cut my hand and left my blood on the bed and on your thighs."

Patrick rose from the mattress and strode across the chamber. He poured water from the ewer into the washbasin. Wetting a cloth, he washed her blood from himself. Then he moistened the cloth again and brought it to Laurie, gently cleaning the blood from her thighs, trying to ease the discomfort between her legs.

The discomfort he caused with his stubborn lack of trust. How would he ever make it up to her?

After returning the cloth to the washstand, he climbed back into bed and embraced his wife. "Now hush, sweetling. Rest."

Laurie absently moved a finger in tiny circles on his chest, twirling the soft hairs. "How did I get drunk last night? I only remember drinking one goblet of wine."

Anger simmered again, but Patrick held it in check. "Only

one?"

"Yeah. Munn gave me the one goblet, a symbol of friendship, or so he said. It must've been very strong wine. Don't you think?"

"Aye, indeed." Patrick wasn't pleased with the direction of his thoughts. Could Munn have used magic on Laurie?

He held her in his arms until she dozed. He rose and donned his garments. Unsure of what madness had overcome his castle, he gazed at the bed where she slept. His emotions raw. He was no longer certain what took place the night past.

He silently left the chamber and searched for Munn.

Caitrina slipped from the shadows of the bedchamber unseen, appearing moments later at the knoll in the Fir-wood.

She smiled triumphantly. The seed was set, the future secure. Victory hers.

The little man had been a fool to celebrate too soon.

While she congratulated herself over her success, she sensed the air around her change—charge with energy. She spun and the queen appeared. Caitrina had never seen such fury on Oonagh's exquisite features. She took a step back, unsure of the queen's intentions.

"Princess, you think yourself the victor? Yet the game continues." With those ambiguous words, the High Queen of the Fae merged with the mist and vanished from sight.

Caitrina cursed. Then she, too, disappeared from the wood.

CHAPTER THIRTY-FOUR

Waking to the sound of soft humming, Laurie discovered Aine moving about the bedchamber, readying a bath. The steaming tub sat before a welcoming fire.

Laurie sighed at the thought of soaking sore muscles in luxurious warmth.

The older woman curtsied. "Good day, Lady MacLachlan."

Laurie stretched and smiled at hearing her new name. "None of that. I'm still only me."

"Nae, lass, you are now the lady of the castle." Aine hustled her into the tub.

"You don't need to stay. I'd like to be alone for a bit."

"I will tend to the bed then—" The woman gasped. "So much blood. What did the brute do to you? Are you in pain, m'lady?"

Laurie's cheeks flamed. Would she ever get used to so many people knowing the intimate details of her life?

"I'm fine," she managed to get out through her embarrassment.

"Beast!" Aine dropped the bloody sheet and hustled from the room.

Patrick searched the castle, but couldn't find Munn. He asked Elspeth. Questioned Duncan and Jamie. They hadn't seen the wee man since the banquet the previous night. Giving up, Patrick headed for his private chamber.

Archibald and Stephen waited for him.

"Now what!" Their unexpected appearance set him on edge.

Stephen leaned nonchalantly against the wall with his arms crossed over his chest.

Archibald stared over Patrick's shoulder. "This message arrived from our Cousin Allain. The gillie who brought the missive was anxious to return. Before he left, he indicated the contents were of the greatest import."

He stepped forward to hand the document over.

Putting aside his quest to find Munn and his resolve to solve the mystery of his wedding night, Patrick gave his full attention to his brother. He placed his hand on Archibald's shoulder. "I was mistaken this past night. I accused you falsely."

His twin hesitated a moment then nodded.

Clearing his throat, Patrick accepted the note. "Let us see what Allain reports."

He broke the seal. Both of the other men watched him. While reading the contents, he kept his features bland.

He held the missive tight in his hand. Heat rushed up his neck and into his face. Crinkling the message into a ball, he thrust the offensive missive into the fire.

Stephen straightened away from the wall. "What did he say?"

"Allain reminds me that Uncle Donald has taken refuge at my keep in Glasrie. It seems our uncle is spreading rumors of my troubles with Lamont, claiming I am unfit to lead. Allain fears Donald attempts to rally support against me."

"He goes too far," Archibald said.

"Aye, he does." Patrick bit back an angry curse.

309

"We can send someone to watch Donald, to follow him should he leave Glasrie," Stephen suggested.

Patrick needed to deal with his uncle himself, but he didn't want to leave Castle Lachlan. Not now that he finally had Laurie as his wife.

"You shall go." He directed his stare at Stephen.

"I did not intend for it to be me. Who will guard you?" His cousin sounded concerned.

"Archie is here, as are Duncan and Jamie. I will be safe enough. Besides, you are well suited to stalk our dear uncle. In addition, I need to ken if Maclay contacts him. The men I sent to search for the cur have found naught."

"What of Lamont?" Archibald straightened at Stephen's question.

"He claims to have washed his hands of the man," Patrick said.

"More the reason for me to remain and guard your back."

Patrick wrapped an arm around his cousin's shoulder. "I trust only you to watch our uncle and uncover any other treachery at my keep in Glasrie. Allain maintains good order there, but he is not accustomed to Donald's schemes."

"Aye." Stephen sighed. "I will keep Donald out of trouble and watch for Maclay."

They exchanged glances, a silent message shared. After some vigorous backslapping, Stephen left the chamber to prepare for his journey. Archibald made to follow him, but Patrick stopped him.

"Stay. I wish to have words with you."

"As you like."

"I recognize the fact it is past time for Uncle Donald to be dealt with. And I should be the one going to Glasrie to handle him. Yet I dinnae wish to leave my lady-wife alone. And I cannae take her with me. The trip is arduous and she would slow me down. I told Stephen you are here. Will you stay?"

"For a wee bit. I plan to take some lads and go to Lamont and attempt to garner his agreement for my marriage to

Isobell. We wish to wed soon. I would have his blessing. However, Alexander will remain here for several months. He plans to stay with Elspeth before he returns to Carrick Castle."

"Good. I trust you to handle Lamont. When I go to Glasrie, I can leave Laurie in Alexander's care."

Patrick embraced his twin and managed a smile of relief. He hated when he and his brother were at odds.

Shortly after his brother left, a gentle tap sounded at the door. He called out and Aine answered. He bid her enter. She stood in the threshold, hands on hips, glaring at him.

What had he done to deserve her irritation?

"Chief, 'tis not my place, yet I must bring this matter to you." She coughed. "You have been overly rough with your lady-wife. She bleeds much. You must be gentle with a new bride."

Heat rose up his neck and into his cheeks for the second time this morning. This was too much. He stared at a stone above her head. "Dammit, woman. It was not all my lady-wife's blood. I cut myself while slicing a piece of cheese and used the sheet to staunch the flow. My lady-wife bled as expected of a virgin. Nae more." Saint Columba save him from the meddling woman.

Aine grinned before she left.

The old woman dared laugh at him. He'd actually blushed under her scrutiny. He growled as he sorted the papers on his worktable. He must be going soft.

Shortly before noon, Patrick ascended the stairs to the upper passageway.

He should stay away from Laurie's bed and give her time for the tenderness from his abrupt possession to fade. Though he could hardly wait to bed her again, to be alone with her, somewhere away from the castle and its over-inquisitive people. He yearned to go somewhere away from the numerous demands on his time, far away from the multitude of people vying for attention.

Ahh! He changed direction mid-stride, headed for the

kitchen and then collected his tail and his lady.

"Where are we going?" Laurie asked an hour later when they stopped on the ridge above the moor to take in the view.

"'Tis a surprise."

She rolled her eyes the way Elspeth often did. "Haven't we had enough surprises to last awhile?"

"This one you will like." He was determined to make up for his callous treatment of her on the eve of their wedding.

The sun slid toward the western horizon. They would need to quicken the pace to reach their destination before gloaming. They traversed a trail through the Fir-wood, riding deep into the forest to a place far from the interruptions of his station, and more importantly, far from the *Sithichean Sluaigh*, the mysterious faerie knoll where Laurie first appeared.

Breaking through the trees, they scattered a small gathering of deer and walked the horses toward the hunting lodge nestled there.

He signaled his guards, who discreetly spread out to keep watch.

With a glance at Laurie, his heartbeat quickened. Aye, the hut would do nicely for a tryst.

Laurie leaned forward in her saddle and eyed the thatched roofed stone hut. "What is this place?"

"We often use it when we hunt in the area." Patrick leapt to the ground.

He grasped her by the waist, lifted her from the horse and slid her down the front of his body, over the hard ridge of his sex. Hers clenched in response.

"Mmm," she purred.

"You are killing me." He set her away. "Let us get settled first."

He held the door and she entered the one-room hut. Well-tended, though sparsely furnished, the bed in the corner drew her attention. The mattress had been dressed with the finest of silks and velvets and furs. Someone created a love nest for them.

"'Tis small, I ken, but away from curious eyes. I will start a fire in the center pit, which will warm us nicely. We can easily tolerate the small amount of smoke. Dinnae you think?"

"It's perfect."

Laurie sat on a rough-hewn bench and admired her new husband while he moved around the quaint room. He secured his sword near the bed and placed their saddlebags on the floor in a corner. When he finished setting the room to rights, he stood before her.

From the pouch at his waist appeared a cloth-wrapped bundle tied with leather strips. He offered it to her. As she reached for it, he gazed into her eyes with a tenderness seldom seen by others. "I am verra sorry." He caressed her cheek with gentle fingers. "Can you find it within your heart to forgive me?"

She placed the package on the well-worn table and returned her gaze to Patrick. Regret clouded his eyes. "There isn't anything to forgive."

"Aye, there is."

His eyes widened when she placed her index finger to his lips. "Hush, now. Let us enjoy this time together without the shadows of the past."

He kissed her finger. His eyes twinkled and a smile reshaped his soft lips, making him appear more handsome and less forbidding.

On tiptoes, she took his cheeks between her hands and kissed his splendid lips. He groaned against her mouth, adjusted his position and enfolded her in his arms. He held her tight against his chest, strong emotions shimmering in the air around them.

Patrick patted her backside and ended the kiss, releasing her from his embrace. He tugged on his shirt. "Warm in here."

She suppressed a smile and reached for the package on the table. After removing the tie, she opened the cloth wrapping. A shiver of delight teased her. He'd given her a present, a beautiful circular brooch of gold with intricate filigree and three lovely, sparkling sapphire stones. The gems were the same color and clarity as the large sapphire set in the hilt of his sword and the one in her betrothal ring.

"The gemstones are the color of your eyes, sweetling. One stone for each of our *bairns*." He winked.

"We don't have any…" She hesitated, clearing her throat. "*Bairns?*"

"Elspeth foresees three. Two boys and a wee blue-eyed girl, sweet like you." He gently wiped a teardrop from her cheek.

"The brooch is beautiful. I'll cherish it always." She clutched the pin to her chest and smiled, though more tears threatened. "Thank you."

Patrick took the brooch from her and placed it on the table. "Come here." He wrapped her in a tender embrace.

The meeting of their lips began with a gentle exploration, tongues seeking and then dueling. The kisses heated to an intensity that burned. They fell onto the bed curled around each other like wrestling lion cubs unable to discern where one began and the other ended. They franticly worked to remove the other's clothing. Fabric ripped here and tore there. Soon they were naked, skin-to-skin, feeling, touching, and discovering each other's bodies, mindless of their surroundings.

All their past petting made Patrick an expert at pleasuring her. He easily brought her to a fevered pitch, her body trembling beneath him with the intensity of her need. When he entered her, she was more than ready to receive him into her slick body. Their lovemaking, wild and frenzied, brought them to an explosive release.

Sated, they cuddled in each other's arms, enjoying the satisfying afterglow.

"Three babies? Really?"

"Aye." Patrick grinned smugly.

Laurie shivered.

"You're cold." He rose from the bed and strode to the fire

to add more peat, presenting his naked back to her.

His body glistened in the firelight. *Magnificent.* His broad muscular back slimmed to a trim waist and a great butt. A firm, nicely rounded backside. The kind she wanted to reach out and squeeze. Her palms itched to touch him again.

He swung around and caught her staring.

Laurie drew in a deep breath. A smile that was purely male gave him a devilish appearance. He flexed his shoulders. Tightened his abs. Her stomach fluttered. A tingly sensation radiated throughout her whole body.

She loved this man. She'd never wanted anything more than what she had now—Patrick. They belonged to one another, completely and without reserve. She wanted to make love to him, again and again.

She curved her lips into what she hoped was a captivating smile, a come-hither look. He shot her a wicked grin before joining her in the bed. This time their loving was slow and sensual. He used all his knowledge and experience to pleasure her.

His lips teasingly skimmed, first one, and then the other of her sensitized, swollen nipples. The gentle caresses sent a tantalizing wave of heat through her, making her tremble. Raising his head slightly, he blew softly. The cool air tickled, the tender skin puckering in response. Taking one pink bud into his mouth, he suckled it into a taut, aching peak.

Laurie squirmed beneath him, craving more of his sweet, seductive kisses. He accommodated. He slowly moved down her body, his lips searing a path along her belly, across a sensitive thigh to tease between her legs. He laved her flesh with his tongue. She savored every kiss, every touch.

Her eyelids fluttered shut. He wrapped her in a sensual web he wove with artful skill.

The final caress of his skillful tongue sent her over the edge. Purple lights flashed before her eyes as she shattered into a million pleasant pieces.

When she came back to herself, she reached out to him. She was never going back to the twenty-first century. She was where she belonged—here, with this man.

She knew in her heart, she'd love him forever. Forever and an eternity.

Her home was with Patrick.

Laurie's taste was sweet on Patrick's tongue. She guided him atop her.

Her feathery touch thrilled him. The lightest pressure of her fingertips grazed the muscles on his back. Slowly she drew circles. Gooseflesh bubbled across his skin, sending throbbing sensations to his groin.

He moaned. No longer capable of restraint, he positioned himself and slowly entered her, giving her muscles time to adjust and wrap tightly around his thick shaft. Milking him. His thrusts were slow and erotic. She undulated beneath him, nearing the precipice. With a bellow, he sent them both over the top. Together they journeyed to an extraordinary place of overwhelming fulfillment.

It was much later before they had the energy to enjoy a repast of the fine food Cookie sent. Even the sharing of food hinted at sensual play.

He'd never been this happy.

With the bliss, a niggling worry tickled the back of his mind. He buried the feeling.

But after spending several idyllic days in each other's arms, the time came to return to the castle and to the realities of their new life as husband and wife, as laird and lady of the castle, and as Chief of Clan MacLachlan and his Lady-wife.

As they negotiated the narrow trail through the Fir-wood, Patrick kept an alert eye to their surroundings. The hairs on the back of his neck stood on end. He had an uncomfortable feeling, a distinct sensation someone watched. He hoped it was his imagination, but he doubted it. Even when they reached the relative security of the castle, he couldn't shake the uneasy suspicion.

CHAPTER THIRTY-FIVE

"*L*et me out." Bolted from the outside, the door wouldn't budge. Seething with resentment, Laurie slammed her fists against the hard barrier. "Dammit. Let me out."

She slid down the wood to her knees. "Sometimes, Patrick MacLachlan, you are *not* a nice man," she whispered, her forehead pressed against the rough oak.

The clamor of activity coming from the courtyard below gave her the energy to rise to her feet. Her chest tight, she ran to the window and flung open the shutters. Several men readied themselves for travel. Patrick joined them, and she glared at his back as the group strode through the gate and made their way to the water's edge.

As she feared, Patrick really planned to leave her behind.

The men hunched in silence, pulling their *plaides* tight against early winter winds. The only sound the gentle lapping of oars on water. Patrick sat on a bench at the aft of the boat, his jaw tight. His last moments with Laurie weighed heavily on his mind.

Earlier in the day, Jamie rushed into his private chamber with the news Maclay had been seen near the Fir-wood.

Patrick ordered his men to prepare, and after the screaming argument with his wife, he and his lads left the castle.

She'd been enraged, angry he planned to leave her behind. His anger fed on hers. The argument that ensued became vicious. They said things neither truly meant. The inhabitants of the castle had sadly gotten an earful. No matter how much Laurie argued though, he ultimately refused to allow her to accompany him. A raid was no place for a woman. Too much risk.

They'd been married several weeks. With time, she'd learn to trust his decisions. He shot his stare at Jamie. "How many ride with Maclay? How many on foot?"

"Ten in total, all on horseback." Jamie sat forward on his bench.

Patrick rubbed his whiskered jaw and scrutinized the other lads. He selected fewer than his usual tail. Only four well-seasoned fighters joined him. On this raid, stealth would be more important than force. In order to flush out Maclay, the warriors would need to blend into the woods and catch him unawares.

The boat beached on the mainland shore where a pair of young lads waited with saddled horses. The warriors swiftly mounted, guiding their steeds northeast along the shore of Loch Fyne.

Refusing to allow himself the weakness of looking back to see if Laurie watched from their bedchamber window, Patrick galloped away. Hardening his heart, he thought only of the confrontation he'd soon face.

The time had come for Maclay to pay for his sins.

Laurie lunged onto the bed and slammed her fists into a pillow, sending feathers flying. After the fit of temper, she swung her legs over the side and sat on the edge of the bed.

Nausea gurgled in her stomach. With a hand pressed to her belly, she rushed across the room to the basin and vomited. Shit, she'd made herself sick.

She grasped a cloth, wet it, and held it to her mouth. She slid down to her knees and leaned back on her heels. Shivers replaced the queasy flush.

With winter spreading its frosty blanket over the land, the weather turned blustery. Brisk raw winds raced along the loch, slamming against the castle's old gray stones, howling through the battlements. The castle held a constant chill, the chambers breezy.

The only time she felt warm was at night when she lay in bed with Patrick. Sleeping with him was like cuddling with a large red-hot coal. He produced more than enough heat to keep them both warm through the bitter nights.

A tear escaped, and she brushed it away with the back of her hand. She wouldn't cry. She pushed up from the floor and sat in a chair near the hearth, wrapping one of Patrick's plaids around her shoulders for added warmth. The fabric still held his pine forest scent.

Her heart clenched. She couldn't really blame Patrick for refusing to allow her to join in the hunt for Maclay. It wasn't as if she could protect him. Now, when she thought about it. He was right. Having to worry about her safety would put him at risk.

Laurie jumped when a cup fell from the mantle to crash on the stone floor. "What the…" She picked up a broken piece and a chill slid down her spine.

"Munn?" Where was the jealous little man? He'd been at the root of most of her recent troubles.

Although Caitrina had gotten her into the mess in the beginning, loving Patrick as she did, Laurie no longer faulted Caitrina for her trickery. If Caitrina hadn't pushed her through the time-gate, Laurie would never have joined with her true soul mate. She never would have learned the true meaning of belonging.

She believed the old woman at the caves had been Caitrina in some sort of magical disguise. Caitrina hadn't made an appearance since, and Laurie wondered why.

Munn, on the other hand, had been the one who gave her

the cursed goblet of wine to drink at the wedding banquet. Token of friendship? Surely not. She only drank one goblet, yet she'd been incredibly drunk. Something must have been in the oh-too-sweet wine, something that confused her, caused her to believe Archibald was Patrick.

It almost cost her…her love.

She should've realized sooner Munn worked against her. When she thought of the many odd occurrences, she should have had cause to question his loyalty to his chief. Whenever Patrick took her into his arms, there had been something not quite right. Each time, something unnatural occurred, stopped their loving.

The wet cloth that landed on Patrick's back while they kissed. The horn in the tower that mysteriously sounded on its own. And the evening in Patrick's study when Munn appeared out of thin air, ranting and raving about doom and gloom, blaming every imaginable misfortune on her.

The only explanation for the insanity was Munn. He was a menace.

Spiraling into another fine rage, she leapt from the chair and marched to the door. She tugged, never expecting to find it unlocked, but this time, the door opened. Hurrying along the passageway, she passed two guardsmen deep in discussion. Although they glanced up and nodded when she passed, they didn't bother to block her way. Confident no one else would attempt to stop her, she quickly made her way down the circular stair, across the courtyard, and through the castle gate. She ran along the path to the garden, blind to everything save her destination.

She found Elspeth sitting in the midst of the frost-dead plants with Alexander.

"Where is that miserable brownie?" Laurie asked. "How do you call a brownie to you?"

Elspeth and Alexander, as one, flipped wide eyes up from the book they read.

"You dinnae," Elspeth said after a moment. "They appear only when they wish."

Laurie glared at the horizon, raised her arm and made a fist. "Damn you, little man. I'll find a way to keep Patrick close to my heart. You'll not force us apart."

Queasiness once again rumbled in Laurie's stomach. Her vision blurred. She clutched her belly and swayed. Was this magic too? Had Munn put a hex on her?

"Laurie!" Elspeth jumped to her feet "What is it? What has befallen you?"

Laurie didn't have the breath to answer. She stumbled over the gravel path and threw out an arm, reaching for the wall, but it was too far away and she was too weak. She slid to the ground and lost consciousness.

CHAPTER THIRTY-SIX

*P*atrick crept through the dense forest on silent feet. Branches slapped at him, scratching his skin. Hearing the screech of an owl and the flutter of wings nearby, he stood motionless. He peered into the dark. It pressed in on him, a heavy weight against his chest.

A terror dream flashed in his mind, an assailant's heavy net entrapping him.

Seconds passed. He drew an uneasy breath. The panic subsided. Comforted by his faith that Laurie remained safely ensconced within his castle's walls, he released the air from his lungs and soundlessly moved forward.

His men skulked close behind.

They were rewarded for their stealth when they came upon a well-lit camp. A large bonfire burned in a clearing. Carefully moving within the shadows, Patrick crawled on his stomach through the brush, getting as close as he dared.

Secure in their arrogance, Maclay's men hadn't positioned a guard to signal their enemies' approach. The horses were also unguarded, tethered haphazardly in a small meadow nearby.

Three men sat huddled together by the fire, passing skins, talking loudly, hurling lewd insults at one another, their speech slurred with drink. Four additional men moved amidst the flickering fire light, stumbling with their drunkenness. Seven inebriated men. They would be easy odds for the MacLachlan warriors.

Disappointment tasted bitter in Patrick's mouth. Maclay was not among them.

Patrick signaled to his men and they silently moved to encircle the camp.

A birdcall sounded. A wildcat howled. Horses whinnied, restless, then free to stampede. Chaos ensued.

Although his men argued against the wisdom, Patrick sent them ahead to the castle with the few prisoners who'd chosen to surrender rather than die. It gave him the chance to scout for Maclay. But he'd never expected to come across something so troubling.

Munn lay in the mud at the side of the trail. Battered and bruised, his clothing torn and singed, the wee man curled into himself. Terrible pain was visible in the creases of his weathered face.

Patrick helped the brownie sit against a tree.

"Ach, chief, I have betrayed you. The *Sithichean* queen, she beguiled me. I vowed to keep the lass from the future away." He hung his head.

"What have you done?"

The wee man didn't answer. He faded as if about to completely disappear. Ever so slowly, he returned to solid form only to fade again. His body convulsed when his form reappeared once more.

Although the flickering repetition was difficult to watch, Patrick found himself transfixed.

When Munn faded again, Patrick touched the brownie's shoulder. His hand moved through Munn's fading image and an unbearable pain shot up Patrick's arm and into his chest.

A strangled scream escaped his throat. Spasms of excruciating pain shook the length of his body. He fell to the ground, paralyzed, unable to move. Relentless pain throbbed within Patrick's chest as if his essence, the substance of his very life had drained from him and into Munn. One last spasm raked Patrick's body and he mercifully fell unconscious.

He regained consciousness a little at a time. He opened his eyes a slit, a bright white light almost blinding him. He tried to move, but his muscles wouldn't respond. With great effort, he managed to shift his head enough to see Munn sitting next to him, watching him through wary eyes.

Patrick hardly believed what he saw. No bruises marred Munn's wrinkled old skin. The man seemed fully recovered. Yet Patrick felt weaker and more helpless than a newborn *bairn*.

Then he noticed the beautiful woman standing over him. A shimmering silver aura surrounded her, the source of the intense light. She moved her hands in intricate patterns, softly chanting in a language ancient as the pagan gods.

Patrick again attempted to move, something as simple as bending his fingers, but even that he couldn't manage. He wasn't capable of forming words to speak either. Fear pooled in his gut and he tried to make sense of the situation. Before he had much of a chance, his vision faded once more.

Sunrays warmed Patrick's face when he woke for the second time. He gingerly moved his fingers. They worked fine. He moved his arm and pushed up into a sitting position. Scanning the area, he discovered he was alone. He almost believed he dreamt the whole thing, yet deep in his gut, he knew he hadn't.

Why did the fae meddle in his life? His thoughts flashed to Laurie. He needed to get home before something else fae-like occurred.

Laurie opened her eyes. The ceiling looked familiar—like the one in the room she shared with Patrick. But that didn't make sense. The last thing she remembered—

A movement turned her attention from the stone ceiling. Laurie blinked to bring the figure into focus. A worried Elspeth stood near the bed. A frowning Alexander was a step back. He was glaring. Laurie moved the multitude of plaids atop her and raised her hand to her forehead, trying to remember what happened.

"You are awake," Elspeth said.

"I'm sorry. Did I faint again?"

"Aye." Elspeth raised a brow. "When do you plan to tell Patrick?"

"Tell him what?"

"About the *bairn*." Elspeth smiled.

Alexander burst out laughing, and Laurie shut her gaping mouth.

"How do you know?"

"My gift."

Laurie reclined against the pillows. *I'm in the motherly way.*

Joy spread from her heart outward. *I'm going to have a baby.*

Nothing could make her more happy.

At the sound of Patrick's voice, she lifted her head to listen. She could just make out the sound of his husky voice while he spoke to Duncan outside the bedchamber door. She sat up, bracing herself against the headboard.

The door jerked open. Patrick stood in the doorway, looking at her quizzically.

She rushed her gaze over him, searching for injuries. He looked fine. *Damn fine.*

"We will leave you then." Elspeth gathered some items from the bedside, flicked a glance at her brother and whispered, "Aine must have told him." She grabbed Alexander by the hand and hustled past her brother.

As soon as they were gone, Patrick crossed the room and pulled Laurie into his arms. His passionate kiss removed every thought from her mind.

When he ended the kiss, he didn't release her. Glancing at his face, she saw something unexpected in his eyes. Hurt?

She needed to apologize for the argument she'd caused

before he left.

"Why did you not tell me you carry my heir?"

Laurie stiffened within his embrace. Men had such fragile egos, and Highland chiefs were the worst. "Yes, I'm with child." She couldn't help the snarky smile that curled her lips. "Our child. Yours and *mine*. I only now learned myself."

Several emotions crossed Patrick's face before he released her and stepped away. "Are you well then?"

"Yeah. Listen, I'm sorry for arguing with you before you left."

"Me too." Patrick rubbed the back of his neck. "You must ken 'twas only to protect you."

"I do understand."

"Good." He sat on the bed next to her, stroking her arm while he spoke. "We found their camp. Maclay wasn't there. He continues to roam free. For that, I am truly sorry."

"Then I'm still not safe." A chill swept her spine at the mere mention of the lunatic's name.

Patrick reached for her and pulled her into his embrace, holding her within the warmth and safety of his strong arms. "I will protect you, sweetling. Always."

❀ ❀ ❀

Shortly afterward, Patrick met with Stephen in the great hall. The warning horn blew loud and clear, interrupting their discussion.

His man, Dunall, hurried into the hall, huffing and puffing. "Archibald approaches the bay on a lathered steed."

Archibald never mistreated a horse. "Something must be wrong," Patrick mused aloud and dashed to the window. A clansman rowed his brother across the bay toward the castle.

"What has happened?" Patrick bellowed as Archibald rushed into the hall, his eyes wide with panic.

Attempting to catch his breath, Archibald gulped large quantities of air. "Lamont refuses to agree to the marriage. He is determined for Isobell to wed a clan chief."

"What else had you pushing your mount? Caused you to

ride like the devil was on your tail?"

"The devil is on my tail. Lamont plans to wage war. He rides with Uncle Donald and more than one hundred warriors."

Patrick's jaw tightened. "How much of a lead have you?"

"Two days. Mayhap three."

Patrick glanced at each person in the great hall, and then at his beautiful wife. He wanted more than anything in this world for her to be happy, and he'd wondered if that were possible here in his time. Now set before him was a resolution for everyone. His brother deserved to have love too.

Patrick grasped Laurie's hand. "Are you sure you know the way home?" He gave her a pointed look. "To the place of your birth?"

"I believe I do."

"Well, then. I have made a decision. If Lamont wants Isobell to wed a chief she shall." Patrick raised his hand to stop his brother's expected retort. "You will become laird of this castle and Chief of Clan MacLachlan."

There was a collective intake of breath from those present in the hall. Archibald's mouth hung open.

"Close your mouth, Archie. 'Tis unbecoming of a great Highland chief."

"What are you saying?"

"That you will be chief. We will leave, Laurie and me. As my rightful heir, you will take my place as chief. Lamont will be forced to approve your marriage. And Archie, if I were you, I would get Isobell to say her vow in front of the priest before Lamont arrives."

"I dinnae understand."

Laurie wrapped her arm around Patrick's waist. He gazed at her and clearly saw her love for him in the depth of her eyes.

"Tonight there is a full moon. I am taking my lady-wife home. We will make a new life for ourselves in her country."

Late afternoon brought with it the threat of storms as they rode northeast along the loch. Laurie clutched the reins. The heavily bearded clouds roiled with thunder and lightning. The sky so murky the water below appeared a dark charcoal gray, the white caps shocking in contrast.

Without warning, unfriendly riders bored down on them.

The small MacLachlan party spurred their mounts, coaxing them into a burst of speed. Their flight was wild and dangerous. Laurie and her mount fell behind. Patrick slowed, risking the time to pull her from her horse to settle her behind him on his.

She wrapped her arms around his waist and held on. They found themselves crossing the moor alone, having been separated from their escort.

Maclay and several warriors rode down upon them.

Patrick spurred their mount and they rode, fast and furious, precariously onward through the storm. The speed of their flight amazed her, as if Patrick's magnificent gray stallion had sprung wings. She clung to Patrick, praying to the saints above for their safety and escape.

He rode a zigzagging course, circling and backtracking in an attempt to lose their pursuers.

Urging their horse to an even greater speed, they galloped across a field, racing toward the dense wood that edged the cleared space. When they reached the first trees, Patrick reined in and glanced back.

"We've gained much-needed distance, but the cur still pursues," he yelled over the din of the storm.

They entered the wood, taking a narrow trail that climbed to higher ground. The storm intensified, the wind hurled stinging sleet. They traveled a narrow and steep track. Hoofs slipped and slid on the loose shale nearly loosing purchase.

Laurie held tight to Patrick's waist, much relieved when they reached level ground. When they traveled a short distance into the Fir-wood her pulse quickened. They were near the clearing at the edge of the faerie knoll.

With Maclay not far behind, Patrick glanced back, and then quickly guided their horse onto the edge of the hillock.

Everything changed as if they'd moved through a curtain from winter to spring.

"We will be safe here. Maclay will not follow us." Patrick helped Laurie from the horse.

She stared in awe. The faerie knoll was a mysterious place. Hundreds of small dazzling white lights flickered around them. The sparkling lights hovered near the ground and up high, in the grass atop the knoll and in the nearby tree branches. The scene reminded her of her childhood, of watching lightning bugs, little glowing fireflies dancing in the night. She thought the sight amazing, and beautiful.

"This place is known as the *Sithichean Sluaigh*. Legend has it the knoll is a habitat for faeries. I have heard the old folk say beams of brightly colored light are seen here on starless nights," Patrick said with a dancing twinkle in his eyes.

"Have you ever seen the lights?"

"Nae." He shook his head. "I have also heard tales that on occasion you can hear melodious faerie music coming from the verra depths of this mound. They say 'tis Finvarra's rath though I believe he resides in Ireland." The corner of his mouth twitched.

Laurie smiled. "Really? Have you heard the faerie music?"

"Nae, though when I was a child and learned about Munn, I was determined to catch a faerie of my own. I would sneak out of the castle and come here. I never succeeded in trapping a sprite, but I have never once doubted the fae's existence." He grinned. "They will keep us safe."

As Patrick knew faeries and brownies existed, he now believed time travel possible. His precious Laurie was proof of that. The mere thought of trying the experience made his knees weak.

She told him about the wonders of her time. He marveled over her explanation of a satellite phone. He could imagine how amazing it would be to have the ability to speak to anyone, anywhere in the world, from anywhere else in the world. She told him about something called a laptop computer. Small enough to sit on his lap, but contained all of the learning from all the manuscripts in the king's library. And something called an MP3 player filled with music. Her stories were well beyond his comprehension.

He doubted he'd be at ease with her time. But for her, and for the *bairns* he planned to father, he'd try. He wanted her safe and he wanted healthy *bairns*. He was doing the right thing. Handing the leadership of the clan to his brother had been necessary to keep the peace and gave Patrick an excuse to take Laurie to her home.

Determined to go through with the faerie magic, he opened his arms to her. She walked into his embrace. They hugged, secure in each other's arms.

"What if we get separated and only I return to the twenty-first century? I couldn't bear losing you." Laurie clung to him.

He squeezed her tight. Stepping back, he held her at arm's length. He gazed into her eyes, exposing for her all of his emotions. "Ach, lass. Nae matter what happens, I will find you. Even if I must travel through time to a thousand different places, I promise you, I will find you."

Patrick gazed around the knoll. The storm through which they had fled didn't exist in this place. He hugged Laurie again before pulling away and clasping her hand. He gave a little squeeze and together they walked to the center of the knoll. He let go of her hand and wrapped his arms around her waist. "Hold on and dinnae let go."

At that moment, the full moon escaped from the clouds to shine brightly overhead, casting its silvery glow on the unusual spring-green grass of the knoll.

Then it happened.

The earth shook, the wind blew and the world as Patrick knew it ceased to exist.

Energy ignited his soul in a jolt of awareness that crowded out every other sense. He fell, falling downward, down…down…down into the swirling maelstrom. Choking against the scream that threatened to escape, he held his eyes closed tight. Yet bright lights flashed, scorching the back of his lids.

His grasp on Laurie weakened. The force wrenched her away from him.

No longer holding her hand, he was alone and lost in the frightening tempest.

CHAPTER THIRTY-SEVEN

Anderson Creek, North Carolina

*F*inn jolted awake, his heartbeat kicking in double time, his innate warning system screaming an alarm. Alert to potential danger, he lay motionless, listening. Noise came from outside, from the garden, muted voices.

Adrenaline pumped through his veins. He'd learned, years ago during his short stint in the military, to channel the energy in a positive way. Taking several deep breaths, he imagined himself the calm warrior.

He reached for his jeans from the chair next to the bed and tugged them on. He padded across the bedroom on bare feet, grabbing his sword from where it leaned against the wall before he left the room.

His grip tightened on the hilt of his claymore, the two handed sword of the Highlanders. The antique weapon cost him a small fortune. Legend spoke of a faerie princess who kissed the moonstone in the middle of the cross-section, bestowing upon the sword magical power. The legend claimed the weapon enhanced the skills of the warrior who possessed it. Iain and Douglas, the men he met shortly after he arrived to search for his cousin Laurie, instructed him in its use. The sword weighed about six pounds, and he'd massed the muscle and strength to wield it. He couldn't best them yet, but he worked hard to acquire the skills.

Had they planned a surprise attack?

Douglas beat him into the mud during today's practice. Finn rubbed the resulting ache at his hip. What was he thinking getting involved with the local reenactment group? The training was more grueling than he'd undergone as a marine.

He crept through the living room and into the kitchen, stopping at the door. Hesitating for a moment, he listened. The voices came from the rear of the garden.

Finn twisted the doorknob and pushed, praying it wouldn't make noise. Very quietly, the door opened. He released the breath he held, thankful for well-oiled hinges. He stayed put until his eyes adjusted to the near darkness. Using foliage for cover, he worked his way through the garden to the stone bench. A large shadow the size of Iain moved near the back gate.

The gate Douglas claimed a conduit of magic.

Gooseflesh prickled along Finn's arms. He dropped into a crouch, balancing his weight on the balls of his feet with the sword grasped in both hands extended in front of him ready to fend off an attack.

He remained motionless. Why didn't Iain make a move on him?

Finn stiffened. Had his friends set him up for a rear attack from Douglas?

The clouds cleared the full moon and a silvery light bathed the garden. The large man who stood before him wasn't Iain. The stranger dressed in one of the most authentic Scottish Highlands' reenactment costumes Finn had seen. If he guessed right, the great kilt was from the sixteenth century. A sight he hadn't expected to see in his cousin's garden tonight.

He strained his eyes to see the other shadowy figure partially hidden. A small woman completely wrapped within a large tartan blanket stepped from behind the man.

With barely a thought to his training, Finn stood straight. Taking his sword in one hand, he rested it point down on the ground while he rubbed his eyes with his free hand. Was he seeing things? Who could these strange people be? Friends of Iain or Douglas?

What were they doing in his cousin's garden? "Hey? Who are you?"

In one swift motion, the stranger pulled a sword from a sheath on his back, and before Finn blinked, the sharp point pressed against his throat.

"Don't! He's my cousin." The woman rushed forward and grasped the man's bicep.

Not daring to move, every muscle taut, Finn looked into the man's dark eyes and recognized the warning. With the slightest pressure, he'd be dead.

Biting back the fear boiling in his belly, Finn refused to glance away.

"Release him."

What the hell? The voice belonged to Laurie. Still, he knew better than to let down his guard. He continued to hold the man's stare, issuing a challenge of his own.

With a chuckle, the stranger let the point of his sword drop and reached out his arm. "Patrick."

Finn looked from the offered hand to the man's eyes, flicking his gaze to his cousin and back to the stranger. Humor now sparkled in those dark eyes. Relaxing his muscles, he allowed Patrick to grasp his arm in what he learned from Iain was a warrior's greeting—a show of honor.

"Finn."

"Aye. I ken that now. Sorry I brought my sword upon you. My lady-wife would be sorely vexed if I killed her kin."

Finn jerked his gaze to Laurie. Her expression dared him to question her. He planned to do just that. Maybe he'd wring her neck while he was at it.

"Where have you been and what are you doing with this brute? Lady-wife? Dammit, Laurie, what is he talking about?"

Laurie grabbed hold of Patrick's hand for moral support. And to restrain him from coming to blows with her cousin. Two men, bristling with pride, positioning for dominance, wasn't something she wanted to deal with after zinging through a time warp.

She shivered and glanced around the garden. Something wasn't quite right, but she couldn't figure out what unnerved her. Plants bloomed in abundance. Cosmos, zinnias, and sunflowers surrounded them. The perfume from the Stargazer lilies tickled her nose. Even in the dim light, the garden showed at its peak.

Flowers?

"Finn, what is today's date?"

He stared at her as if she were crazy. "My darling cousin, I've been extremely worried. I returned from a financial symposium in Beijing to find you gone. Your landlord claimed you left without a word. You paid the rent for a year in advance and then disappeared. What was I to think? Now you want to know the date? What's going on? Where have you been?" He glared at Patrick. "And what are you doing with this man, dressed in that costume?"

Stray hair had come loose from her braid, and she smoothed the strands back with a shaky hand. "I'll answer your questions in a minute. First, tell me the date."

Finn leaned against the hilt of his sword. "Wednesday, July twenty-fifth."

She slumped against Patrick.

He squeezed her hand. "When we left, snow covered the ground."

"I know. I don't understand this either."

Her cousin looked at their joined hands and relaxed his shoulders. "What are you talking about? Snow?"

"Can we go inside? I really need to sit down," she said.

"Sure." Finn gazed off to the east. "The sun will rise soon. I can make a pot of coffee."

"Wonderful." Laurie sighed with pleasure. "I haven't drank coffee in months."

His eyes snapped to her. "What? You survive on coffee. Just where have you been?"

"I'll explain after I have some java."

Laurie held Patrick's hand and guided him along the path to the cottage. His grip was firm, but his features thinned as he checked out the profusion of flowers.

Unreal. The garden was lush and green.

And her Patrick—brave.

He dropped her hand and followed her into the kitchen. "Where are the candles? I've nary a one in my pouch."

Finn flicked on the light as he entered behind them and leaned his sword against the wall.

Patrick yelped. With a backward hop, he hit his backside against the stove. His eyes filled with panic and his gaze darted around the room.

She reached out to him, but he shook his head and raised his chin.

Patrick rubbed his eyes and surveyed the chamber again. Odd. Although the table and chairs looked much like the ones at Castle Lachlan, though less ornate, other items in the room were more foreign than what he'd seen during his travels on the continent. There were several large silver boxes. One nearly as big as a man, and with handles on its front. He raised his gaze to the ceiling and the strange source of light, until his eyes burned and he looked away.

He'd never seen the like before. The extreme brightness made it seem as if the sun hung from the ceiling. He refused to ask his wife's cousin how he'd made the chamber light. He didn't want to appear ignorant.

Many things existed in this time he couldn't possibly understand. Patrick ran a hand through his loose hair. Had he made a grave mistake? He noted the worry in Laurie's eyes and straightened his shoulders, standing tall. He'd made the right decision. She belonged here in her own time, and he would learn how to survive here too.

Her cousin watched him with suspicion. Patrick

suppressed a growl and ignored the man. He unfastened his sword and shrugged it off, leaning the weapon against the wall next to Finn's. He didn't want the man to think he didn't trust him.

He smiled at Laurie, guided her to the table, and helped her sit in one of the chairs. He leaned close and kissed her soft cheek.

"Are you well?"

"Fine." Her radiant smile was his reward.

He'd do whatever it took to make her happy. The glare from the other man was of no consequence.

Patrick stood behind his wife's chair and clenched his jaw. No one need know he clutched the chair back to keep his hands from trembling.

Laurie reached behind her and patted Patrick's hand, feeling remorse for putting him through this. This was the beginning of his adjustment. The transition would be difficult for her Highland warrior.

She removed the heavy wool plaid and folded it on the table at her side.

Finn gasped, his gaze narrowing on her swollen belly. He pointed at her stomach, his mouth dropping open.

"Close your mouth, Finn. You look like an idiot."

"Would you mind explaining that?"

She placed a palm on her extended abdomen, and felt movement. Excitement bubbled up, but she kept it to herself. A secret she'd share with Patrick later when they were alone.

Well, her unborn child showed an odd sense of timing. Laurie had left Scotland barely pregnant and now appeared closer to six months along. With a sigh, she made eye contact with Finn.

"Outside, you shook hands with my husband." Again, she patted the back of Patrick's hand. "We married several months ago. What often happens to married couples happened to us. We're expecting a child."

"Dammit. What were you thinking? With a child on the

way it'll be hard to get an annulment."

She opened her mouth to blast her cousin, but Patrick growled, low and deep. Laurie half expected to hear a battle cry. "We said our vows afore a priest. There will not be an annulment." Taking her by the hand, he pulled her from her seat. "Come, wife. We return to Scotland."

Finn snarled. "You'll not take my cousin anywhere. Least of all out of the country. I'll have my law enforcement friends on you so quick, your head will spin."

Tension strained between the two men as they glared at each other. The testosterone overload was thick in the air. They were two obstinate, headstrong, foolish men, whom she loved, each in her own special way. But right now, she wanted to give them each a smack.

"Stop this foolishness, both of you. Patrick, sit down. You too, Finn. We're married, and Finn, you'll have to get used to the idea. Now, explain to me why you're here, obviously living in my house. And then, I'll try to explain where I've been." She sat in the chair and folded her arms over her chest.

Finn gave her one of his annoyed looks, one she was way too familiar with from when she worked for him.

"I returned from Asia to learn *Trendsetter* magazine named me *Best Catch of the Year*. Believe it or not, women are stalking me. I needed to get out of town and thought this the one place no one would look for me. I drove down. Only, when I called to invite myself, I learned you'd been missing for over a month."

Poor Finn. She almost felt sorry for him. She could imagine the antics women would contrive in an attempt to grab his attention.

"How long have you been here?" She glanced around the kitchen at the junk on the counters, piles of newspapers and magazines, a few paperbacks, dirty dishes. "It appears as if you've settled in."

Finn strode to the refrigerator, removed a container of ground coffee and, using a filter, put some into the drip coffee maker, then added water.

"I've been here a little over a month, though it seems longer." After he flipped the switch, he took three cups from the cupboard and set them on the counter. "I tried to contact Father when I discovered you were missing. He's in Africa, again—somewhere on a dig—and can't be reached."

Finn had always found it galling to have a father who shunned his business responsibilities in order to travel around the globe pursuing archeological artifacts.

"What's up with the sword?" She breathed easier, relieved to see the two claymores—so out of place in the modern kitchen—leaning harmlessly against the wall. Wait a minute. The sword—

"What?"

"Isn't it from the *Celtic Image* shop?"

"Yeah. Before I hired a firm to find you, I searched for you myself. I visited the shop and met Douglas MacKinnon. He told me you'd vanished into the woods behind the cottage in search of your destiny." Finn leaned against the counter. "Can you believe it? He thinks you were spirited away by a faerie princess."

"A faerie? Really?" Laurie sucked back her smile.

Her nose twitched. The aroma of brewing French roast tantalized her taste buds. Steam spewed from the coffee maker. Patrick's eyes bugged. Finn poured the java and put the full mugs on the table along with milk and sugar.

"Douglas has got some unusual beliefs, but otherwise we've a lot in common. He convinced me to join the local reenactment group. He and your landlord are teaching me to fight like a Highlander."

Patrick made an unpleasant noise deep in his throat, and she chuckled. He stared into the dark brew. She added a spoon of sugar and some milk, and pushed the cup toward him. He took a sip and gave her one of his beautiful smiles. As always, her heart tripped a beat.

Finn cleared his throat. "Now it's your turn to explain where you've been." His gaze landed on her belly. "Just when did you get pregnant? You've only been gone a couple of months.

"That's part of the story, though it would be best if I started at the beginning." She felt herself frowning. "And there are a few things I don't understand." Like how she was several months ahead on her pregnancy.

Laurie talked until her voice rasped, with Patrick adding a nod at critical points. The sun had risen long ago and natural light streamed into the kitchen.

Finn closed his mouth. He'd spent a good part of their discussion gaping. "I guessed the story would be long and complicated. I didn't expect the tale to be completely unbelievable." He emptied the dregs from his cup into the sink as if he needed to do something normal. "You're telling me you left the sixteenth century in the winter to arrive here where it's your previous summer, at least measured by the basis of the length of time you were in the past. You know, the story boggles the mind."

"I know." She cocked her head sideways. "I never lie. You have to believe I'm telling the truth."

"I guess I believe you. It's just unfathomable." He ran his fingers through his tousled hair. "Let's get some rest. I need to sleep on this. I'll take the sofa and you and Patrick can take the bedroom. Later you can help me pack and take my things to the inn. The innkeepers will be relieved to learn you've returned safe and sound."

Laurie rose and tugged on Patrick's hand. "I'll show you to our bedroom."

Patrick leaned against the bed-head with Laurie curled against him sound asleep, her belly pressed into his side. The *bairn* growing within her womb filled him with pride. He rubbed his chest in the vicinity of his heart.

Laurie and their *bairn* would be safe here in this time. He glanced around the chamber. The furniture was constructed from good quality wood. The bed was smaller than his at

Castle Lachlan; his feet hung over the end when he laid flat, but otherwise the mattress was comfortable. The cottage was wee, yet serviceable. Laurie's home would shelter them until he built something bigger.

The *bairn* kicked and the wonder of it had him rubbing his chest again. Laurie's eyes opened, her lips curving into a glorious smile. She claimed his heart, and he made a vow. He'd do whatever was required to make a good life for her and their *bairn*.

She rubbed her hand along his thigh. "How's my lover?"

Patrick hardened. With a growl, he pulled her on top of him, pressing his erection against her center. Her eyes flared. "We won't hurt the babe?" he asked.

"Nah." She nuzzled his neck, sending shivers over his skin.

He held her tight against his length. "Are you sure? I wouldn't want to—"

"I'm not fragile glass. I won't break."

He slipped her chemise over her head and slowly entered her. Warmth washed through his body. She scraped her nails along his back, urging him to give her more.

Their loving was all consuming and they exploded in unison with an intensity that shook his soul. He doubted he'd ever get use to the intense pleasure he found within her arms.

But would he be able to provide for her and keep her and the *bairn* safe in this strange time?

Laurie strolled into the living room, straightening the lavender peasant blouse she wore over a black elastic-waist skirt. She'd need to go shopping to get some maternity clothes.

Finn reached for the front doorknob. "My Hummer is out front."

"And you don't understand why women chase after you when you flaunt your wealth like that."

Finn bristled. "I don't."

"You do." She laughed. "I doubt Patrick is ready for a car ride. Our world is overwhelming enough for those born to it. For someone like Patrick, well…all I can do is try to ease the way for him." She pulled her sweater from the chair and tied it around her shoulders. "You take your vehicle. We'll walk. We'll cross the meadow and take the trail through the woods."

She sensed Patrick's presence before he touched her. When he put his hand on her shoulder, she turned around to face him. Her breath caught. He wore a pair of Finn's jeans. They fit him, nice and snug, in a way to make her mouth water. Raising her eyes to his chest, she took in the white polo pulled taut against firm muscle. She licked her lips and gazed into his eyes. They burned with pure lust.

"Ach, wife. Do that again with your tongue and we will never leave this cottage."

She swallowed, stepping closer to him.

Finn chuckled. "We can't have that. I need you both to help me unload my stuff at the inn. Besides, I'm starving and you promised to join me for dinner." He opened the front door and headed out.

Laurie gave Patrick a disappointed pout before turning away to reach for her purse. He stooped down. With his lips grazing her ear, he whispered, "Later, m'sweet. I will make you scream."

A delicious shiver slid along her spine. "I'm doomed to be horny all through dinner."

"*Horny?*" His forehead furrowed.

"Never mind. I'll show you what I mean tonight." Hand in hand, they left the cottage and strolled across the meadow, taking their time along the woodland trail to the inn.

"I think you should explain *horny* now," Patrick said.

"Remember what it was like when Munn pulled mischievous pranks to keep us apart?"

"Aye."

"That frustration is horny."

"We could make love here in the wood."

"Finn would interrupt us."

"Later then." Patrick's sexy smile made her insides flip.

"It's a date."

When they arrived at the inn, Finn's black Hummer was parked in front. Laurie brought Patrick through the side garden, around to the rear door and into the foyer. Since the room was empty, she guided him toward the dining room entrance.

"Welcome back, Miss Bernard. Can I seat you?" Emily worked the hostess stand.

Laurie didn't bother correcting the young woman. Sooner or later, everyone at the inn would learn her new name.

"Thanks." She smiled. "We're supposed to meet my cousin, Finn."

"He's around here somewhere. He's reserved a large table by the windows." Emily beamed.

Large? Whatever.

"Can we wait for him at the bar? He should be along shortly."

"Sure, Kim's tending bar." Emily's eyes popped as if she'd just noticed Laurie's stomach. She recovered quickly and turned away to write something on the seating diagram.

Laurie grasped Patrick's hand and pulled him into the bar, a chuckle on her lips. Everyone would know about the baby soon.

The barroom was masculine with dark wood and leather. A long mirror ran the length of the bar and she smiled at Patrick's reflection. He grinned back.

"Hi. I haven't seen you in a while," Emily's boyfriend, Kim, greeted them. "What can I get you to drink?" He dropped a couple of cardboard coasters in front of them.

Patrick gave the boy a strange look before plastering a smile on his face. Laurie assumed he'd never seen an Asian before. Kim's family fled Vietnam for France and moved to the United States a few years before.

"I'll have water and my husband will have a whisky. The best you have."

Kim placed Laurie's drink on a coaster and poured Patrick a glass of thirty-year old Tamdhu single malt. They were clicking glasses when Finn joined them.

He ordered a whisky and raised his glass when it arrived. "A toast to my new cousin-in-law. May you find kin among us." He clicked both of their glasses with his.

"Thank you, kindly, I appreciate the warm welcome."

Finn's gaze darted to the doorway where Iain stood. "Ah, here's someone you should meet."

Patrick twisted to greet Iain with a wide smile. His face paled to a chalky white and he sagged against Laurie. She reached for his arm. Had the whisky gone to his head so quickly?

"Da?"

She stared at her landlord and then flicked her gaze back and forth between the two men. Her husband looked ill. Iain wore an inscrutable expression.

"Well lad, 'tis about time you got here." Iain broke out into a broad grin.

Oh, shit. She should have seen the resemblance before. Their eyes were the same, both a dark blue that sparked when they smiled.

"Da? Is it you?"

Iain nodded and the two men embraced. A squeal pierced the air and Mairi ran into the room, tears spilling freely down her cheeks. "Oh, Patrick, I knew Laurie was the one…the one who would bring you to us."

Laurie watched the scene play out in stunned disbelief.

An amused smile played on Finn's lips.

Patrick disengaged from Mairi and stared at his father as if the man were a ghost.

"How?"

❀ ❀ ❀

Much later, after Finn had gone up to his room, and the rest of the party sipped some fine port, Patrick decided the time had come for explanations. "Da, how did you and Mairi come to be here?"

His father gave him a weak smile. "That would be a tale for another time. What I will tell you is why we sent Laurie to bring you here."

"You sent me? Why?" Laurie asked, shocked Iain and Mairi were involved. "Please explain."

His father leaned forward. "'Tis a long tale—"

"Your father went to the library in Asheville and looked through some old Scottish history books where he found an entry about the MacLachlan line of chiefs," Mairi said. She looked directly at Patrick. "Your name wasn't there. The manuscript listed Iain as chief and then Archibald, but no mention of you. No mention of a death. Nothing. It was as if you had gone away before becoming chief and not returned."

Patrick ran a hand through his hair. This time traveling, time changing, mystified him. "Mayhap Archibald had my name stricken from clan history."

"Perhaps," his father agreed. "With enough badgering, Caitrina—I assume you've learned of her—finally admitted the faerie queen challenged her to bring you forward in time. For three years, we waited for your soul mate to show up. I guess you probably ken more of the rest of the story than we do," his father said.

Laurie grasped Patrick's hand under the table and gave his fingers a tender squeeze, assuring him she was there for him, and always would be.

He was the luckiest man alive.

He would keep her and their *bairns* safe and prove his worth.

Weeks later, Laurie joined Patrick in the golden-hued cottage garden. The full harvest moon glowed overhead. The rear gate ajar, they could see the faerie knoll just beyond.

Laurie leaned against the warmth of Patrick's hard chest, and he wrapped his strong arms around her, his breath teasing her ear. Tingly sensations traveled the length of her spine.

Even after what they'd been through together, she had a niggling of doubt. Patrick never once told her how he felt. Never once said he loved her. She hesitated before she spoke, not completely sure she wanted to spoil the moment. Yet she needed to know. Otherwise, every full moon would bring with it the fear of him leaving.

Laurie labored to remove every trace of her tumultuous emotion from her voice. "I know it's been difficult to adjust to our new life. Do you wish to go back?"

Having finally asked the question, she braced herself for his answer.

"Nae." He smiled. "Here is where our life is. Here is where our love will grow and blossom. Where our *bairns* will be born. Here is where I can keep you and our *bairns* safe." His arms tightened around her. "My only regret is I let Maclay escape. However, I am sure Archibald will ensure the bastard is brought to justice. You dinnae need to fear I will go running off. I am yours forever... *gu bràth*."

She snuggled against him and he nuzzled her neck. "I love you."

No other words ever sounded as sweet.

"I love you too." She turned in his arms and kissed her Highland warrior with every ounce of love within her heart.

EPILOGUE

One year later, Laurie stood amidst the racks in her new greenhouse, humming to herself while she transplanted young seedlings.

She missed her little guys, but her two baby boys, Young Iain and Scott, were at the inn where their doting grandparents watched over them. Geez. When Patrick informed her they'd have three children, two boys and a girl, she never imagined the boys would come at the same time.

She smiled whenever she thought of them and of the baby girl still growing within the protection of her womb. She took out another planting tray and continued humming.

Patrick sauntered in and grinned. "You sound happy today, m'love."

"Why not? There's so much to look forward to. My garden shop will open soon. Finn should arrive at any moment for a long visit. And did I tell you he plans to stay for the Grandfather Mountain Games and the Gathering of the Clans?"

"Aye. That you did."

"I'll have two gorgeous men to boss around." She batted her eyelashes at her husband.

Patrick wrapped his arms around her, and chuckled softly

into her ear. She leaned into him, enjoying the closeness. Moments like this had become much too infrequent since the twins arrived.

The ringing of the doorbell in the attached gift shop ruined the mood. She pulled away. "Will you get the door? I locked it. Whoever is there can't get in." She brushed the dirt from her apron. "It's more than likely Finn."

She stared at Patrick's firm butt as he walked away and sighed.

Chuckling, Patrick walked through the greenhouse and into the cramped quarters of the gift shop beyond. They'd made good use of Laurie's old cottage.

When he opened the front door, he found a wee lass standing there. The tiny woman jumped back. She slowly raised her gaze to him and her eyes widened. She trembled before she stiffened and glared at him.

He frowned, unable to believe her glower. The woman studied him as if he were some distasteful creature she found under a slimy rock.

Remembering his manners, he forced a smile. "Hello, lass. Can I help you?"

The lass squeaked.

"Who's at the door?" Laurie called as she came to join him.

"Naught but a wee mouse." He spoke over his shoulder.

Returning his gaze to the woman, he watched her bristle at the barb. He chuckled good-naturedly.

Laurie stepped behind him and peeked around his back. "Jillian, what are you doing here?" She pushed him out of the way.

The two lasses hugged.

"Please, come in." His wife gestured for her friend to enter.

The lass hesitated, eying him with uncertainty.

"Ignore my brute of a husband." Laurie grabbed Jillian's

hand and pulled her into the gift shop. "Now, tell me how you came to be here."

"I lost my job." A sob escaped Jillian. "The company laid me off. They've dissolved my department. They're sending our work to someplace called Bangalore."

"Oh, sweet Jillian, as much as this must upset you, it's wonderful news. I've been looking for a partner to help me with the new shop. I plan to call it 'Foxgloves'. It will be a special place, a community space for all the local gardeners to share information. With your customer service experience, you'll be perfect. Please, tell me you'll stay."

Patrick stepped out of the way and the two wee lasses brushed passed him headed for the greenhouse. He'd need to hurry the guest cottage he planned to build, especially if his wife was determined to pick up every lonely misfit who wandered by. Their house would be too crowded once their daughter was born. Then again, the lass could stay at the inn.

With that decided, Patrick strode off, whistling a merry tune.

Tir-nan-Óg

In the queen's chambers, Caitrina forced aside her pride.

"What is your challenge?"

The queen slid the tip of a pink tongue over crimson lips and smiled a beautifully wicked smile. She ran the sapphire gems from a crystal bowl through her slender fingers.

"I believe you'll enjoy my wee dare, you do so adore your twenty-first century mortals. Your task shall involve that sinfully handsome Finn MacIntyre."

"Not Finn!"

"Getting him together with his perfect match won't be too difficult, my princess. Just impossible."

With her hands close to her sides, Caitrina clenched her fingers into tight fists.

"Your eyes spark green fire. Don't make me regret the gift

of my leniency." Oonagh sensuously stretched on the white chase, making soft purring sounds. "Now be off with you."

Just Once in a Verra Blue Moon

A Highland Gardens Novel
Book 2

Also available
from
Dawn Marie Hamilton

www.dawnmariehamilton.com

Turn the page for a sneak peek…

PROLOGUE

Castle Lachlan, Strathlachlan, Scottish Highlands, 1490.

Fae? Mairi stilled, senses alert. Along with stifling afternoon heat, a curious fragrance pervaded the airless bedchamber, making her nose twitch. What interest had the *Sithichean* here? Her faerie protector, Caitrina, traveled far from Castle Lachlan on a private errand. There was nae reason for fae interference.

Mairi MacLachlan shifted the *bairn* nursing at her breast to the crook of her arm and fidgeted with the sleepy babe's wrappings. Angst swelled in her chest. *Could they be after the babe?*

The old folk whispered tales of malicious faeries stealing infants and replacing them with *changelings*—sadly misshapen souls. Mairi scanned the room in panic. She and the *bairn* must escape.

While Mairi struggled to untangle herself from the bedding, a white-haired woman appeared afore her, an elder, a reader of destiny. Mairi held the child close and swallowed uneasily. The *bairn* let out a disgruntled yelp, and she eased her hold.

"M'lady." The fae woman's voice garnered attention.

"You honor us with your presence." Mairi inclined her head briefly in deference to the faerie's status, though apprehension shivered over her skin. She searched the woman's features, hoping to ascertain the intent of the unexpected visit.

A sweet smile curved the faerie's lips and the edges of her ageless, green eyes crinkled.

Mairi relaxed against the pillows. The woman didn't bring warnings of ill fortune. The faerie's gray silk gown reminded Mairi of the ever-present Highland mists—a thought that made her frown.

"Why so sad, mistress? You have a bonnie wee one in your arms." The faerie glided to the side of the bed and peered at the bundle Mairi cradled.

Why, indeed? The answer troubled Mairi more than the woman's sudden appearance. Less than a sennight had passed since their child's birth, yet her husband left this morn in anger. She hadn't meant to quarrel with him, but he had set his course.

"My stubborn man is off to meet with the Campbell to secure a contract for the babe to wed one of his grandsons."

She didn't want such an arrangement for her *bairn*. She begged Iain that when the time came for the child to wed, he allow the lass to choose a husband of her own. Mairi wanted wee Elspeth to find love in the marriage bed, as she herself had.

"Be at peace." The old woman reached down to move the swaddling away from the babe's face, distracting Mairi from her glum thoughts. The faerie ran a finger along the *bairn's* tender cheek. A pleasant smile transformed her as she gazed upon the perfect features of the precious lass. She glanced at Mairi and in a raspy voice said, "Just once in a verra blue moon love will…" The faerie's brow puckered. "Oh, dear." She tapped a finger against her wrinkled chin. "I simply cannot remember what I am to say."

"Ah, yes." Her face beamed. "When three, seven-year cycles of the moon wane…" The wise one placed her hand on the wee babe's forehead and gazed into the infant's eyes. "A strange warrior from an unknown far-off place will come wielding the mighty lost sword of the fae to save you from despair, dear one. *Just once in a verra blue moon love will triumph.*"

As silently and swiftly as she arrived, the faerie woman disappeared. The only evidence remaining from her visit was the sweet, otherworldly fragrance clinging to the air.

Mairi caressed her daughter's smooth cheek, and the child cooed. "Well, my wee Elspeth, your da will not be pleased to learn the fae guide your future."

CHAPTER ONE

Present Day, Manhattan

*H*umid July air slammed into Finn as he rushed from the steel and glass high-rise of his family's prestigious business consulting firm. The fine linen shirt he wore instantly stuck to his chest. He tugged at the fabric and surveyed the heavy afternoon traffic. The shrill horn from a passing vehicle blared, starting a frenzy of honking.

Finn released a heavy sigh and loosened his silk tie. If he didn't find a cab right away, he'd be late for his flight.

He flicked his gaze at the empty curbside stand then hurried along Madison Avenue in search of a taxi. Sudden tingling on the back of his neck alerted him someone followed. A glance over his shoulder confirmed his suspicion.

Damn. To be stalked by beautiful women would be most men's fantasy dream, but it was his worst nightmare and all too real. The debutante following him was only the most recent in a barrage of overzealous females set on making his life hell.

He clutched his shoulder bag filled with his reenactment gear and quickened his pace. He didn't have the time or the inclination to deal with the woman's intrigues.

Finn had a games to attend. Damn good thing he'd sent his claymore on ahead.

In an effort to lose her, he sprinted for several blocks, weaving in and out of hordes of pedestrians, and ducked into a side street. He jumped into the first cab he came across. "LaGuardia, and make it quick."

When he looked back, a second cabby pulled in behind them, the darned woman was the passenger. His gut burned with dread. He told her he wouldn't marry her. Why did she persist in pursuing him?

"You've earned an extra hundred if you lose the yellow following us."

The driver accelerated into the flow of vehicles. The taxi careened through midtown traffic, running red lights and barely missing bystanders. Finn darted glances behind him. The other cab tailed them as if attached to their bumper.

Finn jerked forward. "What the—"

The other taxi had rammed them. Then it rammed them again, several times. His driver yelled a rapid-fire succession of what he assumed obscenities in a foreign language and maneuvered around several cars to get out of reach.

At the Queensboro Bridge, traffic slowed to a crawl. Finn tapped his fingers on the armrest. Antsy, he twisted to see out the rear window. The other vehicle was two cars behind.

Once on the boulevard, things opened up. He checked his watch. "Hurry, dammit."

On the expressway, they raced along straight-aways, darted between cars, skidded around curves. Tires squealed. Horns blared. An abrupt twist of the steering wheel hurled Finn across the black vinyl. He used his arms and legs to brace himself, determined to keep his seat.

When he entered the airport terminal, the woman wasn't far behind. Zigzagging through the crowd, he lost her at security.

Finn boarded his flight, slumped into his first-class seat, and ordered a whisky. While the crew prepared for takeoff, he spied the woman watching through the large plate-glass window of the waiting area. She must have used her security credentials to get through the checkpoint. Her audacity made him shudder.

The 737 taxied, took off, gained altitude. He stared out the small window at the wispy clouds. He could imagine the look of defeat in her dark eyes when the aircraft pulled back from the jetway to speed him off to North Carolina and the Highland games at Grandfather Mountain.

❀ ❀ ❀

Blue Ridge Mountains, near the Village of Anderson Creek

Finn inhaled deeply. His lungs filled with fresh mountain air. For the first time in months, he was free of fawning women. Free of the awkward position they put him in.

Patrick's sword sliced past his face, drawing him from his thoughts. Rain streamed over his bare chest, mixing with sweat. He needed to pay attention. If he weren't more careful, he'd do a face-plant in the mud.

"You fight like a lass, MacIntyre," Patrick taunted.

"Hilt is slippery." Finn cursed under his breath and sought a better grip.

"You must learn to fight under every circumstance. That includes rain. Could save your miserable life someday."

Grunting, Finn barely ducked the next assault.

Patrick pulled back. "Enough!" He dropped the point of his claymore to the ground and scowled. "'Tis obvious you are not paying attention."

Trying to catch his breath, Finn gulped air. He glared at his cousin-in-law. "This is supposed to be just for fun."

"Ach, then. You must try harder to have fun, lad." Humor lit Patrick's blue eyes, and he unloosed the leather strip holding back his long chestnut hair. Patrick MacLachlan was a primitive man; to him a workout with the large two-handed sword was child's play. "At times I forget we live in a modern world."

Finn shook his head. *"You are my fiercest opponent."*

Patrick laughed and placed a hand on Finn's wet shoulder. "Come. The *bairns* are at the inn for Rory's Thursday morning story time. Let us go and warm ourselves by the fire and listen to the old Highlander tell his tales."

Finn yanked on a soaked t-shirt and followed Patrick across the wet lawn.

About twenty-five eagerly waiting children sat on the plush carpet in the parlor of the *Whispering Pines Inn* while gossiping moms relaxed on overstuffed floral sofas. A few dads stood nearby, appearing disinterested. Finn knew better. Everyone loved hearing Rory's stories.

The crackling fire brought much-needed warmth to the dreary mountain morning. Finn joined Patrick at the hearth, hoping his clothes would dry.

Conversation ended when Rory MacNaughton entered from the rear door, his carved walking stick at his side. The elderly gentleman wore dress slacks, a brown tweed jacket with leather patches at the elbows, and a tam covering his white hair. He greeted individuals as he crossed the room and eased onto the tall stool at the center of the parlor. With an age-spotted hand, he motioned for his audience to move closer.

Alert eyes sparkling, Rory glanced at Finn and grinned. One of the men standing nearby snickered. Finn groaned, sure he knew the yarn the storyteller would regale them with.

Taking a deep breath, Rory began…

"The *Sithichean*, the faeries of the ancient Highlands, had a special affinity for moonstones. Enamored by the pale, lustrous, blue color resembling that of moonlight, they found the best of these unique stones on the shores of their sensuous faerie paradise *Tir-nan-Óg*—land o' heart's desire—having washed ashore on the tides when the sun god and moon maiden were in a particular heavenly harmony."

Rory leaned forward. "Ye ken this miraculous occurrence happens only once in three, seven-year cycles of the moon…"

He held up an index finger. "Just once in a verra blue

moon," he whispered.

A hush fell across the parlor.

"Handfuls of these precious stones belonged to a beautiful flame-haired faerie with eyes the color and brightness of the most costly emeralds."

"Caitrina?" a precocious little girl, with red curls and freckles sprinkled across her nose, whispered. Her blond-haired friend giggled, and Rory smiled at the pair.

"She bestowed upon the moonstones magical powers, gifting them to deserving mortals. Some of these charmed stones had the ability to reunite lost lovers. Others gave the bearer the gift of second sight. One especially large gemstone she forged into the hilt of a magnificent Highland claymore, and with a kiss enchanted it with extraordinary power."

His eyes wide, a boy in front pointed at Finn.

Finn glanced down. He must be a sight, his soaked shirt clinging to his chest and his wet kilt slung low on his hips. He'd grown his hair long and now the knotty, wet strands hung around his shoulders in disarray. Beside him, his sheathed sword leaned against the stone of the fireplace, the large moonstone in its cross-section plain to see.

Rory chuckled, locking gazes with him. With tight lips, Finn shook his head *no*. He didn't want the kids to think his sword was the one of which Rory spoke.

"Over the ages, the sword brought many a worthy warrior fame and fortune. That was until the day an evil, dark power used it." Rory's voice rose and his pace quickened. "This could not be borne. With green eyes shooting flames of fire, the one who fashioned the splendid weapon cast it far away to vanish in the *Sands of Time*."

The storyteller lowered his voice an octave and slowed his speech. "There are those who believe the lost sword of the fae has been found."

Finn refused to listen to more of the man's fantasy. He signaled to Patrick he was leaving.

Patrick followed him into the foyer. "Why the rush, lad?"

"My claymore doesn't have supernatural powers. It's just

an antique sword."

"Ach, well. Dinnae take offense. Rory means nae insult. He merely wishes for the *bairns* to believe in a wee bit of magic. Nae harm in that."

Finn shrugged. "Guess not."

"Will you be staying for the midday meal?" Patrick asked.

"No. I'll change out of these wet clothes then head to the mountain for a nap before the festival begins."

"I will meet you at the game field for the picnic along with Laurie and the *bairns*."

"See you there." Finn crossed the parking lot to the truck he kept in North Carolina for when he visited.

Less than an hour later, he walked along the camping area's muddy gravel road past travel trailers, water dripping from his rain gear. Why hadn't he thought to rent an RV? He'd be about to enjoy a dry warm bed instead of a damp sleeping bag. He continued down the road, swerving to sidestep one exceptionally large puddle.

There were few people about. The afternoon rain kept most from exploring. Those who had ventured outdoors huddled beneath ugly blue tarps, sat around smoldering campfires that made him want to sneeze, or were garbed in bright-colored raingear from head to toe.

Striding down the hill past pop-up trailers, he walked into what some had named *Flag Town*. Wet banners and flags flapped in the wind, hanging mostly everywhere, from ropes strung across the road, from poles in campsites, from trees. Stars and Stripes, St. Andrew's Crosses, and Lion Rampants hung together among the multitude of Clan banners. He inhaled a deep breath of moist air. The display roused his ancestral pride.

He waved to a couple of fellow reenactors then jumped over a fast running stream that hadn't been there yesterday. The flow weaved its way across the road, along the edge, through the center of someone's campsite, to cross the road again around the bend. There the water rushed into the woods, into the faerie glen where his friends, the MacRae sisters, camped.

Farther along the road, he eyed his tent where it stood in the woods at the edge of the camping area, behind the campsite of a bunch of good ole boys, alumni of the University of Tennessee. Fortunately, he'd pitched his humble abode on the hill and dug a trench around the upward side. His efforts paid off. The water flowed around the tent instead of through it. But there was too much rain, making it impossible for anything to stay completely dry.

Finn bent to unzip the fly and entered the vestibule. Hunched over, he re-zipped the flap and took off his raingear, hanging the wet jacket and pants on the line he strung inside. After removing his muddy boots, he unzipped the tent and climbed in. His sleeping bag wasn't wet, just damp.

He didn't care. He needed sleep.

Rolling his shoulders, he tried to ease the tension in his muscles from his workout with Patrick. He reached for a ditty bag and took out an aspirin, popped the pill into his mouth, and washed it down with water from his sport bottle.

Wrapped in a fleece blanket, he lay on the sleeping bag and allowed the distant skirl of pipes lull him toward sleep. He began to snore, the sound startling him, almost fully waking him again, before he drifted into oblivion.

She called to him.

The young woman stood alone on a heather-covered hill, as if surrounded by a halo, her long strawberry blond hair aglow in the sunshine. A puff of air blew the sheer gown she wore, causing the gossamer fabric to cling to feminine curves, teasing his imagination.

He wanted to reach out, touch her cheek, kiss her lips, sweep his palms over her sensuous form. Desire pooled low, tightening his groin.

As he strode closer, she floated farther away.

The lilting sound of her voice came to him on the breeze, soft and alluring.

At first, he couldn't make out her words. She spoke a language he didn't understand yet sounded familiar. And then...

"Come to me, my warrior...save me...come to me."

Dawn Marie Hamilton dares you to dream. She is a 2013 RWA® Golden Heart® Finalist who pens Scottish-inspired fantasy and paranormal romance. Some of her tales are rife with mischief-making faeries, brownies, and other fae creatures. More tormented souls—shape shifters, vampires, and maybe a zombie or two—stalk across the pages of other stories. She is a member of The Golden Network, Fantasy, Futuristic & Paranormal, Celtic Hearts, and From the Heart chapters of RWA. When not writing, she's cooking, gardening, or paddling the local creeks of Southern Maryland with her husband.

Visit Dawn Marie on the web at dawnmariehamilton.com.

www.ingramcontent.com/pod-product-compliance
Lightning Source LLC
Chambersburg PA
CBHW051323250626
47155CB00007B/2428